SENTINALS DESTINY

SENTINALS DESTINY

BOOK SIX OF THE SENTINAL SERIES

HELEN GARRAWAY

AUTHOR'S NOTE

Content Warning

This is an adult epic fantasy with mature adult themes. There are scenes of violence, consensual sex, reference to mental health issues, committal and self-harm. Please take care of yourself when choosing to read my book if any of these topics could cause distress.

This book is written in British English.

The name Sentinal was a variation of the word Sentinel. I deliberately changed the spelling from Sentinel with an 'e' as it always makes me think of technology or computer software. I wanted the idea of a protector or guardian so I thought the word was close enough to keep the meaning.

Sentinal with a capital is the person, sentinal with lower case is the sentinal tree.

For my Daughter, Jennifer
I love you x

Thank you to my amazing ARC readers.
My Sentinal Superfans!

Michael, Jan, Daisy, Johnny, Ellen, Dr Pam, Pat,
Chastity, Jackie, Leah, Barbara, Pierre and Kris.

I appreciate all your support

ALSO BY HELEN GARRAWAY

<u>Sentinal Series</u>

0.5 Sentinals Stirring (Novella)

1. Sentinals Awaken

2. Sentinals Rising

3. Sentinals Justice

3.5. Sentinals Recovery (Novella)

4. Sentinals Across Time

5. Sentinals Banished

6. Sentinals Destiny

<u>SoulMist series</u>

SoulBreather

DragonBound

OblivionGate (Spring 2024)

<u>Freedom Series</u>

Familiar Troubles (part of free anthology Men of Magic and Myth)

REMARGAREN
POST-FLOOD
ELOTHIA
TEROLIA
VESPIRI
BIRTOLI
OLD VESPERS
NEW VESPERS
DEEPWATER
GREENSWATER
STONEFORD
EASTWATCH
AGUINTI
MOLINTI
SENTI
DONA
AMRI
AMRILLA
SERBOL
CHERNI
VYR
ASTILLE
RAMIL
ATOLEA
KIKER
SOLARI
GUSAR
KIRSHA
MINER
MISTRA
KHASMA RIDGE
RELARPU

VESPIRI
ELOTHIA
NEW VESPERS
OLD VESPERS
WATCH TOWERS
DEEPWATER
VELMOUTH
GREENSWATCH
KING'S PORT
THE GROVE
STONEFORD
DALEHURST
TWO BRIDGES
EAST ROAD
LINTEL
LOWALSTALL
TEROLIA
MARCHWOOD
EAST FORD
APPLETREE
MORTELIN
EAST WATCH
WOODBRIDGE
MARSHFORD
BIRTOLI

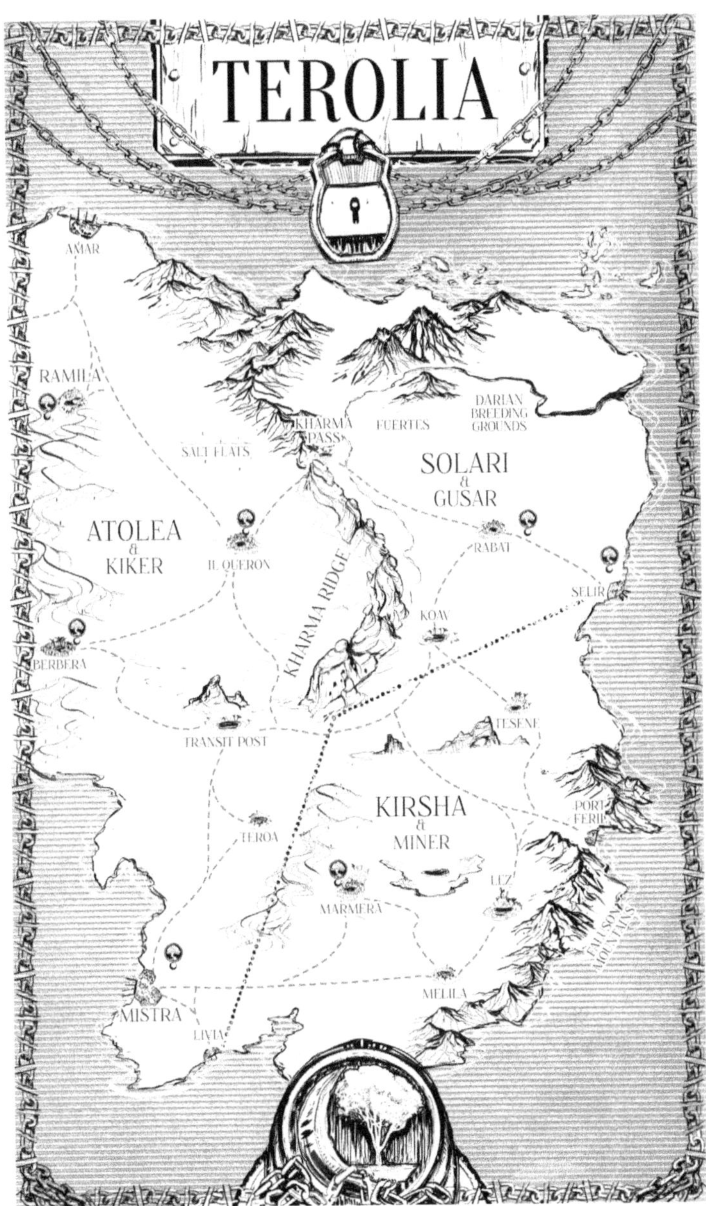

TEROLIA
AMAR
RAMILA
KHARMA PASS
SALT FLATS
FUERTES
DARIAN BREEDING GROUNDS
SOLARI & GUSAR
ATOLEA & KIKER
IL QUERON
RABAT
KHARMA RIDGE
KOW
SELIR
BERBERA
TRANSIT POST
TESENE
KIRSHA & MINER
PORT FERIE
TEROA
LEZ
MARMERA
FALUSON MOUNTAINS
MISTRA
MELILA
LIVIA

BIRTOLI
POST-FLOOD
VESPIRI
MORTELIN
WOODBRIDGE
AGUINTI
MIKRI
MARSHFORD
LAKRI
HARBOUR
MOLINTI
PORLI
SENTI
DONA
POINT
STORM WALLS
AMRILTI
CHERNI
AMRI
EYTI
PAUUL
ASTILLE
SERROL
DUYLI

CONTENTS

1

WESTERMAINE, GREENSWATCH, VESPIRI

Leyarille jerked awake as Birlerion's arm flailed and elbowed her in the stomach. She sat upright as he struggled to draw breath, the frightening noise driving away the last vestiges of sleep. He writhed, his face tense, the creases deepening between his dark brows, accentuating the scar that bisected the left brow as he gritted his teeth.

In the sliver of moonlight entering the room through the uncurtained window, Leyarille saw his eyes were screwed tight, his firm chin squared, the dimple hiding as she tried to corral his arms. Birlerion was having a nightmare.

The small mackerel coloured Arifel, Ari, popped into view, hovering over Birlerion. He chittered in concern, his emerald eyes filling his face as he landed on the bed with a soft thud. The fluffy kitten-like creature had scaly wings and tail which gleamed in the moonlight as he walked up Birlerion's chest to peer at his face.

"Hush, my love, you are home now, safe at home," Leyarille crooned as she tightened her embrace. Birlerion inhaled deeply and shuddered out his breath before relaxing in her embrace. His breathing deepened, smoothed, and he slept. Ari meeped in approval and disappeared.

The sparse light from the new moon caressed their bodies. Legs entwined, wrapped in each other's arms, they couldn't get any closer if they tried. Leyarille watched him sleep, his precious face relaxed. She gently traced the lines engraved on his skin by pain and suffering. The moonlight picked out the gleam of silver that threaded his black hair. She was determined he would never suffer again; she would protect him. The Sentinals would protect him. Relaxing, she drifted back off to sleep.

Birlerion awoke from a deep sleep wrapped in the arms of a beautiful young woman. His lips twitched as he considered how to extricate himself, but he decided he didn't want to. How often do you find yourself in such a delicious predicament?

He firmly shelved the memory of being restrained in a much different manner. This was no comparison. The gentle fragrance of her hair drifted under his nose, relaxing muscles tense from some distant shadow that hovered on the edge of awareness. An insidious presence that caressed his body, persistent and desperate as it searched for something.

Ignoring the sudden chill that shivered through him, he kissed Leyarille's shoulder and inhaled the comforting aroma of her sleep-damp skin. Her hair was loose and clouded around her face. She would be annoyed by it when she awoke; maybe he would offer to tame it for her.

The thought made him smile, and he slid against her lean body as he kissed her, and she stirred. She had her father's thin face, winged eyebrows, and his stubborn chin. The hair was her mother's.

"Good morning," she said, sliding her arms around his back and tugging him closer.

"Good morning," he replied, accepting the offered kiss as he happily molded her into his body. Reluctantly releasing her, he said, "We need to get up unless you want Jaredion to chase us down."

"He is too tenacious for his own good sometimes."

"Can't have it both ways," he laughed. "You would be complaining if he wasn't."

"True," she replied with a smile. Her fingers trailed over his warm skin as he rose and crossed to the bathing room, leaving cool air in his place. Leyarille curled up against his pillow, inhaling the scent of him. She loved him so much it hurt. Her chest ached with the need to be near him, touching him, protecting him. He was still too thin after his recent ordeal; the edges of his shoulder blades jutted out, and she could see every rib. No matter how much she fed him, he hadn't put the weight back on.

Instead of graduating from the ranger's academy, she was now part of an elite group of Lady's Guards, here, according to Birlerion, to protect those who couldn't protect themselves. Leyarille, along with Jaredion and their friend Kayenion, had turned Sentinal during the recent tumultuous months when a rogue Sentinal had abducted and tortured Birlerion to relieve her addiction to the Veil. The Veil that protected their world from wild and uncontrolled magic and which she had nearly destroyed, along with Birlerion's sanity.

Lady Leyandrii had asked for their help, and they had answered her call. As a result, they were now part of her personal guard; ancient uniform, silver eyes, and all. Her lips quirked; of course, she'd already had the silver eyes and name since birth—a gift from her parents.

The Sentinals were from the time when the goddess, Lady Leyandrii, had first called forth her protectors and marked them with silver eyes. She had protected them in tall sentinal trees when she had destroyed the Bloodstone and banished all magic from the world of Remargaren, casting out those who threatened to destroy the world. The Sentinals had slept for three thousand years until she had need of them again to protect her world. Twenty years ago, Leyarille's father had become the Lady's Captain, tasked with awakening the Sentinals. There were a dwindling number of Sentinals across Remargaren; her father had found few to wake all those years ago. New Sentinals had been unheard of, until now.

Her cousin, Jaredion, had the daunting job of guarding Birlerion's back. As the First Administrator of Vespiri, Birlerion was an important man, second only to her father the chancellor, and the king himself.

Birlerion was slowly recovering from his recent traumas, but he was still vulnerable and easily upset. Leyarille and Jaredion were determined to hide his struggle; they would give him the breathing room to recover. It would take time, and they would give him however much time he needed.

Stretching, she observed Birlerion from under her lashes as he returned from the bathing room and began dressing. Reluctantly, she rose, floorboards cold beneath her feet. She needed to get a rug or something, and they needed to choose some furniture; their house was empty. She sighed again. It wasn't a house, it was an estate. It was huge but secluded, and that was what Birlerion wanted, the privacy and the tranquillity.

The mansion was newly built from grey stone and decorated with elaborate cornices and gleaming flint. It had two wings elegantly festooned in clear glass windows which let in lots of light, something Birlerion also needed. The rear of the building opened through wide doors onto a terrace with a grey stone balustrade and looked down an avenue of trees to a small lake.

She had preferred the smaller estate over on the borders with Terolia, but it was much darker inside and more exposed and open outside. It had few trees and was too far from Old Vespers. Though she knew her father would create a waystone for them if they asked. Birlerion felt more at home in Greenswatch; he had a connection, a history with the watch. It was where he grew up, where his family had lived all those years ago. And wherever Birlerion was, that was her home too. At least this house had not been lived in. It was a blank canvas waiting for them to make their mark on it.

New beginnings, that was what they both needed.

They also needed to hire some staff and furnish the house else they would all be eating their food off the floor. Which they had done for the first few weeks, making do with bedrolls and travel rations, but Birlerion needed cosseting. Living rough when he was still recovering was not doing him any good, so she had put her foot down and ordered some furniture from a local carpenter. Now, they had a bed and a kitchen table and chairs. The carpenter was gradually working his way through the house, mansion, whatever it was.

They tended to camp out in the kitchen around the large wooden table. Jaredion would join them for breakfast and take over guard duty from Leyarille. Jaredion took his responsibility for Birlerion's safety extremely seriously; he was like his shadow, always present, watching.

It had taken Birlerion a few months to get used to it; he was more used to being the shadow, usually behind her father's shoulder, but now he was an important man in his own right, and he needed protection. Today they would travel to Old Vespers. The two months he had been granted to recuperate were up, and he had to return to work.

The healers said he was recovered physically and that his nightmares were all in his head; continued counselling would help ease those. Her father said he couldn't justify the loss of three Sentinals and the First Administrator any longer, and anyway, Birlerion was much better. Keeping him busy would do him good. It was time to return to Old Vespers.

When she returned to the bedroom, he was gone. Jaredion must have arrived and escorted him to the kitchen. She hurriedly dressed and descended the imposing staircase. Maybe she would commission a painting of Birlerion to hang on the wall. They needed at least one picture to brighten the place, and he was the one person she could look at all day.

She followed the low murmur of voices and found Birlerion seated at the sturdy kitchen table with her cousin, Jaredion. His hair was as dark as Birlerion's, and he was strikingly handsome if you liked the chiselled features look with high cheekbones and black eyebrows which framed a highly intelligent face.

"Morning!" Jaredion greeted her, his silver eyes bright, his grin welcoming.

Leyarille tried not to smile. She should be welcoming him into her home, not the other way around. "You're a bit lively this morning. What's got you all excited?"

Jaredion laughed. "My sentinal arrived. He travelled overnight. It's nice to be in the same place for once. I can sleep here now." Jaredion had been staying with his parents in the neighbouring watch of Deepwater each evening, trying to give Birlerion and Leyarille some privacy, for which she blessed him whole heartedly. There would be a lot less privacy in the king's palace. She intended on staying with Birlerion in his rooms in the palace instead of the Sentinals' barracks.

"And now we are going to Vespers. Not good timing,"

Birlerion said.

"But we'll be here at the weekends, so we'll be together then," Jaredion replied.

"Toast?" Birlerion offered her a slice of bread. She skewered it on the fork and held it over the kitchen fire as she perched on one of their new chairs and watched the bread slowly brown. The carpenter had done an amazing job, carving decorative swirls around the legs of the table and matching chairs and flowers along the straight edges. A beautiful piece of furniture for such a mundane purpose. An oven sat above the hearth, a sink with running water stood under the uncurtained window, and that was it apart from a few wooden shelves with a stack of crockery and some pans. They needed to do some shopping while they were in Old Vespers.

"Kafinee?" Birlerion pushed a mug towards her. He always called it kafinee; he had never picked up the modern name, coffee, even after twenty years.

Leyarille smiled as she sat and began spreading butter on her toast. "Where did you get the bread?"

"It arrived with Jaredion. Apparently, it was left on the doorstep, along with some milk."

Leyarille tilted her head. "Offerings from the neighbours?"

"They came a long way. It must be at least five miles to the nearest village," Jaredion said.

"Next weekend, we'll go and ask. We should pay for it," Birlerion said. "I would hate for someone to go hungry on our account."

"We need some staff to keep the fires burning when we're not here; otherwise it will be so cold when we come back," Leyarille said, munching her toast.

"We'll ask in Vespers. I know some people who might be able to help us. We need to get on the road. Jaredion, go get the horses ready." Birlerion stood and wrapped up the butter.

Leyarille hurriedly finished her toast and then helped clear the table. She paused beside Birlerion and cupped his face in her hands. "Make sure you don't overdo it. It's only your first day. Take it steady." Smoothing his jacket, she removed a stray thread. He wore the same high-necked uniform both Jaredion and she wore. They were all Sentinals; the Lady's protectors.

Birlerion smiled and kissed her on the lips, his silver eyes gleaming. "I promise I will be good."

Leyarille chuckled as they descended the steps out of the house and raised her face to greet her sentinal tree located by the entrance, along with Birlerion's and now Jaredion's. They were the first thing you saw as you left the house, tall and elegant, smooth silver trunk and emerald green pointed leaves. The contented hum of her tree in the back of her mind was a constant reassurance.

Birlerion paused on the steps, acknowledging his sentinal before greeting Kin'arol, his honey-gold Darian stallion.

"We go to Old Vespers?" Kin'arol asked as he waited for Birlerion to mount.

"Indeed, back to work."

"But we'll come back here, won't we? I like it here."

Birlerion chuckled. *"Of course, every weekend. Westermaine is our home now."* He and Kin'arol had explored every square inch of their estate over the last few weeks. It had been a gift from the king for services rendered, and it was the first time Birlerion had owned a property. In all the years he had been awake, he had never had his own home. He liked the feeling and was reluctant to leave.

There was a lot of opportunity for improvement, and he had many ideas to extend his good fortune to those around him. They would be self-sufficient as much as possible, and he wanted all his people to have their own homes and the ability to fend for themselves. He also had more expansive plans but he hadn't shared those, yet, with anyone.

They rode down the tree-lined track that led out of the grounds and onto the road that wound its way to Greenswatch, Jaredion behind them. It was five miles to the Greenswatch manor and the nearest waystone. They could have asked Leyarille's father, Jerrol, the Chancellor of Vespiri and the Lady's Captain, to create them a waystone, but Birlerion wanted the privacy. Any Sentinal could use the waystone, and he preferred more notice that someone was visiting.

Arriving at Greenswatch, they were confronted by his eldest brother, Versillion, who inspected him keenly before hugging him tight. Birlerion huffed his breath out. "You saw me last week when Val'eria gave me the all clear. If your wife says I'm fine then there is nothing for you to worry about."

"I know, but we almost lost you."

After fending off his brother, he also had to manoeuvre past the Lord Warden, Simeon, without offending him. He only escaped by promising to visit when they returned the following weekend, which looked like it was going to be busy.

They managed to reach the waystone, and dismounting, they shimmered through the portal and stepped out behind the Chapterhouse in Old Vespers. The waystones were a legacy of Lady Leyandrii. An ancient, magical method of travelling between two places almost instantaneously.

Jaredion laughed as he stepped through the waystone after them. "The number of times I threw up behind that bush. I am so glad I don't have that problem anymore." Sentinals had iron guts. They were the only ones who could use the waystones without being affected by debilitating nausea.

Birlerion smiled and led Kin'arol down the street towards

the Justice buildings. Leyarille pecked him on the cheek in farewell and continued up to the palace to report back for duty. Handing Kin'arol's reins to the stable lad, he mounted the steps, and entered the tall grey building, Jaredion at his shoulder.

It took him half a chime to breach the well-wishers, and his face was flushed by the time he reached his office. Warmed by the honest pleasure on the faces of his staff, he sat in his chair and relaxed, grinning as Kayenion filled the doorway.

Curly blue-black hair bouncing, silver eyes bright, he dropped a pile of files on his desk. "Welcome back, Lord Birlerion."

"Why, thank you kindly, Sentinal Kayenion."

Kayenion laughed. "I'm glad you're back. Tom is getting fed up with talking to me."

"I'll go and see him later."

"Please do, he will be most happy to see you."

"Anything I should look at first?"

"I'd recommend you start with the proposal from Elothia. They are offering to increase our fishing quota if we agree to remove the tax on their paper exports. I've been stalling them, but they are pushing for an answer."

"Do we need more fish?" Birlerion asked.

"I'll let you make that decision. Above my pay grade," Kayenion grinned as he left.

Jaredion poked his head in the door. "Kafinee?"

"That would be great," Birlerion replied absently, opening the file.

<hr>

Leyarille sat in the chair opposite her father, the Lord Chancellor. He was only forty-three, yet his brown hair was already streaked with grey and lines creased his forehead and around his eyes and mouth. Leaning forward in concern, Leyarille asked, "Pa, are you alright? You look tired."

Jerrol smiled. "Missing your mother. I don't sleep so well when she is away. She's still up at the Watch Towers, setting up the new chapterhouse."

Leyarille grinned. Her mother was the Scholar Deane of the Chapterhouse of the Lady's Order of Remargaren, the centre of learning located in Old Vespers. "That didn't take her long. She hasn't been in office two months yet."

"She was determined. She always said the Watch Towers were under-appreciated. I promised I would go up this week-end." He leaned back in his chair. "I'm hoping you are going to tell me you've brought Birlerion with you. I need him."

"I left him at the Justice buildings. Don't overwork him, Pa; he is still fragile."

"He's stronger than you think. But don't worry, the healers will be breathing down his neck. They won't let me overwork him. Physically, he's fine. You know that." He grinned as she blushed. "When is he going to make an honest woman of you?"

Leyarille rolled her eyes. "We don't need to be joined, Pa. And don't you dare say anything to him either. We'll get joined when we are good and ready."

Jerrol laughed. "Make sure you do. It's about time he is officially part of the family. How do you like Westermaine?"

"It's perfect. Just what Birlerion needs."

"What about you? What do you need?"

"Whatever helps him recover; I want Birlerion back."

"You need to give him room to breathe … otherwise you will become the cage, not the freedom he so desperately craves."

"Then why is he back at work?"

"He needs routine, normalcy, something to engage his

mind instead of constantly thinking about the past. Help him build a new future, Leyarille. You need to start living your life again, return to duty."

"I can't do that. I need to be with him."

"Of course you can. Your absence will drive him to the decision you've been waiting for; he won't miss you if you are around all the time. And he must see you as a partner, a companion, not a crutch to hold him together. That's not what you want, is it?"

Leyarille sighed, staring at her hands. "No, of course not, but he is so vulnerable, I want to protect him. He is safe with me."

"That is not your place either; he has Jaredion for that. He needs you to love him, to share his life, not suffocate him."

"What do you suggest?"

"Give it a week or so, and then I think you should join your mother at the Towers. She needs help, and Tianerille asked for some leave. I think it might be useful for you to learn more about the Watch Towers. It may help Birlerion let go of his fixation on the Veil if you know more about it."

"It's not a fixation," Leyarille said, her stomach fluttering.

"The healers say he is repressing his memories, that's why they are coming out as nightmares. Talking about his experiences would help him accept that they are in the past, finished. He could put them behind him."

"Birlerion has been candid. He is trying. You have to understand, talking about it all the time just reminds him of what happened. He feels inadequate, weak, and his nightmares are worse after a session."

"They will pass as he accepts that it wasn't his fault; he regained control at the end."

Leyarille stared at her father. Did he really believe what

he was saying? She rubbed her face; maybe he was just attempting to be positive. "Let's see how the next week goes. I don't like leaving him on his own."

"He won't be on his own. You know there are plenty of us around to support him, and Jaredion doesn't leave his side."

Leyarille exhaled. She was so glad that he didn't.

2

JUSTICE BUILDING, OLD VESPERS

Jerrol peered through Birlerion's open office door and inspected his friend. He looked much better, maybe a little gaunt in the face, a few lines around the eyes, but lean and trim. It looked like he had been training. Healer Ewan had signed him off as physically fit. It was the effect on his mind that was concerning.

"Welcome back, Lord Birlerion."

Birlerion looked up in surprise, a smile spreading over his face. *Now that is new,* Jerrol thought in concern. Birlerion always knew when he was being watched; you could never creep up on him, usually.

"Jerrol, come in, take a seat. I was going to come up and see you once I caught up here."

"I doubt you will catch up in one day, and nor do I expect you to," Jerrol said with a grin as he sat in the chair opposite Birlerion's desk.

"That's fortunate then because I haven't finished the first file yet." Birlerion leaned back in his chair. "You look terrible. What have you been doing?"

"Missing you, mostly. I distinctly remember saying I

would only take on the Chancellorship if you were here to help me."

Birlerion twisted his lips. "I'm sure there are others that are just as capable; young Erian, for example. Kayenion was quick to tell me he has been holding my office together in my absence. I am going to promote him to a junior minister."

"An appropriate reward I would think for all his hard work," Jerrol agreed. "Does that mean I can have Kayenion back?"

"Of course. Is Fonorion finally retiring?"

Jerrol sighed. "Yes, he's hung on these last few months, but it's time. He wants to go home to the Grove. Our numbers dwindle. It makes you wonder what the Lady intends."

"The Ascendants are no more, and there is no threat to the Veil; we are not really needed as Sentinals anymore. Maybe it's time for them to retire; let them concentrate on their families."

"Does that include you, Birlerion? Do you want to retire?"

"Never. I promised I'd help you. I told you, I'm in for the long haul. We protect those who can't protect themselves; the Lady's expectation hasn't changed."

"Good, then I need you to focus on finalising the sale of Gillian's assets because the next project is joining off Anders. It's time to find him a bride, and we need to secure his throne."

Birlerion laughed. "And does he have any preference?"

"I haven't asked him, but I thought someone from Terolia. It would bind us together much tighter."

Birlerion nodded thoughtfully. "Maraine's daughter should be old enough, or even one of the Solari, though Atolea would be better."

"You know them best. Can you draw up a list for us to propose to Anders?"

"Of course, though you ought to consider the Vespirian options too; give him a choice."

"I have. Make sure you get that list to me by the end of the week." Jerrol rose. "It's good to have you back, Birlerion."

Birlerion grinned. "It's good to be back."

Watching Jerrol disappear through the waystone outside his office, he waited for the chime that warned a waystone was in use. As the pure tone vibrated in the air, he smiled and returned to his paperwork.

He was debating about going into the city to find his contact, Tom, when a compulsion swept through him, taking his breath away. Gasping, he braced himself against his desk as he shuddered with the need to go to the palace. The king had got impatient and invoked the Oath.

Jaredion rushed in and shut the door. He hovered over Birlerion in concern. "What is it? What's happening?" He grasped Birlerion's shoulders, kneading tense muscles coiled for action. Birlerion's face was grey as he shook with the effort to remain behind his desk, straining against Jaredion.

"Oath. King invoked … the Oath," Birlerion gasped.

"Alright then, we'll go to the palace next. Accept his request, Birlerion; it might ease the need."

"I did," Birlerion whispered, collapsing limply in his chair.

"Is that typical?" Jaredion asked, frowning at him.

"No, I've never experienced such a strong compulsion." Birlerion wiped a hand over his face.

"Maybe you need to ask the king not to invoke it unless it's an emergency; you can't take too many of those."

"Maybe. Come on. I suppose we'd better go and see

what he wants." Birlerion took a deep breath and rose. Jaredion's hand steadied him as he swayed.

"Wait a bit. I'll get you some water."

"No, we need to go now." Birlerion stiffened his knees and left his office, stepping through the waystone in the corridor and stepping out into Commander Bryce's office at the palace. Bryce's aide Deron jumped, scattering papers across his desk as they appeared. His curse died on his lips as he saw who it was. "Birlerion! Sorry, Lord Birlerion. Welcome back. We've missed you."

Birlerion smiled at the captain. "It's good to see you too, Deron." They were interrupted as Bryce joined them.

The stocky grey-haired man had a broad grin on his face. "Birlerion. I'm glad you're here. Come and join me."

"I will, but I need to see the king first. Give me a chime or so?" Birlerion was shuffling towards the door as he spoke. Bryce raised his eyebrows and nodded. "Of course, I'll see you later." Jaredion grimaced at Bryce and followed Birlerion out the door. They hurried through the palace until they reached the king's private chambers, which were guarded by Parsillion, the tall blond-haired Sentinal on duty.

Parsillion gripped Birlerion's arm in greeting. "I'm glad to see you back," Parsillion murmured as he knocked on the door. A stooped grey-haired steward opened the door and ushered Birlerion inside, leaving Jaredion outside with Parsillion.

"How is he?" Parsillion asked quietly as the door closed.

Jaredion shrugged. "As well as can be expected, but if you could stop the king from invoking the Oath unnecessarily it would help; it almost wiped him out."

Parsillion frowned. "It shouldn't, though, should it?"

"I don't think so. I've never seen it invoked before, but he nearly collapsed. He's not as strong as he makes out."

"Look after him, Jaredion. We need him."

"I know, I'm trying. It is not as easy as it sounds."

Birlerion knelt before King Anders as the Oath running through his veins set his blood on fire. He tensed as a weight pressed down on him, brooding and oppressive. The king looked just the same; wavy brown hair curling down to his collar, intent blue eyes inspecting him. He looked more and more like his father, Benedict. Not as broad across the shoulders but well built. Once, he could hold his own in the ring, though he rarely sparred anymore.

"Rise, Birlerion."

Birlerion rose. Staring at the king, he raised his eyebrows. "You called, sire?"

Anders waved his hand in apology. "Sit. I thought it was the quickest way. We don't have spare Sentinals to send through the waystones these days."

"Maybe sending Ari would be a better option? It caught me unprepared, sire."

"That Arifel? He rarely responds; he's always off sunning himself somewhere. He is unreliable," the king replied, sitting behind his desk. Birlerion called the Arifel, one of the Leyandrii's messengers, and waited.

"What was so urgent, sire?" Birlerion smiled his thanks as the steward offered him a glass of water. He took a steadying gulp, still feeling the vibration of the Oath through his body.

"I wanted to speak to you about the Oath, whether you thought it would be a good idea to bring it here to Old Vespers."

"Here, sire? Why?"

"I'm not sure." Anders frowned. "It feels too far away in Senti. It ought to be here with us."

"It's been safe in Senti until now. I wouldn't recommend moving it," Birlerion said slowly, and he tried to ignore the oppressive awareness stirring behind his shoulder, waiting to pounce.

There was a disturbance in the air, and Ari popped into view. Anders lurched back as a fluffy kitten-like creature with reptilian wings and tail hovered in front of him, and Birlerion held out his hand. Ari landed on his palm, flipping his wings back as he curled his scaly tail around his fluffy toes. Large emerald eyes stared at him, and Ari meeped as he flicked his ears.

"He doesn't come for me," Anders complained.

"Maybe you don't ask nicely, sire," Birlerion replied as Ari crooned. Birlerion had the distinct impression that he was worried. "What's the matter?" he murmured, flinching as he received images of the Veil, the vast amorphous shield stretching around the world of Remargaren. It had a voracious appetite, especially for Sentinals, and he had been trying to ignore the Veil's constant call. It wanted him to return; the Veil was desperate for a piece of him. It was the Veil's obsession with him that was draining his resolve and causing his nightmares, he was sure of it.

"Birlerion? Are you alright?" Anders stared at him, and Birlerion curled his fingers into a fist trying to disguise the sudden tremor. Ari crooned, and Birlerion took a deep breath forcing himself to relax. He stroked Ari's soft fur as he settled on his lap.

"Have there been any reports from the Watch Towers, sire? Is the Veil secure?" The Veil Watchers up at the Watch Towers were supposed to keep it under control, monitoring it, ensuring the weave remained strong and true.

Anders frowned at him, and Birlerion gritted his teeth. He knew the king was aware of the healers' reports. Everyone thought he was fixated with the Veil, that he couldn't ignore its call.

"The Veil is fine. I'm concerned about the Oath. Senti is

too remote. We ought to bring it here; the Oath should be in my throne room."

"Why, sire?"

"Why? Because I control it. I invoke it and so will my line after me; it should be here."

"I disagree, sire. Marguerite safeguards the Oath, and there is no reason to move it; it has been safe for many thousands of years."

"You disagree, Birlerion?"

Birlerion stilled at the edge in the king's voice. "My apologies, Your Majesty, but I would strongly recommend against attempting to remove the Oath. Firstly, you would draw attention to its location, and secondly, I'm not sure it can be moved."

"Jerrol moved it. So could you."

"We would still draw attention to it, which I think would be a mistake."

"Bring it here, Birlerion. I command you."

The King's Oath swept through Birlerion and he inhaled, trying to keep the room in focus.

"Did you discuss this with the Lord Chancellor, Your Majesty? What were his thoughts?"

"He agreed with me, and so I'm ordering you to bring it here."

Ari meeped, flipping his wings and settling again as the Oath stirred in the back of his mind. Birlerion had accepted the King's Oath when Anders had invoked it in a time of need. The Oath bound them together, to protect the people and the lands of Remargaren. But the Oath was more than ensuring the king performed his duties; it also bound him to Lady Marguerite and the world itself. The Oath was not something to be trifled with, but he was unable to refuse Anders' command. "Yes, Your Majesty. If it is at all feasible, I will, but I can't guarantee I'll be able to retrieve it."

"Of course you can. I want it here before the end of the year. I know this is your first day back and you have duties here, but by the end of the year, Birlerion."

"Yes, Your Majesty." Birlerion rose, his chest tight and stomach clenching. Holding the Arifel close, he made his escape. The Oath was perfectly safe where it was. Why would Jerrol agree to move it? He strode through the palace to the chancellor's office, intending to ask him, but Jerrol's office was empty.

Pausing, he communed with Ari. Ari didn't know what was wrong with the Veil, he just knew that something was not right. The little Arifel rubbed his head against Birlerion's chest, leaving a trail of white hairs, and blinked out of view.

Birlerion ran a trembling hand through his hair. This was only his first day back. Could it get any worse? Exhaustion pulled at him, and his shoulders bowed as if under a great weight. Jaredion watched him with concern.

"I think that maybe I'll have a rest before we return to my office," Birlerion said, turning away from the chancellor's office. Jaredion followed, exhaling with relief. At least Birlerion was being sensible. They arrived at his rooms in the palace, and Jaredion took up position outside. "Wake me in a chime if I'm not up," Birlerion said as he closed the door, but didn't lock it.

He glanced around the suite. Pale beige walls enclosed a seating area which took up one room, an unlit fire in the grate. Weariness swept through him, and he ignored the comfortable chairs and walked into the bedchamber. His stomach churned at the thought of moving the Oath, and the pressure weighing down on him was exhausting. He placed his daggers on the table, slipped his boots off, and shrugged out of his jacket. Lying on top of his bed, he sighed out a breath.

Kin'arol crooned in his head, concerned. *"Birlerion? What's the matter?"*

"I'm just tired. I'll sleep and then I'll go back to work."

"I'll listen."

"Thank you." Birlerion closed his eyes and drifted off to sleep.

Ten minutes later, Jaredion burst into his room as Birlerion's screams tore through him. "Birlerion, wake up, it's just a bad dream," Jaredion bent over the distressed man and shook his shoulders. Birlerion came out of the bed raging, his dagger in his hand, driving Jaredion back across the room.

"Birlerion, stop, it's Jaredion. Birlerion, STOP!" Kin'arol screeched so loudly even Jaredion could hear him, and Birlerion faltered mid-thrust. He hovered, staring in horror at Jaredion lying beneath him. His hand shook, and he dropped the dagger, grabbed Jaredion and hugged him tight. "Are you alright? I am so sorry. I didn't hurt you, did I?"

"I'm alright, Birlerion, you s-stopped. Kin'arol stopped you in time and I'm fine," Jaredion stuttered as he gripped him back, his breath coming out in terrified gasps. He knew he wouldn't have been able to stop the killing blow. Birlerion was so strong.

"Lady help me," Birlerion moaned as he rocked Jaredion back and forth.

"I'm not hurt. You had a bad dream. It was just a dream."

Birlerion shuddered and released him as Healer Ewan rushed into the room. Bryce peered over his shoulder, along with other palace staff congregating in the corridor.

Bryce turned and shooed everyone away. "There's nothing to see, off with you all, get back to work." He firmly shut the door behind him. Casting a glance at the shattered looking Birlerion, he inspected Jaredion. "What happened?"

"Birlerion had a nightmare, and I tried to wake him. He

thought he was being attacked and woke up with his dagger in his hand. It was instinctive, he couldn't help it. I'm alright; he didn't hurt me."

Ewan helped the shaking Birlerion back to the bed and made him lay on it. "Slow breaths, Birlerion, breathe in deep and out, it's just a panic attack, you'll be fine." Reaching into his bag for an injection, he quickly pushed up Birlerion's sleeve and jabbed him with it before he could protest. Birlerion's breathing evened, and his eyelids drooped. Ewan breathed a sigh of relief and covered him with a light blanket.

Bryce joined him as they stood looking down at the sleeping man. "Will he be alright?"

"I don't know. If he can't control his reactions, he will be a danger to others."

"He seemed fine this morning, a bit anxious, but otherwise he looked like the old Birlerion."

"Time will tell. He'll sleep for the rest of the afternoon. I'll speak to him when he wakes up." Ewan collected his things and quietly left.

"I'll watch him," Jaredion said, drawing up a chair.

Bryce stared at him for a moment and then nodded, turning to leave as Jerrol burst into the room. "What happened?" he asked, taking in the sleeping man on the bed. "Is he alright? Zin'talia said he attacked Jaredion."

"Let's go to your office, and I'll explain. He's sleeping, let's leave him to rest. Jaredion, call for help if you need it. Don't try to deal with him on your own."

Jaredion nodded and leaned back in his chair. The door snicked shut and Jaredion rose. He inspected Birlerion as he slept. Even sedated, he wasn't relaxed. Lines of tension creased his brow, his eyelids moved, and his fingers flexed as if he was reacting to some external threat. Jaredion rubbed his face and sat back down, watching the man who gave his life meaning.

His purpose was to protect Birlerion. Deep in his gut he knew the Lady expected him to stand between Birlerion and whatever threatened him. Only he didn't know the origin of the threat, though he had no doubt there was one.

A chime later, Leyarille dashed in, breathless and distraught. "Kin'arol called me. What happened?" She dropped beside the bed. "What have they done to him?"

"Healer Ewan sedated him, said he was having a panic attack, but I'm not convinced he was, Leyarille."

She gently smoothed Birlerion's tousled hair off his face. She bent forward and kissed him on the lips. "You're safe now, safe with me. You're home, Birlerion, home." Birlerion sighed and relaxed, the visible tension running through his body melting away. Leyarille lay on the bed and wrapped her arms around him, cradling his head on her shoulder. She looked across at Jaredion. "Tell me exactly what has happened since we arrived today," she said.

3

____

KING'S PALACE, OLD VESPERS

Jerrol led the way into his office, sat behind his desk, and gestured Bryce to a seat. "What happened?" he asked, his face creased by lines of concern.

Bryce sighed and explained what he knew. Jerrol's frown deepened as he listened. He leaned forward as Bryce drew to a close.

"Jaredion said it was instinctive. Birlerion thought he was being attacked. The boy was unhurt, but Ewan sedated Birlerion. He was distraught, having a panic attack." Bryce paused his face serious. "Jerrol, if he can't control himself, he's a risk. We'll have to restrain him. He almost killed Jaredion, even if it was by accident."

Jerrol rubbed a hand over his face. "Let's not make any hasty decisions. We'll see what Ewan has to say first. Do you know why Anders wanted to see Birlerion?"

"I never had a chance to ask him. Jaredion might know."

"I'll speak to him later. He won't leave Birlerion now; he's like an over-anxious mother where Birlerion is concerned."

"Do you think we should reassign him?" Bryce asked.

"No, not yet. Let me speak to him first."

Bryce levered himself to his feet and left, leaving Jerrol to stare out of the window, deep in thought.

Healer Ewan returned early and shooed Jaredion and Leyarille out of the room with instructions to go and eat. He heaved a deep sigh as he considered the younger Sentinals and sat in Jaredion's chair. Birlerion's face was pale and strained, shadows stood out beneath his eyes, and he was stirring. Ewan had thought he would fight the sedation; Birlerion was like that. The notes that Healer Francis had left on the multiple injuries this Sentinal had received over the years were like a catalogue of horrors, and every time he had resisted sedation.

He wasn't surprised it was something mental that had brought him down. He had suffered so much physical pain, something had to break eventually. It was obvious Birlerion was still struggling to control his emotions. His lack of control was eating away at him, the guilt and the shame corroding his common sense, causing him to panic and trigger his fight response at the least provocation. Ewan wasn't sure how to help him regain his balance; he was resisting all proven theories.

He leaned forward as Birlerion's dark lashes fluttered and lifted. His eyes were a luminous silver, which solidified and settled as he watched; it was quite unnerving. From a healing perspective, eyes should not behave like that. Which was the other issue; Sentinals were of the Lady, they were from the past, awoken after three thousand years of deep sleep caused by the Lady sundering the Bloodstone and bringing down the Veil, and they didn't always react the same way as ordinary people. They didn't always see the world in quite the same way as the man in the street.

"How do you feel?" Ewan asked, keeping his voice gentle.

Birlerion turned his head and focused on the healer. "You sedated me."

"Yes, you were distressed, upset, you needed time to recover."

"Don't do it again."

"That will depend on the situation. You could do more harm than good if we left you untreated."

"You can't sedate me for the rest of my life."

"I have no intention of sedating you. You have to accept that it's over, you survived. She can't hurt you anymore."

Birlerion closed his eyes, tensing against the rising memories of Elliarille's invasive perfume, the seductive call of the Veil. "It's not her. I can't escape the Veil. It is persistent; it wants more, all the time."

"You're not afraid of the Veil, you're afraid of losing control; that's why you keep overreacting. You are overcompensating. You have to accept that you did escape her— it was your hand around her throat, you squeezed the life out of her. You may not have been able to release the restraints, but no one could. Jaredion couldn't either, remember? And he wasn't injured like you were. You are only human, Birlerion, give yourself a chance."

"I try, honest Ewan, I am trying, but I'm afraid to go to sleep. The Veil seems stronger when I sleep. I feel exposed. Leyarille keeps me safe. I can sleep when she is here, but when she's away, I'm afraid of what I might do."

"That's just an excuse. You're using her as a crutch, and that's not fair on her or you. You can't build a relationship on spurious emotions. You have to be honest with yourself."

Birlerion gritted his teeth though he lay still. *Don't show a reaction,* he thought, trying to remain calm. He liked Ewan, he was a good healer, but Lady help him, if he didn't leave soon, he might do something he would regret. *"Kin'arol? Get Leyarille to come back now or I swear I'll throttle Ewan."*

"She's coming, don't do anything silly. I don't like it when they make you sleep."

"I won't. I'm sorry, I don't mean to upset you."

"You don't, they do." Kin'arol sounded angry. He would have to go down and soothe him.

"I don't need soothing, Birlerion. You are quite sane. They need to listen to you."

Sometimes his Darian was the most clear-sighted one of them all. The thought was reassuring. When he heard the door, he opened his eyes again and relaxed as Leyarille approached his bed.

"What's the prognosis, Healer Ewan?" Leyarille asked. Her voice was light but Birlerion knew that she could tell he was keeping a tight grip on his temper. He was surprised the healer couldn't feel the waves of anger rolling off him.

Ewan stood. "He just needs to rest. We'll speak again tomorrow, Birlerion. Let me know if you can't sleep and I'll prescribe a draft for you."

"Thank you," Birlerion replied, his voice flat.

Ewan smiled and left. Leyarille waited beside him, and even though he was soothed by her presence, he sat up in an explosion of energy. "They won't listen to me; they are not hearing what I'm saying."

"I'm listening. What happened, Birlerion?" She placed a gentle hand on his arm, and his anger drained away. He wrapped himself around her and breathed in her comforting scent.

"You keep me sane. You keep me safe, and I can sleep when I'm with you. As soon as I close my eyes, I can feel it. It waits, hanging over me like a silent threat, and then when I'm vulnerable, it strikes. I have no defence against it; it wants me, and it won't stop until it gets me. Leyarille, I don't know what to do."

"What is threatening you, Birlerion?"

"The Veil."

Leyarille hissed her breath out, her face tensing. She understood what the Veil was like. What it was capable of. She had heard the stories. Her father had warned his children often enough, and her sister, Margareth, was a Veil Watcher. Lips pinching, Leyarille said, "You said you were safe with me; we just have to make sure I'm here when you sleep."

"You are back on duty, and they will assign you away from me. The king could send me away. I need another defence."

"Join with me, make it official, then they can't send me away."

Heat flushed through him at her words. What he would give to join with her, to claim her for his own, to start his own family. But a sense of fear and uncertainty made him hesitate. He had to resolve this last threat before he could focus on what he wanted. "I can't, not while this is hanging over us; it's not fair to you."

"I don't care about fair. I love you, and I want to spend the rest of our lives together. Don't waste the time we have on what-ifs. I don't want to sneak into your bedchamber at night. I want it to be *our* bedchamber. You're mine, and no one is going to say anything different."

He smiled at her fierce tone. "Once we deal with the Veil, I promise we'll get joined." Wrapping his arms around her, he revelled in the lithe body that molded to his. Dropping his head on her shoulder, he nuzzled her neck, and the door opened.

It shut just as quickly behind Jaredion. He glanced at them. "Sorry for the interruption. Birlerion, you need to know, there are all sorts of rumours going around the palace that you tried to kill me. The fact that I am perfectly well doesn't seem to make any difference."

Birlerion rolled his eyes. "We've been here one day and I already need to get out of Vespers. I can't cope with the pressure. I need to speak with Tom, set some things in motion, and then I think we'll leave for Terolia. The king needs a bride. Let's go check out the candidates. It's a good a reason as any to get out of here." And he could catch a ride with Roberion to Birtoli and check on the Oath if they happened to cross paths.

Leyarille nodded thoughtfully. "Pa wants to assign me to the Watch Towers. We could travel together and keep going. I'm not leaving you to the mercies of the Veil on your own."

"What's this?" Jaredion asked.

Leyarille explained about the threat from the Veil hanging over Birlerion.

Jaredion frowned. "What if I protect you when you sleep? I can try and reach the Veil. I'm sure I can keep the Veil away."

Birlerion considered him. "It is vicious, Jaredion. I wouldn't want you to get caught in it."

"I won't be, this is what I'm here for. The Lady sent me to protect you; this is what I'm supposed to protect you against. I know it."

"We'll try it tomorrow, see if you can reach the Veil. I'm too tired now, but it would be good to know if you can hold it off."

"Why won't they believe you about the Veil's threat? You are the Oath Keeper, connected to Lady Marguerite. Surely that should have some meaning?" Jaredion asked, frowning.

Birlerion shrugged, weariness dragging at him. The King's Oath entwined Lady, Land, and Liege within him. He was its current Keeper and enshrined in the Lady's will. He was Leyandrii's intentions in action, linked to her sister, Marguerite, as a protector of Remargaren. It didn't make sense that the very people who invoked it ignored him. "I have too many issues that they can easily explain by their theories. I've been through a traumatic experience that has left other men mindless, and they are expecting me to be the same. But I have the Oath, you, Leyarille, and Kin'arol keeping me sane. I know I am not imagining things, which also means there is a bigger issue at stake. Something is causing the Veil to target me; it wants me, my blood, but why?"

"Maybe it's good I am being assigned to the Watch Towers. If Jaredion can protect you from the Veil, I could spend some time at the Towers and try to find out more about the Veil's history and what it really does. If we can understand what is happening, then we can deal with it," Leyarille said, brow creasing in thought.

Birlerion nodded. "Sounds like a plan. Let's test it tomorrow. But now, I'm starving. Let's go and find some food and show everyone that we are all good, well-behaved Sentinals and maybe lay a few rumours to rest."

The next morning Birlerion sat in the chair in Jerrol's office. Leaning forward, he asked, "Have you seen Ari lately?"

"He flits in now and then, doesn't stay long."

"So he didn't share his concerns about the Veil with you?"

Jerrol sighed. "Birlerion, you have to let it go."

"It is hungrier than usual, have you noticed? It's restless."

"You need to forget it. Stop revisiting it and move on. Dwelling on the past won't help you heal."

"Have you checked it recently? It's hardening."

"It's fine, Birlerion; it's your imagination. The Watchers watch it so you don't need to. They would soon tell us if there was something wrong. Look to yourself. You need to concentrate on getting better. Worrying about the Veil won't help."

Birlerion fell silent. They all thought it was in his head, and sometimes he thought it was.

"It isn't," Kin'arol interjected.

His head ached, and he wanted to go home. The palace set him on edge. They all expected so much of him, and yet they wouldn't listen to what he had to say. He couldn't pretend. Nor could he behave how they wanted him to. Had he changed that much? He closed his eyes, the despair creeping up on him.

"You haven't changed, Birlerion. Circumstances are changing." Kin'arol's soothing voice relaxed the tension flowing through him.

He opened his eyes as Jerrol spoke. "Are you alright, Birlerion?" The concern in Jerrol's voice and expression made him cringe.

"Yes, I'm fine. Thank you."

"You don't look fine," Jerrol said gently. "Let us help you. You don't have to do this on your own; we want to help you, but you have to help us too."

"I know, and I am."

"I'll go and check the Veil myself, though the Watchers would have said something if they had seen a change. I'll also send them a request to keep a closer eye on it. Would that help?"

Birlerion exhaled and briefly closed his eyes against the sheer relief that flooded through him. Thank the Lady, Jerrol was listening to him. "Thank you, yes." Birlerion licked dry lips and changed the subject. "Here's the list for Anders. Do you want me to go to Terolia and sound them out, arrange visits so he can meet them?"

"Would you? Do you think you are up to it?"

"Of course. Using the waystones, it's a short hop. It's time Kino and I went back to the desert. He hasn't had much time there, and the heat will do him good."

Jerrol watched him, nodding thoughtfully. "I have no doubt it will do you good, too. I know you like Terolia and get on well with the Families. Ask Bryce for an escort. This would be an official visit."

"I don't need an escort. I'm just going to check the interest levels. Let's not make this more than it is."

"You're the First Administrator, Birlerion, it goes with the job. Get used to it," Jerrol said with a grin. "Speak to Bryce."

Birlerion gave in; at least it got him out of the palace. Collecting Jaredion at the doorway, he left to speak to Bryce and ended up collecting a whole unit from him no matter how much he argued. Sixteen men to keep him safe. They would be available from ninth chime in two days, and they would escort him wherever he needed to go until he returned to Old Vespers. Alright then. That meant waystones were out. So much for the short hop.

Collecting Kin'arol from the palace stables, they left the palace and rode down the switchback into the city. Kin'arol was ecstatic that he was going to be with Birlerion for the foreseeable future. Birlerion laughed out loud at his enthusiasm as they arrived at the large grey stone building that housed the King's Administration. A young lad led Kin'arol away to the stalls behind the building, but instead of climbing the steps, Birlerion walked down the road past the ranger's barracks and into the city centre. He flicked a glance at Jaredion. "Shall we try the Crown for lunch? Or can you cope with the fare at the tavern?"

Jaredion scowled at him. "Jim will take offence if we don't eat at his place."

"The tavern it is; I was just checking."

"It has improved, you know; he has a proper cook, now. You can tell."

Birlerion threaded his way through the busy market and out the other side, following the road towards the harbour. Veering into the maze of streets in harbour town they eventually reached the nondescript tavern. Filthy windows and stained brick walls concealed a lively bar and many people whom Birlerion called friends. They entered the Docker's Tavern, and Birlerion glanced around the smoky interior. It was quite busy. The large man behind the bar raised his eyebrows in greeting and jerked his head at the door which led off to the side. "He's in there waiting for you. Good to see you, Birler." He slapped a mug on the bar, closely followed by a second.

"Thanks, Jim." Birlerion took the mug of ale and ducked under an even lower door frame and entered the dim room. Jaredion placed the order for their lunch as Birlerion greeted the elderly man seated at the single table. His neatly trimmed grey hair and moustache were a reminder of his military background. "Tom, how is it you always manage to get this table to yourself?"

"Practice," Tom said, his voice gruff. "It's good to have yer back."

"It's good to be back, though I am only in Vespers today; off on the road to Terolia already. Time to find the king a bride."

Tom snorted into his mug. "Think yer'll find one?"

"I'm sure there is someone out there for him."

"Terolian, huh?"

"It would be preferable, but there are a few eligible

young ladies at court. Maybe some competition will make them step forward if they want him."

"About time. He's left it a bit late to secure his succession."

"Are people worried?"

"Not yet, but they will be if he leaves it much longer, so it's good yer going." Tom nodded at Jaredion as he slid into the third chair. "Alright, lad?"

"Yes, thank you, you?"

"Not so bad." He leaned forward. "Birler, yer ought to let the chancellor know, his support of this new Healer's society didn't go over so well. They've taken it as approval to increase their prices; no one will be able to afford their services except those up at the palace."

Birlerion frowned. "Healer's society?"

"It were Tyrone's idea. A way of organising the healer's services so they'd be available for everyone. But the society have changed the rules and now charge for every visit."

"Do they refuse to help if a patient can't pay?"

"Yer have to go to them, and they won't make house visits no more, unless yer pay for it. And they are charging yer just to see them, even if they don't do anything."

"I thought the basic tenant of the healers was to help anyone who needed it?"

"It might've been once, but they've updated it. Help available on payment of fees, appointments only."

"I'll speak to the chancellor. There should be access to basic care available to all, no matter their circumstances."

"Appreciate it, Birler."

"Of course. I have a favour to ask of you."

"Ask away."

Jaredion smiled into his beer. Tom must be pleased to see Birlerion to be so expansive.

"As you know, I have a small estate north of Greenswatch. I need a good housekeeper and a handyman to keep the place running whilst I'm not there. Do you know a couple or a young family who would be interested in relocating to help me? I'd provide accommodation, a good salary. I need someone who can run the house, cook, and clean until I can get some staff and a man to manage the grounds, gardens, fires, and such."

Tom peered at him. "If I were thirty years younger, I'd be there in a shot."

Birlerion smiled. "I wish you were. We would have got on well, I think. You would be welcome anytime."

Tom flushed with pleasure, his skin crinkling around his eyes. "Good of yer to say, but if yer mean it, my son is looking for a new place t' stay. He's just had a kid, and he and the missus are living with us right now as their landlord won't allow children. George is a carpenter, works on the docks, good with his 'ands he is. Have ter learn about the gardens, but he ain't daft; he learns quick. His missus knows her stuff too."

"That sounds ideal. As I say, I'll be away for about a month, so it would be pretty quiet, just keeping the fires burning as they say. When could I meet them?"

"Tonight? I can get them to come here for about seventh chime. My missus will look after the little'un."

"I appreciate it, Tom," Birlerion leaned back as Jim slid a plate in front of him and then Jaredion. The aroma of beef in gravy made Birlerion's mouth water. He smiled up at him. "I hear you have a new cook. It smells delicious."

Jim grunted and left.

"Man of few words." Birlerion flashed Tom a grin and began eating. It tasted as good as it smelt.

Tom watched them. "It does smell good," he said, tipping back his mug. "I'll leave yer to yer food. Tonight at seven." He pushed his chair back, and with a tap to his forehead, he was gone.

After a short silence as he ate the stew, Jaredion asked, "If Tom's son and his wife work out, do you think we'll have time to take them to Westermaine on the way to Terolia?"

"With a baby, it may take longer for them to get organised," Birlerion replied. "I'm sure they can make their own way, but I was thinking of asking Versillion to escort them and show them where everything is when they are ready. That is if they want the job, of course."

"They would be crazy not to. Most people would bite your arm off at the opportunity you are offering them."

"We'll see. You finished? We ought to get back to the office."

Returning to the Justice building, Birlerion spent a quiet afternoon shuffling paper and writing up his report for Jerrol. He had one meeting with a King's Justice, who managed the paperwork for his estate. Once they were finished, the man bowed himself out, and Birlerion leaned back in his chair, staring out the window until he was disturbed by Jaredion, informing him that it was time to leave to meet Leyarille and go back to the Docker's Tavern.

4

OLD VESPERS

Birlerion held Leyarille's hand as they walked through the city centre, across the empty market square and into the misty back streets. The air was cold and damp and a dog barked in the distance; a sharp echo in the deserted streets.

"It's amazing that such a busy city can become so quiet so quickly," Leyarille murmured.

"Everyone has a home to go to. Hopefully, we will too soon. Maybe we should get a townhouse or rooms. I'm not sure I want to stay at the palace; it feels too restrictive."

"It certainly cramps your style, my dear," Leyarille said with a low laugh.

"Wait until tonight and I'll show you how cramped it is."

They entered the tavern with Leyarille gripping Birlerion's hand as he led the way, smiling as they were shown into the back room. A young couple waited with Tom, fresh-faced and nervous. Staring up at the tall Sentinals, they scrambled to their feet.

"Please, sit, I appreciate you coming to meet us on such short notice. This is my partner, Leyarille Haven, and I am

Birlerion. The young man hovering in the doorway is Sentinal Jaredion."

Birlerion drew a chair back for Leyarille and sat next to her. Jaredion, after a quick grin in greeting, turned his back and leisurely watched the bar.

"This is my son, George Baines, and his missus, Mary," Tom said as they sat.

Birlerion smiled, twining his fingers with Leyarille's under the table. "It's a pleasure to meet you. Did Tom explain what we need?"

George bobbed his head. His brown hair was trimmed short, similar to Tom's. Cut by the same hand, Birlerion thought. His round face was sincere and eager, his cheeks rosy with hope. "Yes, my lord Birlerion. You're looking for a housekeeper and a groundsman. We would be most interested in working for you. I'm good with my hands, been working in the docks for the last five years, and they would give me a good reference.

"I ain't done no gardening, but I'm happy to learn if you'll give me a chance. Mary here is a good cook," he reached for her hands, "and kept our house fine until we had to leave it." Mary blushed. She was a slim young woman, with long brown hair coiled into a knot at her neck. Bright brown eyes observed them shrewdly.

"There is just the three of us to look after at the moment, and we won't be back for a month or so, but we will grow, and we'll get more staff as we need them. For now, I just want someone in the house, airing the rooms, making it lived in, keeping the grounds under control. We are still furnishing the house. Most rooms are empty, so I don't think the work will be too onerous. My only concern is whether you wanted to leave the city? My estate is a couple of leagues north of Greenswatch manor. So it is quite secluded. There won't be many people around."

Mary gripped her husband's hand. "We would prefer it. We would like our daughter to grow up where there is fresh air and lots of space." Her voice was low and cultured, at odds with her husband's. Birlerion thought there was a story there.

"You have a daughter? What is her name?" Leyarille asked.

"Sybil, she is five months."

"What a pretty name. I look forward to meeting her."

Mary smiled. "I can cook, clean, sew. I make our clothes, curtains. I know how to make preserves and store them; we just never had the windfall here to make it. I can pickle and salt, so we would never have an issue for stores. And George is a fast learner. He only needs to be told once; he'd soon pick up whatever you need him to do."

"Do you have any experience with horses?" Birlerion asked.

Tom spoke up. "We never had any horses, but I know a lad works at the hostelry would be interested; he is a natural."

"Well, we won't need to worry about the horses until we return. As I said, I'll be in Terolia for about a month, so we can meet him when we get back." He smiled at the couple. "What do you think? Would you like to give it a go?"

George glanced at his wife's face and grinned. "Yes, sir, we'd love to."

"Excellent. You need time to prepare and pack, so this is what I suggest. When you are ready, hire a wagon and charge it to my estate. I'll send you authorisation. Travel to Greenswatch and ask for Sentinal Versillion. He will escort you to Westermaine, give you the keys, show you your rooms and the house.

"Use your best judgement and keep the house for me. We can reassess what we need to do when we come home. I know it's a bit vague, but is that acceptable? The only thing I can't figure out is how you'll get about. Are you prepared to learn to ride or drive a cart? I could ask Versillion to give you some lessons, then at least you'll have some transport to the nearest village."

"We've got legs; we can walk," Mary said.

"But I'll learn if you want me to, sir," George added.

Birlerion smiled. "Very well, I'll arrange it with Versillion, and you can sort the details out between you." He squeezed Leyarille's hand. "Anything else you can think of?"

"No, I think you've covered it—only, welcome to Westermaine both of you. We look forward to the time when we'll all be there together."

Mary's smile lit up her face; it accentuated her high cheekbones and emphasised the delicate structure of her face. She was a beautiful woman. "You won't regret it, I promise. Westermaine will be ready for you when you come home."

Arriving back at the palace, Birlerion led the way to his rooms. Leyarille slid her arm around his waist, and he hugged her tight as they walked down the corridor. He glanced over his shoulder. "Jaredion, we should see if you can reach the Veil before you go off duty."

"Of course. What do I need to do?" Jaredion asked as he followed them into the room.

Birlerion sighed as he sat on the settee and rested his arm on the back. Leyarille sat beside him, and he dropped his arm around her shoulders. "The Veil is a defence, a protection against the wild magic that the Ascendants used. As such it is a complex weave of threads that form a barrier. Only ..." Birlerion hesitated. "Only, over time it has become more. It is not just a protection; it also has its own desires."

Leyarille stroked his hand, and Birlerion relaxed, suddenly realising he had tensed.

"When Leyandrii first brought the Veil down, Lorillion and I helped her. I don't think I realised what was happening at the time, I just remember Leyandrii drawing on me, using my power and Lorillion's to create the Veil." He frowned as Leyarille's fingers entwined with his. "It wasn't until Elliarille took me back up to the Veil that it recognised me."

Leyarille hissed her breath out.

"Ellie and Ellaerion had been trapped in the Veil for thousands of years. The Veil knew them intimately. I think the Veil learned what it could have, and Ellie fed that desire. Now she is dead, the Veil needs a new host. It is insidious, persistent, clever. It calls, constantly, trying to coax me back. I believe it wants to use me as it did Ellie."

"That is not going to happen," Leyarille growled. "You're mine!"

Birlerion smiled at her ferocious expression. "Except, I think it wants more. It is hunting me. A dark shadow hovers over me, watching my every move. I can't explain it, but I get the feeling it wants me for its own purpose. There is a hidden intent within its attacks. Whilst I am awake, I can defend myself, but when I sleep ..." Birlerion shrugged, unease stirring in his belly, "... it knows."

"But when you're with me, I keep it away," Leyarille said.

"Yes. I am safe when I'm with you. I can sleep. But if you are not with me, it attacks as soon as my guard goes down."

"So I need to replicate whatever Leyarille is doing," Jaredion said.

Birlerion wrinkled his nose. "Unfortunately, I don't think it's that simple. Leyarille carries a trace of the Oath and the Bloodstone, inherited from her father. I think that is what enables her to protect me. You don't have that. I think you are going to have to defend me in a more traditional manner, if you are able to reach the Veilspace."

"More traditional as in using my sword?"

"Yes."

Jaredion squared his shoulders. "Let's try and see what happens."

"First, let's see if you can access the Veilspace. Don't try and use your sword, we don't want to warn the Veil." Birlerion twisted his lips. "It will catch on quick enough as it is."

"Is the Veil … alive?" Jaredion asked.

"I think it wants to be," Birlerion replied. He squeezed Leyarille's hand and then stood. He walked behind Jaredion and grasped his shoulder. "You need to relax and focus your consciousness on me. Feel me gripping your shoulder. Focus on that connection."

Jaredion closed his eyes and concentrated. A small crease appeared between his eyebrows as he focussed on the warmth of Birlerion's hand seeping through his jacket. The sense of belief, support, even love, suffused him.

It was surprisingly easy to link with Birlerion. *"Good,"* Birlerion said, his voice soft in his mind. *"Now reach with me."*

"Reach?"

"Yes. Reach outside of your body. Outside of our world. Take your innerself and come with me."

Jaredion felt a wrench, and then he was floating. His link with Birlerion flared a brilliant gold and then he was rushing upwards, aware of Birlerion beside him until they came to an abrupt halt, and he gasped.

Sheer unending beauty spread before him. Sparkling translucent threads wove together in a shield around their world. Deepest black was dotted with pinpoints of light, a rash of sparkles that glittered all around them.

"That is the Veil," Birlerion murmured.

"It's beautiful."

"And deadly. Don't touch it. The strands try to embed themselves in you. Once it has you, it won't let go."

The strands twisted, loose ends trailing, questing in the air, reaching towards them.

"It knows we're here?" Jaredion asked.

"It knows I am near. Watch those tendrils."

Jaredion drifted in front of Birlerion and observed the Veil.

"Don't get too close." Birlerion's voice was a soft murmur as Jaredion watched the Veil undulate. It shivered and stretched towards them, a hint of darkness dulling the weave. It suddenly lashed out like a whip, and Jaredion snapped his sword up in front of him and cut the tendril off before it could reach Birlerion. Another strand swept around him, so fast Jaredion missed it and Birlerion grunted in pain before he lopped the end off and the Veil retreated, hissing and swirling in agitation. *"Return,"* Birlerion said, and Jaredion followed him in a rush back to his body.

Inhaling a deep breath, Birlerion's room solidified around him, and he was horrified to see Leyarille staunching a bloody wound on Birlerion's arm.

"I-I'm so sorry, Birlerion. It was so fast; I didn't expect it to lash out like that." Jaredion collapsed into a chair.

"It was your first experience of the Veil; how could you have known? That's the first time it's attacked like that."

"You don't usually go visiting," Leyarille said.

"True, I try to avoid it. But it keeps coming after me."

"At least we know Jaredion can reach the Veilspace, and he can protect you if needed."

"I'll get better, I swear. I was a little overwhelmed. It is an amazing view." Jaredion inhaled a deep breath, trying to ignore the tremble of fatigue in his limbs. Although they hadn't been there long, exhaustion hovered, waiting to ambush him.

"Forget the view and remember it wants Birlerion dead," Leyarille snapped.

Birlerion hugged her. "It was his first time. Give him a chance."

Jaredion launched to his feet and strode over to them. It was his fault Birlerion was bleeding. He vowed it wouldn't happen again. "No, Leyarille is right. I should have been paying more attention. I won't fail you again."

"You didn't fail me, Jaredion. You protected me. As I said, that was the first time it has lashed out at me. You couldn't have known. You did well. Very well. Now, go get some sleep. Leyarille will keep me safe tonight."

"Is that why the Veil retreated like that? Because of Leyarille?"

"Yes. The Veil is afraid of her. She keeps it away."

Jaredion swallowed at the enormity of the task. "Why don't you tell Uncle Jerrol about the Veil?"

"I did, and he said he would check it," Birlerion said on a sigh. "But I think he said it more to placate me. They believe I am fixated on it, because of what Ellie did to me. The more I warn them, the less they listen to me."

"I'll protect you, I swear. Until they *do* listen to you."

"I know you will." Birlerion gripped his arm. "Go to bed, Jaredion. We'll see you in the morning."

It was much later when Birlerion, lying in bed with Leyarille, stretched, reaching for a scroll of paper. The parchment crackled in his hand, and Leyarille looked up from her contemplation of his chest, her fingers tapping a soft beat on his skin.

"I had this drawn up for you today," he said, handing her the scroll.

She raised herself on her elbow and took it, pulling the red ribbon apart. She gasped as she read the papers. "But why? It's yours."

"It's ours. Westermaine is our home. We will build it together. I promise, Leyarille; we will get joined, just not yet. Until then, I want it to be ours, so no one can ever take it away from you."

Leyarille shivered. "Why would they? It is legally yours. The king bestowed it on you."

"What can be given can be taken away," he murmured, kissing her shoulder.

"Rubbish, they wouldn't dare. You are the First Administrator."

"And you will be the First Administrator's wife once I return from Terolia. You will need a new wardrobe."

"I can't wait." She smiled, letting the scroll roll back up. "Shall I give you a taste of what you will be missing?"

"I want more than a taste," Birlerion replied as he entwined himself around her. He kissed her body as she stretched past him to toss the scroll on the bedside table. She chuckled as she slid against him. "Now, First Administrator, didn't I tell you not to be so needy?" She stopped teasing as Birlerion kissed her, his mouth hot and demanding, his intentions clear.

5

OLD VESPERS

Two days later, they were packed and ready to travel. Kin'arol sidled around Birlerion in the palace courtyard, overexcited in the misty morning air. The scent of damp grass and mouldy leaves were a warning the year was drawing to a close, and the temperatures were dropping.

"*Hasn't anyone exercised you lately?*" Birlerion asked.

"*Yes, it's just we're going home. It's been so long.*"

"*Well, calm down otherwise you'll be worn out before we get down the hill.*" He caught the eye of the grizzled captain detailed to look after him.

"Captain Benson, first stop Greenswatch. I need to speak to Lord Simeon, then, if possible, East Ford, then the Watch Towers."

"Yes, my lord, we are ready when you are."

"Let's go then." Birlerion swung himself up and settled in his saddle. Leyarille and Jaredion closed either side and Benson's men organised themselves around them. The cavalcade proceeded out of the palace courtyard and down the switchback. They walked demurely through the city and picked up the East Road where they could finally pick up the pace on the open road.

Arriving in Greenswatch later that afternoon, Birlerion sat with his brother, Versillion, and Lord Simeon and relaxed with a hot drink. The day had chilled fast and they had all been eager for a break. Leyarille sat next him, and Jaredion had gone off to see the other Greenswatch Sentinal, Frenerion, while Birlerion explained where they were going.

Versillion quirked his eyebrows. "They are sending you to Terolia? I thought Jerrol needed you in Vespers?"

"I was glad of an excuse to leave." Birlerion rubbed his face, already tired at the thought of his impending journey. If only he could have used the waystones, but arriving with a troop of vomiting rangers was not the impression he wanted to make.

Versillion leaned forward. "Why? What's happened?"

"Nothing, I had forgotten how busy Vespers was. The quiet of Westermaine has lulled me into a preferring a peaceful life."

"You certainly deserve one. Jerrol should give you more time to rest before sending you off like this."

"I'm perfectly well."

Gripping his shoulder, Versillion shook his head. "You're not fully recovered. You need to look after yourself first. It takes time to heal. Yes, I know Val'eria cleared you as fit, but that doesn't mean you hare off to Terolia. She thought you'd be sitting behind a desk, taking it easy."

Simeon snorted. "I don't think those words have ever applied to Birlerion."

"Well, it's time they did. He can't keep up this punishing pace forever."

Birlerion laughed. "I can assure you, we will not be racing to Terolia. This is an official visit; I have the honour guard to prove it."

"And that means you'll be at least a month on the road," Versillion said, pinching his lips in concern.

"We'll be fine. Jaredion will keep an eye on me."

Versillion raised an eyebrow. "Not Leyarille?"

"I'm assigned to the Watch Towers to replace Tianerille while she has a break," Leyarille said.

Frowning, Versillion glanced from Leyarille to Birlerion. "And you allowed that? When are you two going to be joined?"

Huffing out a laugh, Birlerion threaded his fingers with Leyarille's. "Soon enough. Leyarille is going to do some research for me at the Towers and check on the Veil. Ari is concerned about something. We'll collect her on the way back."

Simeon sat up. "What is wrong with the Veil? Do we need to be worried?"

Birlerion smiled at Simeon's instant concern. So different to the disinterest in Vespers. "Jerrol said it's unchanged, but I just want to make sure."

"Keep me informed. Not that I can do anything," Simeon said with a scowl.

"Of course." Birlerion looked at his brother. "I wanted to ask if you would escort my new housekeeper and her family to Westermaine, show her where everything is. Mary and George Baines should be arriving within the next two weeks."

Versillion's face lit up. "Finally, you're planning to settle at Westermaine?"

"Oh yes," Leyarille said with a grin. "The palace is too stifling."

"You'll have to get a waystone put in," Versillion said.

"Rather that than staying in Vespers," Birlerion replied.

"We'll be glad to have you as our neighbour." Simeon raised his glass with a smile.

. . .

The journey to the Watch Towers was as every bit as slow and frustrating as Birlerion had expected. The only alleviating factor was Leyarille's company.

Since the first night in Greenswatch, Birlerion had ignored the scandalised captain and made sure Leyarille slept with him. After a couple of chimes of Jaredion protecting him each night, Leyarille crawled into his bed, soothed his agitation, and kept the shadows at bay. Sheltered by her arms and her love, he slept soundly and undisturbed.

Five days later, they rode up the winding road to the Watch Towers, in much the same order they had left Old Vespers.

He was not so eager about leaving Leyarille, but she had her duties as he had his. Jaredion had proved he could reach the Veil and protect him, and he would have to take over once they left the Watch Towers.

With Versillion willing to help settle George and Mary at Westermaine, he mused on his other worry, the Veil, as they travelled through the pine trees lining the road. The resinous scent permeated the clear air, and he inhaled the fresh aroma, unconsciously relaxing.

Ari hadn't returned, but his images were still stark in Birlerion's mind. He had shared everything he knew about the Veil with Leyarille, even how he had been involved in its creation. She would attempt to find out more about the purpose of the Veil and the Watchers.

The Watchers had been created before the Veil ever existed. That reminded him, he must remember to mention that Tagerill had been one of the first Sentinals posted up at the Towers and he'd been there for at least six months. He would be a good source of information.

Arriving at the Watch Towers, they clattered past the

duty guard who waved them in under the archway and into the grey stone-lined courtyard. A stable lad rushed up to take Kin'arol's bridle, his eyes wide as he admired the sleek lines of the Darian.

Venterion strode into the melee of dismounting men. "Birlerion, Leyarille, and Jaredion I see, welcome to the Watch Towers. Come, let me show you to your rooms. You must need to freshen up." He gripped Birlerion's forearm as he reached him.

"Venterion, it's good to see you." Birlerion grinned at the bull-necked Sentinal; he made up in width what he lacked in height. Leyarille paused beside him, and Birlerion wrapped his arm around her waist. "Lead on," he said as he shouldered his saddlebag.

Raising an eyebrow, Venterion tugged the saddlebag off Birlerion's shoulder. "This way, my lord, my lady."

Leyarille laughed and, hugging Birlerion, followed.

They inspected the towers with interest. Four circular, stone towers rose above a central courtyard now festooned with flowerbeds and sheltered seating areas. Evidence of new building works extended off the back of the tower gardens. Taelia, Leyarille's mother, had been in situ for about a month, setting up a new Chapterhouse. "I see the Scholar Deane has been busy," Birlerion murmured.

Venterion's laugh was deep and loud as he led them into the newer, main building and up the stairs. "She's had everyone hopping. But the foundations are laid. It won't take long for the walls to go up. Then we'll have a lot more youngsters up here. It will do us all good; we've been steeped too much in the past. We need some young blood to set us off in the right direction."

"How are the Watchers doing? I know you were hoping to encourage them to socialise more."

"Germaine is the most active; he likes to sit and chat with

Margareth of an evening, and Samuel and Virenne often join them. So we are making progress." He stopped before a door, his eyes twinkling. "This is you, Leyarille. Birlerion, yours is two doors up, and Jaredion is next to you."

Leyarille grinned and kissed Birlerion demurely on the cheek. "I'll see you downstairs."

"Dinner's in the main hall. You remember where that is?"

"Yes, see you there." Leyarille disappeared into her room.

Venterion dropped Birlerion's bag on the floor. "Bathing room is across the hall, shared by all in this corridor. Towels on your bed, see you downstairs."

Birlerion began to strip off his jacket. He grabbed a towel and headed for the bathing room. He met Leyarille at the door. "After you, my dear."

Leyarille chuckled and grasped his arm. "Let's share."

Jaredion cleared his throat behind them. "I'll protect your privacy. Make the most of it," he said, pushing them in and shutting the door. They exchanged a guilty glance then stripped off and made the most of the shower. They were drying each other off, whispering soft endearments, when Jaredion knocked on the door. "Corridor's clear," his muffled voice came through the door. Leyarille grabbed her towel and hurried back to her room. Birlerion took time to shave and then went back to his empty room. "Sorry, Jaredion, you must be desperate for a shower too."

"I'm sure mine won't be half as much fun," Jaredion laughed as he closed the door. Birlerion sighed and rubbed his hair dry as he rummaged in his bag for clean clothes. It was a relief to see the Watch Towers evolving. Tianerille had brought them back to life after the Watchers had stagnated for thousands of years, much like Sentinals in their trees.

Birlerion didn't have particularly good memories of the Towers, not that he had been posted there, but since he had been awoken, the towers reminded him more of his losses than anything positive. The Ascendants had tried to use them to tear their way through the Veil and bring their ancestors back. He had lost his very close friend, Serillion, in the battle to control the Watchers, and Jerrol had suffered much at Ascendant hands.

Shaking off his maudlin thoughts, he made his way downstairs to the dining hall. Tianerille, a large muscular Sentinal with cropped brown hair, was waiting in the foyer with Leyarille. "It's so good to see you, Birlerion; you look well," she murmured as she hugged him tight.

"I am, thank you. Leyarille and Jaredion take excellent care of me."

A faint shriek interrupted them. "Leyarille, when did you arrive? Why did no one tell me?" A slender woman dressed in the golden robes of the Scholar Deane of Remargaren shot across the room and hugged her daughter. She caught sight of Jaredion over Leyarille's shoulder and reached out an arm. "And Jaredion too." Her eyes widened, and she turned. "Birlerion, I wasn't expecting you." She embraced him carefully as if he might break. Birlerion laughed and hugged her back.

"I'm back at work, Taelia. It's so nice to see you. I can't believe you deserted Jerrol for a pile of bricks."

Taelia laughed and set him back from her so she could observe him more closely. He endured her scrutiny with a slight smile on his face. "You *do* look well. I am so pleased."

"As do you. The Watch Towers suit you," Birlerion said, admiring the sparkle in her beautiful turquoise eyes.

"What do you expect? I'm in my element! There is so much history here, and none of it is catalogued. Torsion barely scratched the surface."

"Yes, it's a shame he didn't focus on our history instead of trying to make his own."

"Never mind, let's not talk about him. Come, tell me why you are here. Margareth will be here soon. She was just checking something."

"Is the Veil alright?"

"Oh yes, it was nothing to do with the Veil. Tell us, why are you here, Birlerion?"

"I'm on my way to Terolia. Captain Benson and his men are escorting me to visit Maraine and then on to Fuertes. The king needs a bride, and I get to broker his choices."

Taelia's peal of laughter made them all smile. "Are you sure Anders will be able to cope with a Terolian bride?"

Birlerion shrugged. "I can but offer choices; the rest is up to him."

They sat down as Benson and Margareth arrived, completing their numbers. Margareth gave Birlerion a brilliant smile in greeting, her pale green eyes luminescing as she took her seat. She was a Veil Watcher and Leyarille's sister. She was the one who had saved Birlerion from the attentions of the Veil. "Birlerion, I am happy to see you fully recovered."

"Thank you. May I say, you are looking extremely well too."

"I love it here, there is so much to do, and with the Chapterhouse, it will be even busier."

"And you'll have Leyarille here as well. You will be spoilt for choice."

Margareth smiled at her sister. "I'm glad; it's been ages since we had any time together."

"I'm looking forward to learning about what you do up here and working with you and ma; it's going to be great," Leyarille said as she squeezed Birlerion's hand under the table.

Taelia considered her, then flashed a glance at Birlerion,

but at his bland expression she forbore to comment. "We'll love having you here. Both my girls together, I am so lucky."

The food arrived and the conversation became more general.

The next morning as Leyarille watched Birlerion and Jaredion ride away, she hugged her body, hoping Birlerion would be alright. The previous evening, she had snuck into his room, and they had talked most of the night, finally just holding each other as they slept. It would probably be Birlerion's last night of undisturbed sleep until he returned.

She had been horrified by how quickly the Veil had attacked him when they had tested Jaredion's reach. That it left a physical wound across his arm sickened her, but it was one they could fortunately hide from overzealous healers who would be quick to make assumptions about Birlerion's state of mind. But still, the Veil was evolving and not in a good way. The Veil was not something they should underestimate. It had already proved fatal to at least three Sentinals that she was aware of, if not more. She would find out everything there was to know about it, and they would find a way to protect Birlerion.

Leyarille went in search of her sister. She would start with Margareth, the newest Watcher. Hopefully she would be more open to believing what Leyarille had to say. She found her in her tower. "Looks like you've made yourself at home," Leyarille said, smiling as she looked around the cosy room. Swathes of dark red material were draped over the walls and either side of the window. Her leather reclining seat sat in the middle, and along one wall she had a wooden desk with shelves of books above it. The opposite corner was full of colourful cushions, and Leyarille collapsed onto them.

"Make yourself comfy, do," Margareth said with a grin. "I spend most of my time here, so I wanted it to be like home, even though I sleep up in the main building with the others."

"It's quite amazing that the Watchers slept in their chairs all those years, isn't it? How did we forget about them?"

"My theory is that they slept like the Sentinals; they must have to have survived all those years."

"Have you found out what their purpose was before the Veil? The Lady set their task to watch before she created the Veil, didn't she?"

"We don't know. Their memories are hazy. They only seem concerned about the Veil."

"What about you? Are you only concerned about the Veil? Is it behaving itself?"

Margareth laughed. "It is like a petulant child, but yes, it is fine."

"It must get boring with nothing changing. What else do you do?"

"How can it be boring? The expanse up there is immense. Don't you ever wonder what's beyond?" Margareth's eyes began to glow. "Think, when Birlerion first lived, there was no Veil. What do you think it was like?"

"He says it felt just the same, except there were more Arifels and of course the Lady could do things that no one else could, and that some people had different abilities than those around today."

"Like what?"

"His friend, Serillion, apparently, on occasion, would crackle with energy, as would Guerlaire. They had to exercise to keep it under control, but it strengthened their sword arm. And Guerlaire's sword, of course, that Pa has, was pure magic. Birlerion said it glowed blue. He spoke about them on the way here. I think coming to the towers reminds him of his loss."

"What about Birlerion? He is something special, isn't he?" Margareth asked, watching her sister closely.

Leyarille smiled. "You noticed."

"I knew it; you've been sleeping with him, haven't you?"

"Mags, what a question to ask!" Leyarille laughed, throwing a cushion at her.

Margareth caught it and grinned back. "You have, I knew it. You both seemed so in tune with each other. You can tell me. I'm your sister, after all."

Leyarille glanced towards the door. "Only if you promise it goes no further, not even Ma."

"Promise."

"Well." Leyarille smiled as heat flushed her cheeks. "I can safely say he is physically fine. He's asked me to join with him."

Margareth squealed. "I am glad. He is such a catch. When? Where? Have you told Ma and Pa yet?"

"Not yet, we want to tell them together, and he won't be back for at least a month. As to when, as soon as I can arrange it in the new year. I thought maybe on my borning day. I need to ask Mikke if he'll let us have the ceremony at Stoneford. It is still home for both of us, though of course, we'll live in Westermaine."

Margareth clapped her hands. "Oh, Leyarille, of course Mikke will say yes. It will be great to get everyone together again. I can't wait. Congratulations, I am so happy for you."

Leyarille grinned. "Make sure you keep a close eye on that Veil; I don't want any nonsense from the Veil delaying my Joining."

"Don't worry. I will."

"Have you seen Ari lately? Birlerion said he was all riled up about something to do with the Veil. Something was wrong with it; though he wasn't sure what."

"He came through a few weeks ago, all excited about the Veil, but there is nothing wrong with it."

"Good," Leyarille said, her chest hollow. Why could no one else see what has happening? She hugged her sister. "I'd better go see Ma. Remember, Mags, it's a secret until Birlerion and I can tell them. Don't tell anyone."

"I won't, Leyarille, you can trust me."

Birlerion and his escort arrived in Berbera on the Terolian borders as dusk was falling. Benson drove his men to set up camp while Birlerion, Jaredion, and two of the guards went to find the village Elder. They found him sitting under an olive tree by a well. Birlerion hesitated, remembering a graceful sentinal that used to stand there, now relocated to the plains of Oprimere. His friend, Adilion, had fallen in that final battle over twenty years ago, and he still missed him.

"Elder, Lady's greetings. My name is Birlerion, and I am looking for the Atolea. Do you know where they are camped?"

"Sentinal Birlerion, welcome back to Terolia. You have been much missed." The Elder rose and bowed, clasping his hands against his chest.

Birlerion returned the greeting and sat on the ground in the dust. "It is kind of you to remember me. It has been a few years since I last visited."

The Elder shrugged as he gracefully folded his legs. "One does not forget family, no matter how long they are away."

"Very true. Do you know if Medera Maraine will return this way?"

"Unlikely. She's more likely to be found towards Mistra or Melila. I would recommend you try Mistra first."

"I thought as much, but I thought it best to check before

we head off into the desert. Are any of her patrols in the vicinity?"

"Further south." The Elder peered at him. "You are not going dressed like that are you?"

Birlerion laughed as he looked down at his uniform; he was already perspiring under the thick material. "No, I have a robe in my bags, though I'm not sure about the guards accompanying me." He glanced over his shoulder at the hovering guards. "Peters, did your unit come prepared for the desert?"

"Of course, sir. We have taken our orientation for surviving in the desert."

Birlerion grimaced. Orientation would not be enough to survive. They needed experience. "Jaredion here needs some robes and some extra water canteens."

"I have what you need." The Elder rose and beckoned Birlerion to follow him into the shadowed doorway. "My daughter still makes them. You are fortunate that she hasn't taken them to the market in Mistra."

Birlerion looked at the robes piled on a table and began shrugging out of his uniform. "You are a lifesaver." He grinned at the sweating Jaredion. "Get undressed and take your pick; you will be more comfortable." He exchanged his clothes for a thin white tunic and trousers. He tucked his coins, papers, and map back into the deep pockets and then belted his daggers back on before wrapping a dark brown robe over the top of it all. He slipped his feet into the strappy sandals and breathed a sigh of relief as he immediately felt cooler.

He haggled with the Elder but finally agreed on a price for both his and Jaredion's robes and left his uniform in exchange for a second water canteen and two headscarves, though he kept hold of his boots. Wide-eyed, Jaredion copied him.

"I'll suggest the men come to you to get some extra robes. Don't bleed them dry. Make sure they each buy a water canteen as part of the trade, would you?"

The Elder chuckled. "Of course, my son. My daughter will be most pleased."

When they left the Elder's home, the stocky guard, Peters, did a double-take, his blue eyes bulged in surprise. "I would never have recognised you, sir."

Birlerion grinned. "I recommend you change your clothes now while you have the chance. You'll be much cooler. The temperatures will begin to rise as we travel into the desert. Your uniforms will be really uncomfortable."

"Yes, sir."

Jaredion laughed when they came back out, their uniforms bundled under their arms. They still wore their boots, neither purchasing sandals.

"Here, you tie it like this, that way it doesn't flap open." Birlerion deftly retied the man's robe.

"Appreciate it, sir, I've never served in Terolia before. We've done the orientation, but it's always different when you're actually here. You gonna be able to show us what to do with this? The gentleman inside said we would need it." Peters held up a bright orange scarf.

"I'll show you in the morning. You don't need it now." Birlerion released the bucket in the well and pulled it back up, carefully topping up both his and Jaredion's canteens. He looked at Peters. "Did you bring canteens?"

The men held them like some hard-won prize, and Birlerion filled them as well. "Water is life in the desert. No matter what, always check your water, always top it up when possible, and always make sure you secure it properly. Without water you will die, understand?" He waited until the men nodded. Tying off the bucket, he led the way back to camp, thanking the Lady for provisioning them so well.

Captain Benson glared at his men as soon as he saw them. "I didn't give you permission to get changed yet."

Birlerion spoke up. "Captain. You are in the desert now, and you will find tight-fitting uniforms most uncomfortable. The Terolian robes allow the air to move between the cloth and your body, allowing your skin to breathe. It helps reduce your body temperature so you don't overheat and collapse. All your men should change into robes. You will find it much more comfortable."

"We are the King's Guards. We do not go savage just because we are in another country."

"But Terolia is one with Vespiri; you are not in another country," Birlerion said calmly.

Birlerion watched with interest as one of the guards, a slim young man not suited to wielding the sword hanging at his waist, murmured in his ear. Benson's face grew rigid. "Lord Birlerion, your tent is the smaller one in the centre. We eat in a chime. Peters, break out the packs and hand out the robes."

Birlerion raised his voice. "And make sure you pick up a water canteen. Two if you can afford it."

Benson strode off, muttering under his breath, and Birlerion ducked into his tent. He sighed. This was going to be a nightmare of a journey if Benson was going to ignore his training; he'd be lucky to keep them alive. What was Bryce thinking to saddle him with such inexperienced men? He slung his canteens on the floor and stuffed his boots in his bag.

"Jaredion, I'm going to have a nap. We'll try it in short shifts, just a chime. Wake me up for dinner, alright?" He handed Jaredion his daggers and sword and lay on the bedroll.

Jaredion sat cross-legged in the entrance, shielded by the flap. He rested his hand on his sword and relaxed. His silver eyes glowed as he reached for the Veil and waited, hovering in the breathless expanse as he inspected the glistening strands twisting off into the distance. It wasn't solid, thousands of threads wove into a sparkling material which created a shield around the world of Remargaren.

He felt the disturbance as the Veil warped. It was as if the Veil knew when Birlerion slept, some inner shield or defence must drop, because the Veil sensed the weakness immediately. Birlerion didn't go to the Veil; the Veil was actively searching for Birlerion. Jaredion wished he could protect him like Leyarille could.

He swung his sword and parried the questing strands. The strands pulled back and regrouped. It pondered briefly and then split into two, twisting away in opposite directions. He waited; they wouldn't draw him away. The strands worked their way back towards him, and he lopped them off. Jaredion imagined the howls that would echo through the void if the Veil had a voice as the tendrils burrowed back into the weave. Fortunately, it didn't, and the silence continued uninterrupted.

The Veil retreated, and Jaredion watched.

***

Old Vespers, Vespiri

Jerrol opened the field healer's report and sighed with relief as he leaned back in his chair. Birlerion's party had arrived at the towers safely, and all was well. Birlerion was alright, no erratic behaviour observed. Jerrol felt a little uncomfortable sending a healer disguised as part of the troop, but the Administration were concerned, and it was better to be safe. At least a healer was on hand should he be needed. Captain

Benson had strict instructions to listen to the healer's advice if Birlerion should have a collapse or something.

He opened his next letter, which was from Taelia telling him about Leyarille and Birlerion arriving and how well they were. She wrote that Birlerion had seemed in excellent spirits. She was glad he had recovered; even Margareth said he looked well. Taelia's letter confirmed the healer's report, and Jerrol was reassured. Birlerion would be fine.

He moved on to Birlerion's report from Tom about the Healers changing their policy. He frowned in thought. The Healer's society was becoming more organised, it's members more co-ordinated in the way they provided their services. Healers retained by the king or the Watches assisted those within their remit, but for those outside, the general man in the street, they had extended their services on an as-needed basis. But he could see that changing. Something else to worry about. He jotted a note for his assistant to arrange a meeting with Healer Kirin, the head of the society and a vocal advocate for change and embracing new methods.

He picked up the next report.

***

Watch Towers, Vermouth

Taelia paused on the threshold of the dining hall and observed her daughter. Leyarille had changed. She couldn't quite put her finger on what exactly was different; matured, maybe. She was a lot more serious; she didn't laugh so much, and she worked hard. She was turning out to be a diligent researcher. If she hadn't gone Sentinal, the chapterhouse would have been her calling, Taelia was sure of it. She almost regretted the lost opportunity, to have at least one of her children follow in her footsteps. But the Lady's claim came first.

Taelia slipped into the chair opposite Leyarille and smiled at her daughter's distant expression. "Copper for them," she said softly and watched Leyarille's silver eyes solidify as she focused on her mother.

"Good morning. I was thinking about Birlerion and whether he had found the Medera."

"As in the sooner he finds her, the sooner he can come home?"

"Yes, I miss him."

"And do you have some good news for your father and me?"

Leyarille grinned at her mother. "He has to come back before I can answer that question."

"Then let's hope he comes home soon."

"Absolutely." Leyarille sipped her kafinee. Taelia helped herself to some toast and began scraping butter over it. "Why do we still need the Veil, Ma?"

Taelia jerked her head up and stared at Leyarille, her knife poised in mid-air. "What?"

"The Veil. Why do we need it? Its purpose was to protect us against the uncontrolled magics of the Ascendants. They are all gone now, have been for years. If there is no wild magic posing a threat, why do we still need it?"

"You do ask the most interesting questions. What made you ask that?"

"I was speaking to Germaine about what the Watchers did before the Veil was created. He couldn't remember. They were Watchers before they became Veil Watchers. In that case, they must have been watching something else." She looked at her mother. "So what were they watching?"

Taelia put her knife down. "I don't know," she said, "but that is an excellent question which needs an answer. Do you think you can create a research protocol with that question as the prime?"

"Of course."

"Then do it. Find out for us, Leyarille. It could turn out to be vitally important."

6

DESERTS OF TEROLIA

Birlerion glanced over his shoulder and checked the column of horses behind him. He called a halt and ordered the awnings raised. It was only a day's ride to Mistra, but they still couldn't travel in the heat of the day.

"Water the horses first, then yourselves. Rest while you can, we move in three chimes." He turned to Jaredion and kept his voice low. "Take the time to sleep. I will stay awake, Kin'arol will make sure. I'll sleep tonight."

Jaredion nodded and barely made it to the awning before he collapsed. He was asleep in a muddle of robes before his head hit the blanket.

Peters stopped by Birlerion. "I just wanted to say thank you, sir. If you hadn't made us wear these robes and stock up on water, we would've been in much worse shape than we are."

Birlerion grimaced, watching the men collapse under the awnings, suffering in the heat. The slim guard with the neat hair and sharp eyes moved between the men, offering water and a salve for their burnt skin. Birlerion watched him thoughtfully. "Who's the young lad tending your colleagues?"

"Tarvin? Don't know him, he's not part of our usual unit. He's a field healer, I think."

Birlerion shivered. "Ah, that's good then. Let's hope he knows how to treat sunburn and dehydration."

Peter's grinned at him from out of his orange headscarf. "Am I glad you made us wear these things! And we've only been out in it for half a day. Think what they'll be like by tonight."

"We've got at least eight days of travel if we go to Fuertes. imagine what they'll be like after that."

"They won't make it," Peters replied, watching his peers with better-informed eyes.

"I fear you may be right, Peters."

Birlerion woke them after the worst of the heat passed. Most of the men had succumbed and slept. "A sip of water only, little and often. Don't speak, keep your face wrapped up. If you don't have a scarf, use a spare shirt. It's about three more chimes to Mistra. We will camp there tonight."

The men slowly broke camp, and Birlerion watched them with concern. They were lethargic and miserable.

"They do not look much improved, Birlerion." Kin'arol's warm voice filled his mind.

"This is ridiculous. Why are they not better prepared?" he asked as he paired them up, ignoring Benson's objections. The fitter ones paired with a sufferer. "Keep an eye on them and keep them in the saddle. We can't stop out here any longer, they will die. We have to make Mistra before we can rest."

They dragged into Mistra five chimes later. Birlerion had to chivvy them on, rounding up stragglers. He took them straight to the Terolian Guard barracks. Men came running to take the horses and help those suffering from heatstroke.

"Birlerion, what's happened?" An assured, thin-faced officer strode through the crowd.

"Oscar, thank goodness. Nothing more than heat exposure, fortunately. Which we could have avoided if they had listened to me."

Oscar Landis, the Commander of the Terolian Guard, frowned. "Why wouldn't they listen to you? You are the First Administrator; they should follow your orders."

"Good question, Oscar, one I'll try to answer after I've had a cold shower, if that's possible."

Landis scanned the scene. The healer and his assistants had arrived and were dealing with those worse affected by the heat. "Come with me, you can use my quarters. It looks like you'll be leaving some of your guards here."

Birlerion thankfully handed over the unit to better-qualified people and, dragging Jaredion with him, followed Landis to his quarters. "How is Kayerille?" he asked as they entered the cool stone building. He eased off his scarves now that he was out of the blazing sun.

"She's fine, thank you. I'll take you home, and you will stay with us tonight. She'll be happy to see you. Jaredion, I didn't realise it was you, though I should have known. It's good to see you, lad. I am glad you at least listened to someone who knows what he is talking about."

Jaredion grinned. "I always listen to what Birlerion has to say."

Birlerion scowled. "One of very few these days."

Oscar led them to the shower room. "Jaredion, you go first. You looked like a boiled ham; get cooled down. Birlerion always acclimatises quickly." He found a couple of towels and gave them to Jaredion, pushing him into the room. "Birlerion, sit. I'll get you some water."

Birlerion sat and sipped the cold water. He rested the beaded glass against his temples. "I may acclimatise, but I still get hot."

"Don't we all." Oscar grinned. He originated from Greenswatch and struggled to cope with the heat on occasion, though not so often as he used to after fifteen years in the desert. "Tell me why that officer would not listen to you."

Birlerion grimaced. "They all think I am still affected by my recent traumas and that I will collapse in the middle of the street, a moaning wreck," he said somewhat bitterly.

"Bullshit."

"My thoughts exactly. They won't listen to me. I keep having nightmares about the Veil, and the healers believe it is my inner repressed feelings trying to escape."

Oscar scowled. "Which, of course, it's not."

"No, there is something wrong with the Veil. It keeps attacking me in my sleep. But they won't believe me. It's all in my mind, apparently."

"If they believe you to be unstable," he paused as Birlerion winced. "Sorry, poor word choice, but you know what I mean. If they are concerned, then why are you out in the middle of a desert with a crowd of deluded guards depending on you to keep them alive?"

"You always ask such excellent questions."

Oscar gave a crack of laughter and leaned back in his chair. "You always manage to find the most ludicrous problems."

Birlerion shrugged. "Welcome to my world."

"What do you need?"

Birlerion relaxed at Landis' calm acceptance of the situation. It had always been one of his most valuable traits. "I need to find Maraine; do you know where she is?"

"Last I heard she was out past Melila. I believe she was going as far as Lez before returning here."

"In that case, we may as well head towards Melila and hope we meet her on the way back. Any chance you can send her a message and tell her we are on our way and to meet us in Melila?"

"Why do you need to speak to Maraine?"

"I'm searching for a bride for Anders." Birlerion paused, sipping his water as Landis laughed again.

"They think you are not coping and yet they send you to find a bride for the King of Vespiri and Terolia? Are you sure they are not the ones who are unstable?"

Birlerion grinned. "Makes you wonder, doesn't it?"

"I assume you are after Mir'elle?"

"Yes, it's years since I last saw her; what has she been up to?"

Oscar chuckled. "I'll let Kayerille give you her opinion tonight; I'm sure it will be more …" he paused, "more accurate shall we say."

Birlerion rolled his eyes, and Jaredion came out of the bathing room. His dark hair was still damp, and he looked a lot younger dressed in his cotton tunic and trousers. Birlerion stood and picked up the towel. "I look forward to continuing this scintillating conversation with your wife." Oscar's laugh followed him into the shower.

Kayerille embraced Birlerion as he stepped through her front door. "Birlerion. Please be welcome in our home; what we have is yours."

"May your home be blessed and the Lady watch over you," Birlerion replied, hugging her back.

"Jaredion, please be welcome in our home."

"Lady bless you," Jaredion replied as he hugged the beautiful woman who was his friend Kayenion's mother.

Kayerille's home was bright and colourful, the grey stone interior softened with rugs and cushions. But she led them through the room and out into a shaded courtyard. The scent of roses perfumed the air, and Birlerion stopped. "Where did you find them?" he asked, looking up at the trellis above him. Tiny pink roses twined around the wooden strut work, providing a living ceiling of pink and green.

Kayerille laughed. "They are the closest I have found."

"They smell just like Leyandrii's." His shoulders relaxed at the familiar scent, and Kayerille pushed him onto the cushions.

"Relax, tonight is a night for reminiscing with old friends. Tomorrow is soon enough to pick up duties."

The evening passed in casual conversation, easy topics without weighted expectations, and he blessed Kayerille for her consideration. She introduced Jaredion to his first tanjia, a slow-cooked meat stew that melted in your mouth, flavoured with exotic spices that overwhelmed the taste buds. Birlerion hoped he would be able to stay awake after such an amazing meal.

Kayerille laughingly described the daughters of the Families who were of marriageable age. Oscar had obviously told her of Birlerion's mission. "Your most obvious choice is Mir'elle. She's intelligent, exquisite, and twenty-seven."

"Why hasn't she joined with anyone?" Birlerion asked.

"She was supposed to join with the eldest son of the Kirshans about four years ago, but he died in an unfortunate accident. She mourned his loss and then stayed to support Maraine when Viktor became so ill. They offered her the second son, but she refused; they didn't wait long enough. She has stayed with Maraine since Viktor passed. Her elder sister Elis'ande is due to take over as Medera later this year. I think the timing would be right for Mir'elle. A new beginning would suit her, and she deserves some happiness."

"What about Sim'intha of Gusar?"

"Another beautiful woman. She's elegant, poised, has a sharp tongue, though. She is older, past thirty. She has been the hand behind the Medera for years. She refused a couple of offers because she wanted to be the next Medera, but she miscalculated. Her sister joined before her, and her mother chose her. I'm not sure she would be prepared to take the back seat to Anders."

"And would be offended if Anders didn't choose her?"

"Very. I think you take a risk inviting her."

"Yet if I don't would that not be seen as an insult?"

Kayerille wrinkled her nose. "I'm not sure which is the lesser insult, but you are probably right. Does that mean you are travelling up to Fuertes?"

"Don't know. I think we'll ask Mir'elle first. If she is agreeable, we'll return to Vespers; if not then I'll try Sim'intha."

"Most of your men won't make it," Oscar said with concern.

"I know. I was wondering whether I could leave them here and take a few of yours? I don't need a whole unit; just a patrol would do."

Oscar considered him. "I'll be having words with Bryce. Why is he providing you with ill-trained troops? There are plenty of units that have rotated through the Terolian Guards and know how to go on."

"I didn't have a choice, and I didn't want to bring any of them. I would have used the waystone, but Jerrol wouldn't hear of it."

"Well, I can understand that. You can't travel on your own; you have a position to uphold. I'll assign you a patrol."

"Thank you, Oscar. I appreciate it."

"I'll go with you," Kayerille said.

Birlerion stared at her. "Why would you come with me?"

"There is no way Maraine will allow Mir'elle to travel without a woman companion, so unless you want a trail load of Atoleans, I'll come with you. In fact, she will probably bring her guard. You need a woman with you."

"She's right, Kayerille should go with you. She'll lead the

patrol," Oscar said. "Decision made." Birlerion knew he wouldn't make them change their minds.

He was blessed with his friends, and his chest tightened with emotion.

"Now," Kayerille said softly, "explain what is happening with the Veil."

Birlerion ran a hand through his hair and shrugged. "I don't know. I started having nightmares about the Veil attacking me. The healers think I have repressed feelings that are coming out through the dreams, but it's nothing to do with Ellie.

"Ari dropped by a couple of weeks ago. He was worried about the Veil, something wasn't right; he showed me images of it blackened and brittle as if it was diseased or something. But the Veil Watchers say it is fine. Jerrol thinks it's all in my head, and that's why no one is listening to me.

"Now it is actually attacking me when I'm asleep. I can sleep when Leyarille is with me, but when she is away …"

"It is like his defences drop when he is asleep," Jaredion explained. "The Veil can't reach him when he is awake, but when he sleeps, it knows he is vulnerable. It is actively watching for his defences to drop. I have been guarding his sleep. I go up to the Veil." Jaredion glanced at Birlerion. "It is getting more difficult. The Veil has some basic intelligence; it learns. It keeps trying to draw me away so it can get in behind me."

"So the Veil thinks Birlerion has something it needs?" Oscar said thoughtfully. "But what? And what does it want it for?"

"I don't know, this has all escalated since I left Old Vespers. We have no proof of anything. And with my recent traumas, the healers believe my concerns are all in my head. If I start saying the Veil is physically attacking me, they will certify me."

Kayerille rose and came to sit next to him. "We believe you, Birlerion. Anything is possible, and the Lady asked you to do many things that the rest of us couldn't. Jerrol and Bryce don't know you as I do, they don't understand. Even after everything that has happened, there are still things they can't possibly imagine. This is one of them. The Veil looks fine, therefore, they believe it must be fine, even if it isn't."

Birlerion closed his eyes. "Thank you. You don't know how much it helps to hear you say that."

Kayerille hugged him tight. "We will always believe in you, Birlerion; you are the last stand, the Lady's shield between us and whatever threatens us."

Jaredion slept while they talked late into the night until Birlerion reluctantly retired. "It's getting to a point where I'm afraid to go to sleep, but I can't stay awake forever."

"Leyarille will discover something at the Towers," Oscar said, "and you have Jaredion guarding you. He is a good lad. He won't let you down."

Kayerille woke Jaredion as Birlerion prepared to go to sleep, and he made sure they took his weapons. "If I wake up in fight mode, it will be safer if you take them."

Kayerille and Oscar watched as Birlerion lay down. He heaved a deep sigh and relaxed. Jaredion stiffened, his face draining of expression as he closed his eyes. Kayerille reached, but she couldn't see where he had gone. She couldn't reach the Veil the way Jaredion could.

Jaredion sat still and silent. It was if his body was vacant, waiting for a new family to move in. As they watched, Birlerion flinched, Jaredion tensed, and then Birlerion groaned. A red welt appeared on Birlerion's right arm. Kayerille and Oscar exchanged horrified glances. "They need help, Oscar. You have to go and tell Jerrol that you've seen the Veil attacking Birlerion and he needs to find out why. He needs to find Marguerite."

As dawn broke, they woke Birlerion. They argued about waking him earlier, but this was the only sleep he would get, and he needed it. Once Jaredion's face began to grey with exhaustion, Kayerille said it was enough and woke him. He was distraught when he realised Birlerion was injured. Kayerille had slathered the welt in a salve and bandaged it, but it was deep and angry. "I'm so sorry. I didn't think any got through."

Birlerion gave him a reassuring hug. "You're doing great, Jaredion, sleep while you can. Oscar will accompany me whilst I check how the men are faring and see if any are fit enough to travel with us. Kayerille will bring you with her when we are ready to leave."

7

OLD VESPERS, VESPIRI

The practice to use waystones to transfer messages daily was a definite improvement and also an indication that life was more peaceful with Sentinals reduced to messengers. But it did mean Jerrol was inundated with more information and requests.

Leaning back in his chair, he read Tarvin's latest report about Birlerion taking charge in Terolia. That sounded more like the Birlerion he knew. Jerrol was relieved his friend was coping so well. He would have to speak to Bryce, though. Benson should be abiding by Birlerion's advice, even if Benson was in command of his unit. Expert advice should be sought not ignored, especially if the men had little experience with the terrain.

Another project for them; time to start rotating the men again. They had become lazy. All soldiers should be trained in necessary survival skills in Terolia, Elothia, or Birtoli. Owen, Bryce, and Landis could organise it between them. Birlerion shouldn't have to teach them on the trail. They were lucky he had been with them. Jerrol frowned in thought; maybe it was time to set up a ranger station in

Berbera, make sure anyone entering Terolia either had experience or a guide.

Reaching for a quill, he began writing notes, though he had no doubt that Landis would already have his own suggestions for improvements. He looked up as his assistant hovered in his doorway. "Healer Kirin, your eleventh chime meeting is here, sir."

Jerrol rose as a thin, gangly man took his assistant's place. His high forehead and grey hair straggling around his face made him look a bit absent-minded. Jerrol extended his hand. "Healer Kirin, thank you for responding to my request for a meeting so promptly." Kirin's handshake was firm, not at all what Jerrol expected. He met the man's sharp grey eyes and began to revise his opinion of him. "Please have a seat. Would you like coffee or tea?"

"Mint tea, if possible. It helps focus the mind."

Jerrol nodded at his assistant and sat down. "I understand you have stepped into Healer Tyrone's position now that he has retired. They are large shoes to fill."

Kirin bobbed his head. "Fortunately for me, Healer Tyrone was my mentor for many years. He was most generous in sharing his wisdom and knowledge. The Healer's society is only in existence because of his vision. His efforts to bring forth consistent training methods and procedures have revolutionised our services, and there is much more we can do."

"What is your area of expertise, Healer Kirin?"

"Traumatic anxiety disorders. I have been working extensively with the King's Rangers and the King's Justice to treat anxiety issues resulting from life-changing injuries. The mind is just as important a part of our body as the limb that received the physical injury, yet we often overlook its impact on our behaviour. Losing a limb, for example, like Captain Deron did, was a traumatic experience. These men need someone to talk to, just to be able to comprehend and accept what has happened. Until they do, it is impossible to continue with their lives."

"A commendable effort. I wish we'd had something available like that when I suffered my injury." Jerrol clenched the remaining three fingers on his right hand.

Kirin smiled in sympathy. "Tyrone's work, I believe? He was highly skilled. It all takes money, of course, and facilities. I have invested some of my own money into an estate in Marchwood. These people require peace and tranquillity to adjust to their situation. By providing a haven for them to recover in, we can return them into society much quicker, but of course, it all needs funding, and that is just one facility."

"Is this why you have changed your policy for offering basic care? I understand that the Society is now charging a fee for appointments and, subsequently, any treatments that are identified."

"Unfortunately, yes. The healers have absorbed this burden of cost for years, but the population of Vespiri has grown; there are many more people with health issues. We need chapterhouses to educate new healers and facilities to provide these services."

"And yet, the Lady has always said help will be given to those who ask, whether they have the means to pay for it or not."

"That may be so, Lord Chancellor, but help costs money, and we are running out of it." He cleared his throat delicately. "I have a request coming up before the administration for state funding for my healeries and for a new law to provide free help for those who are deemed unable to care for themselves. I propose that the state takes the burden of care off the families. Families are rarely equipped to provide the support needed, and the stress causes issues within the family, which further compounds the problem. If we commit them to the healerie for treatment because they are unable to look after themselves, then I believe the state should fund it.

"If the Society received consistent funding yearly, then we would be able to use economies of scale to offer a basic level of support to everyone. Obviously, the more complex treatments would need to be fee-based, but common ailments and midwifery could be covered for free if state funding subsidised us." Kirin paused, his blue eyes gleaming.

"Forward me your proposal and I will review it."

"I gave a copy to your assistant when I arrived."

Jerrol smiled. "You came prepared, Healer Kirin."

Kirin laughed. "Healers are prepared for all eventualities; we never know who is going to come through our doors next. I was extremely fortunate to meet your wife, the Scholar Deane. Lovely lady. She was very interested in my proposals for an extension to her Chapterhouses for healers. The more structured we can make the training, the more consistent our healers will be in the service they offer."

"You sound like the right man for the job, Kirin. Let me read your proposal and I'll get back to you. When is it due before the administration?"

"Within the week, your lordship."

"Very well, I will make sure I read it today. It was a pleasure meeting you. I look forward to seeing how you continue to improve on the services available to us all."

"I appreciate you taking the time out of your busy schedule, and truly, we have the best interests of all our people at heart. We do endeavour to provide help to all who ask."

Jerrol rose and shook his hand. His assistant escorted the healer out, and when he returned, he handed Jerrol the proposal. Jerrol sighed. There were pages and pages of it; it was at least an inch thick. Before he started reading it, he would check the Veil, just to reassure himself that Birlerion was mistaken.

He relaxed in his chair and concentrated for a moment, reaching for the Veilspace. Immediately, he broke through and hovered in the vast expanse. It was beautiful and serene. Glistening strands twisted in an arc of protection around their world.

Inspecting the weave, he searched for a sign of hardening or distress, but found nothing. After a period of unending silence and no discernible change, the silence became oppressive and he returned to his body, aware that staying too long while he was on his own was foolhardy.

Straightening, he pulled the healer's report towards him and began reading the first page.

Watch Towers. Velmouth, Vespiri

Leyarille sat with Germaine in the library at the base of the west tower. Her mother had plans for a much bigger library in the new chapterhouse, but she liked this room; it was small, cosy. The homey scent of beeswax drifted in the air. Leather-covered books lined the shelves and a central oak table was surrounded by comfortable chairs.

Germaine reminded her of her grandfather Jason, with his cloudy white hair and distant pale blue eyes. They luminesced on occasion like Margareth's, or maybe it was Margareth's that luminesced like Germaine's.

"Germaine, why did you become a Watcher?"

"Oh, my dear girl, it was so long ago, I hardly remember."

"But you must have had some ambitions when you were

growing up. I wouldn't have thought Watcher was the profession that would spring to mind."

Germaine chuckled. "None of us understood what it meant, at first. Lady Leyandrii said the Land was protected and now the skies needed protecting too. She was concerned the magic would be twisted out of recognition and could be used to threaten the whole world."

"Did you see when she brought the Veil down? Did you know what she was going to do?"

"We didn't know, but you couldn't miss it. It was as if the very stars themselves exploded and the resulting splinters descended in a mist around Remargaren."

"I've heard it called a weave. My father and Margareth say to repair it they have to weave the strands back together. Were you able to repair it?"

"No, only the Captain and, it seems, those of his children with the bloodstone in their veins can repair the Veil."

"That would include me then," Leyarille said, her brow creasing. "My brother Mikke was born before my father absorbed the bloodstone, but Margareth and I were born after."

"Now, that may be true, but don't you go gallivanting up there on your own; you could get into difficulty. It is dangerous."

"I know, Birlerion occasionally speaks of his friend, Serillion, who was killed by the Veil." And if she didn't find out something soon, Birlerion could be killed by it as well. "You've watched it for so long, Germaine, have you ever seen it harden? I always thought of the Veil as pliant."

"Never. It has been abraded, worn out, strands snapping as they weaken, but it doesn't harden. If it did, it would break, and it would make the strands very brittle."

"Is there anything that might cause it to harden?"

"Not that I know of, and it never has, so we don't have to worry about it happening."

"Would you notice it if it did harden?"

Germaine peered at her, his bushy eyebrows drawn down over his nose. "I assure you, missy, the Veil is fine. We would notice soon enough if it weren't."

Leyarille gave up. She would try Margareth again. Maybe she would be more open to the possibility, not being engrained with three thousand years of stagnation.

8

DESERTS OF TEROLIA

They were two days into the desert and surrounded by featureless dunes and flat baked dirt when Birlerion called a halt. It was disorienting and relentless. Intense heat beat down on their backs, burning fiercely. Breathing was like inhaling air heated by a furnace, and it dried out mouths and eyes.

As the men watered the horses, Birlerion, Kayerille, and Fer'ilan, one of Oscar's captains, struggled up the incline of a nearby sand dune, their feet sinking into the loose sand. Flopping to their bellies, they crawled to the top and peered into the shimmering distance.

Even keeping still as Birlerion was, lying at the cusp of a ridged dune with hot sand shifting beneath him, sweat dripped down his back, stinging as it ran down the edges and into the welt at base of his spine. He squinted across the rolling desert, trying to ignore the discomfort. Faint white creases lined the corners of his eyes, already a sign that the sun had found his skin through his scarves.

Birlerion watched the group of heavily armed riders who

had been following their trail since they had left Mistra. Steel flashed in the sunlight. "Who do you think they are?"

"Difficult to tell. But with that many weapons, they are not a local patrol," Fer'ilan replied.

Birlerion frowned. "They are between us and the road to Melila. If we don't want to meet them head-on, we're going to have to veer towards the ridge, head for Marmera, and try to go around them."

"If they push us any further south, we'll be up against the Telusions," Kayerille said from beside him.

Birlerion peered back at the men waiting below. There were five of his original guards, and five of Oscar's but he would prefer to avoid a hand-to-hand conflict if he could. "Thoughts on who they are? We could try and out manoeuvre them."

"The only travellers out here are Kirshan patrols or bandits. If they were Kirshan, they would have approached us instead of keeping their distance," Fer'ilan said. Oscar's chosen captain was a typical Terolian, dark skinned with black curly hair and alert black eyes. He had a curved scimitar at his waist, and Birlerion knew he was skilled in its use. "We've had trouble with raiding parties recently, though last report said they were further north. It's possible a group have come south. We should try and avoid them, just in case."

"They already know we are heading for Melila. What if we continue trying to head that way, but tonight, make a dash for Marmera instead? They won't be expecting us to head north. We should be able to pass them in the dark," Birlerion said.

Fer'ilan frowned, busy calculating. "We'd have to ration the water. It's an extra day's travel, and it's bare rock where the tail end of the ridge is exposed. They may hear us even if they don't see us. Depends how close they get before they camp."

"We have two choices, we either hit them head-on, or we try to go around them," Kayerille said.

"Or we could go back to Mistra," Fer'ilan suggested.

"If we go back, they are likely to attack," Kayerille replied. "They wouldn't have spent so long following us if they were going to let us go unmolested."

Birlerion exhaled. "Let's try and go around. We won't impress the Medera riding into Melila all banged up. If that doesn't work and they do attack, then we'll have to fight and hope there are not too many more of them than us," Birlerion said.

"We can travel for another chime or two until dusk and then set up camp, get a few chimes rest. We won't be getting much sleep later by the sounds of it," Ferilan said.

Birlerion nodded in agreement, and they slithered down the dune back to the waiting men.

Under the cover of darkness, they slipped around the travellers' camp, muffling their horses' hooves with their scarves as they crossed the rocky shelf before dipping back down into the dunes. The night was black, and the moon hid behind a swathe of thick clouds that would burn away come morning. The chink of harness travelled quite clearly in the night air. Birlerion cursed under his breath as he led Kin'arol across the open rock. The camp, although quiet, was much closer than expected, but there was nothing he could do now.

Their luck held out until the last horse and rider were crossing the smooth rock. A scarf must have slipped because the metallic clang of the horse's hooves suddenly echoed and the peaceful night shattered as men rose, shouting in alarm.

Fer'ilan urged them on, and then wheeled his horse around to shout a challenge. A harsh voice yelled a reply, and

Kayerille swore under her breath. "Bandits," she muttered to Birlerion as the Terolian guards unsheathed their scimitars.

They had no choice but to engage. It was a very scrappy fight, and they were outnumbered, but they had three Sentinals and much better trained men.

Kin'arol pirouetted, squealing as a dark shape bore down on them. Birlerion parried the strike, aware of his men engaging around him. Jaredion loomed beside him and forced the bandit back.

Birlerion turned, sensing a presence behind him as a bandit barged into Kin'arol, pushing them away from the main fight. Riding the blow, he tasted the tang of blood in his mouth, and tangling with the man, they both fell into the sand and rolled down the side of a steep dune.

They struggled, grappling in the sand. Birlerion gripped the man's wrists and, trying to keep the knives away from him, he twisted. The man grunted, dropping his blade, and he brought his knee up. The robes fouled the movement, but Birlerion managed to get a leg around the man's and flipped him over. Pushing his face into the sand, he scrabbled for the knife, but no matter how hard he strained, it was just out of reach.

Pain spiked in his shoulders, he was at full stretch restraining the man, but at last, the man's struggles beneath him weakened as he suffocated in the sand. He grabbed the dagger and rose as another pair of tangled men rolled down the dune. Unable to tell friend from foe in the darkness, he grasped the robe of the man nearest him. "Name," he hissed as he raised the knife to his throat.

"T-Tarvin."

It was the field healer. Birlerion pushed him away and turned to Tarvin's opponent, diving in as the man rose from the sand.

Birlerion's breath was coming out in gasps. His chest

hurt, as did his cheek, which had caught the edge of a blade. He had made the man pay for that, but he was tiring. He had to end it quickly. Feinting, he ducked under the swinging arm, threw his other arm up, blocking, and thrust his dagger upwards. The man faltered and sagged to the sand as warm blood spilt over his hand; he must have hit something significant. He tugged his blade out and stood, straining to see who was nearby. He couldn't hear any other fighting. A shadow moved. "Tarvin?"

"Lord Birlerion, are you alright?"

"Yes. Let's see if we can find the others." Birlerion tried to lead the way back up the sand dune, but their feet sank into the shifting sands. "We'll have to go around. Let me just get my bearings." Birlerion breathed in deeply, catching his breath. He began the movements for the first stage of Apeiron, the disciplines which aligned body and mind, and steadied as his mind calmed.

The sky above was swathed in cloud, as dark as the land, and he couldn't tell where one stopped and the other started. He rotated, but there were still chimes till morning, and there was no indication of where the sun would rise.

"Oh, for a compass and a flame to see it by," he whispered.

"W-what?" Tarvin's teeth were chattering. Birlerion wasn't sure if it was cold or fear.

"Are you alright, Tarvin? Not hurt?"

"N-no, just cold."

A bit of both, Birlerion thought, and a touch of shock to boot. The lad had probably never been in a fight before. "It can get cold at night. Tuck your hands in your sleeves and keep your mouth shut. Chattering teeth are very loud."

"Kin'arol?"

"I come. Where are you?" Kin'arol's voice was faint.

"I don't know. I can't see anything. It's too dark. Who is with you?"

"Jaredion and Fer'ilan and some of his men. We just came across the camp; we have injuries, so we stop here."

"No sign of Kayerille?"

"Not yet. Who is with you?"

"Tarvin."

"We are missing four men, including you and Kayerille. Fer'ilan intends waiting until dawn, and then we search."

"Did we get them all?"

"Difficult to tell. It's possible there are still some out there."

Great. Not only did they have nothing on them except a blade, but they might also come across more bandits.

"Tarvin, do you have anything on you? Water? Weapons?"

"J-just my sword."

"Give it to me. I've lost mine."

"Kin'arol? We have no water."

There was a brief silence. *"I will come as soon as you tell me where."*

Birlerion turned towards the shadow that was Tarvin. "I can't tell which direction we need to go. I think I was driven south of their camp, but I'm not sure. It looks like we are surrounded by high dunes. Let's see if we can find a way out, and then we'll bed down until dawn. Melila is east and the sun rises in the east. When the sky begins to lighten, we'll know which way we need to go if we can't see anyone."

"Alright."

"Come on then, stay close." Birlerion followed the dune around its long curving edge and it kept going. Stumbling in the deep sand as it shifted beneath them, it was slow going and tiring. After about a chime, Birlerion called a halt. It didn't feel right. Instead of guessing the direction, they would wait.

"Let's stop here, scoop out a bed in the sand, try and get some sleep. The sand will keep you warm; it retains some of the sun's heat. I'll keep watch. I'll wake you at dawn."

"What about you? You need sleep too."

"I'm not tired. I'll sleep tomorrow."

Birlerion huddled in the sand next to Tarvin. He listened, straining to hear any movement in the sands.

It was silent except for the slow breathing of the man lying beside him. There were no birds, no skittering lizards searching for food, no stealthy shifting of sands of someone trying to creep up on them. A gentle desert breeze stirred, felt more than heard, caressing the tender skin of his sore cheek. He stared up at the sky and thought about Marguerite.

She should be vibrant and present, but she wasn't. Was that something to do with what was happening to the Veil? Ought he divert to Senti instead of lingering here in the desert chasing a fool's hope? If he had known the Veil would escalate its attacks so quickly, he wouldn't have come. His priorities would have been somewhat different.

His gaze focused on a shadow flitting across the sky, followed by a second. He stood, trying to see the direction they flew; tiny desert bats out on a foraging spree. They lived in cool caves, deep in the stone. Were they coming or going? He couldn't tell.

His body ached, so he spent a chime working through 'Acknowledgement', warming muscles before they stiffened in the cold. He paused, breathing deep, and listened. Silence. Was the sky beginning to lighten or was it his imagination? He started 'Understanding' and flowed into the moves. When he finished and looked around, the sky was definitely lighter to his right than his left. The black sky was easing to a deep grey but still not light enough to see anything. Another chime then, time for 'Awareness'.

. . .

Tarvin woke in the lightening gloom, shivering in his robes. Darkness pressed in around him, but it wasn't so dense; dawn was approaching. He watched Birlerion moving through some sort of slow exercise and stiffened as his sleeves fell back and revealed dark marks instead of the gleam of smooth white skin. Birlerion came to a halt and dropped his hands, the sleeves concealing whatever he was doing to himself. Tarvin's stomach fluttered. He had begun to think the healer's concerns were unfounded, but here was evidence that Birlerion was not in as much control as he ought to be.

He didn't know where anyone else was; they had become scattered very quickly in the melee. He had no idea where he was, and Birlerion was his only hope of survival. At least someone would come looking for the First Administrator.

Birlerion stilled, listening. There were no sounds on the night air; there was no one in their immediate vicinity. They needed to get to higher ground and see what they could recognise. His neck prickled and he looked over at Tarvin. He was awake. His eyes gleamed in the dim light. His sixth sense was returning. That was a relief.

"Let's try and get out of these dunes. East is that way; as long as you keep the sun in your face, you will be heading east." Birlerion led the way through the shadowy dunes. Finally, they climbed one of the lower mounds, struggling through the sands. Birlerion rotated. "I don't understand how we can be so far from the bandit's camp. I don't remember us being forced this far away."

Tarvin shrugged.

Birlerion deliberated. Head for Melila without water or try to find the Bandits' camp, which in theory was closer?

"Kin'arol?"

"Yes?" His voice was even fainter.

"I still don't know where I am, and the dunes seem endless. I don't know whether to head towards the sun and hope to hit Melila or head west and hope to find you."

"You are going away from us. If you go much further, I won't hear you. Stay where you are, and we will come to you. We are packing up camp and moving towards Melila. We managed to round up enough horses. Wait for us, Birlerion."

"Alright, we'll just get out of the dunes and then we'll wait. If I can find the flats or a trail marker, I'll let you know."

"We come."

Birlerion eased his shoulders and stared at Tarvin. "Help is coming; let's get out of these dunes."

"Your face, it's covered in blood."

"Caught the edge of a blade. Nothing we can do now unless you have your kit on you?" He wrapped his scarves around his face as Tarvis shook his head.

"Ignore it, then. Come on, we'll go this way." He led the way down the other side of the dune and followed the curve towards what he thought might be a gap. He froze as the sliding sands ahead warned of another movement. Friend or foe?

He waited. The other person had stilled waiting too. Keep silent or call out?

The silence stretched.

Decision made, he raised his voice. It came out as a croak, and he tried again. "Kayerille?"

"Birlerion? Thank goodness." Kayerille appeared over the dune and half stumbled, half slid down towards them. Birlerion helped her to her feet, and then he hugged her with relief.

"Are you alright? You're not injured?"

"No, I just got separated somehow. Do you have any

water?"

Birlerion grimaced. "I was hoping you did."

"No. Well, we made a fine mess of that, didn't we?"

"Do you know where we are? I was heading towards that gap over there."

"They are called the endless dunes because that's what they are. They stretch from Marmera down to the Telusions. There is a road that winds through them, but half the time it's covered in sand so not used much. I think we are in the middle, and the road should be through that gap. If it is, we might find the marker."

"Or not, knowing our luck. Kino is bringing the others, and they at least have water; they just need to find us. They rounded up some of the horses, and they have injured men, so we need to get Tarvin back to them."

They walked as they talked and came out on a flat stone expanse before more dunes rose the other side, and Birlerion heaved a sigh of relief. It was a much easier footing, if more exposed. "Kino wasn't sure if there were more bandits still around, so I don't think we can just sit here and wait. We can either hide behind that dune and watch for them or we walk towards Melila. What do you think?"

"I'd prefer to be doing something until it gets too hot. Let's walk until the sun rises and then we'll wait."

"*Kin'arol? I've found Kayerille and the road. We're going to walk toward Melila until the sun rises and then we'll wait for you.*"

"*We come.*" He sounded closer.

Birlerion snorted into his scarves. His Darian was a horse of few words.

They turned onto the sometimes road and began walking towards the sunrise. It was another chime before Kin'arol reported they were on the road, and they stopped walking. The sound of many horses drew nearer. Tarvin tensed, and Birlerion smiled. "It's Fer'ilan and the troops," Birlerion murmured, his voice gruff. Kin'arol had been getting louder in his head for the last chime. At least it kept him awake.

Jaredion slid from his horse and grabbed Birlerion, checking him over, half frantic with worry, though he calmed down as he realised Birlerion wasn't seriously hurt and the Veil hadn't carried him off. "Thank the Lady you're alright!"

"Thank goodness you found us, or we might not have been," Birlerion replied as he hugged him back and then accepted a water skin. The water was tepid, but Birlerion thought it had never tasted sweeter. "Did you manage to recover everyone? I found Kayerille and Tarvin, but there were more missing, weren't there?"

"Everyone is accounted for," Fer'ilan reassured him.

Dragging out the healer's kit, Jaredion insisted Tarvin treat Birlerion's face. Open sores festered fast in the desert. After cleaning the wound, Tarvin ended up pressing a pad against Birlerion's cheek and wrapping a bandage around his head.

They had lost most of their supplies, but fortunately, the water canteens were still tied to the mounts they found. Tarvin was able to clean and dress the cuts and contusions. Luckily there was nothing more serious.

It took them another two days to reach Melila. Two days of trying to sleep in the baking heat and travelling at night. Birlerion sincerely wished for a waystone. He could barely stay awake. Kayerille and Jaredion were taking turns poking him in the side. He couldn't risk going to sleep until most of the men had bedded down, and only then for a few chimes, and he struggled to stay awake day and night.

Birlerion was conscious of Kayerille's growing concern. If he was overtired, Jaredion was showing signs of prolonged exhaustion. He was drooping in his saddle, his face strained and pale under his scarves. His body was beginning to show signs of the Veil's attentions as it struck out at him in frustration.

He was also aware of Tarvin's scrutiny. He observed them all from a distance. Birlerion had been unable to hide the new wounds on his arms quick enough and he was sure Tarvin had seen them when his sleeves had fallen back as he mounted his horse.

As they approached Melila, Birlerion was relieved to see the Atolean camp on the approach. There was much activity, and Birlerion grimaced as Kin'arol said it was for them. Landis had managed to arrive before them accompanied by a search patrol.

Landis strode through the men and Kayerille gasped in surprise. "Oscar, what are you doing here? You are supposed to be on your way to Vespers."

Oscar's face relaxed at the sight of her. He reached for her and hugged her tight. "We had reports of bandits on your route before I left, so I sent a message to Vespers instead and came looking for you. We were trying to intercept you, but we couldn't find you. I was so worried."

"We tried to slip around them and had to divert further south, but they attacked us instead."

"I've run my men into the ground searching for you, and we didn't find the bandits either, so they are still out there as well."

"Not all of them. We dealt with most of them," Fer'ilan said.

Oscar nodded, drawing Kayerille away. "Give me a quick report and then go get checked out by the healer. The Medera offers her healer's services."

Tarvin gawked as the Atolean Medera embraced Birlerion and then Jaredion before leading them into her tent, throwing out instructions for water, food, and more.

Tarvin followed the men, offering to help the healer. Kin'arol was led off with the other horses and was happily anticipating baliweed, a grass he was most partial too.

"Birlerion sit, you look exhausted. Drink, you are dehydrated, and you, Jaredion. Tell me what happened," Maraine said as she fussed around them. She was a small woman, her glossy hair, now more grey than black, still piled on top of her head.

"We were attacked by a group of bandits west of here, and they forced us south off the route. We were lucky to find our horses; otherwise we wouldn't be here," Birlerion said, unwrapping his scarves.

Maraine winced as she saw his face. "And found trouble, I see."

"It's only a scratch. Not worth fussing over."

"Don't be silly, Birlerion. An open wound should not be left unattended in the desert. You know that." She called for the healer.

Cringing, Birlerion tried to persuade her his wound wasn't serious. "Maraine, the men are more important; they have worse injuries. Let her look after them first."

"You are the First Administrator, and a son of the Atolea. As if we would not offer you the assistance you need." She fussed over him until the healer arrived, and Birlerion let her.

He sat through having his face treated. Arguing would only have delayed the healer longer.

Jaredion grimaced at him. "Looks worse."

The healer grinned. "The bruising will fade. Drink plenty of water both of you, small sips. You are on the edge of dehydration; you're lucky it's not worse."

"And the men?"

"Cuts and abrasions, dehydration like yourself, nothing serious."

The healer bowed out, and Maraine smiled at him. "Why are you here, Birlerion?"

Birlerion sighed out a breath. This was not how he had intended having this conversation. "I came to get your opinion on a state issue. Anders is looking for a bride, and I wanted to know if Mir'elle would be interested in meeting with him."

Maraine blinked. "That was not what I was expecting you to say."

Birlerion laughed. "You did ask. Anders needs to secure his succession, and I wanted to propose a Terolian bride. One who would bind Terolia and Vespiri tighter together. But I wasn't sure of Mir'elle's circumstances."

"You'll have to ask her yourself. I have no concerns in principle, but this is a discussion you should have with her."

"Of course, but as her Medera, and her mother, I wanted to speak to you first."

"I thank you for it, but I have handed over to Elisande. My heart isn't in it now that Viktor is gone. The younger ones need to pick up the reins now."

Birlerion wasn't surprised. "I understand; it can't be the same without Viktor. He is much missed. Where will you go, Maraine?"

"I haven't decided. Mistra possibly; it's time to stop travelling. Elisande will manage fine, and her husband, Andisse, is a good Sodera. I will introduce you to them when they arrive. They went with Mir'elle up to Lez, and they will return in a couple of days. See, already I am staying put. I don't have the energy anymore."

"Will Medera Elisande need to approve the match?"

Maraine grinned. "No, I am the mother. But it will be Mir'elle's choice. I will not force her."

"Of course not, and this is just to meet him. If she

decides it won't work, there is no shame. There are other women in the world, after all."

"You will just have to find them," Maraine said with a twinkle in her eye.

Birlerion chuckled. "I will be asking you for suggestions. I do not want to be spending all my time matchmaking."

"Understood. Be welcome in our home, Birlerion. Bathe, rest. Mir'elle will be back soon."

Birlerion stood. "Thank you, Maraine, Lady bless your home."

9

MELILA, TEROLIA

Birlerion and Jaredion discretely bathed, and Kayerille reapplied the salve and bandages where possible. Jaredion was also beginning to collect scores inflicted by the frustrated Veil much to Birlerion's dismay. Birlerion sent Jaredion off to catch up on some much-needed sleep whilst he sat with Oscar and Kayerille in the guesting tent, feeling much refreshed, if still tired.

"What is the plan?" Kayerille asked.

"First, speak to Mir'elle, and if she is agreeable, head back to Old Vespers. Then I need to start working on the Veil. See if Leyarille has discovered anything, speak to Jerrol. I can't go on like this, that's for sure. Then check on the Oath; it is too quiet. I need to speak to Marguerite."

Oscar nodded thoughtfully. "I need to head back to Mistra. I'm just waiting on the men to recover before I leave, you need some sort of guard. You can't appear weak to the Atolean."

"I appreciate your concern, though I would prefer not to have to travel back to Vespers across the desert. We certainly can't use a waystone. I shudder at the thought of Mir'elle and her entourage arriving and promptly vomiting every-where. Not the first impression she needs to give to the citi-zens of Old Vespers. I was wondering if you could see if there was any word of Roberion? If we could use his ship to take us home, it would be much quicker."

"Now there is a thought," Kayerille said, sitting up. "If you want, I can ride up to Feril and check for you if you like whilst you're waiting for the Medera. And leave word if he isn't."

"Thank you, Kayerille, that would be a great help."

"In that case, we'll bid you good night, seeing as I haven't seen my husband for a while. I'm going to make my time count before he departs again."

Birlerion laughed and let them go. He wished Leyarille would walk through the door, not only because he needed a good night's sleep but because he missed her. He could use her help to figure out what was going on. Hopefully, the time spent at the Watch Towers would prove valuable. Musing on the Veil and the Oath, he tried to remember everything he knew about them.

He had been involved at the beginning, and it looked like he would be involved at the end if he could stay awake long enough. The Lady had sundered the Bloodstone to create the Veil, and when she'd destroyed it, he had been linked to her as he projected a shield over the people of Vespers, protecting them. The Lady had drawn on him and his power when she'd created the Veil. He remembered the vast expanse, his exhaustion as she drew him in, and the descending sparkles twisting into the weave that became the Veil before everything went dark. If some part of him was in the Veil, then maybe that was why the Veil needed him, possibly to replace something it was losing?

But what? And why now?

No, that didn't make sense. Jerrol had absorbed the

pieces of the Bloodstone, and the Lady had used him to repair the Veil the second time around. He should be suffering the same way Birlerion was. They had both contributed to the Veil. Why was he affected but Jerrol wasn't?

He mulled over how the Oath could be connected. The only connection he could see was him. He held the Oath, and the Veil was trying to consume him; was it him or the Oath it was after? The thought made him go cold. Could the Veil be trying to drain the Oath out of him? Was that what it was after?

He didn't know, and it was making his head ache.

"You need to sleep," Kin'arol said, his voice gentle in his mind, his concern palpable.

"Not yet, give the boy more time."

"You need the time too, Birlerion. Don't forget."

"I know, I won't."

Giving up, he went to find Jaredion, then collapsed into his borrowed bed, readying himself for the nightly onslaught. Although he was sleeping, he wasn't getting any rest, and each night was a test of resolve, his body the battleground. It was as if someone was whipping him every night, which he supposed was the case. The Veil would wrap its strands around him, trying to draw his blood, and left angry welts in its wake. As Jaredion said, it was intelligent to a degree and learnt from its mistakes.

Chancellor's Office, Old Vespers

Jerrol read the report, and his heart sank. Self-harm? He couldn't believe it. And now reports of similar injuries were being observed on Jaredion. Could Birlerion really be attacking Jaredion too? Not deliberately, surely. There was no way he would ever hurt Jaredion if he could help it.

"I am sorry, Lord Chancellor," Healer Kirin's voice broke through his thoughts. "We didn't want to say anything before we were sure. We reconfirmed with Healer Tarvin, and as you see, he has reported seeing similar injuries on Sentinal Jaredion as well. He reports that Lord Birlerion won't allow anyone but Jaredion to guard his sleep, and Jaredion is obviously too afraid to speak to anyone, so he is concealing what is happening. We are concerned Lord Birlerion is unable to control his actions; he is a danger to himself and others. Lord Chancellor, I assure you, we wouldn't approach you if we didn't have incontrovertible proof."

"I can't believe it. Birlerion wouldn't harm anyone, least of all Jaredion."

"He has already attacked Jaredion, certainly once that we know of. He didn't mean it then, but he couldn't help himself. It is often very difficult to believe ill of one you love. I know Birlerion is a very close friend of yours. But as a friend, a good friend, it is your duty to ensure he is given the care he needs to protect him from himself.

"As Lord Chancellor, it is your duty to remove the danger from society. He is unable to control his behaviour, and he could harm others as well. There is no telling what he could do. Birlerion is a trained killer; his levels of violence and the havoc he could wreak are terrifying."

"He wouldn't. Just because he has the skill doesn't mean he will use it. You could say the same of every soldier that is trained."

"He is uncontrolled, my lord. He no longer sees the line he shouldn't step over. The rules of society no longer bind him. If they did, he wouldn't be inflicting harm on others to ease his pain." Kirin considered the Lord Chancellor. "You are the Captain of the Sentinals. Would you want one Sentinal's behaviour to tarnish the reputation of all the others? For your Sentinals to be feared just because they have silver eyes like Birlerion? For you to be feared? You can't allow your emotions to overrule what you know is the right thing to do."

Jerrol stared at the healer.

"Consider it, Lord Chancellor. Reconfirm if you must. But recall Lord Birlerion to Old Vespers before it is too late. I'll leave the papers with you." Healer Kirin bowed and left. Jerrol stared in concern at the seat he had vacated.

Watch Towers, Velmouth

Leyarille was getting desperate. They wouldn't listen to her suggestions. No one was concerned; no one was worried. They weren't even looking. What could she do? She couldn't do anything, apart from going to look for herself, but she wouldn't know what she was looking for.

She was tossing ideas around as she approached the dining hall. Her sister and her mother were already seated with Venterion. They were laughing, *laughing*. Something snapped within her, and ice-cold anger ran down her veins.

She greeted Venterion and smiled at the women seated at the table. "How is the Veil today?" she asked, her silver eyes glittering and an edge to her voice.

Taelia glanced at her as Margareth replied, "It's fine, Leyarille, why do you keep asking?"

"Because I keep telling you there is something wrong, and you don't seem concerned."

"Because there is nothing to be concerned about. Stop trying to borrow trouble, Leyarille," Taelia said.

"You keep telling me it is dangerous; why? You say,

'Don't go up on your own, Leyarille, you may not come back'. If it is so dangerous, then why are you not concerned that Birlerion, Ari, and I have told you that there is something wrong with the Veil?"

Taelia stared at her daughter. "What has happened, Leyarille; what has upset you?"

"I am not upset." Leyarille spaced out her words, unable to restrain her fury any longer. "I am angry at your complacency."

Margareth stared at her sister in wide-eyed awe. She had never seen her so magnificently furious, and it made her sit up and listen.

"If you do not start looking then I will. I will not let the man I love die because complacent people like you, who think they know it all, can't be bothered to do their jobs."

"Leyarille. There is no need to be insulting." Her mother's voice was sharp.

"Are insults the only way to get a response out of you?" Leyarille dashed away an angry tear.

Margareth gasped. Her sister was genuinely worried about Birlerion. "Leyarille, I swear we are monitoring the Veil, but I have seen no issues. No hardening, no abrasions. Nothing out of the ordinary."

"Just because something looks alright, doesn't mean it is."

"But if we can't see anything wrong, how can we tell?"

"Look for something else, like signs of Jaredion in the Veil. He shouldn't be there, but if he is, then that is an anomaly, isn't it?"

"What does Jaredion have to do with it?" Taelia asked frowning at her daughter.

"He is defending Birlerion. From the Veil. I would have thought you would have noticed that by now."

"Don't you think that is taking it a bit too far Leyarille?"

Leyarille spun on her mother and Taelia flinched back

from the anguished expression on her face. Leyarille shook with restrained fury. "I haven't taken it far enough. I thought if I played the game, then you would listen and believe me, but I was mistaken."

"Played the game?" Her mother's voice grew colder.

"Yes, Mother, let you and Pa push me around as if my opinion doesn't matter. I am here because Pa thinks I am a crutch for Birlerion. He thinks Birlerion won't ask me to join with him unless he has time to miss me." Leyarille gave a crack of laughter that made Margareth shiver. "He has already asked me, and I accepted, but he won't join with me until he figures out why the Veil is attacking him. Does that make it plain enough?"

Taelia stared at her, horrified. "But there is nothing wrong with the Veil. It can't be attacking him. Birlerion must be imagining it."

Margareth thought Leyarille might explode, but she contained herself.

"Birlerion is not imagining anything," Leyarille said, her voice so low it made Margareth's hair stand on end.

Venterion sat open mouthed.

Margareth stood. "Leyarille, come with me, and I'll go and look."

"Margareth, you haven't had your dinner yet; you must eat first."

"No, I must go and look. Birlerion is more important." Margareth ignored her mother, grabbed her sister's hand, and dragged her to her tower.

Margareth made her incandescent sister sit on the cushions and crouched before her. "Now tell me exactly what is happening to Birlerion, every detail."

Leyarille exhaled and began talking.

Melila, Terolia

Medera Elisande and Sodera Andisse arrived in Melila two days later, accompanied by Mir'elle. Birlerion and Jaredion had survived another two nights, only just. Jaredion was barely able to keep his eyes open, and Birlerion forced him to lie down and sleep. "Jaredion, please, sleep is the best healer. Take it while you can. I am so sorry I cannot help you fight off the Veil."

"Then there would be no point you going to sleep. If you fought the Veil in your sleep, then you wouldn't get any rest, would you?"

"I'm not resting anyway, and you bear a burden I would not load on anyone."

"Birlerion, I wouldn't trust it to anyone else. I will protect you until my dying breath."

Birlerion smiled sadly. "My champions, my last defenders. I hope it will never come to that. You and Leyarille, what would I do without you? Know that I can never repay you enough for all you do for me. Thank you, Jaredion."

"You don't have to thank me, just fight, don't give up. That's all we ask, we need you."

"I'll do my best. Rest, Jaredion. The night will come for me all too soon." Birlerion ducked out of the tent and joined Maraine as she waited for the confusion of horses and riders to resolve itself.

Elisande jumped down from her horse into the arms of her Sodera, laughed as she patted his face, and turned to greet her mother. Birlerion smiled as the two petite women embraced. He scanned the riders for Mir'elle, Maraine's youngest daughter, and found her astride a grey Darian mare.

Her black hair was scraped up in a high ponytail, and her scarves were pulled down off her face and gathered around her neck like colourful necklaces. She wore the shapeless dusty travelling robes of the Terolian, which made it difficult to see her. She reminded him of Leyarille.

Jumping down lightly enough, she instructed the boy who came running up to take her horse to look after her well. She strode off after them without pausing to speak to her mother. Birlerion grinned as Elisande turned to him. "Birlerion, we are so glad to see you and looking so well. Welcome home." Her fingers hovered over his cheek. "Apart from your face … you must tell us how you gained such an injury." She reached up to embrace him, and Birlerion stooped over her to hug her back.

"Medera, congratulations. It suits you."

Elisande laughed and tucked her arm in his. "You haven't met Andisse, have you? Andisse, meet my brother, Birlerion. Birlerion, my Sodera, Andisse."

Birlerion shook hands with the lean black-haired warrior watching him. "I've heard a lot about you, Birlerion; it is good to meet you." His voice was low and deep, and his teeth gleamed white in a brief smile.

Birlerion grinned. "All good, I hope?"

Andisse laughed.

"What brings you all this way? Not that we aren't glad to see you, but we didn't expect you," Elisande asked.

"He's here to see Mir'elle. Where did she go?" Maraine said.

Elisande glanced behind her. "Per'enne was complaining about something, as usual. I expect she went to sort her out."

"Then send someone to get her or she'll be head to toe in dirt. Sorry, Birlerion, Mir'elle still loves to muck in with the horses."

"Don't worry, I'll go and meet her down there. I need to look in on Kin'arol anyway."

"Well, don't take too long. I want to speak to you too," Elisande pouted.

"Your wish is my command," Birlerion said, bowing extravagantly, and Elisande laughed.

Birlerion found Mir'elle scowling at Kin'arol, her hands on her hips. Viktor had once called her his surprise package. Shy and retiring as a child, she had grown into a vivacious and unexpectedly sharp young woman. "Is something the matter?" Birlerion asked, and she spun in surprise, the scowl on her face transforming into a brilliant smile.

"It is you. I thought I recognised Kin'arol, but I wasn't sure." Her smile faded. "Birlerion, what have you done to your face?"

Birlerion raised his hand to his cheek and winced. "Met some trouble on the way here. Bandits."

"Andisse will be furious."

"I'll let Fer'ilan give him the details. He saw more of the fight than I did. How is Per'enne? Elisande said she wasn't happy."

"She's alright. She's not happy unless she's complaining. But what are you doing here? How are you?" She reached to hug him and then peered up into his face. "You look tired. Aren't you sleeping properly?"

"Not really, I'll explain later. But you look great, Mir'elle."

Mir'elle scrunched up her face. "Don't start. Elisande is always telling me to dress more appropriately, attract a man, but really, we live in a desert. What does she expect me to wear?"

Birlerion chuckled. "You could wear a sack and you would be beautiful; she is just jealous."

"Now, now Birlerion, you be careful, or Leyarille will scorch you like the sun on a midsummer's day, roast you long and slow."

"How did you hear about her?"

"We do get news, you know, and anyway, Kayerille keeps us informed on what you're up to."

"Well, I suppose if it were Leyarille doing the roasting, I'd probably enjoy it."

Mir'elle laughed and rapped his knuckles. "Behave." She suddenly looked serious. "You are truly alright, Birlerion? What happened to you was so terrible; it would have destroyed lesser men."

"Well, I have Leyarille, Marguerite, and Jaredion and even Leyandrii still keeps an eye on me. I am fine, I promise."

"Good, I am so relieved. So why are you here?"

"I came to see you. Anders needs a queen, and I thought you would be the best woman for the job."

"What? Me?"

"Yes, you. You are smart, beautiful, you hold family close and can hold your own against opinionated men."

"But Birlerion, I am Terolian. I have never even been to Vespiri."

"Anders has never been to Terolia. I will escort you. I can show you Vespiri. You would like Anders, I think. He needs someone who he can test his foils against; he needs the exercise."

"Are you sure his guards will let me get close to him if I'm holding a sword?"

"Not all swords are made of metal, you know."

Mir'elle chuckled and flicked a glance at him from under her lashes. "What if I don't like him?"

"You come home. No one is forcing you to join with him. Just meet him, see what you think."

"Won't he be offended if I say I don't want to join with him?"

"Would you be if he said the same?"

"Maybe."

"I ought to warn you. You are not the only lady on the list; you are just my first choice."

Mir'elle blushed. "I take that as a compliment, coming from you."

"So you should. You would make a queen we would all be proud to serve, and Anders may surprise you. He could be a great king, if he had someone to help him. Anders honours the Lady and his Oath, but he needs a partner, someone who will rule at his side and support him."

"When do we leave?"

"What?"

"Give over, Birlerion. I want to meet this paragon of a man."

"He is no paragon. He needs someone to rule beside him, someone to provide him with the insights that help him make the right decisions."

Mir'elle smiled. "My dear brother, my life has been on hold for many years. You offer me an opportunity to begin living again. I would be a fool not to take it, and besides, I would get to see you more often. We have missed you. You have been lax in visiting; how many years is it since you last came home?"

"I don't remember."

"Exactly, you should. You don't treat family that way."

"You are right. My apologies, my dear sister."

Mir'elle's laugh pealed out, and Birlerion smiled; it was just one of those infectious laughs. "You always make such a good recovery, Birlerion. You are so honest, and I love you for it. You are quite my favourite brother."

Birlerion's smile was a touch cynical, but he let the comment go. "I am waiting for Kayerille to return from Feril. If Roberion was to port, I was going to ask him to take us back, but if you wish we could leave for Old Vespers tomorrow."

"Then leave we shall." She patted Birlerion's uninjured cheek. "You have tarried here too long already; you have much to do."

Birlerion smiled. She would be perfect.

10

MELILA, TEROLIA

Mir'elle didn't waste any time organising her guard. Andisse insisted his brother, Cor'ilno, choose the men, and Mir'elle smiled and told them to hurry up.

Birlerion sent Fer'ilan to try and manage the escort, hoping their party wouldn't expand by too many more people. Fer'ilan returned, twisting his lips as he reported, "I think there will be at least ten of them including Cor'ilno. They do not trust us to protect Mir'elle."

Birlerion frowned. "Are bandits that big of a problem?"

Fer'ilan nodded. "Water is getting scarcer. The oases are shrinking. There is more contention over who controls access. The more they try and regulate who can draw water and when, the worse it gets. The bandits are stealing whatever water they can find."

"Who is controlling the access?"

"Depends. Some places it's the Mederas, in others it's the town Elders. If everyone only took what they needed it would be fine, but people are panicking and trying to hoard water. It puts more pressure on the springs."

"Will we be a greater target because we are a relatively large party?"

Fer'ilan shrugged. "Difficult to tell. It could work in our favour as there are more of us. But we'll also be carrying more water. We'll just have to remain alert."

"Very well. What about Benson's men? Are they all recovered?"

"Even if they are, Commander Landis said they would not be part of the escort. They need to stay and acclimatise before they'll be ready for the return journey. My men and I will accompany you to Old Vespers, in their place."

Benson would not be happy about that. Birlerion would no doubt have to put up with his complaints. Sighing his breath out, he went to join the Medera and sat on a rug by the fire next to Mir'elle. Elisande smiled in welcome, waving the piece of bread she held at him. "I hear you are leaving. You should stay a little longer. It has been so long since we last saw you."

"I thank you for your hospitality, but I've already been away from Vespers for over a week. It will take another week to travel back. I am sure there is plenty of work piling up in my absence." He smiled his thanks as Fer'ilan passed him a plate of bread and meat. He inhaled the aroma of warm spices, and his mouth watered as he tore off a piece of flatbread and wrapped it around the chunks of meat. An explosion of flavours filled his mouth, and he moaned in appreciation. Elisande laughed and stuffed another piece of bread in her mouth.

Jaredion joined them, and Birlerion was relieved to see the few chimes of sleep had done him good. His eyes didn't look so heavy and he attacked his meal with a healthy appetite.

Relaxing on the rug, Birlerion smiled at the happy faces around the fire. The men were swapping stories, each trying to best the other. Tales from the past, more myths and legends, than real history. Birlerion wondered how long it would be before they asked him for a tale. He hoped they wouldn't. Much of his time in Terolia had been a time of strife. When he thought about it, he didn't have very many happy stories to share.

His thoughts drifted back to Leyarille. He hoped she would be able to meet him in Vespers. His chest ached; he missed her so much.

"You're wrong," Fer'ilan chimed in, and Birlerion paid more attention to what they were talking about. "It was the Falusion mountains where the Mother rested after she created the deserts of Terolia."

"No, it wasn't," Andisse argued. "There was the arena in Kharma. That's where the tests were held and her guards competed. They entertained her as she rested. Competing for her favours."

Jaredion leaned forward. "Wasn't that the arena where the All Mother tested those who thought they were good enough to serve her? Uncle Tage used to tell us the tales about the men who had to prove they wanted to help others to gain her grace." He grinned. "He usually descended into a parable about helping those less fortunate and not yourself!"

"There is no sign of an arena in Kharma or anywhere else." Fer'ilan reached for the waterskin to refill his mug. "No ruins or even any suggestion that it might have been there."

Cor'ilno rolled his eyes. "Of course there isn't. Her arena is not here in our world, it's someplace else. It's said you had to transcend time to reach it. The *entrance* to the arena was in Kharma. You can't win a god's gift here."

Fer'ilan snorted. "There is no place called Kharma, only the ridge. You can't tell a story that is not possible. We're talking about things that actually happened. Like Captain Jerrolion bringing forth the spring in Il Queron. That's a feat no other man has achieved. The Lady must have been at his shoulder."

"It was Lady Marguerite," Birlerion murmured.

Elisande tilted her head. "I wish Lady Marguerite would create a few more springs. That would solve much of the current angst within our people."

"I'll mention it next time I speak with her," Birlerion said, and he grinned at the wide gazes and open mouths around him.

Mir'elle laughed and clapped her hands to break the silence. "You wanted true stories. Birlerion is the only one of us here who has met the gods. You should be asking him what actually happened."

"Was the Kharma arena real?" Cor'ilno asked quickly.

Birlerion shrugged. "I have no idea. That was before my time. Though I can confirm that Jerrol did create the spring at Il Queron."

"Did Lady Leyandrii create the bridge which stretched from her palace to the Chapterhouse in Old Vespers? It was said to be alive; it glowed so brightly," Healer Tarvin asked. Birlerion had forgotten he was still with them.

"That was Guerlaire, not Leyandrii. And yes, he built a crystal structure between the Chapterhouse and Leyandrii's palace. It was very beautiful."

"Could you tell us about our ancestors? Medera Yannis and Sodera Arkan. You met them, didn't you?" Mir'elle asked, her voice a soft whisper in the darkness.

Birlerion shifted to make himself more comfortable. "Your mother is very much like Yannis. Petite, glossy black hair piled on her head to give her those few extra inches." He smiled in memory. "Her Sodera, Arkan, was whip thin, but so powerful. He crackled with energy. If you got too close your hair would stand on end. Yannis often sent him away to work it off before she would allow him in her tent."

Cor'ilno leered at his brother. "See, Sodera. That's where you get it from."

Laughing, Andisse shoved his brother away. "You can't talk. You're just as bad."

"I'll have to remember that," Elisande murmured.

Mir'elle laughed and patted Birlerion's arm. "It seems quite amazing that you knew them."

"Their son, Tiv'erna, was a good friend."

"Oh," Fer'ilan piped up. "He was the Atolean who first forged the relationship with Greenswatch."

"That was Yannis and Arkan, though Tiv'erna travelled to Greens to meet my parents. I wouldn't have my Darian if it wasn't for him."

"Kin'arol is gorgeous and his colour is so distinctive," Mir'elle said.

"He'll get big-headed if you continue."

"No, I won't."

Birlerion's lips twitched, and he was glad when the conversation moved onto Darians in general and their blood-lines. A little while later, he wished them all the Lady's blessing as he and Jaredion retired to their tent. Birlerion handed Jaredion his weapons before he settled down to sleep.

Sighing out his breath, he tried to get comfortable, but he couldn't relax. Old memories hovered near the surface, and he remembered travelling the deserts and sharing a hearth with his friends Tiv'erna and Adilion all those centuries ago.

A memory of Marguerite surfaced, of her accompanying him into Terolia. *"Marguerite? I need your help,"* he called. He really needed her assistance. Maybe she would know what was going on. It wasn't like her to be absent so long.

Sometimes, it was difficult to remember which time he was in and who he would wake up to the next morning. Jaredion hummed under his breath as he polished his sword, readying for another night of defending him. Birlerion didn't know what he would do without him. He stilled. Jaredion truly was his sword and Leyarille his shield. Since when had he needed such protection? He drifted off to sleep as his brain tried to comprehend what that meant.

Jaredion stiffened as the Veil immediately stirred, and he reached for the Veilspace, intent on protecting Birlerion, no matter the cost.

11

MISTRA, TEROLIA

rriving in Mistra after two days of travelling across the burning deserts, Birlerion commandeered the large tavern that had been built on the outskirts of the town. They had all luxuriated in the baths, washing off sand that stuck to sweating skin and rubbed it raw. They now rested for the night before they continued their journey the next morning.

Birlerion had just laid down, Jaredion preparing to return to the Veilspace, when they heard the clash of swords in the corridor. Rushing out of his room, Birlerion skirted Fer'ilan fighting a man dressed in brown desert robes and hurried to Mir'elle's room. Kayerille rushed down the corridor behind him. Mir'elle was struggling in the grip of two men who were trying to drag her out of the room.

Birlerion didn't hesitate. He grabbed a glass bowl from the table, and threw it at one of the men threatening Mir'elle, and launched himself at the other. The men released Mir'elle and shoved her at Birlerion as they turned and leapt out the window.

"Are you alright?" Birlerion asked, and not waiting for an

answer, he climbed out the window and set off across the rooftops as Kayerille dragged Mir'elle to safety. Jaredion stormed after Birlerion.

Leaping to the next roof and clambering over the ridges, Birlerion flew across the wooden fretwork of a covered court-yard, barely touching the woodwork. Scrambling up the side of the building, his bare toes gripped the rough rock wall, leaving the wisteria blossoms trembling. A pleasant perfume drifted in the warm night air, the only sign of his passing.

He hesitated, straining to see over the jumble of roofs and screens of Mistra. A slight movement and he was in motion veering across the flat roof and leaping the alleyway.

"*I'm here,*" Kin'arol said, and Birlerion peered down into the dark passageway and dropped between the buildings, landing on Kin'arol's back.

He grabbed Kin'arol's glossy mane and leaned over his neck, his bare chest gleaming with sweat. "*West side, two men.*" The heat from the honey-gold stallion warmed his thighs as his powerful muscles moved under his legs. Birlerion was suddenly conscious of his lack of clothes. He only wore the light linen shorts he slept in. He was thankful he had been wearing them.

"*Birlerion, you have nothing with you; you're not even dressed. What are you going to do if we catch them?*"

"*I want to see who they are, where they go. We need to know why they want Mir'elle.*"

Kin'arol huffed but kept up his pace as he thudded through the alleyways of Mistra.

Kayerille stopped running, her sides heaving as she tried to regain her breath. "You can't say he isn't fit. He's twice your age, and if you can't catch him, I doubt anyone else will."

"We can't leave him on his own. He hasn't any

weapons, remember?" Jaredion replied. Birlerion still made sure Jaredion took his sword and knives away at night, without fail.

"You go back to the tavern, keep an eye on Mir'elle. I'll find him," Kayerille said, searching the shadowy rooftops. The faint sliver of the waning moon had almost disappeared, and the night was thick and dark. She so wished Roberion had been in port. They would have been safe aboard his frigate on their way to Old Vespers. Instead, she was chasing Birlerion over the rooftops of her hometown without a clue why.

Why did Birlerion always seem to attract trouble? A flicker drew her eyes, and she leapt across the narrow gap onto the next roof and took off—a slender shadow darting across the Terolian skyline.

Kayerille slithered down the trellis, snagging an annoying splinter on the way. She sucked the side of her hand as she peered around the end of the alleyway. The market square spread out before her, shadowed and still. Where had Birlerion gone? The hum from her Sentinal, which was usually a soft presence unobtrusively sitting in the back of her mind, increased, and she headed in his direction. It was as good a direction as any.

She found Kin'arol hiding in the shadows behind her tree. She smoothed his nose. *"Where is he?"* she thought, not really expecting a reply.

"Inside; there are two others. He shouldn't be on his own," Kin'arol replied.

"He wouldn't be if he called for help on occasion."

Kin'arol's sigh was more an impression than a sound, and she grinned. Easing the wooden door of the temple open, she slipped inside and paused, listening. Voices came from near the altar. Birlerion was speaking.

"… and just because we are in the Lady's temple doesn't

mean I won't hurt you." A low moan followed Birlerion's words. "Why were you after Mir'elle?"

"Go fuck yourself."

"I swear I will break your arm, in multiple places. What do you want with Mir'elle?"

"To leave is to die."

"What do you mean?"

"She can't leave Terolia. A filly like that needs protecting."

"From the likes of you, obviously," Birlerion leaned harder.

The man moaned louder. "Others have prior claims, expectations."

"Like who?"

"Why should Terolia only get the dregs? It's not fair. A bloodline like that should be mounted by a Terolian, not some weak Vespirian."

"And which Terolian stud would that be? Kikeran? Like yourself?"

Birlerion flicked a glance up as Kayerille approached. The man sensed his distraction and twisted out of his grip; the man's arm broke with an audible snap as he tugged free. Birlerion hissed as he blocked the man's desperate kick. Kayerille saw a second dark mound stir, and she slid between him and Birlerion, striking the groaning man over the head before he could rise.

Birlerion had his man back in an arm lock, and the man stilled, his face grey with pain.

"I'm sorry, Birlerion, I didn't mean to give him an out."

"Don't worry. He isn't going anywhere."

"Kiker," Kayerille said thoughtfully, "worried about bloodlines and not prepared to take no as an answer. You must belong to Mar'inder."

The man tensed.

"Mir'elle has refused him how many times? You should have waited after Bor'anser died. You moved too quick, didn't give her time to grieve."

"Bor'anser?" Birlerion asked.

"Kiker's eldest. He and Mir'elle were betrothed, but before they could join, he broke his neck in a riding accident."

"Maybe it is more pique at being refused, rather than anger at Vespiri."

"Possible, but still, how did they expect to get away with an abduction? Mir'elle's brothers would not have allowed that to go unanswered." She leaned over the man, "And nor would I." She clipped him around the head, and Birlerion let him slide to the floor.

Birlerion exhaled. "It's getting late; we need to get back before Jaredion panics."

"You can't go back like that, people will see you. Spend a few chimes in my sentinal; let him heal you and get some sleep. He'll protect you. I'll tie these two up until we can get Cor'ilno to pick them up." Kayerille jerked her head towards the door, and Birlerion left.

He returned after a chime, wearing a black robe over his shorts. Kayerille squinted at him. "Was that long enough?"

Birlerion dragged his hands through his hair. His sleeves fell back, revealing pale, scarred skin. "Yes, more than enough; I thank you."

Kayerille glanced down at the trussed up men and then met Birlerion's eyes. Her lips twitched, and then they burst out laughing. "I shouldn't laugh, really," Kayerille said, wiping her eyes. "Mir'elle would be so insulted by their references to a brood mare; you can't tell her." She carefully latched the temple door until the Atoleans could collect them. Kin'arol followed as they began the walk back to the Atolean camp.

"I wouldn't dare."

"But how did they know she was leaving?" Kayerille asked. "You only spoke to her a couple of days ago. Before that she had no intention of travelling anywhere."

"I don't know. No one except Jerrol and Bryce knew where I was going. I suppose they must be making arrangements to receive her at the palace, as it wasn't a secret. Maybe the men have spoken to someone; we left some of our original guards here to recover from heatstroke. It could have been anyone."

"Well, at least we are forewarned. Let's hope that was the only attempt."

Birlerion went to speak with Oscar and Cor'ilno; Andisse's brother, who headed up Mir'elle's guard, discussing the best way to protect Mir'elle and escort her safely to Old Vespers. Dawn had arrived by the time he left them hatching a plan and sending out scouts to check if any strangers had entered Mistra, relieved to let someone else figure it out.

Arriving back at the tavern, he found Jaredion seated in the courtyard, staring blindly at the small fountain in the centre. After a closer inspection, he sat next to him. "Jaredion, you are not looking well. Why don't you go and get some more sleep? Spend some time in Kayerille's sentinal. I'm sure he would oblige."

"I'm fine." Jaredion leaned back in his chair.

"You're not fine; no more am I. It's getting worse, and I don't know how we stop it. I'm exhausted, and I'm just sleeping. You are expending energy every night."

"And it still gets through."

"You can't do any more than you already are. I'm indebted to you forever for what you are doing now. But we can't go on like this. Once we escort Mir'elle to Old Vespers, we need to go to Senti and find the Oath, find Marguerite."

"What has she said about it all?"

"Nothing, she isn't responding."

Jaredion frowned. "That's not right, surely?"

"No, it just makes me think there is more going on than we are aware of."

"Then, after Old Vespers, Senti it is. Can you send a message to Roberion and ask him to meet us somewhere?"

"No reason why he can't meet us in Old Vespers. I'll send Ari." Birlerion leaned back in his chair, smiling as he thought of the little Arifel. Jaredion ordered them some coffee as Birlerion stared off into the distance. Almost immediately there was a disturbance in the air, and a black and white Arifel appeared; Lin, Ari's mate. She settled on the table in front of Birlerion. She rubbed her fluffy ears against Birlerion's hand and meeped. "I need you to find Roberion."

Lin chattered, her green eyes wide.

"I know, but you'll find him. He's probably at Cherni. Ask him to meet us in Old Vespers the week of the new moon. And make sure you come back and tell either Jaredion or me if he says yes."

Lin scolded him and popped out of view. Jaredion chuckled. "Are you sure she will do as you ask? Maybe you should have written a message."

"She is perfectly capable," Birlerion replied, sipping his kafinee.

"Everyone always says they are unreliable."

"Not when she's worried, and the Arifels are worried."

"I wish more people were. No one seems concerned about the Veil."

Birlerion rubbed his face. "It must be getting whatever it needs from me to sustain itself. Otherwise, there would be signs of degradation that the Watchers could see."

"Are you sure it's not getting it from anywhere else?"

"Don't," Birlerion held his hand up against the thought,

"the only other place would be the Oath, and Lady forbid the Veil gets its teeth into that."

Jaredion leaned forward. "Can you ask Ari to find Marguerite?"

"He would have already if he could."

"What about sending a message to Uncle Jerrol to check?"

"He said he would. Without any proof, he'll just think I'm fixated on the Veil. That's what he believes anyway." Birlerion stood up with such force his chair skittered away. "I can't believe no one will listen." He strode over to the fountain and stared down into the water, the pattering water drops soothing his sudden anger.

"They will listen, soon," Jaredion said, trying to reassure him.

Birlerion sat on the side of the stone rim and dipped his hand in the basin. He rotated his hand, watching the play of the water. A blue sparkle flowed over his skin, and he stilled. The power gifted to him by Leyandrii was returning; he wondered why now. He straightened and glanced back at Jaredion. As if the boy didn't have enough to worry about. He stood, deliberately relaxing, and forced a smile on his face. "Come on, let's go and see what Oscar and Cor'ilno have decided. It's time we went home."

Tarvin peered around the corner and frowned after them. He hadn't understood half of what he had heard. None of it made sense. And Birlerion had been talking to himself for some of it, most concerning, along with his display of anger. He would report what he had heard, especially the bit about going to Senti to retrieve the Oath. He was sure the chancellor would be interested in that.

· · ·

The next morning, having survived another night of the Veil's onslaught, Jaredion watched Birlerion strap on all his weapons, his bow included; better to be prepared than not. Cor'ilno had his men scouting out front, and Oscar had assigned Fer'ilan as point. His captain got all the best jobs.

As the sun began its march across the sky, they finally left Mistra, Birlerion and Jaredion riding on either side of Mir'elle. It was at least three day's travel to Berbera, and then they would cross into East Watch and begin the journey across Vespiri to Vespers.

Jaredion wished they could go up to the Watch Towers and collect Leyarille, but that was a day's travel in the wrong direction. He was exhausted, and Birlerion was not much better. Between them, they would probably fall off their horses as soon as swing a sword.

He eased his shoulders under his black robe and ignored the trickle of sweat working its way down his back. If he was uncomfortable, he dreaded to think how Birlerion felt with the new welts scoring his skin.

Watching Birlerion shift in his saddle, Jaredion could tell he was suffering, not surprisingly. He had been horrified when he woke Birlerion up and found blood staining his bed sheets. He had bandaged the wound low on his back, but it had still been sluggishly bleeding.

If it weren't for his tan, he would have been noticeably pale. The Veil was taking it out of Birlerion, and Jaredion wasn't sure how much longer he could hold out. If it came to it, he wasn't sure how much longer he could defend Birlerion, not when he was failing so badly.

Jaredion idly observed the column, and as he watched, one of the horses jinked out of line as an apparition rose out of the sand beneath it. The horse pirouetted to face the opposite direction. In the time it took for Jaredion to shout a warning, Birlerion unshipped his bow and Kin'arol had also pirouetted to meet the attack from the rear.

Men were rising out of the sands around them, tugging unprepared riders off their mounts and dispatching them just as quickly.

Jaredion silently cursed as Birlerion ran out of arrows and unsheathed his sword. Where were they coming from? Fer'ilan charged past him, followed by at least three riders, and Birlerion blocked a wild strike. Jaredion leaned down to grab some arrows from slumped bodies on the ground.

"Where is Mir'elle?" Birlerion yelled as Kin'arol pirouetted again.

"Next to us, don't worry, I've got her," Kayerille shouted.

Jaredion forced his way beside Birlerion and passed him the arrows. Birlerion grabbed them and relieved Fer'ilan of his pursuers. Fer'ilan waved a hand in acknowledgement and charged back into the fray.

Birlerion glanced at Mir'elle and saw her sway in the saddle. He reached across and pulled her onto his lap. "Mir'elle?"

"I'm fine; please put me down, you can't hold me."

"Where are you hurt?"

"It's nothing, a mere scratch. It just caught me by surprise."

Birlerion swept a glance around them; Fer'ilan and Oscar were mopping up the stragglers. He pulled Kin'arol over to the side and, holding Mir'elle, carefully slid off. Her knees collapsed as they hit the sand, and Birlerion sank down with her.

"Tell Jaredion to find the healer, Tarvin," Birlerion told Kin'arol as he tugged open Mir'elle's robe, her right shoulder was soaked in blood. He ripped off the bottom of his tunic and clamped it against the slice across her arm. "What sort of idiots are they to attack the woman they

supposedly want to save?" Birlerion muttered under his breath.

Mir'elle smiled up at him. "Sun-scorched idiots I expect. Thank you for saving me, Birlerion."

"It wasn't just me. Fer'ilan and Oscar's men had something to do with it."

"And you, my dear brother. Here is Jaredion with the healer."

Birlerion gave her up to the healer's ministrations and, leaving Jaredion to guard her went to check on the men. Fer'ilan began setting up camp some distance from the worst fighting, erecting awnings for the injured. Men congregated around the camp, checking their horses, equipment, each other.

Birlerion returned to find Mir'elle seated alone in the shade, watching him approach. They sat quietly until Oscar joined them.

"How bad?" Birlerion asked.

"Bad enough. Six dead, two serious, plenty of walking wounded."

"Enough horses to get us to Berbera?"

"Maybe, if your Darians can tell us when any other horses find their way back to us. We'll stay here tonight," he paused, his eyes gliding over Mir'elle, "say our farewells, and see what's what in the morning."

"Did any of the attackers get away? Can we expect more trouble?"

"If they did, Cor'ilno will run them down. They won't be coming back. He was furious that Mir'elle was injured. He was muttering about conclaves and such."

"Let us hope saner minds prevail. We do not want the Families warring. I would suggest they have paid the full blood price and it should end here," Mir'elle said, her voice calm. "I will advise the Medera so."

Oscar bowed. "As you say, my lady. I apologise for not protecting you adequately."

Mir'elle waved her hand. "Don't be ridiculous, Commander Landis. Your men could have done no more. I thank you for your continued efforts to protect us. And now you must all be exhausted. Rest. We are safe here." She frowned at Birlerion as Landis left and pulled at his robe. "You're still bleeding though," she said, pulling the material away from his skin. "Didn't you see the healer?"

"It's nothing."

"No, it isn't," Jaredion said.

Mir'elle rolled her eyes. "Jaredion, there are some bandages and ointment in my saddlebag. Could you get them for me, and get him some clean clothes? Birlerion, strip."

Jaredion rushed to do Mir'elle's bidding, and she helped Birlerion out of his robe. Her hands were cool on his hot skin. "What is this?" she asked from behind his shoulder.

"The Veil. It is hunting me. When it gets past my defences, it scores my skin. Jaredion is trying to defend me, but there is only so much he can do."

"Why is no one else helping you?"

"They don't believe it's the Veil. They think it's all in my head."

"They are fools."

"Indeed," Birlerion replied.

She poured some water over the welt, rinsing it off, and Birlerion sighed with relief. When Jaredion arrived, she patted it dry and smoothed the salve over it before wrapping a bandage around him.

"Thank you," Birlerion said.

"Don't leave it so long next time," Mir'elle scolded. "Let's get you covered up before anyone sees you. Remember, Birlerion, always; we are here for you, and none of us will ever let you down. The Lady believes in you, as do I, and even in your darkest moments she would not forsake you."

Birlerion hugged her as the growing uncertainty and doubt melted away. "Lady bless you, Mir'elle." He rose as Cor'ilno came to find him, and Jaredion stared after him.

"How do you always know the right thing to say?"

"He is the Lady's, a Sentinal; he holds the Oath of the King and Remargaren. He is my brother. Why would I ever doubt him?"

Jaredion stared at her in awe. "My lady, I wish they were all like you."

Mir'elle smiled. "They will be one day, you watch. They will all drop to their knees as they realise the treasure that stands before them."

12

OLD VESPERS, VESPIRI

A week and a half later, Birlerion collapsed into the chair opposite Jerrol's desk with a grunt.

"Welcome back."

Birlerion smiled. "It's good to be back. I'd forgotten how large the desert is and how long it takes to cross Vespiri when you can't use a waystone."

"You managed to find some trouble as well I hear?"

"Don't we always?" Birlerion smoothed his healing cheek. It had bruised spectacularly and was now a sickly yellow. "We survived, though you need to consider some training for our men to cope in Terolia; they didn't have a clue."

"I know. I already raised the point with Bryce and Landis. We should start rotating the men again."

"You knew? Well, it can only help. And then the trouble on the borders. It was unfortunate the Kikerans took matters into their own hands; a delay we didn't need."

"Yes, how is Mir'elle?"

"She is well; she is tough. I think the courtiers will find

she is a match and more for them. I am looking forward to Anders and Mir'elle's first meeting."

Jerrol scowled. "It's taken up most of my time arranging everything. Imagine what the Joining will be like? They haven't even met yet, and it's taking over our lives!"

Birlerion shifted under Jerrol's keen inspection. He knew he looked tired. So would anyone after the long journey they'd had, but Jerrol's open worry for him was concerning.

"How have you been?" Jerrol asked.

"Fine."

"And Jaredion?"

"He's fine too."

"You would tell me if there was anything wrong, wouldn't you? If you need any help? You know I'm here for you."

Birlerion twisted his lips. "There's nothing wrong with me; it's the Veil."

Jerrol stood with a huff of breath. "For goodness sake, Birlerion, how many times do you need to be told? The Veil is unchanged. I checked it. The Watchers checked it. There is nothing wrong with it. You need to move on."

"Why do you not believe me, Jerrol? When did you stop listening? When did you forget what being a Sentinal, being the Captain really means? You've lost touch with what is going on around you."

"Don't start casting blame just because you cannot manage your own fears. I know you've been through a terrible experience, and if you need more time to recover, then take it. You need to move past the Veil. You will never be free until you do. The healers can help you, Birlerion. Please, take the time to look after yourself. If you are not ready to return to us, I will understand, just be honest with yourself."

Birlerion considered his friend. Jerrol was convinced it

was all in his head; he was not listening, nor would he, at least not to Birlerion. When had their paths diverged so completely? Who he would listen to was beyond Birlerion's control, and he shivered at the thought. He gave Jerrol what he wanted. "Of course, I will speak with Ewan."

"Good, take care of yourself, Birlerion. I'll see you later at the reception." Birlerion rose, taking it as a dismissal. He was glad to leave. It seemed he was on his own.

Stepping out of the waystone inside the Justice building, he entered his office. A new pile of files awaited his attention. Sighing, he pulled a fat file towards him. He was behind in so many projects, and yet the pull of the Oath distracted him. He needed to go to Senti and find out what was going on. It wasn't in his mind; the Veil was desperate, and he knew the answer lay with Marguerite and the Oath.

First, though, he needed to support Mir'elle through her first meeting with Anders, and then he would be free to go to Senti. The words on the paper danced in front of him as his thoughts drifted to Leyarille. He wished they were back in Westermaine with only each other to worry about, but his life had never been that simple.

He ought to go and speak to Tom, see if he had heard from his son, and he ought to go to Westermaine and check his new employees were alright. Dropping his head into his hands, he closed his eyes as his temples throbbed. There was so much he ought to do. Where to start?

"Birlerion?" Jaredion's voice was tentative as he peered through the door.

Birlerion looked up, and he grimaced as Jaredion winced at what he saw on his face. The onslaught was unrelenting, and he knew he was beginning to show the effects. Even his uniform was looser, not fitting so well, and he had already been too thin to begin with.

"The healer is in the building and coming here."

Birlerion closed his eyes. That was all he needed. Jerrol hadn't waited; he had sent him anyway. "Very well, interrupt us after half a chime, say I have an appointment waiting or something." Returning to his file, he picked up his quill, dipped it in the ink and began making notes.

He was buried in the papers when a tap on the door interrupted him, and he looked up into the face of Healer Ewan. Birlerion leaned back and smiled. "Ewan, please come in." Ewan's searching inspection pierced his defences, but he kept his face calm.

Ewan shut the door and sat opposite him. "How are you, Birlerion?"

"Good, thank you, just tired. Terolia's climate can be tough."

"More like exhausted. Still not sleeping properly?"

"Some nights are better than others, like most people."

"I need to check you over. The chancellor was concerned that you might not have been ready to return to work."

Birlerion frowned. "Then why did he send me off to Terolia?"

"I don't think he realised how fragile you still are."

"Fragile? I've just been through two weeks in the desert, two attacks, and you are calling me fragile?"

Ewan smiled. "No one doubts your physical recovery; it is your mental condition we are concerned about."

"My mind is fine, Ewan. I have plenty to do to keep it busy."

"You can't hide from it by keeping busy. You have to face it and deal with it."

"And what do I need to face, exactly?"

"The trauma you suffered. You need to accept that it is in the past and can no longer hurt you, that the Veil cannot hurt you. You need to accept these truths so you can move on."

Birlerion tried not to snarl. "And if I can't?"

"Then I will refer you to a colleague of mine who is more experienced in these matters. I have helped you as much as I can, but it seems I can only take you so far."

Leaning forward, Birlerion concentrated on remaining calm. "Ewan, you have helped me. I know the Veil is no longer a threat, and I have accepted that Ellie is long gone and can no longer hurt me."

"Show me your arms. Push your sleeves up. I want to see your arms."

"Why?"

"Because I am worried about you, Birlerion. You are saying what you think I want to hear, not what you feel."

"Maybe you are not listening to what I am saying; we have been over this for months, and I am fed up of discussing the same thing."

Jaredion opened the door. "Five minute warning, sir, your next appointment has arrived."

Birlerion waved a hand in acknowledgement. "Ewan, I am busy. I have a full day. I will come and find you when I am not so in demand."

Ewan stood. "Make sure you do, Birlerion."

Birlerion waited for Ewan to leave and then leaned back in his chair with a deep sigh. He had only put him off, not reassured him as he had hoped. And what was it about his arms? He pushed his sleeve up and inspected the faint silver scars, a consequence of the Veil's attention that he was supposedly imagining. Pushing his sleeve back down, he shrugged and returned to his file.

That afternoon, he escorted Mir'elle to meet Anders. He smiled in appreciation as she joined him in the outer chamber. She wore a traditional flowing Terolian robe, which fell in soft folds around her body, the cloth a deep amber that set off her glowing brown skin. The scarves draped around her were threaded with gold that glinted in the light and accentuated her curves. Glossy black hair curled over her bare shoulders, framing her beautiful face.

She looked vibrant and very different to the pale-skinned court of Vespers. Birlerion hoped Anders would be appreciative of the woman he was about to meet. A small smile hovered over Mir'elle's mouth as she observed Birlerion's reaction.

"You'll knock him dead."

"Oh, I hope not. I would not want to be accused of killing the king."

Birlerion laughed. "You look beautiful, Mir'elle."

"Thank you, dear brother, but I think you may be biased."

"My words are true, even if you claim me as a brother."

Mir'elle frowned at him. "You know perfectly well that you are, so don't pretend you're not. The Atolea claimed you, and they do not allow Family to be forgotten because of a few trivial centuries." She rested her hand in his arm and gestured her fussing maids away. "Shall we?"

Birlerion led her through the hallways and down carpeted stairs, her honour guard of Cor'ilno and one of his men behind them. The rest of his men were hopefully not causing trouble in the guesting barracks, though Birlerion wasn't betting on it. The dark eyes and lean physique of the Terolians had caught many a lady's eye when they had first arrived.

Walking through an ornately decorated arch into a glass-roofed atrium, they skirted a tinkling fountain, the tang of water in the air complementing the profuse greenery climbing the columns and arching above them.

Anders was standing with Jerrol in a small alcove, and Birlerion's lips twitched as Jerrol continued to talk fast, keeping Anders still and in place.

Anders froze as Birlerion led Mir'elle into the sunlight. Her robes glistened as she sank into a deep curtsey. "Your Majesty." Her soft voice curled around them, rich and inviting.

"Lady Mir'elle," Anders breathed. "You look exquisite." He took a step forward and offered his hand to help her rise, a smile spreading over his face.

She rose and smiled back at him, and Birlerion saw the moment Anders fell in love. Their eyes met and he was lost in their mysterious depths. She came to his shoulder, dainty and serene, and very much in control.

"Please." Anders indicated a small walkway. "Accompany me."

Jerrol grinned as they walked away. "That went much better than I expected. He was ready to bolt."

"I saw you were talking fast."

"I hope Mir'elle didn't notice."

Birlerion shrugged. "If she did, she wouldn't say. She is a lovely woman, thoughtful, considerate, and Anders will be very fortunate to have her. As will Vespiri."

Jerrol flicked a sharp glance at Birlerion. "You hold her in high esteem."

"Indeed. I wouldn't have suggested her otherwise. As will you when you get to know her. You met her when she was a child after all; you are old friends."

"Not as old a friend as you, I think."

Birlerion frowned at the edge in Jerrol's voice. "I visit Terolia more often than you do."

"You always were more comfortable there, weren't you? Are you sure you don't originally hail from Terolia?"

Birlerion laughed. "Vespirian through and through."

Twenty minutes later, Anders led Mir'elle back to them and, bowing, he kissed her hand. "I look forward to extending our acquaintance this evening, my dear."

Mir'elle bestowed a blinding smile on him that made him blink. "I look forward to it, Your Majesty." Mir'elle extended her hand to Jerrol. "Lord Chancellor, it is a pleasure to meet again after all these years."

"Mir'elle, the pleasure is mine. I hope you will spare me a dance tonight?"

"I would be honoured." Mir'elle placed her hand on Birlerion's arm, and he led her away.

Birlerion waited until they arrived back at her rooms. "Well?"

Mir'elle grinned at him. "Very well, I think. I like him. He was refreshingly honest. And he was appreciative of you, so that is always a good mark in his book. I am glad you are his Oath Keeper. It means you will be around to remind me of my Family. I would miss them more, otherwise."

"You will build your own family here, Mir'elle."

"Yes, in time, but for now, you are it." She leaned forward and kissed him on the cheek. "Thank you for being here, Birlerion."

"It is my honour, and may I request you save a dance for me tonight too?"

"Of course, straight after the king and the chancellor."

Birlerion laughed. "I am glad you know my place in the scheme of things. I will see you later."

13

______

KING'S PALACE, OLD VESPERS

Birlerion stood waiting to escort Mir'elle to the ball. He had bathed and had his hair trimmed, and he was freshly shaved. He wished he was waiting to escort Leyarille.

"Oh, my," Birlerion whispered as Mir'elle entered the room.

Mir'elle smiled, satisfied with his dazzled expression.

"You look like a queen," Birlerion said as she rested her hand on his arm.

"Quite so," she murmured in response. She glittered, and yet, not a single piece of jewellery adorned her.

They swished their way through the corridors, sentries standing to attention as they approached, and Birlerion knew their eyes followed them. As they descended the stairs, the faint strains of music grew louder. They paused in the antechamber and gave their names. The doors opened, and they were announced over the din. People turned to see the woman being touted as their future queen, and the ballroom stilled as they passed.

"Satisfied?" Birlerion murmured through rigid lips.

"Absolutely," Mir'elle whispered back, holding her head high. The king rose from his throne and took a step forward.

She was a vision in gold, shimmering and magical, an explosion of vibrant colour in the king's court and yet feminine, and oh so very desirable. Birlerion sank to his knee as Mir'elle sank into her curtsey, and they both rose at the king's command. Birlerion smiled as he handed her to Anders, and they spun off onto the dance floor as the other dancers made way.

Birlerion caught Parsillion's eye and joined him behind the throne. "That was some entrance," Parsillion murmured, watching the king.

"That was all her, nothing to do with me."

Parsillion snorted. "She's something special; where did you find her?"

"She's my sister, of course she's special."

"No one is going to believe that. You look nothing like her."

"Families are made up of all sorts, and if the Medera says it is so, you do not argue with her," Birlerion replied, his hands loosely clasped behind his back.

"Anders is smitten."

"Long may it continue."

"What about you? Where's Leyarille?"

"On her way here, hopefully." Birlerion couldn't keep the longing out of his voice.

Parsillion smiled at him. "Then she will be here soon." They watched Jerrol cut in for his dance, and Mir'elle twirled away as the courtiers crowded the floor.

Anders sat on his throne. "Birlerion."

"Yes, Your Majesty."

"Good choice," he said, watching his future wife dance with his chancellor.

"I am happy for you, Your Majesty."

"Well, I don't know her that well yet, of course. Bring her to the atrium tomorrow so we can continue our acquaintance."

"Certainly, Your Majesty."

"And tell her more about you being the Oath Keeper; I don't want her surprised by the link between us."

"Of course, Your Majesty."

"I believe it is your dance. I expect her back afterwards."

"Always, Your Majesty."

Birlerion waited on the edge of the dance floor as the dance came to a close and Jerrol handed her over. "One more dance, Mir'elle? Then I'll get you a drink."

"You would be a saviour. It is getting warm in here," Mir'elle replied as they spun away. She cast a cheeky glance at him. "Up for the reverse?"

"Of course my lady, your will is my command," as Birlerion let Mir'elle take the lead and she led them through a variation of the dance that left her eyes sparkling and both in laughter as they finished. Birlerion led her back to the king and went to find her a drink. He finally convinced the waiter that he only wanted water when Commander Bryce paused beside him.

"You need to be careful, Birlerion," Bryce murmured.

"Why? What has happened?"

"You get on too well with Mir'elle."

"We are friends. I am her brother."

"It didn't look like that when you were dancing with her. She was very happy in your arms."

"Don't be ridiculous, we were just dancing. We are family; why shouldn't she be happy?"

"It's how rumours start. You know how it is."

Birlerion huffed. "Don't people have better things to do?"

"You know better than that. Don't give them any excuse to talk about you."

"That is a little difficult when I am her escort in this dance until the king speaks for her."

"I know, I'm just warning you."

"Can't you scotch it?"

"I am, just don't give them any more opportunities."

Birlerion rubbed his neck. "I wish Leyarille would come home; she would stop them straight away."

"Maybe you should ask her to. We don't need any confusion over the woman the king is going to join with, now do we?"

Birlerion gave Mir'elle her water and attempted to keep his distance for the rest of the evening, dancing with Lady Olivia, Bryce's wife, and various other titled ladies before eventually leading Mir'elle back to her rooms at the end of her triumphant night.

"What happened to you, Birlerion? Why only one dance? It was such fun!"

"Apparently we had too much fun and people are suggesting there is more between us."

"What? No, eeew!"

"Thank you so much for holding back," Birlerion said with a grin.

"Oh you, you know I love you to pieces, but as my brother, not in any other way." She wrinkled her nose. "What do we do?"

"I sent a message to Leyarille, asking if she could come and meet you. I think you will both be great friends. At least I certainly hope two of the most important women in my life will be friends."

"I can't wait. What else?"

"Keep your maids in the room when I am present. That way, you'll have a chaperone."

"I should not need a chaperone when I am with family. Don't they know the rules?"

"Sadly, no. No one here has any idea of the rules that bind the Family."

Mir'elle frowned in thought. "If they did, no one would dare insinuate what they are. Maybe it's time I educated them on how the other half of this kingdom live."

"I think that might be a very good idea."

Mir'elle nodded. "Very well. You are dismissed, dear brother," she said, her black eyes gleaming.

"Until tomorrow, my queen." Birlerion grinned as he left.

Birlerion found squeezing in his day job around escorting Mir'elle to the atrium and the balls each evening extremely difficult. In the end, he resorted to sending Jaredion with a message for Tom, hoping to catch him the next day.

He considered asking Jerrol to create a waystone on the edge of Westermaine. At least it would mean he could visit more often. Taking a day out of his schedule now was not an option.

Leaning back in his chair, he hissed as a new welt caught the wood. He needed his Sentinal, even if it was just to heal his skin. Maybe they could sneak away one night after Anders made his decision known; Jaredion needed a break as well.

The days passed, and the balls, dinners, and entertainments began to ease. Anders and Mir'elle spent more time together, and the court waited like expectant pigeons brooding over their eggs for the announcement.

At last, the announcement was proclaimed. King Anders and Lady Mir'elle were to be joined on the 1st of Janu in the year 4146. The new year would be welcomed in with the crowning of a new queen. Birlerion watched them and relaxed. They had achieved a mutual understanding, and he thought they would rule well together.

His responsibility for Mir'elle was over with the king's claim now public. King Anders was now responsible for her, and Birlerion would be able to step back. Well, as far back as Mir'elle would allow him, which would not be far, he knew.

They would celebrate with a ball in one week; time for Maraine and other members of Mir'elle's family to arrive. They would stay until the Joining, and as a result the palace would be full.

Birlerion met with Jerrol daily to discuss arrangements and plans. They spent more time in Jerrol's office at the palace than in the Justice building.

Jerrol came round and sat on his desk and leaned towards Birlerion. "You still look tired."

"It's been hectic. Though I suppose I'll have to go to Senti next."

"Senti? Why Senti?"

"I need to check on the Oath."

Jerrol suddenly leaned forward, grabbed his arm, and pushed his sleeve up, revealing the faint silver scars and a new welt scoring his inner arm. "What are you doing to yourself, Birlerion?"

"It's not what you think."

"Birlerion, you are my friend, my brother. I'd do anything for you, you know that. But this is beyond me. You need help."

"No, honest Jerrol. It's the Veil. It attacks me when I sleep. Something's wrong with it. Jaredion is trying to protect me; he defends me when I sleep. I think it's after the Oath. That's why I need to go to Senti; the Oath is at risk."

"The Oath is fine, as is the Veil. When are you going to admit that you need healer care? Harming yourself and others won't ease your pain; it only causes more."

"I'm not, I wouldn't. How could you believe such a thing

of me? I am a Lady's guard, her Sentinal, I would never betray her trust. I would die first."

"You are deceiving yourself, Birlerion. The first step to healing is accepting that you need help. Let me help you. Let the healers care for you. Ewan said you never followed up with him."

"I haven't had time; you know that."

"You have to accept that you need support. You can't go on like this."

"No, the first step is Acknowledgment, you should know that. Yes, I acknowledge I have been through some terrible things recently, and I have struggled to overcome some of it, but that doesn't mean I can't tell when the Veil is acting up." Birlerion stood and caught sight of the healer's report on Jerrol's desk, and his heart sank. After all they had been through, it had come to this. No matter what he said, Jerrol was not going to believe him.

Opening the door, he paused, his chest tight and tears rising, though he blinked them away. Staring at his friend, he searched Jerrol's face. He supposed Jerrol was doing what he thought was right, but it hurt. The betrayal hurt so much. The thread of family and friendship connecting them snapped and shrivelled; the pain of losing a brother shivered through him. "I am a Sentinal, and I remember my purpose. At the Lady's behest, we protect those who can't protect themselves." Ignoring the pain growing in his chest, he said, "We die so they don't have to." He turned and left the room.

Jerrol stared at the doorway, at a loss, and then saw Jaredion take a step to follow him. "Jaredion, a moment," Jerrol called as Birlerion strode down the corridor. Birlerion waved his hand, and Jaredion hesitated. "Sit, we need to talk." Jerrol sat behind his desk. "How are you, Jaredion? You've been on Birlerion's detail for months; you must need a break."

"I'm alright. He needs me."

"You have needs too. He doesn't own you."

Jaredion laughed. "Of course not. When he gets a break, I'll get a break. You shouldn't work him so hard if you want others to be able to relax."

Jerrol smiled. "He is dedicated. Jaredion, is there anything you want to tell me?"

"About what?"

"About Birlerion and what he is doing to you."

Jaredion stilled. "I don't know what you mean."

"I know he has been self-harming for months, which is bad enough, but to start abusing you too is not acceptable."

"How could you think such a thing? It's the Veil. You know Birlerion better than that; he would never abuse anyone."

"I know you think you need to protect him, but you can't protect him from himself. You need to tell us everything so we can help him properly."

"Is that why you made us come back? So you can drive him mad with some more counselling sessions? They won't stop the Veil from attacking him."

Jerrol exhaled. "Jared."

"It's Jaredion," he interrupted softly, watching his uncle with trepidation.

"Sorry, Jaredion. Look, I know Birlerion means a lot to you; he means a lot to all of us. But I think you've become too emotionally involved. You need some time away from him, and I am reassigning you to Elothia. It's time you experienced a different culture. Go home for a couple of weeks, have a break, and then move on to Elothia."

"No, I refuse the assignment. I need to protect Birlerion."

"It's not your choice. I am your Captain, and I decide your duties. He needs healer help; he is a danger to himself and others and you can't protect him from that."

Jaredion froze as fear spread through him. "What have you done?"

"He will get the treatment he needs. The healers will see to that. Maybe once he is rehabilitated, you can see him again."

Jaredion lurched to his feet and slammed his hands on Jerrol's desk. "What have you done to him?"

"Jaredion, stop. It's for his own good."

"No, you don't understand. You of all people, after everything he's d-done for you," Jaredion stuttered with anger, his silver eyes flashing as he tried to absorb what his uncle was saying. His voice deepened as he leaned over Jerrol, and Jerrol flinched back from his fury; the air crackled with it. "What have you done to him?"

"Jaredion, don't make me restrain you too. It would not look good on your record."

"Where is he?" Jaredion gasped and spun for the door. "You deliberately delayed me here. I want to see him. Now."

"You will return to your barracks and prepare for your new assignment in Elothia."

"I resign."

"You can't resign; you are a Sentinal."

"I just did. I will protect Birlerion. From the likes of you, if necessary. I swear by the Lady you are making a mistake, and if *anything* happens to him, if he dies, I'll never forgive you." He strode out of Jerrol's office, back straight, anger coiling around him, blue sparks crackling in the air. Stopping in the hallway, he looked back, his face hewn by his fury, and Jerrol held his breath. "Does Leyarille know?" His face set at Jerrol's expression. "I thought not."

Jerrol exhaled, staring at his empty doorway, shaken by the depth of Jaredion's anger. He hoped the healers had managed to restrain Birlerion peacefully. It was for the best; his friend needed help. He couldn't go around hurting people just because he had some issues. Carefully straightening the papers on his desk, he calmed his breathing. He looked up as Bryce hovered in his doorway. "Are you sure this is the right way to go about this?" Jerrol asked. "It leaves a bad taste in the mouth. Jaredion just stormed out of the palace swearing vengeance on all of us if something happens to Birlerion, and I'm inclined to agree with him. This feels too heavy-handed. It shouldn't be necessary."

Bryce shook his head. "We've tried to reason with him, counsel him, but he is too violent for this to be managed any other way. The healers said this was the best way to ensure he wasn't hurt. He would have panicked."

"Just because the Healer's society has come up with a name for this type of trauma doesn't mean he's caught some disease." Jerrol frowned at the report on his desk, his heart still thrumming from Jaredion's horror. It resonated in his bones. "He's still our friend, someone who has suffered immensely protecting our world. Putting a label on him doesn't make him any different to the rest of us."

Bryce sighed and rubbed his face. "I was listening. He was trying to blame his scars on the Veil, of all things; he can't admit he has a problem. It's obvious he is still fixated on the Veil, and then he started saying there was an issue with the Oath, threatening to go to Birtoli. More diversions. Jerrol, you know we can't take the risk."

Jerrol pursed his lips. "Are you sure he would threaten the Oath? Birlerion *holds* the Oath. He understands perfectly well what it does."

"Are you confident enough about that to let him go to Birtoli?"

Massaging his temples as if it would help his pounding headache, Jerrol said with a groan, "I don't know."

"What does Anders say?"

"I haven't told him yet. I wanted to make sure Birlerion

was alright first. I was going to go down to the infirmary now, if you want to come."

"There's no point. The healers caught Birlerion completely unaware, and they managed to sedate him before he could stop them. No one was hurt. Healer Kirin has already left with him; he got spooked by Jaredion. I had to call the guards to hold Jaredion back."

Jerrol grimaced. "He resigned."

"What?"

"Jaredion. He resigned as a Sentinal."

"He can't resign."

"Well, he has. Apart from locking him up for a court-martial, which seems pointless, there isn't much I can do."

"Ask Jennery or Tagerill to speak to him."

"I'm hoping that's where he's gone. Home. To cool off before he does something we all regret."

14

———

OLD VESPERS

Jaredion literally saw red when the King's Guards barred him from the infirmary. If Kayenion hadn't hauled him down the corridor with some well-placed warnings ringing in his ear, he didn't know what he might have done.

He couldn't help Birlerion if he was locked in a cell himself. It was enough to calm him down, but his fury simmered, ready to explode at any moment. What had they done to Birlerion?

Healer Ewan came out of the infirmary and held his hands up in front of him.

"If you harm a hair on his head," Jaredion growled.

"You know we won't. It's for his own good, Jaredion."

"You'll regret this. After everything that man has done for you, for Remargaren, this is how you treat him?" Jaredion flung his hand towards the infirmary. "He trusted you. *I* trusted you. You were our friends!"

"We're still your friends. When you calm down, you'll see nothing has changed," Ewan soothed.

"Everything has changed," Jaredion snarled, tears of anguish and anger streaming down his cheeks. "And even if he forgives you for betraying his trust, I never will." Storming out of the palace, he headed towards the stables, not knowing what else to do with himself.

"Jaredion? What have they done to Birlerion? I can't reach him."

Jaredion stiffened as a Darian's rich voice filled his mind. *"Kin'arol?"* He hadn't expected Kin'arol to speak to him.

"Where is he? Why aren't you with him?" Kin'arol's voice was edged with fear.

"The healers ambushed him while Jerrol delayed me in his office. They won't let me near him. They say," Jaredion drew in a harsh breath. *"They say it's for his own good. That he is a danger to others."*

There was a tense silence and then Kin'arol roared in his head. It was such a deep and anger-filled sound that Jaredion ran down the path and into the stable block, where the racket of Kin'arol bashing down the door to his stall echoed through the yard.

"Stop, Kin'arol, you'll hurt yourself. And if you're hurt you can't help Birlerion."

The banging stopped, and Jaredion hurried up to his stall. He raised his hand as stable lads came running. "Saddle him up for me. I'll take him for a run while the First Administrator is with the Lord Chancellor. We could both do with the exercise," Jaredion said as he opened the door.

He cringed at the sight of Kin'arol's rolling eyes. *"Calm down. If they see you like this, they won't let me ride you. If we can get out of here before the guards come, we can follow wherever they take Birlerion."*

Kin'arol nodded his head. *"Let's go now. How dare they treat Birlerion so."* He stamped his foot, and Jaredion took the saddle as the stable lad froze.

"He's just eager; I'll do it," Jaredion said and lifted the saddle onto Kin'arol's back. He tightened the straps and then stroked Kin'arol's neck. *"Steady now. We'll rescue him. Between us, we'll find a way."*

Jaredion took the bridle off the lad and quickly slipped it over Kin'arol's nose. Checking over the straps to make sure all was tight, he led Kin'arol out of the stall and launched himself on his back. They headed out of the yard before anyone could stop them.

Birlerion stirred, and his head thumped, vibrating through his temples. His mouth was thick and dry, and he was thirsty. He tried to move his arm and couldn't. Convulsing, he realised he was strapped down.

"No," his voice croaked, and he stared around at the unfamiliar surroundings. It was rocking; they were moving.

"He's awake."

"Already? Dose him again."

The carriage faded.

Awareness returned painfully. The expanse of the Veil dominated his mind, and he shied from it. He shuddered, trying to push it away, and then swung his sword and felt it connect. Tightening his grip, he opened his eyes. The Veil writhed in front of him, strands grasping, wriggling towards him, separating, trying to divert him. He backed up, senses questing, but there was no Jaredion.

Harsh voices intruded, and he woke, rising out of his bed instinctively. Hands held him down, and he struggled against them. His mind tracked the snarling Veil as his eyes snapped open and flicked about him; small square room, strangers hovering over him. He didn't recognise any of it.

A sharp voice continued, high with fear, for him or because of him? "Hold him down, quick, Serna, inject him. How did he cut himself? Did you not search him properly? He must have a blade somewhere."

Birlerion thrashed as straps bit his skin. What was happening? His mind spun, trying to grapple with reality. He forced words out of his dry mouth. "Stop, don't …" a sharp prick in his shoulder and his words slipped away, along with the room.

The next time he awoke he couldn't move; he couldn't raise his arm. He flexed his hand; no sword. Opening his eyes, he glanced around the empty room in horror. He was trapped, restrained. Painful memories overwhelmed him; the scent of her perfume, the sound of her voice, her hands, her hands all over him. He convulsed again, struggling against the restraints.

"Birlerion, calm down or we'll have to sedate you again," a disembodied voice echoed above him.

They had sedated him, no, no, no, not again. He squinted. "What are you doing? How dare you? Let me go!"

"It's for your own good. You need to relax before you do yourself an injury."

"Unstrap me and then I'll relax."

"No, not until we're sure you have control of yourself. We know your violent tendencies; your safety and ours are the main concern here. We are here to help you, but you have to let us treat you."

"Where am I?"

"Somewhere safe. Rest, Birlerion, we'll talk later."

"Who are you?"

"Your friends; we're here to help you."

Birlerion strained. The leather straps were secure and

buckled around his chest, waist, wrists, and ankles. At least it wasn't rope; he wasn't back with Ellie being tortured. This was something new. He was dressed in a thin, pale blue wrap-around robe and nothing else. He shuddered at the thought of people touching him, undressing him.

His mind raced as he stiffened; tension ran through his body as memories surfaced. The last thing he remembered was Jerrol calling Jaredion back. He had walked down the corridor, and Ewan had appeared out of a side room and jabbed him in the neck. Ewan!

He tried to swallow, but his throat was tight. And Jerrol. Jerrol had conspired to ambush him. He hadn't even had the guts to tell him face to face. They had sedated him, again, knowing how much he hated it, what it reminded him of, and they had still sedated him. Why?

Anger licked along his veins at the betrayal, at the injustice of it all, and the air crackled around him. Staring up at the ceiling, he tried to control his terror. He mustn't sleep; how long could he last without sleep? Maybe he should make them sedate him; at least he would be safe from the Veil whilst he was sedated. But if they didn't sedate him deep enough, the Veil would get him. He would be defenceless, and he wouldn't be able to escape. His mind spun, trying to figure out the least-worst scenario, reminding him of his recent trauma they were all so insistent he needed to forget.

He drew a blank. He didn't understand why they would treat him like this. As if he was a dangerous animal, out of control. It didn't make any sense. He had escorted Mir'elle around the palace without incident; there was no reason for it.

Jaredion would be upset, more likely frantic. Jerrol would find his hands full with that one. He hoped Jaredion wouldn't do anything stupid. And Leyarille, she would go incandescent when she found out. He knew she wouldn't take it well either; his two champions. They would wreak havoc. He had to escape before this spiralled any further out of control.

The question was, where was he? If he got out of the straps, could he get out of the room? Rolling his head, he inspected his prison. It was square, empty, except for a door on his right-hand side. The walls were smooth and painted blue. Cold, sterile. Not friendly at all.

He listened, but there was silence. It was creepy. No voices, no birds, nothing. The air was still and warm. No aromas drifted in of food or medications. He had no idea how long he had been sedated and no idea how far they had travelled. For all he knew he could be in a cell under the palace or on a remote island in Birtoli. It was all the same to him. No one knew where he was. No one knew he had been restrained against his will; no one would try to find him.

Except Jaredion and Leyarille.

They would find him and rescue him. He just had to hold on.

For how long? He didn't know how long he had been awake. His thoughts tumbled into a cascade of confusion, not getting him anywhere. The silence was oppressive; it would drive him mad, and now the thought filled his mind. He would go mad from being trapped in a silent, sterile box. Never breathing the fresh air or seeing the Lady's moon ever again.

There was a thought. *Marguerite? Can you hear me? I need help. Marguerite? Leyandrii? Help me, please. Leyandrii?* More silence. It pressed in on him. Leyandrii was quiet these days; a mere memory since they had resealed the Veil all those years ago. She was barricaded more firmly on the other side of the Veil, but Marguerite usually responded. Where was she?

His thoughts were diverted worrying about why Marguerite

hadn't warned him what was happening. Now he thought about it, he hadn't heard from her for months. He had been so busy he hadn't noticed. He should have gone straight to Senti and checked the Oath. As soon as he got out of here, wherever here was, that was where he would go. Decision made, he felt better.

He began Apeiron, stepping through the movements in his mind, focusing on acknowledging the predicament he was in. Apeiron was a discipline he had used all his life, a way of aligning the mind with the body to enable clear thought and control. He couldn't physically perform the moves, restrained as he was, but he could imagine the motions. His lips twitched as he gentled his mind so that it relaxed and allowed thought instead of panic. His heart stuttered as he thought the word; so he started again. The first discipline was acknowledgement, so he would acknowledge the chaos incapacitating him.

He was on his fifth rendition of 'Acknowledgement' when the door rattled and opened. Turning his head, he stared at the man on the threshold. He didn't recognise him, nor could he see out of the door; it was shadowed, and there were no windows. No draft stirred the air as the man dragged a wooden chair across the stone floor. The screech grated against his ears.

The man was thin, bordering on skeletal. His head was too large for his body and covered with straggly grey hair. Sunken blue eyes observed him from under bushy black eyebrows peppered with white.

"Are you supposed to be reassuring or a warning of what I will become?"

The man smiled, his eyes brightening, and intelligence firmed his face. "My name is Kirin. I am your friend."

"That's nice. Do friends bring water?"

"Certainly, a moment." He stood and opened the door.

He spoke to a person outside - so there was a guard on the door - before returning with a cup and straw.

Birlerion drank quickly, just in case he took it away. The cool liquid soothed his throat and cleared the crud. The man smiled and held it steady. "No rush, you just need to ask and we will bring you water."

"Thank you."

"Of course, this isn't a prison, and you are not a criminal."

"Oh? What is it then?"

"A place where we care for those who can't care for themselves."

"And who makes that decision?"

"In your case, the chancellor, with the advice of the Healers. You see, Birlerion, you are a conundrum. You seem physically fine; you act completely normal, yet your mind is affected, causing odd aberrations in your behaviour. You are suffering from a disorder caused by trauma-induced anxiety. We need to understand what is causing your underlying distress, remove it, and give your mind time to recover. Then you will be safe to go back into society and able to go home again."

"And you make that decision?"

"Along with others. We have a team who will work with you, help you uncover your hidden terrors, help your mind heal."

"I don't think you really want to know all the terrors I have experienced. They are better left untouched."

"There, you see, I knew you wouldn't understand. I said as much to Ewan when he asked for my advice."

"About what?"

"Why you weren't responding to the treatment for Trauma Anxiety Disorder. It's often referred to as TAD. There were too many distractions at the palace. Too many expectations on you, they weren't allowing you to understand your inner motivations and deal with them. Here, there are no distractions. Nothing is expected of you but to acknowledge your fears and release them so they don't trouble you anymore."

They had a name for it, even a nickname. Lady help him; they had stuck him in a box and nailed down the lid. *Marguerite, if you don't hurry up, I am going to cream this guy.*

"Why am I strapped down?"

"For your safety." The man leaned over Birlerion. A musty scent drifted under his nose as the man opened his robe above the waist restraint, revealing deep red welts on his skin. "This cannot continue, Birlerion. Your body is covered in these marks. Our first task is to understand why you feel the need to hurt yourself. Once you acknowledge how wrong this is and you start respecting yourself and your body, we can begin to build the trust that will allow you to be released." He closed the robe back up.

Birlerion considered him. That sounded like it might take a very long time. He was sure it would take even longer to convince them he wasn't a threat. They wouldn't be so over-anxious, otherwise. And he wouldn't be strapped down.

"How am I supposed to eat, use the bathing room, exercise?"

"We will help you. For now, it is safer you are restrained."

"You do know that my last most traumatic experience included being restrained and tortured by a madwoman. How is this any different? How is this supposed to help me get over it?"

"Don't worry, we have plenty of time, and we will get to that."

"This is not helping me."

"Dinner will be served soon. Rest. We have a busy day tomorrow." Kirin patted his shoulder and left, taking his chair with him. The door clicked shut, though he didn't hear a lock or a bolt engage. Silence descended. More people who would not listen to him. He couldn't stay here; he would go insane within the week. Heaving a deep sigh, he began the disciplines again. He had some new chaos to acknowledge.

15

MARCHWOOD WATCH

Jaredion and Kin'arol waited behind the Chapterhouse, watching the road that led to the port or deeper into Vespiri. He didn't think they would take a ship. The healers were Vespirian; they would take him wherever their healeries were, he hoped.

When a heavily guarded carriage rumbled down the road, he knew it must contain Birlerion. There was no other reason for it to be guarded. The blacked out windows made him even more certain.

They had followed at a discreet distance, but no one really checked. They were more intent on ensuring their prisoner didn't escape. The guards' focus was on the carriage, not on their surroundings.

Kin'arol's low snarl echoed his own. They were both beyond words.

He had sent Ari with a terse message to Leyarille explaining what had happened. He hoped she would have more luck with her father than he had, though he doubted it. It would be down to him to rescue Birlerion.

It took the carriage three days to reach their destination,

and each night, Birlerion had been carried into an inn and back out in the morning. That first night, Jaredion had been relieved that they were following the right carriage, but the relief fast turned back into unadulterated fury. His head ached with the tension running through him, and he wanted to hit something. Kin'arol wasn't much better.

The escort of Kings Rangers guarding the perimeter averted their eyes as the stretcher passed, uncomfortable at the sight of the incapacitated Sentinal. Had they kept him sedated the whole time? When he woke up, he would not be well.

Jaredion crouched in the undergrowth, watching the building by the light of the moon. The carriage had pulled up in front of the red bricked mansion earlier in the day, and he had watched them carry Birlerion inside. He had been unconscious and strapped to the stretcher. Shortly after, the guards had left. Returning to Old Vespers, no doubt. Now, the moon bathed the landscape in a soft silver glow, picking out movement and deepening shadows. Jaredion took it as a sign of the Lady's concern.

His fists clenched at such treatment. He was the First Administrator of Vespiri and Terolia, the Oath Keeper. Did it mean nothing? He had been tortured, badly injured, and this was how they treated him? Jaredion would never work for the Vespirian administration again.

Grappling with his anger, he stoked it deep inside as he regained his composure. Now was not the time. He scouted the building. It was a small manor house set in an estate about twenty leagues south of the Grove, deep in the forests of Marchwood. It was quiet, secluded, fenced off. It hadn't been difficult to scale the fence; more to keep people in than out, he thought.

The building had tall windows on either side of the door, but they were dull and lifeless, not providing light. Jaredion wasn't sure what they were, but they weren't acting like windows usually did. The second floor had windows that opened, pushed up to let the night air in … or maybe a horrible smell out. It was a bit cold for open windows.

He watched the comings and goings, servants going about their business, muscular gardeners chopping wood or turning over the soil ready to lie fallow for the winter. He counted six servants; four in the house and two in the grounds. There was a tall, gangly, grey-haired man who had escorted Birlerion's stretcher into the house, and he had been met on the steps by two more, a man and woman, both in healer garb.

How many patients are there, he wondered, *apart from Birlerion? And who owns this house?*

Nine of them against him, and he didn't know whether Birlerion would be conscious or not, and he wasn't exactly light. He needed help. The question was, should he wait for help or take a chance? Leyarille still hadn't responded. He imagined she was still trying to control her own fury.

Kin'arol waited in the trees behind the fence, ready to whisk them both away once he figured out how to rescue Birlerion. He couldn't remember what he had said to Jerrol. He had never been so angry in all his life. It was the first time he had literally seen red and known what it meant. It wasn't a pleasant experience. He was quite sure he would have gone berserk if anyone had tried to stop him. Taking a deep breath, he calmed himself, even the memory set his heart racing.

He would wait another day, see if Leyarille responded, try and guard Birlerion overnight if he could reach him, and then break him out when he had thought of a plan. It would come to him by morning, he was sure of it.

Watch Towers

Leyarille hugged the Arifel to her chest and rocked. Tears streamed down her cheeks. How could they? They were destroying the man she loved. Ari meeped, and she relaxed her grip, apologising profusely. "Do you know where Birlerion and Jaredion are?"

Images of leafy green forests, a mansion house, and Lord William's face flashed through her mind. Somewhere in Marchwood Watch. "Could you keep it secret?" she asked.

Folding his wings, Ari meeped. The images disappeared. "Thank you. He isn't mad. He is the sanest man I know."

Ari crooned in agreement, and pictures of the Veil tarnished and black with brittle edges invaded her thoughts.

"Why does no one else see this? Have you shown my father?"

Ari chattered, pushing images of the palace at her, and then after staring at her, he popped out of sight.

Leyarille pushed her anger down deep inside. She would save it for the one who deserved it; her father would pay for betraying Birlerion. Gritting her teeth, she deliberately thought of something else. If she thought about her father's actions, she might not come back whole. She sighed. What to do? She was supposed to be assigned to the Watch Towers. She had found some information about the Veil, but was it enough?

Birlerion was more important. They had to rescue him. Her mother might understand, but would she keep it from her father? Her mother would not lie to her husband, but she might delay. And that was all Leyarille needed; time.

She went in search of her sister first. Margareth was in deep discussion with her mother. She threw the message on the table. "He is being attacked by the Veil and now by Vespiri."

Margareth stared at her as Taelia picked up the scrap of paper. "Leyarille, the Veil is fine. The weave is strong and pliant; there is nothing wrong with it."

"I told you, it is using Birlerion to heal itself. That's why you haven't been able to find any signs. It's healed before you can see it."

Taelia passed the message to Margareth. "I am so sorry, Leyarille. We all know what terrible suffering Birlerion went through. Is this really surprising? He needs help, darling, and the healers are the best people to give it to him. Surely you want what's best for him?"

"The Veil cannot be explained by healers."

"They can help Birlerion adjust, accept what has happened. You need to stop worrying about the Veil. Move his thoughts to a new project, like Westermaine. He needs to move on."

Leyarille quivered. This must be how Birlerion felt when he spoke with the healers; when people didn't hear the words you were saying. Was she saying it wrong? Why wouldn't they listen? "That is a bit difficult, Ma, when they have committed him to an institution. Pa passed a law that takes away all his rights. He is being attacked by something they do not understand, something they cannot possibly comprehend or explain."

Taelia rubbed her face. "Leyarille, darling. Maybe you ought to go and speak to your father. There must be details you are not aware of. Birlerion is our family. You know your father would never do anything to harm him; he must have believed it was the right thing to do."

"We've received an invite to the king's engagement ball. He is joining with Mir'elle of the Atolea. We can all travel together. You can speak to Pa then," Margareth suggested.

Kirin's Healerie, Marchwood

Birlerion smelt soap. It was the sharp, medicated smell of disinfectant. They had washed him. They must have sedated the food they had forced him to eat because he didn't remember going to sleep. Lady help him; this was more degrading than Ellie. At least he knew she was insane; what excuse did these people have? They were supposed to be healers, compassionate, helping him. They were going to sustain his body, keep him alive so the Veil could feed on him longer. The healers would drive him into insanity.

He had been good as well, very docile, answering their questions, inoffensive as possible. But they were all watching him suspiciously for some reason. Was he not behaving how he ought to? He didn't know, and it was too exhausting trying to double think it all. Nothing made sense, he had to get out. He needed a piss, and he wasn't asking one of them to help him.

Healer Kirin returned after breakfast and Birlerion moved on to *Understanding*. He didn't understand anything; maybe Apeiron would help.

"How are you feeling this beautifully sunny morning?" Kirin asked.

"Is it? Why aren't there any windows? Isn't light supposed to be good for recuperation?"

"Light is a reward. As you progress, we'll open the window so the light can enter."

"I thought this wasn't a prison. Deprivation is a kind of torture, you know."

"You aren't deprived. Your bodily needs are cared for. We are protecting you; you are quite safe."

"I am quite capable of looking after my own bodily needs. I do not need your assistance."

"You are extremely placid. I thought you might be more upset."

Upset? He would give him upset when he got his hands around his throat. "Really?"

"Yes, our patients normally rail against their situation for the first few days. You are very accepting."

Nice to see Apeiron works. *Acknowledgement* was the path to *Acceptance* after all. "I have been in this situation before, as I said, and railing did not help."

"Tell me about it."

"What do you want to know?" Birlerion concentrated on *Understanding*. He was sure understanding would come in time.

"Tell me how it felt being restrained."

Was this man for real? Really? "Painful."

"Why?"

"The ropes burnt my skin. I railed so much they burnt through the layers of my skin until the ropes got embedded. Any movement was excruciating. That's what caused the scars on my wrists and ankles."

"Why did you struggle so much?"

"Because I wanted to be free."

"And did you free yourself?"

"No."

"Now you know that isn't true, Birlerion."

Birlerion broke off his mental exercises and stared at him. "I was unable to break the ropes. I couldn't free myself."

"Yet when your rescuers arrived, your hand was strangling that young woman. You freed your hand and freed yourself from her attentions. Repeat after me, Birlerion: I freed myself."

"I freed myself," Birlerion repeated, watching the man in

case it was a trick. Maybe he was going to try and *Mentiserium* him; a bit of brainwashing maybe.

"There," Kirin smiled as if he had made a breakthrough. "Well done. Acceptance of behaviour is the first step. We will continue this afternoon. As you confront each of your traumatic experiences, we will draw out the latent fear and expose it so we can help you manage it."

Acceptance was the fourth step. You needed acknowledgement first, but he'd go with it if it made this crazy man happy. He was glad when the man left, and he went back to *Understanding*.

Morning came, and Jaredion hadn't come up with a brilliant idea. He hadn't found Birlerion out in the expanse of the Veil overnight. It had been quiescent, empty. They must have sedated him, which would have angered Jaredion more except it protected Birlerion from something worse. Jaredion crept nearer to the fence. The tall, gangly man was walking the perimeter, accompanied by the woman healer, and they were discussing Birlerion.

"He is far too quiet, distracted. He should be railing against his restraints; it's not natural."

"But it is good he is calm. Maybe he is not as damaged as we thought. He seems quite centred to me."

"We don't use the word 'damaged', Rose, we say affected; it's not so judgemental."

"Sorry, Kirin, but still, quiet is good."

"No, he is hiding, and we need to bring him out. We need the real Birlerion to face his horrors. Only then will he be released. I think purging may be what we need to consider."

"Surely not. He's only been here two days. You can't possibly have assessed him in that time."

Kirin stopped and frowned at her. "Are you questioning my judgement?"

"Of course not, Kirin, but we still have many other options before we resort to purging. It's barbaric, and if he has suffered what they say, it may make him regress. It is too primitive."

Jaredion's chest squeezed painfully. Had the man not suffered enough?

"I am leaving for the palace in a chime; the chancellor wants my initial report. Keep him restrained at all times and sedated in between sessions. Don't underestimate him. Serna knows what to do. He is still self-harming. The chancellor will be upset if he is hurt any further."

"Of course, sir."

"Good, I will be back in a week, and then we will reassess him. The chancellor expects results, and fast."

16

KING'S PALACE, OLD VESPERS

Leyarille stepped through the waystone into Commander Bryce's outer office and left her mother and Margareth paling alarmingly as their stomachs revolted against the waystone. Deron leapt up and hurried to steer them out the door and offered a bowl he kept handy for unsuspecting travellers. He'd had too many accidents in his office and he hated the smell.

Bryce came out of his office at the commotion and hurried to offer his assistance. "Who brought them through the waystone?" he exclaimed.

"Leyarille," Deron replied. "She went storming off as soon as they all arrived."

"Lady help us," Bryce murmured, as he steered a limp Taelia to a chair and Deron offered a glass of water.

"We should have come by road," Taelia said, rubbing her face with a shaking hand. "But I didn't like to leave Leyarille on her own. She is upset."

Margareth snorted. "Furious more like."

"I'd better go check …" Bryce said as he hurried out the door.

Taelia's face tightened as she watched him leave, but she remained seated and sipped her water. She smiled wanly at Deron. "My apologies for disrupting your office, but we were in Leyarille's hands …" She shrugged.

Leyarille stormed into her father's office without knocking, barely noting Kayenion skittering out of her way. "What have you done to Birlerion?" she demanded.

Jerrol looked up in surprise. "What are you doing here? You're supposed to be with your mother."

"Did you seriously think I wouldn't find out about you attacking Birlerion?"

"I did no such thing. You don't know what you are talking about."

"Ambushing a man without warning, sedating him so you could abduct him, restraining him, after everything he's been through. How could you?"

Jerrol flinched back from the disdain in her voice. "He is in good hands. They will help him. He wouldn't listen …"

Leyarille's anger poured over him. "It's you who won't listen. Where is he?"

"He's in safe hands. He needs time to recover. The healers will help him."

"How many times does he have to tell you there is something wrong with the Veil?"

"You know that's not true. The Veil is fine. I've checked it, multiple times. Birlerion needs to let it go. The healers have recommended a new therapy for him. It will help him manage his anxiety."

"How can you be so stupid? There is no anxiety to manage," Leyarille yelled, slamming her hand down on his desk. "He needs protection against the Veil."

"That is enough!" Jerrol's voice echoed between them

as he stood and leaned on his desk, his jaw clenching as he glared at her. "I have granted you some leeway because you are my daughter and I know you care for Birlerion. But I will not put up with your behaviour. I am your Captain and the Lord Chancellor of Vespiri and Terolia. As such, you will speak to me with respect or suffer the consequences."

Leyarille's lip curled. "You mean you'll lock me up as well? Is that your answer to everything?"

"No one is locked up."

"Then why won't you tell me where he is?"

"The healers are caring for him. He needs time to concentrate on himself, and he doesn't need any distractions."

"What does Birlerion say to that?"

"It's what the healers prescribe."

"Healers, healers, healers. Anyone would think they are your only source of wisdom these days. When did they over-rule your compassion, your common sense?"

"Leyarille, I'm warning you. If you can't control yourself, I'll send you to a post far away where you can spend some time considering your behaviour."

"Don't bother. Where is Jaredion?"

"He went home. He needed a break."

"Back to Deepwater? Just like that? Shouldn't he be at Birlerion's shoulder? The Lady made him his protector, you know."

"He was exhausted. Not thinking straight. He's been on Birlerion's detail for far too long. He stole Kin'arol. If he knows what's good for him, he'll return him immediately. He is already under threat of a court martial."

"Do you seriously believe anyone could take Kin'arol from the palace if he didn't want to go? And why are you threatening Jaredion with a court martial? Did he say something you disagreed with? Is that your answer for dealing with people who don't follow your line?"

Leyarille scowled at her father. Kin'arol wouldn't have gone with Jaredion unwillingly, which meant he was just as concerned. Of course he was. If Birlerion was sedated then Kin'arol wouldn't be able to reach him.

"He was out of line, disrespectful," Jerrol almost snarled, his control on his temper slipping.

Leyarille bit her lip against a smirk. Good for Jaredion. Her mind spun as her concern for Birlerion ratcheted up another notch, not that her body wasn't already screaming with fear for him. She knew perfectly well that Jaredion wasn't in Deepwater. He was somewhere in Marchwood searching for Birlerion. His faithful defender. But if her father didn't know that, then she wouldn't be the one to tell him.

Taking a deep breath, Leyarille reined in her anger. She needed to be sensible, her father was right about that. It would be far more difficult for her to find Birlerion if he banished her from Old Vespers. She needed to be smart. "When do the healers say we can visit him?"

At his daughter's calmer voice, Jerrol exhaled the breath he had been holding. "Once they have assessed him. I expect a report by the end of the week. We'll know more then."

"Very well, I'll wait, but Captain, know this: you are making a grave mistake." She looked up as Bryce hovered in the doorway, and she glared at him before returning her gaze to her father. "I want my protest against your action and my concern for Birlerion's safety officially noted. I do not agree with what you've done. You've set a precedent that puts all Sentinals at risk, not just Birlerion. All of us. Think on that, why don't you, instead of listening to men who don't know what they are dealing with." Leyarille turned at the door as Bryce backed up. "You were once the Oath Keeper. Have you forgotten what that meant? What you did? Could all *your* actions have been explained by a healer's theory?"

Leyarille left, still seething. The air crackled around her as she brushed past Bryce and strode down the corridor. She ignored her father calling her back; she needed to find a target to hit before she exploded. Her feet found the way to the small training ground behind the barracks. A Terolian soldier was already training, his muscles rippling as his scimitar danced in the light, his dark skin gleaming with sweat.

She shrugged out of her jacket, took a deep breath, and stepped up to the target. She pounded out her frustration until the target disintegrated. Taking a deep breath, she stepped into Acknowledgement and smiled as she thought of Birlerion. The familiar moves calmed her breathing and soothed her mind. Birlerion had taught her Apeiron, just as he had taught her everything else she knew, her father often being too busy with the Watch or the king.

Birlerion's face hung before her as she turned. *Hold on, my love. We are coming; we are searching for you.*

She smiled as she imagined his answer. *Search faster.*

She opened her eyes to find the Terolian watching her, his dark eyes questioning.

"It's called Apeiron. Birlerion taught me."

"You know where Lord Birlerion is?"

"No, they won't tell me."

The Terolian nodded. "My name is Cor'ilno, brother of Mir'elle."

"I'm Leyarille, Birlerion's …" She paused. What was she? Lover, friend, colleague? They hadn't formally announced their intentions after all.

Cor'ilno smiled. "Ah, my brother's intended; he speaks of you often."

A smile crept over her face. "He does?"

"Of course, we share his joy."

"Can you help me find him?"

"Speak with Mir'elle. She is already looking. We await a direction, and we will go and get him."

Leyarille grinned at the confidence in his voice. Her shoulders relaxed; she wasn't on her own, nor was Birlerion. "Even though it goes against the wishes of the Lord Chancellor of Vespiri and Terolia?"

Cor'ilno shrugged, the movement fluid. "Birlerion is family."

"I haven't had the honour of meeting Lady Mir'elle yet."

"Then let me rectify that. She will be in the sheltered garden. Come, I will introduce you."

Leyarille grabbed her jacket as Cor'ilno splashed himself with water before covering his muscular chest under a black robe. Smoothing her cloudy hair off her face, she retied it out of the way and followed him out of the ring.

They found Mir'elle seated by the fountain, a hand trailing in the water as she stared down into it, deep in thought. Leyarille thought she had never seen a more beautiful woman. She was not surprised Anders had fallen for her. Her black hair shone as it curled around her bare shoulders, warm golden-brown skin glowed, though a red scar marred one smooth arm, recent and not yet healed to a faint silver, or more likely gold in Mir'elle's case.

Mir'elle looked up, and Leyarille met eyes of inky black, expressive and welcoming, and Mir'elle stood, a smile lighting her face.

"Cor'ilno, who do you bring to me this fine morning?" Even her voice was low and rich. It wasn't fair.

"Leyarille, Birlerion's intended."

"Leyarille? My dear, I am so glad to meet you at last. Birlerion said I would love you, and I can see he was right. Please join me. After all, we will become sisters so we must make sure we get to know each other well." Mir'elle drew her to a bench under a leafy tree. Leyarille felt clumsy beside her; Mir'elle was so petite and elegant.

"You claim Birlerion as a brother too?" Leyarille asked.

Mir'elle's laugh peeled out. "He is a son of the Atolea. Of course I claim him as a brother."

"He is fortunate in his family, though I didn't realise he was an Atolean. I thought he was from Vespers."

"He is, though that doesn't mean he is any less my brother. Family, after all, comes first."

"I'm not sure I understand," Leyarille admitted.

"I suppose not. In Terolia we do not live in individual houses or within cities. We live in Families, as a group. The Medera is our mother and her Sodera our father, and they are responsible for all in the family. My sister, Elisande, is our Medera now, because although our mother still lives, she is old and frail.

"You will meet my mother when she arrives. I will make sure of it. But for now, the Medera speaks with the voice for the family. If she declares a man or woman a son or daughter of the family, then it is so.

"Birlerion was declared a son by one of my ancestors, and it was recorded in the Family's book, in ink so it would not be forgotten. The Family does not forget."

"So he was a son of the Atolea before he was encased in his sentinal?"

"Oh yes, it is recorded that his life was threatened whilst under the Family's protection, and he saved a son of the Family, twice over, so he is owed. Though Birlerion brushes it off."

Leyarille smiled. "He would. Protecting is as natural as breathing to Birlerion." She looked at Mir'elle. "But *he* needs protecting now, and I hope you can help me find him. He is in danger, and the healers can't help him."

"I have been asking questions, though no one knows

what happened. It is said he had a relapse and the healers are caring for him. But no one knows where he is or who is looking after him."

"I know, my father wouldn't tell me where he was taken."

"Oh." Mir'elle's eyes widened. "If he won't tell you, Birlerion's intended, then it's worse than we thought."

"We need to find which healer has him. Ewan is still here, but he wouldn't talk to me; he ran in the opposite direction when he saw me. I was going to try Kayenion next; he must know who has been to see my father."

"Kayenion? Kayerille's son?"

"Yes, he is now my father's bodyguard. He would know which healers my father has met with."

"Good idea. I could ask him to come and see me. Kayerille did ask me to pass her love to him. If I can draw him away from your father, maybe you could ask your questions?"

"He is a friend of mine and Jaredion's; he would speak to me."

"I am so sorry, but I don't know what has happened to Jaredion either. He disappeared along with Birlerion's Darian."

"He's somewhere in Marchwood. He thinks Birlerion is held there."

"So we need a Healer from Marchwood." Mir'elle tapped her lip. "I think we should work the ball tomorrow night. Everyone will be there. Someone must know what is going on. I can ask Kayenion for a dance; that should be quite easy."

"That may be best. My father would be suspicious if I danced with him. I can speak with Bryce and his wife Olivia and members of the Administration," Leyarille said, her face intent and full of purpose. She fidgeted, barely able to sit still as the need to act raced through her.

Mir'elle reached out to rub her shoulder. "Leyarille, we will find him, I promise."

"They've had him for days. He's been through so much already. When will they leave him in peace?"

"I know, but you have to keep it contained. Burn some more of this energy off before tomorrow night else you will draw the wrong attention. You are too vibrant, my dear. We need to lull them, so they don't expect us to do anything."

"I would be honoured to spar with you," Cor'ilno spoke from beside the fountain, silent but listening.

"Thank you, maybe that would be best." Leyarille ran a trembling hand through her hair. "I wouldn't want to scare anyone off, after all."

Mir'elle squeezed her arm. "I will see you tomorrow night. Let us pretend we haven't met. Then no one will suspect we are working together when we start to ask questions."

The following evening, Jerrol stood beside King Anders, Kayenion at his shoulder as he watched the dance floor. He knew both Kayenion and Parsillion were appalled by his decision because they had both taken the time to tell him. They refused to believe that Birlerion would harm himself or anyone else for no reason. Kayenion had even gone as far to demand that his name be added to Leyarille's protest. Jerrol cringed at the fact that he had heard their argument and had agreed with Leyarille.

He was thankful Taelia had arrived to bolster him. Only the thin veneer of good manners and respect for the king and Mir'elle kept Leyarille in check, but only just. He had never seen his daughter so furious, and an inkling of concern stirred in his gut. She was usually so level-headed. For her to react so strongly was unlike her. Margareth had simply hugged him and reassured him that the Veil was fine.

Every time Leyarille had the opportunity, she demanded to be told where they had taken Birlerion. She had the right to see him. She wanted to make sure he was alright. But Healer Kirin had warned against distractions. Birlerion needed peace, time to adjust. Jerrol would give him that; it was the least he could do. He missed him. His absence was more notable since he had only just returned.

Taelia stopped before Anders and Mir'elle, dropping into a curtsey, their daughters behind her. Jerrol avoided Leyarille's accusing glare as Anders smiled. "Taelia, welcome home. I am so glad you were able to join our celebration. Let me introduce you to Mir'elle. Mir'elle, Scholar Deane Taelia Haven."

"Scholar Deane Taelia, a pleasure, and these must be your lovely daughters."

Taelia smiled into the sparkling black eyes. "Yes, Leyarille and Margareth."

"Leyarille? You must be Birlerion's intended. I am so pleased to meet you; my brother spoke of you often."

Leyarille curtsied. "My lady, the honour is mine."

"You must miss him so much. So sad that he is unable to be with us at this joyous time. How goes he? If you don't mind my asking."

"Unfortunately, they won't tell me, my lady."

"Why not?" She turned to Jerrol. "Lord Chancellor, why won't you tell Birlerion's intended how he is?"

Leyarille struggled to keep her expression blank; her father's face was a picture. He cleared his throat. "I wasn't aware that Birlerion and Leyarille were getting Joined."

Mir'elle's hands flew to her face. "Oh no, Leyarille, I am so sorry. Was it a secret? I didn't mean to spoil your announcement." Mir'elle's glance caught Margareth's smirk and Taelia's smile.

"You haven't, my Lady. We were waiting until my mother and father were in the same place. Such a rare event these days, but as you know, events superseded us."

"Oh, my dear, I hope he is brought home to you soon."

Jerrol swallowed. "We only do what is best for Birlerion. The healers care for him so he can return to us as soon as possible."

"Good," Mir'elle patted his arm, and Taelia led her daughters off the dais.

The evening progressed, and Mir'elle hovered over her mother, Maraine, as she introduced her to Anders and smiled as Anders set to win her over. She watched the ebb and flow of the room and observed as Leyarille circulated, alternating between simmering violence and sugar-sweet conversation.

The Lord Chancellor paused beside her. "Mir'elle, may I have this dance?" He offered her his right hand. "Enjoying your evening?"

"Very much so, it has been a wonderful ball. I appreciate all your efforts. I know it must have been a lot of work." Her fingers clasped his mutilated hand. "How do you manage without your good right hand?"

"Oh." Jerrol flexed his hand beneath hers. "I don't notice the lack anymore; it's surprising how well you adapt."

Mir'elle tilted her head. "Don't you find that you still miss your fingers?"

"Sometimes," Jerrol admitted as they twirled around the dance floor.

"There are some things that adapting just can't replace, aren't there? Maybe at the time, it seemed the right thing to do, that the changes you made helped you feel better, but then you realise it didn't solve the problem. That possibly, it has made the problem worse. What do you do then, dear Lord Chancellor?"

Jerrol frowned. "I'm afraid I don't understand your point, my lady."

Mir'elle pouted at Jerrol, her black eyes wide. "What is lost can often leave an echo, a reminder of what once was; surprisingly painful at times I'm told. Have you ever experienced that? No? You are fortunate. The question is, if you did, could you do anything about it? I sincerely hope your decisions are not irreversible, Lord Chancellor."

The music came to an end, and Mir'elle gave him a small smile and moved away, leaving Jerrol staring after her perplexed.

"Is something wrong, Lord Chancellor?"

Jerrol started and smiled at the tall, elegant woman standing before him, draped in shimmering robes of gold and yellow. His brain started working, and he put a name to her elegantly made-up face. "Ambassador Kaplan, forgive me, no, nothing is wrong, not at all."

"No doubt you're missing the First Administrator, Lord Birlerion." Jerrol's chest tightened as the Birtolian Ambassador continued, waving a slender hand. "I was so distressed to hear he had a relapse. We all miss him dreadfully, don't we? Such an intelligent man, so in tune with the people. We can but hope that the Lady watches over him in his difficulties."

"Yes, I'm sure she does."

"Good, we need him back in office. There are some people you just can't replace, aren't there?"

Jerrol forced a smile onto his face, his stomach congealing.

Taelia paused beside him as the ambassador moved away. "Jerrol? Is something the matter? You're not feeling ill, are you?"

"No, not at all."

Leyarille passed them, a cynical expression on her face. "Be careful, Pa. You wouldn't want us deciding you are not a good judge of your health, now would you? We could take the decision right out of your hands." She moved on, her eyes glittering in the lamplight.

Taelia squeezed his arm. "Don't listen to her, love, she is still angry. You did what was best for Birlerion. He will thank you for it when he is all recovered, you'll see."

"Will he?"

"Of course. You only want what's best for him. He knows that."

"I'm not sure I would be so understanding. We could have done it differently, *should* have done it differently. Maybe given him more time to adjust before we made such an important decision."

"If you had waited, Jerrol, he could have killed someone, and then how would you have felt?"

"We don't know that he would have."

"It was a possibility. You can't worry over it. Don't doubt yourself. The decision is made, it is irreversible, you said so. You must have thought he was dangerous to have made the decision in the first place."

"Dangerous, yes, that's right. He was a risk, a danger to himself and others. But I still miss him."

"Of course you do, he is your friend. Maybe if you go and see how he is progressing, it will make you feel better."

"Healer Kirin said to leave it a couple of weeks, let him settle in, get used to the new routine."

"Then that is what you should do. Now cheer up, this is supposed to be a party. You'll worry people if you go around looking like that."

. . .

Leyarille watched the room, silently simmering. How could this be happening? All these people without a care in the world. It was because of people like Birlerion who made their safe little lives possible that they could glide around a dancefloor in their elegant clothes.

Yet, when it came down to the crux of it, deep down, they were afraid of the Sentinals, of what they were capable of. The slightest sign that any of them might be affected by what they had done or seen and they would lock them up. Birlerion was only the first. They had done it once, and they would do it again. They needed to get him out.

"Breathe, Leyarille. You will go up in smoke if you don't breathe." Leyarille gave a brittle laugh as Mir'elle paused beside her.

"Come and sit with me tomorrow. In the sheltered garden, at the eleventh chime. We should talk." Mir'elle squeezed her hand. "Don't let them know they've upset you. You don't want them watching you."

Leyarille let her breath go and tried to relax her shoulders. Mir'elle was right; take it easy and slow. She pasted a smile on her face and approached a slim young man standing by the wall. His blond hair was neatly trimmed, his vivid blue eyes watching the dance floor; Birlerion's assistant. "Minister Erian, I need a partner. Would you do me the honour?"

"Sentinal Leyarille, of course." The young man smiled and, taking her hand, led her onto the floor. They made a few circuits, and Leyarille smiled. "How is the Ministry treating you, Erian?"

"Very well. I enjoy the work, though I miss Lord Birlerion. Have you heard how he goes on?"

"We hope he will return to work soon. I think he overdid it in Terolia."

"It was surprising they sent him on such a long journey

his first week back. We miss his insights. He does see to the root of an issue very quickly."

"I am glad you are looking after his office for him. I know he was very pleased with your work."

"Yes, he said he was putting me forward for a promotion. I appreciate his support, Sentinal Leyarille."

"He appreciates his staff; you can trust him to have your best interests at heart." They twirled past Jerrol and Taelia. "He would never betray your trust."

"I know, he is a role model for all of us; so committed."

"Make sure you tell the Lord Chancellor; he needs to hear what is going right in his Administration. Maybe it will make him consider his next actions more carefully."

"Of course, Sentinal, of course."

"Thank you for the dance, Erian." She smiled as she saw Mir'elle dancing with Kayenion. Leyarille moved on to her next prey.

17

MARCHWOOD WATCH

Healer Kirin set off on his journey to Old Vespers with one of his assistants, later that morning. Jaredion had to get Birlerion out of this terrible place. He couldn't think of a word bad enough for it, and if his uncle had been within reach, he would have happily strangled him. But he wasn't, so instead, he was going to ride up to the house and rescue his friend.

Once the activity from Kirin's departure dissipated, he drifted up to the house. If he was sensible, he would wait for darkness to fall when the servants would be asleep, but the thought of leaving Birlerion in this place a day longer than he needed to drove him onwards.

He entered through the open wooden doors. The hallway was empty, and he silently crossed it to the first door. It opened easily. The room was divided into three smaller cubicles, each with a bed, smooth blue walls, and nothing else. The windows had been boarded over and painted like another wall.

Moving on to the second doorway, it was much the same, though one of the beds was occupied by an emaciated woman curled on her side, whimpering. Jaredion backed out without disturbing her. He walked to the other side of the corridor and tried the door; more of the same. Footsteps echoing in the hallway had him darting inside the empty room, and he knelt by the door, holding it open a crack.

Two women passed. "After the morning session, make sure he is medicated. Just for two chimes; enough time for us to change him and his bed. Prepare rooms four and six. They will be arriving in a chime. Serna should start the next …" the voices faded and Jaredion peered out. The women had turned the corner and passed from view.

Taking a deep breath, he returned to the corridor and opened the final door. Three more rooms, painted blue, a single bed in each, one occupied. His heart stuttered as he saw Birlerion. He looked catatonic, his gaze fixed on the ceiling. Straps restrained him at wrist and ankle, and Jaredion felt his own anxiety stir at the sight of them. What Birlerion must be going through, confined for days, he dreaded to think.

He darted to the bedside. "Birlerion, we need to leave." He started unbuckling the leather wrist strap. Flipping off the blanket, he halted at the sight of more straps holding him down across chest and waist. Face tightening, he started work on the buckles, six silver buckles, cinched across his abdomen. They were taking too long; there were too many of them. His fingers fumbled as he panicked. "Slow down," he breathed, slow and sure. The final buckle released. "Birlerion?" He leaned over, and Birlerion blinked, making him jump.

Birlerion focused on his face, his silver eyes confused. "Jaredion?" he whispered.

"Yes, yes it's me. Come on, help me with these buckles; we have to get you out of here."

Birlerion shuddered and frowned for a moment before

realising his hand was free and that Jaredion really was beside him. His hand wavered, and then he gripped Jaredion's arm just to make sure.

"Thank the Lady," Birlerion said, sitting up. He started to work on his other wrist. "Where did you come from? How long have I been here?" He blinked again. "Where is here?"

Jaredion grinned. He sounded so normal. "Marchwood, about twenty leagues in. I followed them from the palace. It's been four days."

"It felt like much longer. Bless you, Jaredion." He froze as the door rattled. Jaredion flipped the blanket back over him and ducked down the other side of the bed. Birlerion lay back down, tucking the cuff around his wrist and staring up at the ceiling.

Jaredion listened as Birlerion calmed his panicked breathing, amazed he could calm himself when escape was so close. He was sure Birlerion would not want to stay here another day.

"Here we are, Birlerion, a nice cup of coffee for you." The woman positioned the straw by his mouth.

"Thank you, but I'm not thirsty at the moment."

"Of course you are. Come on, drink it. You wouldn't like me to tell Healer Kirin you were difficult now, would you?"

Birlerion sipped it, and Jaredion willed the woman to leave.

"Hurry up, Birlerion, I have other patients to look after." Birlerion rolled his eyes and drank the liquid. "Good boy." She patted his shoulder and left.

"We have about fifteen minutes before I go out like a snuffed flame. They put something in it, so I sleep for a while. I'm not sure how long."

"Two chimes," Jaredion said, attacking the buckles on his ankles. "You got that one?" The final buckle was released, and he put his arm around Birlerion's waist and helped him stand. Birlerion swayed. "Is there a piss pot? I need to go."

Jaredion bit his lip, and leaving Birlerion balanced against the bed, darted out the room and returned with a chamber pot. "I never thought to bring you clothes," he said, holding the pot in front of him.

Birlerion relaxed in relief. "I'm sorry, Jaredion. I've been dying to go for ages; it's just the thought of them ..." He shuddered.

"It's fine. I understand, truly." Jaredion ignored the stink, and the embarrassment, and shoving the pot under the bed, he helped Birlerion out of the room. Voices came from the rooms on the other side of the corridor, and Jaredion hustled him down the passageway. Birlerion began to weave.

"I fear the sedative is upon me quicker than expected," he murmured as he veered off into the wall.

Jaredion righted him. "Could you call Kin'arol? He's waiting at the end of the drive. If we can get you on him, we'll be away."

"Kin'arol? You rascal, what are you doing here?"

"Birlerion. I'm here. We rescue you."

"Come and get me then, because I'm not coming to you. I'm about to fall asleep."

"Again? Stay awake, Birlerion. You sleep too much."

"He comes. He says I sleep too much."

"You do." Jaredion grunted, taking his full weight as Birlerion sank to the floor. "Birlerion? Wake up!"

Birlerion struggled onto his knees. "He reminds me of Kaf'enir," he mumbled to the floor. "She used to complain a lot."

"She is my many times great, great dam. Of course I'm like her. Get up, Birlerion."

Jaredion helped him up. Wedging his shoulder under Birlerion's armpit they staggered out the door. They paused at the top of the stone steps. "Sorry," Jaredion said as he eased Birlerion to the ground and let him roll down the stone steps. He landed in a heap at the bottom.

"Ow," Birlerion said.

"What are a few bruises compared to a lifetime of restraints?"

"Nothing," Birlerion said, his voice slurring. "You're forgiven."

Kin'arol came barrelling up the drive as the gardeners rushed around the side of the house. They gaped at the honey-gold stallion nudging the man lying at the bottom of the steps.

"Hey, you there, what do you think you're doing?"

Hauling Birlerion's body up, Jaredion heaved him up on his shoulder and then over Kin'arol's back like a sack of grain. He slapped Kin'arol's rump and turned to the men, unsheathing his sword. "You're too late. Go find someone else to torture." And he ran after the horse.

Jaredion pushed Birlerion's limp body out of the way and launched himself up into the saddle. Pulling Birlerion back against him, he hugged him tight and urged Kin'arol into a canter. A second horse waited behind the screen of trees. Jaredion had 'borrowed' it from a neighbouring farm. He fully intended on returning it so it wasn't really stealing. Grabbing the travel rug off his back, he flung it over Birlerion's scantily-clad body and, grasping the horse's reins, he tugged it after him as he urged Kin'arol towards the road.

He knew Birlerion and Anterion went way back so he headed for Marchwood Manor, hoping the Sentinal would help them. He needed to find somewhere safe for Birlerion to sleep off the sedative, and a sentinal tree sounded like the ideal place to him.

A swirling mist descended as they arrived in Marchwood, the winter's day providing some cover. The scent of damp vegetation and deep green winter foliage permeated the air. Their breath plumed in the cold air; it was frigid, and Birlerion was freezing. He needed to find him someplace warm. He hid Kin'arol and his burden on the outskirts of the manor grounds.

Approaching the graceful sentinal trees, Jaredion placed his hand on Anterion's tree and called.

In moments, Anterion hurried down the manor steps, peering into the gloom. Broad-shouldered and blond-haired, he was a giant of a man. "Jaredion? Is that you?"

"Anterion, I need your help."

"Of course, what's happened?"

"Birlerion's in trouble."

"Where is he?"

"There's been some sort of misunderstanding, Jerrol had Birlerion locked up as a danger to himself and others."

"He did what?"

"You can't tell anyone I came. They'll be searching for him. Promise, Anterion."

"I would never betray Birlerion," Anterion said, offended.

"I would have said the same about Uncle Jerrol, but he has. If it comes to it, you'll need to lie to the Lady's Captain."

"Lie about what?"

Jaredion grimaced. "I rescued him, but he's been sedated," he explained as he led Anterion to Kin'arol, and the big man gently lifted the unconscious Birlerion off the horse. Anterion carried him to his sentinal tree, shimmered inside, and laid him on the cot. The sentinal immediately spun golden threads around him.

Collapsing to the floor, Jaredion wrapped his arms around his legs, rested his head on his knees and began rocking. Anterion sank into a chair and watched the threads thicken. "What happened?" he asked, dragging his eyes away from Birlerion.

Jaredion explained what he knew, his voice muffled as he spoke to his knees. Anterion gaped at him, lost for words. "I don't understand. Why would they think Birlerion capable of abusing anyone? It's just not in him."

"They think he is unstable, fixated on the Veil. But Anterion," Jaredion looked up, "the Veil is attacking him. I know, I've been protecting him. It attacks him in his sleep. It's trying to coax him back; it wants him, and it will suck the life out of him one strand at a time.

"There is something wrong with the Veil, but only Birlerion can see it. Everyone else says it's fine; the Watchers, the Captain, all of them. They think it's in Birlerion's mind, and on top of everything else, it just confirms their opinion that he is mad." Rolling up his sleeve, he revealed the fine silver scars and a new deep red welt. "The healers believe this is Birlerion hurting me, but it is the Veil. The same marks are all over Birlerion. I can't stop it. It is insatiable."

"What does Birlerion intend to do?"

"I don't know. We haven't had the chance to discuss it. When we got back from Terolia, they blind-sided him with the healers." He rose from the floor and swayed.

Anterion grabbed him. "Stay here and sleep, Jaredion. My sentinal will watch Birlerion. No one will know you were here."

"I need to look after Kin'arol and my horse. They must be just as tired."

"I will look after Kin'arol. No one will know they are here either. Rest Jaredion. You've done well, he would be proud of you." Helping Jaredion to another cot, he watched the golden threads spin around the exhausted man. Anterion looked down at him for a moment, a tense expression on his face, and then he checked Birlerion, who he was received to see, looked a lot more relaxed. He went out and led Kin'arol into the stables. Stashing the horses in a loose box at the back out of sight, he filled the trough and a couple of hay nets, and sprinkled some Baliweed in Kin'arol's hay. Kin'arol immediately dipped his head in the net, and Anterion grinned as he smoothed his back. "Well done, Kin'arol, well done. Birlerion will be back on his feet tomorrow."

18

KING'S PALACE, OLD VESPERS

Leyarille met Mir'elle in the sheltered garden as planned the next morning.

"His name is Kirin. Apparently, he is the head of the Healer's society and a leading exponent of a new treatment for what they are calling Trauma Anxiety Disorder. I imagine he couldn't wait to get his hands on Birlerion to try out all his unusual treatments," Mir'elle reported with relish.

"Kirin." Leyarille mused for a moment. "I'll go to the Chapterhouse and check what property he owns. I expect he is quite proud of it, especially if it's related to his profession."

"I think he was at the ball last night. He turned up very late. I remember being introduced to him. Such a strange looking man. If he is here, maybe you could follow him?"

"Could you find out when he is due to leave? I need to check he is from Marchwood first."

Mir'elle nodded. "I will go and visit the Lord Chancellor to thank him again for last night. No doubt, I'll bump into Kayenion and he'll tell me if he knows. When I spoke with him, he was angry about the way Birlerion has been treated."

"He's always with my father, so it's impossible for me to speak to him without my father knowing. I'm so sorry to drag you into this, Mir'elle. This is your happy time. It's obvious Anders thinks the world of you; I've never seen him so attentive to any woman."

Mir'elle gave her a shy smile. "He makes me happy. I wish the same happiness for you, my dear."

Leyarille shook as a surge of emotion rushed through her, and Mir'elle hugged her. "Leyarille, what is the matter?"

"Forgive me, I don't mean to be, but I'm so envious. He's waited so long. Birlerion, I mean. He waited for me, found me, and now he is suffering instead of living his life with me. I can't help it."

"I understand. I wish you were with him. My joy can only make your situation worse, but I am so happy. I've never met anyone like Anders before. He just makes my heart smile."

Leyarille smiled. Who could ever deny this joyful woman any happiness? "Then he is the right man for you, but I should go. I don't want to spoil your Joining."

"You couldn't. Just promise me you will come back. You are my friend, as Birlerion is my brother. You are family. Whatever happens, please do not become a stranger."

"I promise."

"Then go. Take my horse, Per'enne. She is only languishing in the stables. She will help you track down Kin'arol. Find my brother and don't let anyone take him from you. In the meantime, I will protect his reputation so you can bring him home."

Leyarille smiled. "Thank you. I'll always appreciate your support. No matter what happens."

Mir'elle silently hugged her in farewell.

Taelia massaged Jerrol's shoulders. They were stiff with tension as he tossed files into untidy piles. "Love, this is getting ridiculous. You must learn to delegate. You can't do it all. You'll make yourself ill."

Jerrol stopped shuffling papers and relaxed into her hands. "I know. It just seems that everyone wants my opinion. I can't keep up with it all."

"Why don't you ask Tagerill and Miranda to help you? They are coming for the Joining anyway; they could come a few days early. He could assist you as well as Birlerion could."

Jerrol exhaled. "That's the crux of it, isn't it? I should never have given Birlerion to the healers. Everything has descended into chaos since."

Taelia moved around to face him and leaned against his desk. "Jerrol, tell me. Why did you agree to let Kirin take Birlerion?"

"Kirin is the expert. He knows what's best for him; how to treat him. He couldn't continue like he was, hurting people and himself."

Taelia stared at him. "Do you truly believe Birlerion would harm someone for no reason?"

"I saw the scars."

"Birlerion has a lot of scars; he nearly died many times, saving you. He adjusted to a world that he had no choice but to adapt to. He coped with all of that. What changed, Jerrol? What made you think that this time, this time Birlerion couldn't cope?"

"He was having nightmares."

"So did you, for many months."

Jerrol met her turquoise eyes, so like the seas of Birtoli. "It was the Oath. He was threatening to go and get the Oath."

"Why?"

"He said he was concerned about it. He wanted to check it, to bring it here."

"What is threatening about that?"

"He is unstable. The healers said he no longer knew when he crossed over the line. I couldn't trust him with the Oath. The risk was too great. I had to protect the people of Remargaren."

"Go and speak with him at this healer's retreat. Understand why he is concerned about the Oath. If Birlerion is worried about the Oath, then you should be too. Birlerion understands more about the Oath and the Veil than we ever will; don't throw away the one person who has always helped you."

Jerrol sank his head in his hands. "What have I done?"

"I don't know, my love, but there is still time to put it right."

"Chancellor," Kayenion stuck his head around the door, "there is an urgent message from Healer Kirin."

Jerrol held out his hand. A sharp pain pierced his chest as he broke the seal and ran his eyes down the hurried script. "Birlerion's escaped," he said, staring at the words dancing on the page before him.

"Let me see that." Taelia snatched the paper out of his hand. "Escaped? From a place of healing? Why would he need to escape?"

"I don't know."

"Maybe you should find out. Call Ari, see if he knows where Birlerion is." Taelia paused. "Jerrol, this is not from Kirin, it's *to* Kirin. It looks like it's from one of his staff."

Jerrol called the little Arifel. "I don't understand. Even if Birlerion was angry at being forced to deal with his problems, why escape?"

Taelia grimaced. "Maybe there were bigger issues he needed to address."

"We need to find him and fast." Jerrol started to write out orders, scribbling furiously. He sat back as Ari appeared. "Where's Birlerion?" he demanded, holding his hand out.

Ari squawked, scolding him, and blinked out of view, leaving the image of a roiling Veil covered in blood in Jerrol's mind.

Jerrol rose. "I need to speak to Bryce."

Arriving in Bryce's office, Jerrol frowned at the commander as he sat. Leaning forward, he kept his voice low. "We've got a problem. Birlerion got away from the healers. He's escaped."

"I knew we should have left the guards there," Bryce replied. "Just in case."

"He was not a prisoner," Jerrol exclaimed. "I know I agreed to the healers taking him, but it was to help him heal. To give him time to adjust, as Kirin said. But I think there may be an issue with the Veil, and if there is, then we need him back here."

"You are contradicting yourself, Jerrol. If you know Birlerion needs help, why would we bring him back here?"

"Because if there is a problem with the Veil, then it's not a problem with Birlerion, and everything he has been saying about the Veil is true and I should have believed him from the beginning."

Bryce sighed and inspected Jerrol closely. "You said the Veil was fine."

"I know. I went and checked the Veil, just to reassure Birlerion, and I didn't see anything out of place. It's just, I don't know, Birlerion was so adamant, and Ari was upset, and I have a feeling that something is not quite right."

"A feeling?" Bryce quirked an eyebrow.

"Yes. Don't look at me like that. I used to have odd

instinctive feelings all the time, and I didn't typically ignore them. I'm not sure why I did this time." Jerrol scowled at his hands. "Some of them saved my life. I think I may have put too much credence on these healer theories."

"That's because they are good theories. They are new; it takes time for them to be generally accepted."

"That doesn't mean they apply to Birlerion. He is a Sentinal, the Oath Keeper. He has been through worse situations than this and come out whole. I think I forgot who he is for a moment." He flexed his fingers and exhaled. "I think we made a mistake … I made a mistake allowing Kirin to take him."

"Jerrol. I agree Birlerion has survived many injuries, but don't you think eventually he is going to break? He can't keep bouncing back from all these traumatic events and be unaffected. You saw the healer's reports of his behaviour."

"I know, but if I think about his behaviour from the perspective that the Veil is behaving differently and attacking him, then his reactions makes sense. It *all* makes sense. Even to the point of breaking out of a place of healing if he is desperate enough."

Huffing his breath out, Bryce shook his head. "Listen to yourself, Jerrol. If Birlerion is desperate, then we should be worried about what he will do next. He is a threat to Vespiri."

"No," Jerrol said slowly. "He is our protector. Whatever he is doing, he is doing it for us." Jerrol stood. "We need to help him. I'll draft some orders. We can get the guards searching for him."

"We need to keep it quiet that he's escaped. We should be trying to return him to the healers."

Jerrol clenched his teeth against an angry retort. He had been saying the same not long ago. "We should be offering him some assistance." On that note, and leaving Bryce shaking his head in disagreement, Jerrol strode back to his office.

Sitting behind his desk, he pulled the order pad towards him and picked up his quill. He frowned at the blank page. Hadn't he started writing an order already? He flicked through the pad; all the pages were empty.

A wave of dizziness rushed through him, and he blinked at the blank page. His stomach fluttered. He knew he had begun writing an order, so where was it?

"Henry?"

"Yes, sir?" His aide appeared in his doorway.

"There was an order on this pad. Where is it?"

"Oh, the one regarding Lord Birlerion? I copied it out, logged it, and sent it for distribution, sir." Henry smiled, pleased with his efficiency.

Blood drained from Jerrol's face, and he broke out in a sweat. What had he written? It wasn't what he meant, he was sure. "Bring me the copy."

Henry darted back out the door and returned with the ledger. He spun it around and slid it in front of Jerrol. Jerrol blinked at the page as the words swam. Rubbing his eyes, he slowly read the order he had written, and he whimpered.

Fingers clenching, he whispered. "Recall it."

"I'm sorry, sir? What was that?"

"Recall it, now." Jerrol's voice cracked through the office, and Henry flinched.

"I-It's too late, sir. The couriers have left."

"That order was not complete; it should never have been sent."

Henry swayed, his face paling. "But you signed it. I always send your orders once it has a signature."

Jerrol took a gulp of water and then tried to breathe. What had he done? "Go and check if the couriers have left.

And prevent them from leaving if they haven't. Go now while I write a replacement order for them to take."

"Y-yes sir." The ashen-faced Henry dashed from the room.

Breathing deeply, Jerrol tried to calm his racing heart and then he read the damming words again.

Attention all officers.

Be advised, Sentinal Birlerion has escaped from the Healer's care and is now at large. Please approach carefully; his state of mind is unknown.

Detain Sentinal Birlerion at all costs and return him to Old Vespers.

Signed

Jerrol Haven, Lord Chancellor of Vespiri and Terolia, etc, etc.

Rubbing a shaking hand over his face, he shoved the ledger away and pulled the pad towards him. He had to put this right. Taking a deep breath, he began writing.

<u>URGENT</u>: This order supersedes all orders previously received.

Jerrol underlined it twice.

All care and assistance to be provided to First Administrator Lord Birlerion Descelles.

Under no circumstances is he to be detained or harmed.

Advise Lord Birlerion, all Vespiri's resources are at his disposal should he require aid.

Report any sightings and last known whereabouts to the Chancellor's office immediately.

Signed

Etc, etc

Exhaling, Jerrol leaned back in his chair and wiped his brow with his trembling hand. Exhaustion swept through him and he closed his eyes.

"Captain?" Kayenion's soft voice came from the doorway. "Is everything alright?"

Jerrol opened his eyes and cleared his throat. "No. It's not. I accidentally sent out an order to detain Birlerion at all costs …" Kayenion's gasp of horror went straight to his gut, "and I need to stop it. If Henry can't catch the couriers, then, once he has copied this new order out, you must hand deliver it to everyone. We need to be helping Birlerion, not hindering him."

They were interrupted as Henry skidded back into the office, pushing Kayenion out of his way. He bent over, gasping for breath. "It was … too late … sir," he gasped out. "The couriers … had already left."

Jerrol closed his eyes, all his newfound calm disappearing in a flash.

19

MARCHWOOD WATCH

Jaredion watched Birlerion awake with concern. He saw the moment he tensed as the recent events intruded. The lines around his mouth deepened as he gritted his teeth.

"Birlerion?" Jaredion hovered over him.

Jaredion's chest constricted as Birlerion stared at him in momentary confusion. His eyes glistened as they filled with tears and overflowed to leak down his cheeks. "Jaredion?"

"Yes, I'm here. You're safe now, Birlerion. Please don't cry. You are safe, I swear."

"Promise me, if they ever lock me up in a box again, you'll kill me. I couldn't stand it. It would drive me mad."

"Birlerion, please, they won't lock you up." Jaredion gripped his shoulders, wanting to hug him but afraid to shatter his fragile control.

"Yes, they will. Promise, on the Lady, you will find a way to kill me. Don't leave me there to suffer in the dark. Please, Jaredion, as my friend, please promise me."

Jaredion couldn't take his eyes off Birlerion's strained face; the stark expression of fear, of betrayal, cut him open, and his heart broke into tiny pieces. They had done this to the man who had sacrificed so much for Remargaren. This final betrayal would destroy him; Jaredion could see it as if it had already happened. "Birlerion, listen to me. I will never let them lock you up again, I promise."

"You won't be able to stop them. Promise me this one thing, please."

"I promise I won't leave you there. I'll protect you, always, Birlerion. I promise."

Birlerion stared at him for a moment as if debating whether to believe him or not, but he finally released his breath, and Jaredion exhaled with him as he realised he had been holding his breath as well.

"Thank you," Birlerion said as he relaxed and looked over Jaredion's shoulder. "Anterion."

"Birlerion, thank the Lady. We were worried you slept so long."

"How long have we been here?"

"Two days. It's the second evening. We were discussing moving Kin'arol. We nearly got caught earlier."

"We should leave." Birlerion sat up and pushed off the blanket. "They'll be searching for us. Word will have reached Vespers by now."

"What's going on, Birlerion?" Anterion asked as he engulfed Birlerion in a hug, and Jaredion relaxed as Birlerion hugged him back.

Birlerion's face was sad as Anterion released him. "I don't know, but you don't want to be involved any more than you already are. Thank you, Anterion, but it's for the best if you don't know where we are going."

"What do you need? Money? Maps? Weapons?"

"All the above and some clothes if you have any spare." Birlerion plucked the thin robe. "I'll freeze in this." Birlerion hurriedly dressed in his borrowed clothes.

Jaredion declined the Sentinal uniform Anterion offered and changed as well. Fingering the shimmering cloth regretfully, he stiffened his shoulders. He had resigned; he no longer had the right to wear the uniform. His allegiance was to Birlerion and *then* the Lady. In that order. He hoped the Lady would forgive him.

"Kin'arol says there's someone about to find him," Birlerion said as he buckled on a sword belt. His hand hovered over the hilt, and Jaredion wondered what they had done with his sword.

Anterion cursed and shimmered out of the sentinal. Birlerion grimaced as he strapped on daggers and then followed, wrapping the thick cloak around him, Jaredion at his shoulder. They managed to slip Kin'arol and Jaredion's horse out unseen as Anterion distracted the horse master.

They cut through the Marchwood countryside, Birlerion following a path only he could see. Jaredion followed. He realised where they were going as they passed through Woodbridge; a village he recognised. Birlerion was heading towards the coast. The night was cold and still, the stars glittered in the clear sky, and ice rimed the puddles as they rode. Their breath plumed in the air, the only sign of their passing. The sharp crack of ice breaking made them flinch in the silence of the night.

They arrived in the port of Mortelin as dawn broke, grey streaks lightening the sky and promising another cold day. Birlerion made Jaredion wait at the end of the quay with the horses as he negotiated for a berth on the only boat large enough to take them and two horses out to the island of Senti.

Jaredion stirred as the clatter of hooves broke the early morning silence. He leapt onto Kin'arol's back, yanked his head around, and cut back across the quay as a group of armed men skidded on the cobbles of the harbour.

"That's his horse! After him!" the lead man yelled, trying to turn his horse in the cramped space.

"I don't think so," Jaredion murmured under his breath and barged into them, knocking a pile of barrels over and causing chaos. In the confusion, Jaredion managed to push his way through, drawing the men away from the harbour.

Birlerion poked his head up out of the hold as Kin'arol screeched in his head. *"We lead them away from you. Stay hidden."*

"No, Kin'arol, be careful. They might have crossbows. They could hit you or Jaredion."

"They won't catch us."

Birlerion watched the fight unfold on the quay. There was little he could do except make it worse for Jaredion. If he showed himself, all their efforts would be for nothing, yet he couldn't stand and watch the lad be overwhelmed.

Searching the boat, he looked for anything that could be used as a weapons. He glanced at the captain, who climbed up beside him. "You don't have a sling by any chance?"

The man grunted and ducked back down below. "Use it for bait."

Birlerion grasped the sling and the hard bait balls the man gave him. "Looks like it's just me joining you; I'll pay you the same if we leave now."

The captain squinted at the chaos on the quay. Barrels rolled down the cobbles and onto the horses and some even into the water, bobbing like aquatic spectators. The captain nodded. "If we get caught up in that it'll be days before we leave." He started shouting instructions, and his men jumped down on the quay and untied the ropes, coiling them up as they climbed back on board. The boat began drifting away from the wharf, and the ropes creaked as the men pulled up the sail.

Birlerion aimed and fired a bait ball at the man trying to pull Jaredion off Kin'arol. The man dropped as if he had run headfirst into someone's fist. Birlerion raised his eyebrows, and as Jaredion pulled Kin'arol around, he released his second bait ball at the man blocking his way; the man slid out of his saddle, and Jaredion charged out of the harbour, flinging a desperate glance over his shoulder. The remaining men regrouped and followed him.

Birlerion watched Jaredion ride off with the men in pursuit and sent him the Lady's blessings. "Stay safe, Jaredion." Birlerion turned away and met the captain's stare. "I'll pay you double if after you drop me at Senti. You don't return to Mortelin for a month or so."

The captain grinned. "We never did like Mortelin that much. Ale's too acidic for our taste."

Birlerion smiled, and as the wind caught the sails, he gripped the railing as the boat gathered speed and the harbour of Mortelin began to recede.

Standing on the incredible walls of Senti harbour, Birlerion knew the Oath had gone. The stone was dull and lifeless, not a sparkle in sight. He swayed as disappointment ambushed him. Sinking to his knees, he lay his hands flat on the stone, but there was nothing. It was empty, no welcoming hum, no Marguerite greeting him. Where was she? And what had she done with the Oath?

He leaned back on his heels and swept a glance around the harbour. It was busy enough. The skeleton of a new keel rose out of the sands, and the echo of hammers on wood vibrated across the water. Colourful boats bobbed as a small sailboat manoeuvred by, the steering tiller disturbing the smooth water. Disappointment swept through him as he rubbed his face. He couldn't stay here; people were staring at him.

Leaving the harbour, he walked up the main street and

climbed the steps to Marguerite's temple, though he knew she wouldn't be there either. He knelt at the feet of the statue of a young woman, Marguerite's altar, and reached. There was a resounding silence. Where would she go? His mind was sluggish. Taurillion would know, but he was at the other end of the world in Elothia, too far away.

Who else would know where she might be? His brain slowly creaked into action. Roberion and his wife Lilith; they might know. He needed a boat to take him to Cherni. Resting a moment, he prayed to the Ladies of Remargaren. "Please, Leyandrii, Marguerite, help me."

"Birlerion? What's the matter?"

At first Birlerion thought he imagined her voice, he was so desperate for her help.

"Birlerion? Dearest one? Are you alright?"

"Marguerite? Oh, thank the Lady. Where have you been?"

"Resting. I slept long and deep. I told you I would."

"I'm so sorry to wake you, but … but …" Tears trailed down his cheeks as his voice choked and warm arms held him tight as she manifested beside him. He relaxed into her embrace, inhaling the scent of meadow flowers.

"Hush," Marguerite whispered, and she held him close until his shudders stopped. "Now tell me what has happened." Her vivid blue gaze sharpened as she inspected him. "Oh, Birlerion," she gasped in horror.

"It's the Veil. It wants me. As soon as I sleep, it attacks and I have little defence. Jaredion has been guarding my sleep, but we got separated." He hesitated. "I think it's after the Oath."

Marguerite stared at him, her eyes widening. "Tell me everything."

Birlerion began explaining.

Marguerite swore viciously, and Birlerion winced. "They mean well," he said.

"I'll be speaking to Jerrol, you mark my words, though that doesn't help you now."

"Where's the Oath, Marguerite? It's not here."

"I moved it," she said absently, her brows furrowed in deep thought. And then she snapped her gaze to Birlerion. "I had a feeling it needed closer watching."

"The Tu'ani?" Birlerion asked, thinking of the clan who had first protected the Oath all those years ago.

Marguerite nodded, and her expression became more pensive. "Elder Tuan took the burden, but I'm not sure he was the right choice."

Birlerion sighed. "He is fragile."

"Stronger than you think, though I thought he might pass it to one of his sons, but ..." Her gaze became speculative as she watched him.

"I can't," Birlerion said, knowing she was expecting him to take the burden from the Elder.

"The Land likes you."

"I said no last time. I doubt it liked being rejected."

Marguerite shrugged. "I think it is waiting for you. It's in Cherni."

Birlerion nodded, unsurprised.

"I'm sorry, Birlerion, but from what you've said, I think the Oath will be the only way you can protect yourself and Remargaren."

Silence followed her words. He didn't know what to say, but his heart was eased by her company. He had been Leyandrii's since he'd first heard her name as a skinny street brat, and Marguerite had at some point squirmed her way in and snagged his heart too.

"If I go to Cherni, can you go and speak with Jerrol? Try to make him understand the threat? Get the healers off my back?"

"Of course. I ought to stay with you, protect you until

you get the Oath." She frowned. "Though I don't think I can stop the Veil from attacking you. I can't reach the Veilspace as I'm bound to Remargaren. We need Leyandrii's help. I'll do what I can and meet you in Cherni. I'll go and speak with Jerrol after."

Her presence disappeared, and he knelt to say a quick prayer, asking the Lady to protect Jaredion, Leyarille and Kin'arol. To help Jerrol find his way out of the maze he had lost himself in. To protect them all from whatever was happening to the Veil.

It was dark by the time he left the temple and returned to the harbour. He sat on the steps, and spent the night watching the waning moon, a mere sliver traversing the sky. It would be year end soon. Mir'elle and Anders would be joined. He wished he could have been there to see it and that he was with Leyarille, young and carefree, and looking forward to the excitement of a ball at the palace.

He frowned. He had never been carefree. All his life he had protected others. A faint sense of dissatisfaction stirred. When would it be time for him and Leyarille? Didn't he get to be happy too?

"Soon."

He lifted his head at the soft whisper, but maybe it was just the cool night breeze ruffling his hair. A thin mist hung over the still waters in the harbour, softening the edges and blurring the boats' rigging. Birlerion could almost imagine himself in his tree, the hazy mists wrapped around him. The soft hum was a mere memory. He was too far away to reach his sentinal.

He blinked as his head jerked; he had almost fallen asleep. The Veil snarled, and images of destruction and chaos flashed through his mind, images of Remargaren under siege. The places he loved destroyed. Gasping out a horrified breath, he shook the images away. The memory of his sword in his hand made him stiffen as he faced the Veil.

"No, you cannot have me and you certainly cannot have Remargaren." Birlerion made his stand. It would not be his last; he was adamant. "We don't need you anymore; your time is over."

The Veil undulated, and Birlerion advanced. "It's time you realised your place." Birlerion snarled. "I've had enough, no more." The Veil shimmered, paused, and then struck.

King's Palace, Old Vespers

Margareth shuddered. Her luminous eyes flew open as the shriek woke her up. She panted as she realised the echo of the scream was her own. What had frightened her? She remembered dreaming of Birlerion. He had been fighting the Veil, on his own. The Veil had attacked him. The blood; there had been so much blood.

She reached for the Veil, and the roiling weave spread out before her, agitated and blood-smeared. She recognised Birlerion's essence; he had been here. The Veil was absorbing his blood; hardened patches flexed as the blood lubricated it. The red smears disappeared as she watched the Veil suck it up.

Margareth stared about her in horror, seeing the Veil through new eyes. Faint shadows marked the twisting weave; were they the memory of Birlerion's battle? There were so many of them. Was Leyarille right? Was everything she had said true?

It couldn't be. They would have *seen* it.

She listened; her senses stretched. The Veil was upset, angry even. Why would it be angry?

20

MARCHWOOD WATCH

Leyarille smoothed Per'enne's neck and peered down the tree-lined track. It reminded her of the road to Westermaine and how she wished they had never left. Kirin had disappeared around the bend not fifteen minutes earlier. She slid off Per'enne and led her into the leafy screen.

They crept closer to the fence, watching the entrance of the main building. Per'enne rubbed her cheek against Leyarille's, and Leyarille felt some of her tension ease. Kirin had dismounted and was surrounded by a group of excited people, voices high in the still air. Kirin exclaimed in shock and rushed up the steps, followed by most of the people. Leyarille frowned.

Something was not right.

A disturbance at the back of the mansion resolved itself into a young lad galloping around the side of the building and off down the road—a courier. Leyarille's heart dropped. Had something happened to Birlerion? She had to know.

She led Per'enne back out of the trees and, remounting, rode up to the front door. "Wait for me," she whispered, and

Per'enne's grey ear flicked. Leyarille mounted the stone steps and entered the mansion. A large hallway with high ceilings and bare walls greeted her. It was cold and empty, but voices shrill with fear came from down the corridor. She followed the voices.

They were gathered in a sterile room with a single bed. The walls were painted blue, and there were no windows, no light. She gasped at the sight of the straps. They had strapped him down body and limb, restrained him. What had they done to him?

"Where is he?" she demanded, her voice rasping with anger.

Kirin spun, his forehead wrinkling as he glared at her. "Who are you? You should not be in here. Escort her out." Kirin flinched back as Leyarille advanced. The air crackled around her. She would kill him. She would kill them all.

"Where is he?"

"He's gone," one of the helpers squeaked, ignoring Kirin.

Leyarille's heart jumped, and she took a sharp breath as she stilled. "You killed him?" Her voice broke on the words as her brain clamoured with the words. She had failed; she had lost him.

"No, no," Kirin flapped his hands weakly. "He left."

Leyarille sagged against the doorframe, her knees trembled. "Left? To go where?"

"We don't know. A young man with silver eyes helped him escape." The helper was breathless with excitement.

"When?"

"Two days ago. We sent a message, but it must have passed you on the road, Healer Kirin."

"That's enough. Escort her out. She should not be here." Kirin went to grab her arm, but changed his mind and pointed out the door instead. "Leave."

Leyarille glanced around the room. "Gladly. This is inhumane. I will be reporting to the Lord Chancellor the condition you keep your prisoners in."

"They are not prisoners. They are guests. They are here for their safety; look, there are no locks on the doors." Kirin held the door.

"Why would you need locks? Leather straps work just as well, don't they?" Leyarille held Kirin's gaze, and his eyes dropped as he fidgeted with the door. Leyarille gripped her temper. They weren't worth it, and she needed to find Birlerion.

Per'enne was still waiting at the foot of the stone steps, and she hurried down to her; she couldn't wait to leave. Where would Jaredion have taken Birlerion? How was he? She didn't think he would have coped well with Kirin's idea of care. He wouldn't have been in great condition.

"Can you hear Kin'arol? Are they close?"

Per'enne shook her head. They weren't at Marchwood manor then. Leyarille pursed her lips. She needed help. Jaredion needed help. She would go to Deepwater, Tagerill would assist them. He would do anything for Birlerion; they were brothers, after all.

Decision made, Leyarille started the long slog back to pick up the East Road. She eased Per'enne into a loping canter, fear riding her shoulder. What would her father do when he found out Birlerion had escaped? She didn't know.

Per'enne's long legs ate up the miles, but it was still late in the afternoon before they reached the big East Road. Her stomach ached; a combination of anxiety and lack of food. She had forgotten to provision herself with anything edible. She was sure Jaredion would have been better prepared.

She turned east, following the wide road which wended its way to the Terolian borders. Would Jaredion have taken him there? No, no, it was too inhospitable unless you knew where the Families camped. Maybe he would have fled to Deepwater, where he would find safety and guaranteed help. Would she find them there?

A spark of hope kindled deep inside. What if they were waiting for her in Deepwater? Lady please, she prayed. Protect them, help them. She gave Per'enne a breather as they approached the turning to Deepwater. She reined Per'enne to a walk, smoothing her hand down her neck. "Good girl. What do we have here?"

A flock of sheep blocked the road, mindlessly milling about, bleating in confusion, fat puffs of grey wool butting into each other. Yellow eyes rolled as she neared. "Clear the road, you're blocking passage," she called out, scanning the surroundings. Riders were backed up on the other side of the flock, and although some watched with amusement, others did not.

"If you don't move them, you'll be eating them for the rest of the week," a thick-set man was threatening the skinny lad with a crook. The shepherd maybe. The man shifted his crossbow suggestively.

"These are Lord Marcus' sheep. You have no right to threaten them. And they have as much right of way as you do." The boy was holding his own as the men pushed their way into the sheep.

"They do not have the right to impede the King's Guard."

Leyarille's eyes narrowed and searched the tree line again. What was the King's Guard doing on the road?

The man stared down his nose at the boy. "We are in pursuit. Move your animals, or we will move them for you." They were surrounded by sheep, snared as if in a trap, and held just as tightly.

Per'enne pulled her off the road, and Leyarille let her take them into the dense forest, wending her way through the tightly packed trunks. The thick matting of leaves muffled Per'enne's hooves. She kept going deeper into the woods, her grey ears pricked forward. Leyarille caught a flicker ahead of her, and she urged Per'enne forward, peering into the gloom. Low branches flicked in her face, scratching, drawing blood as she ducked and weaved. On impulse she called out. "Birlerion?"

The rider ahead faltered to a stop, a shadow in the gloom. He was slumped over the horse's neck, and the golden horse pirouetted towards them.

"Birlerion? It's Leyarille."

The rider shuddered and slowly fell out of the saddle, landing in the soft matting of leaves. Leyarille gasped and flung herself off Per'enne. She knelt beside him and gently rolled him over, her heart beating so hard she was sure the soldiers would hear it. A bolt pierced his shoulder, and his jacket was red with blood, his face a shocking white. "Jaredion? What happened?" He was not in uniform. Why was he not wearing his Sentinal uniform?

Jaredion's long lashes fluttered, and pain-filled silver eyes stared up at her. "Leyarille?" His voice was the merest whisper as if the effort was too much.

"Yes, yes, it's me. Where's Birlerion? Why do you have Kin'arol?"

Jaredion's eyes rolled, and Leyarille gripped him tight. She wrapped her handkerchief around the bolt, but it wouldn't staunch the blood for long, she swallowed against rising bile as she remembered another man pinned down by a bolt. She had nearly lost Birlerion. She wouldn't lose Jaredion.

Kin'arol nudged her shoulder and bent his knee. Leyarille stared at him before galvanising into action. She dragged Jaredion over to him. He was so heavy, but she managed to pull him up and lean him over the saddle. It was the best she could do. She made sure his shoulder wouldn't bump the bolt against the leather as Kin'arol struggled back to his feet. "Thank you, thank you. Kin'arol, you are amazing, and I love you."

She rubbed Kin'arol's nose and he whuffled into her hair, making her hug him tight. His soft skin was warm and reassuring under her cheek, and she sighed a shuddering breath out. "Where have you been?" she murmured as she struggled to pull a bolt out of his saddle. He had been fortunate the leather had held. She remounted Per'enne and, gripping Jaredion's arm to keep him in place, led Kin'arol through the trees. They were still quite a distance from the manor house of Deepwater, and she glanced worriedly at Jaredion and behind her frequently as they travelled through the forest.

There were no crashing noises heralding his pursuers. Hopefully, they were still sheep-bound, and she thanked the Lady. She prayed to the Lady to watch over Jaredion because she couldn't staunch the blood and lead him to safety.

The road leading up to the manor house was lit by gleaming lamps hanging from stakes in the ground; the flames flickered inside the suspended glass bowls. Leyarille stayed in the shadows, working her way nearer. She was glad she had as the clatter of hooves pounded up the road behind her. She flinched back, stilling as the King's Guards skidded to a halt in a flurry of gravel in front of the peaceful manor entrance.

Peppins, Lord Jennery's steward, appeared at the top of the steps. The leader of the group dismounted and stomped up the steps, his back rigid. The guard was not having a good day. He entered the mansion as his men milled about, waiting.

Jaredion groaned, and she hushed him. "We're nearly there; you've got to keep quiet."

"S-Senti ..."

"I'll get you to your Sentinal as soon as I can," she promised, her eyes on the guards. She glanced back and realised he had slipped back into unconsciousness. Dark streaks trailed down Kin'arol's belly, dripping down his leg, and she bit her lip.

"Hurry up and leave," she muttered under her breath, afraid to move.

Lord Jennery himself escorted the guard back to his men. Tall, broad-chested, his voice was loud in the evening air. "We'll search the forests at first light. It's no use now. It's too dark. But I expect he is long gone."

"We appreciate your help, your lordship."

"Of course, we are all here to preserve the peace. I'll send a message to the chancellor if we find anything."

The guard bobbed his head and scuttled down the steps.

Jennery watched them leave, standing at the head of the steps until the guards rode from view. He hesitated, and his gaze swept the grounds, across the encroaching trees and down the lamp-lit road. Leyarille waited an excruciatingly long moment, and as Jennery turned to go back into the house, she broke cover.

Jennery spun, squinting as he caught the movement, and then a tall blond-haired man came hurrying out the door behind him. "It's Jaredion and Leyarille," Denirion, his Sentinal, murmured as he dashed down the steps towards Leyarille.

"What?" Jennery gasped before he hurried after him.

Denirion lifted Jaredion off the horse.

"Mind the bolt in his shoulder," Leyarille said, her face pinched and drawn in the dim light.

"Bolt?" Jennery dropped to his knees beside his son. "Jared? Jaredion?"

"We need to get him inside," Denirion said as he looked over his shoulder. "Just in case."

"By the Lady, Guards are now hunting Sentinals? What is Jerrol doing?" Jennery muttered as he gently lifted his son and carried him up the stone steps into their home. "Call Clennin. Hurry." He glanced at Leyarille. "Are you alright?"

"Yes, I'm fine. The horses, they need care."

"Peppins, see to it."

"Of course, my lord." The grey-haired steward hurried back out.

Jennery carried Jaredion into the drawing-room and laid him on a settee, his face tightened at the sight of his blood-soaked jacket and the bolt protruding from his right shoulder. A soft gasp had him rising as his wife Alyssa dashed into the room, her eyes fixed on her son's face.

"What happened? Is he alright?" She collapsed beside him and moaned. "Lea, what have they done?"

"Alyssa, let the healer pass. Leyarille brought him."

Alyssa rose, her hands outstretched. "Leyarille, my dear, are you alright?"

"Yes, I found him in the woods off the East Road. The King's Guards were chasing him. I don't know why. He-he was with Birlerion."

"Birlerion? But where is Birlerion?"

"I don't know. Nowhere near according to Mir'elle's Darian.

"Mir'elle's Darian?"

"She lent her to me. To go and help Birlerion."

"Mir'elle? As in King Anders' future bride?" Alyssa asked, screwing up her face in confusion.

"Why does Birlerion need help?" Jennery frowned down at his son. "You'd better start at the beginning. None of this is making any sense."

"Is Uncle Tage here? I was coming here to see him."

Jennery nodded. "Denirion, go find him and meet us in my study."

Clennin looked up. "I need to remove the bolt; we should move him to the healerie."

"He wanted his sentinal," Leyarille said, watching the men lift Jaredion onto a stretcher. Clennin had his hand clamped around the bolt, his face grim.

"Go with Lea, I'll stay with Jaredion," Alyssa said, shooing them out. "I'll send some food; you don't look like you've eaten." Her voice followed them out of the room.

Jennery wrapped an arm around Leyarille's shoulders. She was road weary and tense. "Come, you need to tell us what's happened." He led her through the halls to his study; a comfortable room with a large desk and shelf-lined walls filled with books. He sat her in a deep chair and poured her a drink.

"You've had a shock. Drink." He looked up as Tagerill entered with Denirion behind him. Another tall Sentinal, red hair now more burnished and streaked with grey, but he was still wide across the shoulders and trim waisted; his silver eyes alertly inspected Leyarille.

"Leyarille? What is my favourite girl doing dragging in at this time of night?"

"Uncle Tage, Birlerion's in trouble."

Grimacing, Tagerill crouched beside her and hugged her. "When is he not? Tell us. Last we heard he had escorted Mir'elle back to Vespers to meet the king and all was going well."

"Pa had him locked up by the healers as mentally unfit," she said bluntly.

Tagerill froze. "He did what?"

Leyarille rubbed her face. "It's the Veil; it is attacking him. Jaredion has been trying to defend him, but it leaves wounds, marks on his skin. The healers believe Birlerion is self-harming and has begun to attack Jaredion as well."

"Impossible. Who could believe such a thing?" Tagerill hissed.

Leyarille gripped his arm. "Pa does. The healers have convinced him that Birlerion is suffering from anxiety, that he is traumatised by what he has been through. They've convinced Pa that he is a danger to himself and others." A tear squeezed its way down her cheek. "Uncle Tage, they locked him up in a tiny room without windows, strapped him down, restrained him."

Tagerill cursed violently. "How could they? Do you know where he is? We'll go and get him."

"He's not there anymore. Jaredion rescued him two days ago."

Tagerill and Jennery exchanged worried glances. "Do you know where Jaredion has been? Where Birlerion might be?"

"No. Jaredion was unconscious when I found him. I don't know where he is. But don't you see? If Birlerion sleeps, the Veil will attack him, and he is defenceless without Jaredion. It will kill him. Something is wrong with the Veil, and it wants his blood. Only my father won't believe us. The Watchers say the Veil is fine. He believes them, not Birlerion."

"Your father wants his head examined," Tagerill growled.

Jennery paced. "It's all dependent on Jaredion then. Until he is conscious, we have no idea where Birlerion is, and we don't know how he is." He dragged his hands through his hair. "But why would Jerrol doubt Birlerion? I don't under-stand it."

"It's been gradual, I think, combined with the rise of the Healer's society. There's a new master of healing since Healer Tyrone of Stoneford stepped down. He has new ideas on how trauma affects the mind and how it should be treated. My father listens to him; a lot it seems. I read up on the healer; that's how I found his healerie in Marchwood."

"Well, we need to tell him he is wrong. Alyssa and I will go to Vespers. We're due to go for the Joining anyway; we can go earlier."

Tagerill smiled down at her. "Don't worry, we'll find him."

Leyarille relaxed back in her chair, watching the tall Sentinals. They had believed her. Their concern for Birlerion was warming; they hadn't doubted him for a minute. The warmth eased the chill that had been creeping through her. She nibbled a roll Denirion placed beside her. The smell of coffee made her eyes tear up, reminding her of Birlerion smiling at her over a cup of Kafinee, as he called it.

"Where are you, my love? Lady keep you safe," she whispered.

21

KING'S PALACE, OLD VESPERS

Mir'elle stood on the dais and opened her arms. "Your Majesty, lords, ladies, and all gentle people. Welcome to our Terolian evening. King Anders has graciously allowed me to share some of the history of our Family in Terolia. I hope you will enjoy the spectacle.

"As you are aware, Terolia joined with Vespiri over twenty years ago, under the auspicious reign of our beloved king's father." She smiled at Anders, and he grinned back at her.

"But Terolia has a history as long as all the other kingdoms. One of mystery, one of nomads, one of the desert. The desert can be a harsh environment, but if you spend the time to look closely enough, you'll find it is very beautiful, and one of its greatest beauties is the people."

She paused as Cor'ilno and three of his men entered the room, ornately dressed in glittering costumes of blue waistcoats and pantaloons that set off their dark brown skin and muscular bodies. Barefoot, they padded around the room, gleaming curved knives at their waist, allowing the audience to observe them.

"The people of the desert learn early to respect their environment. The sun is a demanding taskmaster, water the blood of life. The Family is created to nurture, to hoard, to protect. Everyone is responsible for ensuring the other is safe and well." She paused as the men began to move, slow controlled lunges that the opponent accepted and gracefully returned, the give and take a complimentary dance as their hands swept the air and their bodies twisted.

Mir'elle continued. "The Medera is the mother, the Sodera, our father. They rule the Family and protect where protection is needed, guide where guidance is required, judge where judgement falls, and teach our children the Family way of life. Children are the future and as such, are treasured as the gems they are."

The men started to move faster, and the audience gasped as they unsheathed their wicked swords as they spun, the metal gleaming in the lamplight.

"The rules of the family are sacrosanct; they cannot be broken. They bind us as a Family and hold us all account-able. No son, no brother, no daughter, no sister would ever betray the Family. The consequences are a life debt. A life for a life."

The swords clashed as the men whirled in a complicated dance of attack and defence. An elegant dance of control and strength. A show of trust. Mir'elle stepped off the dais and walked into the middle of the floor, and the audience gasped. King Anders launched to his feet in shock.

The men spun around Mir'elle, adjusting without think-ing, never coming near enough to touch, though to the audi-ence it looked like she walked straight into their path and there was no way they could avoid striking her.

"At no time will a brother injure a sister, nor a sister injure a brother. It is not possible. It is not the way of the Family. We honour and protect one another." She turned and walked back through the flickering knives, the men spinning around her, sweat gleaming on their skin, betraying the effort. As she cleared the floor and stepped onto the dais, they spun to a graceful stop, breathing heavily as they raised their swords in front of their faces, palm flat against the blade.

"I honour my brother, Birlerion, named a son of the Atolea by Medera Yannis over three thousand years ago and remembered until this very day. The Family honours a debt. It is never forgotten. And that, ladies and gentlemen, is the Family."

The audience was silent, awestruck. Mir'elle smiled. "You have just witnessed the formal accolade, rarely seen outside of Terolia. You have been honoured; a memory for you to treasure, forever. I am honoured to join your family; welcome to ours. I thank Cor'ilno, Lan'adir, Jer'issel, and Por'assa for their dazzling display." She swept her hand towards the sweating men.

The audience began clapping.

Mir'elle waited and then flapped her hands at them. "Please, let it be known that amongst these brothers of mine, I count the First Administrator, Lord Birlerion. As an honoured member of the Atolean family, he understands and abides by the rules of the Family.

"At great risk to himself, he has guarded my safety ever since I travelled to Vespiri. My brother values family and he is treasured for it, and I miss him. He will return to us, and we will welcome him home with open arms.

"I hope you enjoy the rest of your evening."

Mir'elle sat as the people clapped, standing to show their appreciation.

Anders leaned over. "You are amazing, you know that, don't you?"

"It wasn't me. It was Cor'ilno and his men. They did all the work. The accolade is extremely difficult. It takes a huge amount of concentration; few can perform it."

"We are honoured that you shared it with us."

"We are Family. You will be joining with the Atolea as well, Your Majesty. You need to know what that means."

"You do realise that Birlerion can no longer be First Administrator though, don't you? Jerrol needs help now. I am appointing Lord Cerenna to the post."

Mir'elle smiled. "I expect Birlerion will be too busy when he returns. You never did give him any time to sit behind his desk, always sending him off on errands. And anyway, he will want time with Leyarille. They are getting Joined too, did you know?"

Anders blinked. "I didn't. Will he be well enough?"

Mir'elle laughed and patted his cheek. "My love, of course he will be well enough, but don't expect him to come running back. I think you'll find he has other things to do."

"He is my Oath Keeper; of course he will come back."

"As you say, my dear. Shall we dance?"

Senti, Birtoli

Birlerion curled into himself as awareness shuddered into his body and pain slashed through him as he shivered on the quay. The warm trickle of blood ran down his chill skin, and he breathed deeply, trying to calm his racing heart. The Veil had not taken well to his challenge. He was a fool.

Marguerite held him, her soft voice berating him constantly.

"You idiot, why didn't you wait for me? I said I would help you."
She helped him sit up. "The Veil is growing stronger each time
it leaches your blood. We need to get you to the Oath as soon as
possible, but first, you need to sleep in the sentinal. He will heal
you. You can get a boat to Cherni in the morning."

A soft murmur penetrated his haze, and he looked up.
The Senti sentinal was glowing. He felt the offer glissade
through him, and he staggered to his feet, leaning on
Marguerite as she wormed under his arm. Swaying, he took
a step and the sentinal's murmur grew encouraging, another
step, followed by another, one foot in front of the other.

Pale sunshine burned through the hovering mists by the
time they reached the sentinal. He extended a shaking,
bloody hand and touched the glowing bark. He collapsed on
the bed as the sentinal hummed around him and Marguerite
hovered over him in concern.

Golden light filled his vision and he slipped away into
darkness.

When Birlerion next opened his eyes, his mind was filled with
a comforting hum. Awareness flooded through him, and he
sat up. His skin was smooth, silver lines in place of raw welts.
"How long have I been here? I can't stay."

The sentinal's hum deepened.

"I know, I thank you for your care, but I can't be found."
Birlerion stood. His clothes were in tatters, red-rimmed
slashes marring the cloth. He looked down at himself with a
wry smile—and he used to accuse Jerrol of being hard on his
clothes.

A cupboard materialised before him, and he opened the
door. A selection of islander shirts and trousers were folded
on the shelf. He pulled out the top two and hurriedly
stripped. Changing into the clean clothes, Birlerion smiled as

he remembered Jerrol sailing to Vespers back in the day, dressed in similar attire. So long ago.

He gripped the cupboard as a wave of emotion sped through him. He was on his own, but for Marguerite. She had come when he'd called. Thank the Lady. Her promise to meet him in Cherni resonated through him, and for the first time in many days he relaxed. There was plenty of help out there. They just weren't with him now. Pondering on whether there was a reason for that, he shook his head, constant uncertainty was making him doubt them. He was sure they would turn up at some point.

Thanking the sentinal, he shimmered out of the tree and paused, looking out over the headland. The sentinal curved over him protectively, and Birlerion smiled up at the branches and patted the trunk. "Don't worry, I will be careful," he said before striding off towards the harbour.

He chuckled under his breath as he stopped by a boat with the name *Island Scout*, which bobbed at the mooring. Another name from the past. He grinned at the black-haired young man who captained the vessel.

"I'm looking for a ride to Cherni."

The young man grinned. "You're in luck then, we're about to cast off."

Birlerion thanked the Lady and jumped down onto the deck. "How much?" he asked as he felt in his pocket.

"For you, two molintis."

Birlerion removed his hand and stared at the coins. He grinned wryly. "It's your lucky day. I only have obols. Could you take me on to Terolia after Cherni? I won't be staying there long. One obol for the trip?"

The man smiled. "For one obol, you can choose to go anywhere."

Birlerion relaxed. "Cherni first, then I'll decide if it's a port in Terolia or Elothia."

"Fine by me. I'm Airen."

"Birler."

"Welcome aboard, Birler." He turned away and yelled at a young girl upon the quay. "Cast off, Gianna."

She scampered along the quay and untied the ropes flinging them into the boat. She jumped down and began coiling them as Airen leaned on his steering tiller, sculling away from the quay. "No wind in here, the walls keep it out. Takes us a few minutes to clear the barriers."

"I know," Birlerion said as he leaned against the rail.

"You swim alright or do you need a belt?"

"No need, I can swim. Thank you."

"Alright then, Cherni here we come. Don't often get asked to carry passengers to Cherni. Beautiful island."

"It is. Do you know if the *Miracle* is still berthed there?"

"Roberion's ship, you mean?" Airen shrugged. "No telling. He gets about." His black eyes inspected Birlerion. "You a friend?"

Birlerion smiled. "Yes, we go back many years."

"Thought as much. You got the eyes, same as the Captain."

Gianna began hauling up a bright blue sail.

Birlerion watched it rise. "You didn't keep to the red?"

Airen laughed. "Sometimes; depends what's available when we need a new one. Only blue this time around. But she prefers the red sail, I must admit." Patting the mast affectionately, he looked out across the sparkling seas.

Birlerion inhaled the fresh salty air and relaxed as the sun warmed his skin. Birtoli was such a beautiful place; all sun, sand and seas. Somewhere he wanted to take Leyarille once they were Joined; just them and a peaceful island. He promised himself they would come.

Staring out over the rippled sea, he wondered if she was still at the Watch Towers? Had she found out anything useful? She was so tenacious; she wouldn't give up on him, he knew. He sat dreaming about when they would meet again. He wouldn't let her go next time, no matter what anyone else said.

He startled when Airen threw a hat at him. "You're turning pink," he grinned.

"It's been a while. In Terolia you are usually covered up, so it's not a problem."

"Yeah, its deceptive, this balmy air, relaxing. You forget the sun can burn, even in the winter."

"It's freezing in Vespers and snowing in Elothia. This heat doesn't seem real, does it?" Birlerion said as he tugged on the cap.

"This is the place to be," Airen agreed. They fell silent as the *Island Scout* skimmed across the waves, the blue sail billowing. Three chimes later they tacked into the bay at Cherni. An empty wooden quay stretched out into the turquoise waters of the bay. Birlerion's heart sank; there was no *Lady's Miracle* anchored in the bay.

King's Palace, Old Vespers

"Pa, I need to return to the towers. Can you take me through the waystone?" Margareth burst in her father's office, cheeks pink with her haste.

Kayenion hovered in the doorway. "Sorry, Captain, but she said it was urgent."

"It's alright. You'd better come in." Jerrol waved him in and turned to Margareth. "You don't travel well, sweetheart. Are you sure you want to go via the waystone?"

"We don't have time, Pa. We need to find out how we can help Birlerion. I saw him in my dreams fighting the Veil, and it was angry. It wanted Birlerion's blood. I saw it absorbing his blood; it repaired the Veil."

"That's not possible."

"I'm telling you it is, and you need to check the Veil. Birlerion was right. The Veil is damaged; it keeps hardening like it is brittle. I've never seen anything like it. I need to go back to the Watchers and see if anyone has ever seen it behave like that before."

"It was unchanged when I last checked, and you've said it was fine every time I asked."

"I know, but it isn't. It has been targeting him."

"The Veil doesn't have a mind, Margareth. It doesn't think."

"Are you sure? It's angry, and you've often called it petulant, voracious. It feels emotion. It knows what it wants. And it wants Birlerion."

Jerrol sat at his desk, lost for words. "Are you sure?" he finally asked.

"Yes. You need to take me back *now*. And Pa? You need to find Birlerion before the Veil kills him."

"I already have orders out to search for him and provide whatever help he needs." Jerrol rose. "Let's get you back to the towers. Kayenion, we'll use Bryce's waystone." He led his daughter to the waystone outside Bryce's office. They stepped out inside the Senti Sentinal.

Margareth spun, squinting up at the swirling mist above them. "Pa! What are we doing here?" She swallowed, her face paling. The sentinal hummed, and the nauseous sensation disappeared. Margareth straightened.

"Sorry, I was thinking of Senti. I'm worried about the Oath. I was intending on coming here after I dropped you at the Towers, but seeing as we're here, let's just check it's alright." Jerrol stepped out of the humming sentinal and looked out over the harbour. He froze; there was no welcoming vibration, no glitter to the walls. No Marguerite. "It's not here," he said, running down the headland, Kayenion on his heels.

"What's not here?" Kayenion asked, searching their surroundings, trying to understand why the captain was so upset.

"The Oath isn't here."

"How do you know? It looks quiet enough to me."

The only movement in the calm waters of the harbour was a single mast fishing boat, sculling its way out of the harbour between the curving walls.

Jerrol skidded onto the wall, collapsing to his knees as he patted the stone as if he could wake it up. Nothing. It was just inert stone.

"Captain Jerrol, sorry, Lord Chancellor, welcome back to Senti." A thin middle-aged man hurried up and stood over him. Kayenion tensed and moved between him and Jerrol, even though the man seemed inoffensive.

Jerrol rose. "Harbourmaster, have you seen Birlerion in the last week?"

"Lord Birlerion? It's funny you should ask that. Someone like him was seen up at the temple, but he was out of uniform, thinner. He kept to himself, didn't speak to anyone. We didn't think it was him."

"Lady help us," Jerrol breathed.

"If he took it, it would be to protect it, Pa. You know that," Margareth panted as she skidded to a halt beside him.

"But according to you he can't protect himself from the Veil; how can he protect the Oath? He should have left it here." Jerrol scanned the busy harbour before turning away. They walked more slowly back up the hill.

"You don't know that Birlerion has it," Margareth said.

"Who else would have it?"

"What about Lady Marguerite? She is the Lady of the Land. She holds the Oath."

"Birlerion intended on coming here; he must have it."

"Why are you so determined to believe ill of Birlerion, Pa?"

Jerrol stopped in surprise. "I don't."

"Yes, you do. You won't trust him. Why?"

"I *do* trust him. He's family. But he is not quite himself at the moment. He is struggling with the effects of a trauma we can't imagine. It affects how he thinks, how he reacts. I need to make sure what he is doing is for the good of Remargaren."

Margareth stared at him, her face sad. "Are you sure it hasn't affected how *you* think of him? Birlerion hasn't changed; he is still the same man. I think it's you that sees him differently."

Jerrol stood staring after her as she walked across the headland to the sentinal. After a moment of stunned silence, he followed her.

Having escorted Margareth to the towers, Jerrol stepped out of the waystone outside Bryce's office and collapsed into the chair opposite his friend. Kayenion waited in the outer office, chatting with Deron. "I went to Senti. The Oath's not there," Jerrol said.

"Any indication of who took it? I wouldn't have thought Birlerion was in a fit state to travel so swiftly."

"I don't know, though the harbourmaster thought he saw a man who could have been Birlerion in the harbour."

Bryce shook his head. "He amazes me at every turn. How did he get there so quickly?"

"It doesn't matter. We need to help him get back here as soon as possible." Jerrol dropped his head in his hands. "How did I get this so wrong?"

Bryce grunted. "Nothing about this has made much

sense. But then anything to do with the Oath or the Veil rarely does, if I remember right. What are the healers saying?"

"Nothing different; they say we need to detain Birlerion as soon as possible and return him to their care. They will not be responsible for him while he is on the loose."

"Well, that's convenient, seeing as they were the ones who lost him."

"I think we lost him long before that. *I* lost him. You know, I can't sense him anymore? Not like Sentinals can usually sense each other."

"Is that usual?"

Jerrol lips flattened. "I don't know."

"Have you checked the King's Oath? It normally reflects Birlerion's health."

"No, I suppose I ought to go and look. In the meantime, send out more orders. Find him at all costs, but with care; we don't want him hurt. Get them to escort him back here. I need to speak to him, urgently."

Jerrol walked through the palace to the throne room; the words of the Oath were carved in the marble wall above the king's throne. He stared at it, tilting his head. There were some residues of pink in the grooves, normally a sign that the Oath Keeper had been hurt. As he watched, they faded, and it returned to the usual golden glow. Except the glow didn't quite reach all the way to the edges. He hadn't noticed it before. Was that new? Frowning, he tried to remember. He would have to ask Anders.

22

DEEPWATER WATCH, VESPIRI

Leyarille sat beside Jaredion's bed in the Deepwater infirmary and watched him open his eyes and groan, a deep, pain-filled groan that made Alyssa call the healer. His face paled as he tried to move, and then he stiffened as he obviously remembered what had happened.

"Jaredion?" Alyssa's voice was soft.

He rolled his head and breathed a sigh of relief. "Mother," he whispered. He cleared his throat.

"Here, drink, it will ease your throat." Alyssa held a straw to his mouth.

"How long?" he whispered. He didn't have the strength to raise his voice.

"What do you mean, love?"

"Here. How long?"

"Leyarille brought you here last night. It's late afternoon now."

Leyarille tensed. One night; was Birlerion able to hold out for one night without Jaredion to protect him? She wasn't sure. She knew the moment Jaredion reached for the Veil to check on Birlerion and knew what he would find as he gasped, and then his expression emptied. The Veil had been a roiling mess when she had last checked. It was antagonised, angry, but there was no Birlerion caught in its trap and Jaredion wouldn't find him there.

"Jaredion? Are you alright? Clennin, what's the matter with him?" Alyssa's voice rose.

Jaredion shivered, and his expression firmed as he returned to his body. "Don't, don't knock me out, must stay awake."

Alyssa hovered over him in concern.

Desperation made him stutter. "I n-need to speak to Leyarille. Where's Leyarille?"

"Here," Leyarille said. He rolled his head, and she leaned over him, Tagerill hovering behind her. "Is Birlerion alright, Jaredion?"

"Yes, on a boat, to Senti."

"Senti? Why Senti?"

"Oath. King sent him; no choice, he needs the Oath, but the Veil is after it." He swallowed, and his mother silently offered him the straw again. Jaredion sucked up the water before spitting the straw out. "Leyarille, he needs help. The Veil is after him, will kill him, help him."

"Of course we will. Uncle Tage and I will leave for Senti."

"He needs to rest," Alyssa said, the worry clear in her voice as she watched her son's pale face.

"I'll carry him to my Sentinal. You'll recover quicker, Jaredion, don't argue," Tagerill said as Jaredion tried to protest. "Then Leyarille and I will go after Birlerion. Your mother and father will go to Vespers and stop Jerrol from chasing him. So once the worst of your injury is healed you can go to your sentinal and just relax and concentrate on getting your strength back, alright?"

"Fine," Jaredion whispered and closed his eyes. His black lashes were stark against his pale skin.

Leyarille kissed his cheek. "Thank you, Jaredion, for rescuing Birlerion. I'll never forget what you've done for him, and nor will he."

"He won't be able to sleep. You have to protect him until I can."

"I will, I promise. We'll find him, Jaredion."

Leyarille stepped back as Tagerill scooped him up, blankets and all, and strode out of the healerie, Alyssa following.

Leyarille returned to her uncle's study. "Uncle Lea, do you think my father will listen to you? He wouldn't listen to me."

"Don't worry, my dear, he will listen to me, I can assure you. How was Jaredion?"

"Tagerill took him to his sentinal. We need to leave for Senti. Birlerion's gone to get the Oath."

"Why does he need the Oath?"

"The king told him to get it."

Jennery stared at her. "The king invoked his Oath?"

"Sounds like it. According to Jaredion, Birlerion didn't have a choice."

"How could they? How could they lock him up when the Oath is in force? Are they mad?" Jennery shot out of his chair, his face tight and his fists clenched. He turned on Tagerill as he entered the room. "Did you hear this? Anders invoked the Oath on Birlerion and then locked him up. Jerrol should know better."

Tagerill nodded, his face as cold as Jennery's. "I heard. Jaredion is asleep in my sentinal. He won't be released until he can stand on his own and his shoulder is healed."

"Good, that will reassure Alyssa. We'll be leaving for Vespers in the morning, but I know she was reluctant to leave him. But we can't wait; we need to find out what is going on and stop it. You two need to leave for Senti, now. You need to find Birlerion."

Leyarille shivered at the unspoken 'before it's too late' hanging in the air. She leaned forward, speaking quickly. "There's something you need to know. The Lady created the Watchers long before she created the Veil. Their purpose was to watch the beyond, to watch the others, to ensure that Remargaren would stay safe. The Veil was created when the Lady destroyed the Bloodstone. Birlerion was there and was part of that creation."

"Whoa," Tagerill interrupted her. "Others? What are you talking about?"

Leyarille scowled at him. "We don't have time for this. I spoke with Germaine at the Towers; he said he didn't remember what was before the Veil, and then he said something weird, that there were other worlds out there and that we weren't the only ones. And they watched them. When I pressed him, he became confused."

"They are old men, Leyarille. You can't trust what they say."

"But what if he was right? Why would we be the only ones the Guardians created? The Lady and Guerlaire went somewhere, didn't they? Her family before that went somewhere. Where? We don't know."

"That is a bit far-fetched Leyarille."

"Is it? Birlerion helped to create the Veil over three thousand years ago. How? He never speaks of it; he says he doesn't remember, but he does. I know he does. He helped my father repair the Veil with the Lady twenty-odd years ago. If he didn't remember, how could he have helped? What did he do? Did you know that the records state not a single person died in Vespers when the Lady destroyed the Bloodstone, yet every building was destroyed. How was that possible?"

"The Lady protected her people."

"It was Birlerion."

"Leyarille, Birler was a scrawny underfed kid off the streets of Vespers, a nobody. He was dying on those streets, starving, no family. He had nothing when he joined the rangers."

Leyarille stared at Tagerill. "Then why did the Lady choose him? Why did she pluck him off the streets and induct him into the rangers?"

"Who knows. The Lady did many charitable things."

"Yet he was her first Sentinal, and she spent a lot more time with him than any other Sentinal."

Tagerill stilled. "How did you know that?"

"Niallerion told me. And about how he used to stagger out of her chambers almost every day, exhausted to the point of collapse. Niallerion said she was teaching him something. That he did things no one else was able to do. That he could reach. Birlerion did things even the Lady was frightened by."

Tagerill paced. "Birlerion was no different to any other Sentinal."

"Then why was his Sentinal the only one in Vespers? And shielding her temple at that."

"He had a connection with the Lady, that is true; the temple recognised him."

"Do you hear what you are saying, Tagerill? The temple is a stone building; how could it recognise Birlerion if there wasn't something different about him?"

"What is the point of all this, Leyarille?" Jennery interrupted impatiently. "That Birlerion is special? We know that already."

"You know he is more than special. He is part of the Veil. He is the Shield of Remargaren. While he lives, he will protect us. That is his purpose, to protect us. You know that,

Tagerill. That is why the Veil recognises him, why it is targeting him."

Tagerill frowned. "The Shield of Remargaren? Where did you hear that?

"My father said it once; that he was the Lady's sword and Birlerion was the shield."

"But if his purpose and the Veil's is to protect us, then why is the Veil attacking him?"

"The Veil has figured out a way to be free."

Jennery sat up. "No way. The Veil is not alive, and it doesn't think. It doesn't have life; it doesn't even understand the concept of freedom."

"It is aware. It must be. Margareth says it behaves like a petulant child. My father says it is voracious. It kills people, especially Sentinals. It knows what is in the beyond, while we don't. Maybe it saw something it wanted, I don't know, but it is trying to kill the one person who anchors it here. Why?"

Tagerill stared at her. Running his hands through his hair, he paced the room again. "If all that you are saying is true, then my brother is the only thing that is preventing the Veil from cutting us loose and doing what? Flitting off to another world to protect them instead?"

"The Veil doesn't want to protect. It has never wanted to protect us; it wants to destroy us."

Jennery held up his hands. "Bollocks. I'm sorry, Leyarille, but really? How did you come to that conclusion?"

"Why would we need the Watchers? They monitor it, and they control it, corral it or whatever. They ensure it is repaired. That it does its job. If it wasn't a threat, why would it need constant observation?"

"Because it's their job."

Leyarille closed her eyes and took a deep breath. She opened them and exhaled on a hiss. "Because the Veil was forced by the Lady and Birlerion to shield our world."

Tagerill shook his head. "I'm sorry, Leyarille, Birlerion would have said. He wouldn't have kept this secret for all these years. There would be no reason to."

Leyarille smiled. "Birlerion is the Lady's. He would do whatever she asked him to."

Jennery rubbed his face. "It would explain why the Veil is so single-minded in its pursuit of Birlerion. And I must admit, he has always been the quiet one. He doesn't lie, but he omits to speak of things. It would explain much."

Tagerill gaped at him. "But-but he's my brother."

"So?"

"He would tell me."

"Why? What difference would it make? The Veil is the Veil. Telling you wouldn't change anything. And if the Ascendants had ever found out, it would have been worse for him."

"So he let Jerrol be the bait? I don't think so."

"But who was always at his shoulder protecting him?" Jennery asked quietly. "Is it really so far-fetched? Look how many times Birlerion almost died protecting Jerrol."

Tagerill's jaw dropped. "I'll kill him."

"Join the queue." Leyarille gave a sharp bark of laughter. "We have to protect Birlerion, no matter what. If we don't …" she shrugged, "our world might not be around for much longer. If the Veil gets past Birlerion, once it's free, it will consume us all."

"I'll fucking kill him." Tagerill was incensed. "All these years, and he never told me."

"Tagerill, get over it," Jennery said. "We have more important things to worry about. Like, how do we keep him alive?"

"We have to find him first," Leyarille said. "And that is down to Tagerill and me. We'll take the waystone to Senti and, if necessary, track him from there. Once we find him, I can protect him from the Veil. We need to speak to him. He must know what is going on. If the king invoked the Oath, he will have no choice but to head back to Vespers. Uncle Lea, you need to make sure they don't kill him on sight when he arrives."

Jennery tried to hide a smile. She was so like her father. "Send a message with Ari if anything changes. You'd better get going. He may have left Senti by now."

Leyarille stood. "Tell Jaredion to meet us in Vespers; there's no point him trailing us through the territories."

Jennery nodded. "Just find him, Leyarille."

"Don't worry, I will."

23

CHERNI, BIRTOLI

irlerion strode up the white sandy beach eyeing the green fronds of the palm trees curving above him. Airen and Gianna cast off to set some nets while they waited for him. He followed the trail through the broad-leafed plants and foliage towards the home of the Tu'ani clan. They had once lived on the island of Geteril, located a lot further south, before the Ascendants had destroyed it. Jerrol and Roberion had saved them, brought them through time, from the past to the present day, and there his friend Roberion had joined with the Elder's daughter, Lilith.

The Tu'ani had once guarded the Oath before Jerrol took it to Senti and built that incredible harbour. It didn't surprise him that Marguerite had taken the Oath back to the Tu'ani.

Birlerion paused on the edge of the clearing. A communal fire pit was dug in the centre, and a small boy dressed in just a pair of shorts rotated a spit above it; a huge fish roasting made his mouth water. He couldn't remember the last time he had eaten properly, just for pleasure. When had his life imploded so badly?

Large dwellings were built around the edge of the clearing, made of bamboo walls and roofs of palm leaves woven into an impenetrable mat, keeping the weather and the heat out. A slender woman ducked out of the largest dwelling and walked towards him, her arms open wide, a huge smile on her lovely face. Her black hair was plaited off her face and fell in a coil around her neck. The largest brown eyes twinkled at him from a face finely lined and belying her age.

"Lilith," Birlerion breathed as he hugged her. The woman who had waited for Roberion in the past and followed him into the future with her clan when Jerrol and Roberion had rescued them across time.

"Birlerion, we have been expecting you."

"You have?"

"My father said you were on your way. Please, join us." Leading the way back to the largest hut, she gestured for him to enter.

He bent his head, passed through the door and blinked in the dim interior. Palm fronds covered the floor, rustling under his feet. Kicking off his boots by the entrance, he padded over to the elderly man lying on a pallet in the corner.

"Elder Tuan, forgive my tardiness."

The ancient man chuckled, his voice a raspy whisper on the air. "You are not late, my son."

"Yet you have been waiting for me."

"Not me, the others; they grow impatient."

Birlerion sank to the floor beside him. Gently, he took the old man's hand in his. His skin was so soft, paper fine, and creased with age. He lay in a muddle of light blankets and robes, swaddled as if already dead and waiting for the Leaving ceremony.

The frail hand squeezed his, and the pale eyes searched his face, no doubt noting the deep lines engraved around

Birlerion's eyes and mouth, the silver threads in his hair, the hollows of his cheeks. "It has been a long time. You are suffering, struggling with your burden; why don't you set it down here and join me?"

Birlerion grimaced. "I am not finished yet; I still have a life to live."

"My son, if you do this, there will be no life for you."

Birlerion collapsed in on himself. "I have no choice," he whispered.

"There is always a choice," Elder Tuan replied.

"Not for me."

The Elder smiled. "Of course there is. I will take your burden. Come, lay down beside me. My time is soon. I will release you, and you will be free to live your life as you desire."

He could lay down and rest? Pass the burden of protecting Remargaren onto someone else? After all these years? Be finally free of the pain and pressure and the need to survive one more day? To be able to curl around Leyarille and never let her go? He smiled at the thought and slowly lay beside the old man.

"Are you ready?" Elder Tuan asked.

"Yes," Birlerion replied, and as he closed his silver eyes, the old man clasped his hand, and a soft hum filled his mind.

Birlerion opened his eyes, and Marguerite stood before him. Their surroundings were hazy; he couldn't tell where they were, but he was no longer lying in a Tu'ani hut on an island in Birtoli.

"You need to make your choice, Birlerion. I am so sorry, but the only way you can fend off the Veil is with the Oath. It's power will strengthen your defences. I tried to reach the Veilspace but I can't."

Birlerion exhaled. "Anders invoked the King's Oath," he said slowly. "I have to take the Oath to Old Vespers. He wants it with him."

"I think you already know that may not be possible. Jerrol passed the Oath to me when we created the harbour in Senti, and I have been hosting it ever since, but the Oath is restless. It knows it needs someone stronger and it's time to pass it on."

"No," Birlerion breathed.

Marguerite gave a wry smile. "What do you think I have been doing all these years? The Land and the Oath are entwined. They are a balance like all else, but it is exhausting."

"Could you take the Oath to Anders?"

Marguerite shook her head. "The last time I manifested was difficult, and moving the Oath here was draining. I don't have the strength. It will take me weeks to recover."

Fear stole down Birlerion's back like a silent assassin. "What would that mean? Hosting the Oath. Can I not just carry it like Jerrol did?"

Marguerite shook her head. "No, you are going to need to bond with the Oath. That is the only way you can use it to protect Remargaren against the Veil. The Oath is the only protection we have left." She glanced up and sighed. "You should really bond with the Land as well, to help sustain you, but you need my mother's permission for that. It would be much easier without the Veil. The lack of magic makes it difficult to contact her or Leyandrii."

"Why would I need to bond with the Land?" Birlerion's heart fluttered as he remembered his last interaction with the Land all those centuries ago. It hadn't gone well when he refused to bond. The Land had not been pleased. Fortunately, Marguerite had bonded with it instead and soothed the sentience back to sleep.

"The Oath protects. The Land sustains. If you use the Oath to destroy the Veil, you'll need the Land to help sustain you."

"Well, I can't reach the All Mother, so we'll have to make do with the Oath."

"Is this your choice?" she asked, her eyes pools of regret.

"There is no choice," Birlerion replied.

"There is always a choice; you've done enough. Tuan offers you an honourable option, with Leyarille waiting for you at the end of it."

"Like consolation for the exhausted hero? Do you think that is what she wants to be?"

"She would never be a consolation and you know it."

"Tuan is not strong enough, he would not survive the Veil."

"He is stronger than you think. There will be no going back. Bonding will change you." Marguerite twisted her lips as she cupped his cheek. "Dearest, if anyone should bond with the Oath it is you, but if you truly do manage to suppress the Veil, the ramifications will be immense, and they will impact you too. I do not know if you will survive it."

Birlerion grinned wryly. "I'm not going to survive the Veil without the Oath. I can't sleep. The minute I do, it tries to suck the life out of me. Passing the responsibility to someone else will not solve that. The Veil is after *me*. It sees me as its jailer. I am the one who anchors it here."

"Think, Birlerion. If you choose to bond with the Oath and fight the Veil, you may not see Leyarille again. You'd be losing everything you ever worked for; your friends, your family, everything."

"But without a world for us to live in, what would be the point? I've lived a long life, maybe not to its fullest extent, but it's been longer than most."

"Birlerion, be sure."

"What do I do?"

Marguerite sighed. "Birlerion, please, wait a bit longer. Think of Leyarille. Let me contact Leyandrii."

"I *am* thinking of Leyarille. If you could have spoken with Leyandrii, you already would have," Birlerion said, unable to keep the edge from his voice, and Marguerite winced. "What other choice do we have? Have you figured out how to stop the Veil? If you have, then please, share it. After all, why take a risk if we don't have to?"

Marguerite wavered. "Taurillion will be jealous. If anyone it should be him."

"Go and get him then, if you think he'll have a better chance of surviving than me."

Marguerite looked away. "No," she whispered. "He doesn't have your strength, your passion. Nor your understanding of the Veil."

"I can't wait. It's me that it's after. I can't go on like this. No matter what, it will drag me there anyway. It wants what I am; the Sentinal that anchors it here, the Shield. I hold its leash and in me it sees its opportunity for freedom. A sacrifice of one is better than sacrificing the whole world, isn't it? Tell me what I need to do."

Marguerite patted his arm and gave him a sad smile. "I'm sorry for the catechism. I had to make sure you knew what you were choosing. You know what to do. You are already here."

Birlerion turned and saw nothing. The darkness was absolute and without texture. The air was thick, a weight pressing down on him, consuming; he was trapped. "Marguerite?" He reached out in front of him, and his fingers passed through empty space. Concerned, he stamped his foot and he fell into the void below. Fresh soil filled his mouth, and he choked.

"His pulse just went mad; it's all over the place," Lilith

said, hovering over Birlerion in concern. His face was taut, the skin pale and tight over his cheekbones; his jaw firmed as he gritted his teeth and he struggled to inhale a breath.

"The choice has been made. He has taken up the Oath and will bear its burden for all of us. He has begun. We must wait."

"Father, was this wise?"

"Wise? Maybe not, but the choice was not ours to make." Elder Tuan lifted his head as the wind rattled the wooden frame of their shelter. His gaze dropped, and he met his daughter's eyes. "Prepare for a storm, a bad one."

***

Tagerill gripped the railing of their vessel and looked out at the dark grey waves in concern. He had only ever seen the blue waters calm and crystal clear. These seas were all riled up and battering against the wooden hull.

The captain offered him a rope, his face grim as his gaze flickered around the boat. "Tie yourself to the railing in case you get swept overboard. I don't know where this storm came from, but it's going to be rough."

Tagerill scowled at the young man. Rough? His stomach already thought down was up and up was down; how much rougher could it get? He tied the rope around Leyarille's waist and then the railing and then did the same for himself. "Maybe we should have waited?" he yelled over the howling wind. The deck canted down into a deep swell and then back up before they were launched into the air as the hull crashed back down into the sea. They hung onto the railing with a death grip.

The young captain was fighting with his sail; the wind kept tugging it out of his hands, and Tagerill loosened his rope so he could stagger over to help. The wind gusted, billowing the sail, and Leyarille curled in on herself as it drove them into an approaching wave. The water thundered down onto the deck, sweeping their feet out from under them. Foamy waves boiled around them, almost drowning out the horrendous ripping sound as the sail tore, and part of it wriggled off into the sky like a demented flag fighting for its freedom before the greedy sea snagged it and it was lost.

Tagerill and the young man grabbed the remaining canvas and hauled it down before they lost the mast, which was creaking ominously. The deck bucked as the boat rolled into another breaking wave, and the youngster on the tiller shrieked as he was tossed overboard. Leyarille flung a belt after him more in desperation than hope. He was lost in the grey swells, and she lunged for the tiller, though what she was supposed to do with it she wasn't sure. She held onto it grimly as the sea tried to roll them over.

The captain slid down the deck and braced himself against the stern. He grabbed the tiller from Leyarille. "Shorten your rope," he bawled.

Leyarille frowned at him as the wind tugged the words away. "What?" she yelled as she wiped the water off her face and looked where he was pointing. Her rope had snagged around the nets that had escaped from a locker. Staggering as the deck canted again, she dropped to her hands and knees and slid the length of the deck. The nets came too, swiping Tagerill's legs out from under him, and they all collected in a tangled mess in the bow.

Tagerill grabbed for her, his other arm braced against the railing, but she was torn from his grasp as a deluge of water thundered onto the deck.

Leyarille was swept away into the torrent of foam; the roaring of the sea was all she could hear, even though Tagerill's mouth was open, screaming something at her. The nets tangled around her and then she was gone, a wriggling mass sinking into the depths. She struggled to free herself, bemused by the eery silence beneath the waves, such a contrast to the chaos above.

Her ears hissed, but it was softer than the ferocious wind. Jerking to a halt, she tried not to gulp. She heaved as her body tried to breathe, and she refused to allow it. She couldn't untangle herself, but she kicked upwards, towards the frothing water above her. A tug dragged her through the water, and she almost exhaled. She heaved again, her body desperate for her to take a breath. The hissing was increasing. She couldn't see which way was up, and the nets dragged at her as her eyes darkened, and she struggled to untangle herself from its grip.

Warm arms gathered her close, and she was being kissed; much-needed air was breathed into her lungs, and she opened her eyes. Shuddering, she realised she was still under the water, her body jerking as it was tugged in long pulls back towards the boat.

"Birlerion?"

"Hold on, my love."

"We're trying to find you."

"Don't, my love; it's too late now."

"Nooo," she screamed as he left and she broke the surface, inhaling much-needed air. The wind had dropped and the sea was still, the waters as calm as the harbour at Senti in the early morning. Tagerill and the captain hauled her in, nets and all.

Flopping on the deck, she choked out water, gasping for breath, and the young man stared at her in shock. "She should be drowned; she was under too long."

Tagerill gathered her close. "Leyarille, my dear, I thought we'd lost you," he murmured as he rocked her in his tight embrace.

"I can't breathe," she managed to squeeze the words out.

"Sorry, by the Lady, I don't know what I would have said to Birlerion; you nearly drowned."

"He saved me," she whispered, shuddering in his arms. "He's in the water."

"Who was?"

"Birlerion, he was under the water with me."

"He couldn't be." Tagerill looked at the captain, who was wringing his shirt out whilst scanning the waters. "We need to get her to port; she's delirious."

Leyarille coughed, her chest wheezing, and Tagerill wrapped a damp blanket around her. "Everything is soaked, but it's better than nothing."

The young man peered around the boat. "Sebastian?" he yelled, shielding his eyes against the brilliant sun.

A faint cry responded, and the man lurched to the other side of the boat. He tied a rope around his waist, kicked off his shoes and dived into the water, swimming strongly towards the boy bobbing in the gentle swells. He tugged him back, and Tagerill helped pull them both back on board.

"Seb, I thought I'd lost you." The young captain hugged him close, tears streaming down his face, his hair and trousers dripping.

Seb wheezed. "Not this time. I heard a man's voice; he said it wasn't time, and he apologised for the storm."

Tagerill's eyes widened.

"Told you he was here," Leyarille said, shivering in her blanket.

"Do you think it was the Fisherman?" Seb asked, awe in his voice.

Leyarille smiled as she leaned against Tagerill, exhausted. "I'm sure it was."

"Ahoy there! Do you need assistance?" a deep voice interrupted them. They all looked up in surprise as a graceful three-masted frigate drifted towards them, its oars raised either side, water dripping from the wood.

Tagerill gasped and stood. "Roberion?"

An equally surprised voice bellowed back. "Tagerill? Ascendants balls, Tagerill, what are you doing here?"

"Trying to reach Cherni," Tagerill yelled back, helping Leyarille to her feet.

"Leyarille? Is that you too?"

"Hi, Roberion." Leyarille waved as the frigate's prow towered above them; the carved face of the Lady smiled down at them, her hand stretched towards them.

Netting was thrown over the side as the oars were raised higher, and the young captain threw a mooring rope up towards eager hands. The small vessel was soon tied securely bow and stern and snugged tight against the *Lady's Miracle*.

Tagerill boosted Leyarille up the netting and then the young lad, following close behind. Eager hands pulled them onboard, and Leyarille found herself engulfed in another hug. Roberion was as broad-chested as Tagerill. His brown hair was bleached by the sun, his face weathered, and creases surrounded his silver eyes.

"Are we glad to see you," Tagerill said as he hugged his friend. "We got caught by a storm; blew up from nowhere."

Roberion nodded as he shook the young captain's hand. "Yeah, we did too. Came out of nowhere and disappeared just as fast."

"Didn't seem that fast to me," Tagerill said with feeling as he rubbed his ribs. "We almost lost Leyarille and the young'un here; they both went overboard."

"The Fisherman saved us," Sebastian piped up.

Roberion and Tagerill exchanged glances. "I'm sure he did, young man," Roberion said, ruffling the boy's hair. "We're headed for Cherni; we can take you. You can get your boat repaired there. Let's get you all some dry clothes. Is anyone hurt?"

"Just bumps and bruises, I think," Tagerill said as they followed Roberion to his cabin. Seb and his brother followed Roberion's first mate down into the depths of the *Miracle*.

Once Roberion had his unexpected guests dried out and settled in his day cabin, he frowned at Tagerill. "What is Jerrol doing down here? Hasn't he got his hands full with the Joining?"

"It's not my Pa. It's Birlerion."

Roberion wrinkled his brow. "How can it be Birlerion?"

"I don't know, but we think he is in Cherni, and he saved me when I was drowning."

"Leyarille, it couldn't have been."

"It was, I know his voice. He said we were too late."

"Too late for what?" Roberion asked as Tagerill stiffened.

"I don't know, but he needs us." She hesitated and then poured out everything she knew, about Birlerion, her father, and the Veil.

Roberion sat aghast. "Jerrol wouldn't do that to one of his own."

"He would if he thinks there is a threat to Remargaren; and the Oath is gone; it's not at Senti," Tagerill said.

"But, Birlerion? No, I don't believe it."

Leyarille twisted her lips. "Believe it. Jaredion was injured saving him. He took a bolt in his shoulder, and he's recuperating in Deepwater, which means Birlerion is exposed. I must find him. I can keep the Veil off him."

"If he went to Senti looking for the Oath, then he is now on Cherni. That's where Marguerite took it," Roberion said.

"Lady Marguerite?" Leyarille gasped. She knew Birlerion hadn't stolen it.

Roberion rubbed his chin. "And that explains the storm.

The Oath caused the storm to protect Cherni; it may not let us berth if it feels threatened."

"Then why is it calm now?"

Roberion shrugged. "We're in the eye of the storm; we have to get out the other side. Let's hope we can reach Cherni and Birlerion and find out what is going on."

"Hold him down," Elder Tuan snapped. "He'll hurt himself."

Birlerion writhed under the men holding him still and then just as suddenly went limp. "Don't release him, it could be a trick," the Elder said, watching Birlerion's face carefully. Birlerion's eyes flew open, luminous, and he twisted in their grip.

"He is so strong," one of the burly men he managed to throw off gasped.

"He needs to be," the Elder said, closing Birlerion's unseeing eyes.

Birlerion spread his thoughts like wings, slowing his descent through the Land, reaching for a sign of the essence that thrummed inside him. He knew it was here; the air crackled with the Oath's presence, and it made his nerves tingle, teasing him, just out of reach.

He reached further than he ought, completely open, exposed. Bringing all his defences down, he waited. It was a gentle breeze to begin with, stirring the darkness like eddies of mist, offering pockets of light in the unending darkness. Birlerion waited. The Oath needed to embrace him. He couldn't force it. He didn't know why he thought this, but he did.

As he waited, a ripple of images flickered in front of his eyes. Remargaren as he remembered it before the Lady broke the stone and the Land buckled. The mountains of Terolia, jagged red teeth against the vivid blue sky before the volcano erupted and blasted the mountain to pieces and then threw up a new range to be weathered by sun and wind.

The Birtolian mainland, vibrant and busy, dusty trails connecting it to Vespiri and Terolia. Swirls of low-lying islands off the coast, offering the best fishing in this world. Now all drowned, except for the highest ground. An archipelago of islands in a turquoise sea where people used to live and breathe.

Rolling Elothian plains of rich grass grazing for the herds of deer and cattle, dissected by clear burbling streams and flower meadows, replaced by rising ridges scarring the plains and blocking the way as the land rose under the stresses of their world. Ice and snow blanketed the land, forcing it into hibernation.

And finally Vespiri and the Watches; Vespers, Greens, Deepwater, Stoneford, East Watch, and Marchwood all had special meaning for him, some more than others, and then the destruction of the palace in Vespers. His heart stuttered as Leyandrii and Guerlaire fell into the vast hole that swallowed the palace leaving him holding a shield over the people of Vespers. The image held, of him being battered by the storm, whipped bloody by debris, but still, he held, until the land beneath him collapsed and he too had been lost.

"Why?" the question lingered in his mind.

Birlerion resisted the temptation to ask, why what? He knew what. *"It is what I do. I protect people."*

Images scrolled before his unseeing eyes. His memories of all the people he had tried to protect over the years; his injuries, his horror when he failed, his happiness when he succeeded, but underlying all, his deep-rooted belief in the

Lady and his reason for existing. To protect those who could not protect themselves.

The images stopped on one; the Veil. He flinched as it struck, and Lilith gasped as a bloody slash appeared on Birlerion's chest, his shirt turning crimson before her eyes. Birlerion flexed his hand and reached. His sword firmed in his grasp. *"Its time is over. It only wants to destroy; we don't need it anymore."*

As he struck, the Oath sat at his shoulder watching. The Veil fought back, tangling itself in its effort to reach Birlerion. Birlerion calmly lopped its strands off. *"It wants you,"* he said. *"It believes you will free it."*

"To do what?"

"To destroy Remargaren."

"Why?"

"Because it can. It has been restrained for years, but now it sees its chance to be free."

"You can stop it?"

"With your help."

The Oath dug a little deeper. *"You would give Leyarille up?"*

"Not if I don't have to."

"But if you had to?"

"Then, I would already be dead."

The Oath pondered at his shoulder. *"She could be dead with you."* The image of a small boat being tossed around like a piece of driftwood coalesced before his eyes. A huge wave swept the people on board down to the bow, and then the boat corkscrewed as a wave swept a mass over the side.

Birlerion dove after her; he knew it was Leyarille. Collecting her in his arms, he pushed her back to the surface, kissing her as if it was his last chance. He heard another vibration in the water, and as soon as she was up, he went to find the other disturbance, aware that the Oath followed.

His body flinched as another strike shredded his shirt and

blood welled as a new welt cut his body. "What is happening?" Lilith gasped as she staunched the bleeding.

"I don't know," her father replied, tightening his grip on Birlerion's hand. Chimes passed, and the men released him, watching in horror as he lay on the floor, his body a battleground beyond their comprehension. Birlerion's fist clenched, and he struck again, his blood slick across the strands of the Veil.

"Why wouldn't you let her die?" the Oath asked.

"It is not her time."

"How do you know?"

"Because we have a life to live together."

The Oath chuckled in the back of his mind. *"You'll do,"* it said, and Birlerion spasmed as the Elder gripped his hand and the Oath penetrated every cell in his body. Birlerion went rigid, absorbing the Oath and the burden that went with it. His mind grappled with the awareness now taking residence and then he went limp.

Lilith panicked as she felt his neck and pressed her head against his chest. "He isn't breathing."

"What?" a bedraggled Leyarille gasped from the doorway. "Birlerion?" she cried as she rushed forward, collapsing to her knees beside his limp body. Water dripped on the mats around her.

She gathered him in her arms and smoothed his damp hair off his face. He was covered in blood. Her grip tightened, and she reached. The Veil was a swirling mass of confusion; how anyone could not see this was beyond her. In the middle, Birlerion swung his sword. He was glowing; a golden glow that expanded as she watched. It was blinding. She cut her way through the strands, and once she reached him, she wrapped her arms around him, resting her head against his back. "It can't have you," she said out loud, and Birlerion's body shuddered in her arms as he inhaled deeply.

Leyarille was aware of the hut solidifying around them and after a moment he opened his blood-drenched eyes. They were a deep indigo blue where they weren't bloody, and as she watched, they luminesced, a myriad of colours which coalesced into a golden glow.

"Birlerion?" she whispered. "Please join with me, now, before it's too late. Please."

His eyes solidified into an indigo blue, and she knew he could see her. He reached a bloody hand and gripped her head. Drawing her down, he kissed her.

"I take that as a yes," Tagerill grinned, his silver eyes wild in his pale face.

Birlerion's hand wavered, and he released Leyarille. He squinted at the doorway. "Tage?" he whispered as he tried to sit up, but the Elder placed his hand against his chest.

"Not yet. Drink," the Elder gestured, and Lilith moved in front of him blocking the view of Birlerion's face. Birlerion stared at him as he drank out of the gourd; the liquid burned his throat, and his eyes shone with the golden glow of the Oath. "So," the Elder nodded. "Welcome, my son; you have been long-awaited. You must rest. There is much still to be done."

Birlerion relaxed into Leyarille's arms as a wave of exhaustion flushed through him. She was here, he was safe at last, and he closed his eyes.

The Elder shakily creaked to his feet, slowly straightening his back, the burly young men supporting him. "He will sleep."

"He doesn't like being sedated," Leyarille and Tagerill said in unison.

"He is not sedated; he is sleeping. He is exhausted. Let's leave him in peace."

"I can't. The Veil will attack him." Leyarille clutched Birlerion closer.

"The Oath protects his sleep. He is safe for now. Come, you must all be hungry. Join us for a meal. He will wake when he is ready."

The Elder was insistent, and as Birlerion was sleeping peacefully, she allowed herself to be coaxed outside.

24

CHANCELLOR'S OFFICE, OLD VESPERS

Jennery and Alyssa arrived in Vespers late the next day. They had left instructions with Miranda for when Jaredion awoke to meet them at the palace. Jennery hoped he would abide by them, but they couldn't wait to make sure.

Alyssa refused to wait in their room and accompanied him to the chancellor's office. He could tell she was ready for a fight; her child had been injured and she was out for explanations. She listened to his request for restraint. They needed to protect Birlerion, that was their goal; she nodded and pushed him out the door.

Jennery managed a smile for Kayenion as they met him outside Jerrol's office. Alyssa gave him a hug and whispered in his ear.

Kayenion's worried expression deepened. "I hope the Captain will listen to you. He is causing tension between the Sentinals and the King's Guards with some of his decisions."

"He'll listen to me," Jennery growled as Kayenion opened the door.

Jerrol rose, a smile of welcome on his face as they entered his office. "Lea, Alyssa, it's so good to see you."

Jennery hugged him. "It's good to see you too." He frowned at his friend in concern. He looked tired and careworn, lines etched in his forehead as if he wore a perpetual frown. "Jerrol, this office doesn't suit you. It is ageing you."

Jerrol grimaced. "I must admit, it is more stressful than I expected, but then I thought I would have more help."

"Delegation is the key." Alyssa said, her eyes bright. "You can't do it all yourself. First lesson of management."

Jerrol twisted his lips. "Have you seen or heard from Birlerion? I'm trying to find him."

"Find him?" Jennery asked, his voice strained. "He's your First Administrator. How can you not know where he is? Doesn't he have a protection detail?"

Taking a deep breath, Jerrol indicated the chairs. "Please sit." Jerrol leaned on his desk and hesitated for a moment. "Don't yell at me, but I agreed to the healer's request to commit Birlerion." He winced and held up his hands as Jennery launched to his feet, an explosive "You did what?" leaving his lips.

"I thought Birlerion was fixated by the Veil, couldn't let go of it. The healers said he was suffering from an anxiety disorder, a result of his episode with Ellie. There were reports that he was harming himself and Jaredion. He needed help."

"Birlerion wouldn't harm Jaredion. You must be mistaken."

"The healers reported it was happening on the trip to Terolia. Didn't Jaredion tell you?"

"No, he never mentioned it."

"Have you seen him? He was a little upset when Birlerion was committed."

Jennery hissed out his breath. "A little? What did Jaredion have to say about that?"

"He threatened to resign. I hoped he went home, and you were able to talk some sense into him."

"He resigned from the Sentinals?" Jennery repeated, exchanging glances with Alyssa. A flash of cold shivered through him at how desperate his son must have been to do such a thing.

"I know he didn't mean it. He was upset." Jerrol stopped talking as he registered their shock. "Has he not been home?"

"Yes," Alyssa said, "but he never mentioned anything about resigning, though we thought it odd he was out of uniform."

"Was Birlerion with him?"

"We haven't seen him. We thought he was here with you," Jennery replied, unable to keep the growing anger out of his voice.

Jerrol waved a hand. "It doesn't matter. Tell Jaredion I'll ignore his insubordination this one time. Though his reassignment stands. I should have rotated him before now. He has become too emotionally involved with Birlerion. He can't protect him with that mindset."

"Reassigned?" Jennery growled. "You cannot reassign him. He is the only one keeping Birlerion alive. The Veil is trying to kill Birlerion. Jaredion's job is to protect him. How is that being insubordinate?"

"There are more important things to worry about if Birlerion is right and the Veil is acting up."

"If?" Jennery asked. "Birlerion wouldn't make this stuff up. Haven't you listened to anyone? How many different people have to say it before you will believe it?"

"The Watchers say the Veil is fine. That's why I accepted the healer's assessment and agreed to his committal. I thought his irrational fear was all in his head. But it's possible there is something wrong with the Veil. I need to speak to Birlerion, but now he's escaped from the healers. We must find him."

Jennery was on his feet again. "Escaped? Why would he need to escape from people who are supposed to care for him?"

"I don't know. He's removed the Oath from Senti. We need to find him so I can ask him why.."

"Because the king ordered him to get the Oath; he had no choice. Did you not speak to Anders, Jerrol? Anders ordered Birlerion to get the Oath. Invoked his Oath and *then you locked Birlerion up*. How could you?"

"That's not possible. He would have told me." Jerrol's mouth dropped open in shock.

"Check with the king, Jerrol, before you make assumptions next time. If there *is* a next time." Jennery leaned over Jerrol's desk. "Do you even register the words coming out of your mouth? Since when did you ignore a threat to our world? Why would you not believe Birlerion? He is the Oath Keeper, for Lady's sake. Who else would warn you?" Jennery straightened and glared at Jerrol before helping Alyssa rise. He escorted his horrified wife to the door. "You had better reassess your priorities, Jerrol. I think you have forgotten what the purpose of your office is. It certainly isn't to persecute your friends because they tell you something you don't want to hear.

"Oh, and by the way, I think you may find that the King's Guards are no match for the Lady's Sentinals, and you should be ashamed of yourself for setting them against each other. They shot my son with a crossbow. He is recovering in Deepwater, no thanks to you. If you are prepared to set the King's Guard on your own nephew, I dread to think how you will treat the man you once called your brother." He left in disgust, leaving Jerrol staring after him in horror.

Alyssa scuttled down the corridor beside him. "Lea, that was restraint? I thought we were supposed to be persuading him to help Birlerion."

"His is not the kind of help Birlerion needs."

"But what do we do?"

"Pray that the Lady manages to show him how he has made a mistake and how he can help Birlerion," Jennery replied.

Jerrol went in search of the king. He found him in his chambers.

"Anders, did you tell Birlerion to go and get the Oath from Senti?"

Anders averted his eyes. "I might have."

"Why?

"I was in one of my insecure moments, and with everything going on, I wanted it close."

"Why didn't you tell me?"

"Afterwards, I realised it was a mistake, so I didn't mention it. And after Birlerion was detained, I didn't think any more of it."

"How did you ask him, Anders? If you invoked the Oath, he wouldn't have a choice, would he?"

"I didn't invoke the Oath, or not intentionally."

"So, you did?"

"Well, he refused to begin with. Said it was a mistake, and he made me angry. So I commanded him to go and get it by the end of the year."

Jerrol closed his eyes. His hand trembled as he held his head. "You do know that the healers used it as an argument for him being a threat to our security and the final reason why I agreed to him being restrained and removed from office? The reason why your guards and my men were out searching for him, with orders to detain him at all costs."

"No, I didn't realise," Anders said in a small voice. "Can't you recall them?"

Jerrol glared at him. "I rescinded the order immediately, but you know perfectly well it's easier to give a command than stop one." He waved his hand in frustration. "There are some units of guards still chasing him. It could take weeks for the new orders to reach everyone, and by then it could be too late. And we have no idea where he is."

"He'll have to come back here though, won't he? So you can just wait for him to turn up, save you chasing him."

Jerrol stared at him, aghast. Was the king serious? They would have a discussion about what invoking the Oath really meant later. Storming back to his office, his mind worked furiously as the realisation sank in that Birlerion's behaviour was perfectly understandable when you knew the facts. His stomach churned as he realised that meant Birlerion must be correct and something was terribly wrong with the Veil.

Only he didn't know what, and the only person who did was currently on the run, being chased at every turn. One thing he could do was confirm if the Veil was acting up. Kayenion rushed after him.

"Where are you going, Captain? What did the king say?"

"Sorry, the Watch Towers. I need to speak with the Watchers." Stepping through the waystone to the Watch Towers, he went in search of Margareth, aware of Kayenion's growing concern at not knowing what he was doing.

Jerrol found his daughter with one of the elderly Watchers, Germaine, in his tower. Margareth was pacing up and down, her fingers busy twirling the end of her hair into a knot, unravelling it and then doing it again. Something he hadn't seen her do in years. She must be really worried.

"What's happened?" he asked, his stomach sinking.

Margareth rushed to him and grabbed his arm as Germaine stood. "Pa! The Veil! It's showing clear signs of damage. It's angry."

"The Veil doesn't have emotions; it just is."

"You go and have a look and then say that."

Jerrol clenched his jaw as Margareth pushed him into Germaine's seat. "Margareth, this isn't your room."

Germaine waved his hand. "Go ahead. You need to see it, or you won't believe it."

Leaning back in the chair, Jerrol concentrated for a moment and then broke through to the Veil. Agitated threads roiled and undulated, shorn strands questing to grasp something. It stilled as he approached, and Jerrol had the distinct impression that it waited.

Weaving the strands back into the twisted pattern, he inspected the overall viability. It looked strong and flexible, though patches of the weave were darker, as if shadowed. Other than that, it looked normal to him. He inspected a bit further and sensed Jaredion in the strands. The Veil twisted away from him, and the essence was lost. Maybe he'd imagined it?

The Veil undulated in the distance, a complex weave of magic shielding them for millennia. He breathed a sigh of relief and then froze. Margareth had been worried, seriously worried, and she was not one to panic. What was he missing?

He remembered a saying of Jason's. *Just because it looks alright on the surface, doesn't mean it is.* Jason, the previous Lord Stoneford, had always told him to look deeper, to look past the obvious and understand the motivation. Margareth had no other motivation but to watch the Veil. She wouldn't lie about there being a problem. Birlerion was the ultimate professional. Even if he was half-dead, he still performed his duty, as Jerrol well knew. You could rely on him, and he had repeatedly raised concerns about the Veil.

Why would the Veil conceal where it was weakening? How would it hide it?

Jerrol grasped an area that was shadowed, and the essence of Birlerion flooded through him. Strong and recent. The Veil snarled in his head. It *snarled* at him! He commanded it to be silent, and it backed off, watching once more. Opening his eyes, he struggled to control his panicked breathing. Margareth and Germaine stood either side of him, holding him down.

"What's wrong?" Jerrol asked.

"You almost jerked out of the chair, Pa."

"Why didn't you tell me about this sooner?"

"It's only just become noticeable."

"You should have been looking closer," Jerrol snapped as he sat up.

"I *was* looking closer, because of what Leyarille said was happening to Birlerion; that was the only reason I saw what I did. The Veil is clever. It is hiding what it is doing."

Jerrol took a deep breath. "The Veil doesn't think. It reacts. Only go up in pairs. It almost attacked me, but it didn't. If it is hiding whatever Birlerion and Jaredion are doing up there, then until we know what is going on, take extra precautions, understand?"

"Yes, Pa."

He struggled out of the chair, and then, straightening his clothes, he strode out of the room, leaving Margareth and Germaine staring at each other.

Jerrol returned to Vespers, stepping out of the waystone behind the golden Chapterhouse. He paused, inhaling deeply, trying to calm his speeding pulse. A vein throbbed in his forehead. Did no one understand the seriousness of the situation? The Veil protected them. It had always protected them. They were supposed to be watching it. They should report every discrepancy. Why hadn't they listened to him?

Kayenion trailed after him. "You said Jaredion had been up in the Veilspace? How is that possible?"

"I don't know. It shouldn't be possible. Only the Watchers, myself, and Birlerion should be able to reach that far. Jaredion certainly shouldn't be up there on his own. It's too dangerous. No wonder he was receiving injuries no-one could explain."

"I don't understand. You said the Veil didn't think. How can it be dangerous?"

"The Veil is a contradiction," Jerrol admitted. "It exists to protect Remargaren. It is an inert form, a protection around our planet, but it can snare the unwary in its weave, and it is difficult to escape. Like the twins, Elliarille and Ellaerion, for example; they were trapped for centuries." He paused, his brow furrowing in thought. "And the Veil hid what it was doing," he said slowly, "as it is now. It knows how to hide its actions." He shook his head. "I would never have said that deceit was a trait of the Veil, but it seems I was wrong."

Arriving at the Chapterhouse, they enquired of the porter the whereabouts of the Scholar Deane. "Grab yourself a coffee or something. I won't be long," Jerrol told Kayenion as he went in search of Taelia, and he found her in her office at the top of the tower.

She was staring at the wall. A report sat on her desk in a neat pile. She slowly turned to Jerrol, and he shivered at the worried expression on her face. "Leyarille left me a report of her findings. You need to read this, Jerrol. I'm afraid it could be worse than you think."

"Worse? How can it get any worse? Taelia, Anders invoked the King's Oath, ordered Birlerion to go and get the

Oath from Senti, and then I ordered him to be restrained. Can you imagine what that did to him? No wonder he broke out of the healerie." She stood as he dragged his fingers through his hair. "What have I done? How did it come to this?"

Taelia gathered him in her arms. "It's not your fault, Jerrol. There were a series of events that all conspired to give you the wrong information."

"I didn't help him. Why did I doubt him? He was my friend."

"You put the safety of our world before your friendship. Birlerion would not fault you for that."

"Leyarille will."

"What do you expect? You would have been the same if it was us. Why should Leyarille be any different? She loves him, and he's under a death sentence. You made a mistake, Jerrol. It happens, you are human. Accept it and put right what you can and help the poor man. He is the only one trying to protect us from whatever is happening to the Veil; help him." She pushed him into her chair. "Read it, Jerrol. Your daughter knows how to write a conclusion."

Jerrol rubbed his temple as he began reading. He read faster as he bent over the pages. He shook his head. "It's not possible," he murmured.

"Why not?" Taelia asked.

"It can't be; I couldn't have been so blind."

Taelia bit her lip. "We weren't looking for it, and there was no reason to think Birlerion was anyone other than who he said. He is not only a Lady's Sentinal, he is the protection Leyandrii left for all of us. The second shield no one knew was reinforcing the Veil, anchoring the Veil to Remargaren. If you *had* known, would it have made any difference?"

"Of course it would. I would have believed him."

"Why, Jerrol? What did he ever do to make you doubt

him? You shouldn't need the Lady to remind you to trust your friends."

Jerrol raised his head from the pages, and Taelia stiffened at the sight of his face. His eyes were hard, glinting silver. "He kept important information from us; he lied to me about who he was."

Taelia exhaled, carefully. "Jerrol, love. He never lied to anyone. We never asked him outright. We didn't know to ask any of this. And honestly, we didn't need to know. It was safer that we didn't know."

"That wasn't his decision to make."

"Oh? Why? Because you are the Lord Chancellor? When did the power go to your head? Are you aspiring to be king next?" Taelia's voice pierced him as if she stabbed him with a knife.

"No!" Jerrol flinched back in shock, and then he stiffened, his hand slapping the papers. "Her conclusion is ridiculous. We need the Veil; why would we try and destroy it?"

"Because it would prefer to destroy us?"

"It's protected us for thousands of years; why would it stop now?"

"Leyarille told you, it's in section three. Because the Veil recognised Birlerion."

"That's just her opinion; it doesn't make it correct."

"Why are you being so stubborn, Jerrol? Why will you not consider it *is* possible? Is it because your feelings have been hurt? Because you didn't know everything about your friend?"

"Of course not."

"Leyarille's report explains what is happening to Birlerion. Her reasoning is quite brilliant, in fact. She explains why the Veil looks normal even though it isn't. Her conclusion is clear. The Veil has changed its purpose, and it is targeting Birlerion in an effort to free itself. What we once thought was a mindless protection has evolved over time, and now no longer wants to protect us; it is more interested in destroying us. We can't let that happen. Ascendants are no longer attacking us with wild magic. We don't need the Veil anymore. It is redundant."

"I can't make such a decision. This affects the whole world. We would have to take it before the king, the Administration, the other leaders. This is a theory, unproven at that. It has to be validated."

"Really? Since when?" Taelia leaned forward, her turquoise eyes burning into him. "By whom? That never concerned you before. You seem to have forgotten the issue here. Birlerion has carried this secret for years, centuries, on his own. The only reason that Veil is still protecting us is because of him. He anchors it here so you can control it. Has he ever wavered? No. Has he wavered now? No. Our friend needs help. Birlerion needs your help. What are you going to do about it, before the Veil figures out how to kill him and then kills us all?"

25

___

CHERNI, BIRTOLI

Birlerion awoke to the low murmur of voices. They drifted on the night air, and he identified Leyarille, Tagerill, and Roberion. He was warmed by the concern he could hear in their voices. Easing upright, he looked down at his shredded shirt. A bowl of water and a pile of clean clothes sat waiting beside him. His hand shook as he rinsed off his blood. The Veil had been antagonised by the nearness of the Oath; it knew he had it now, and it would be even more dangerous.

A sudden bout of light headedness made him sway, his stomach lurching; *loss of blood*, his mind supplied. *Scared*, he admitted deep within himself. *You are a sane person, of course you're scared*, he thought, *who wouldn't be?* Uncertainty about what his next steps should be hit him, and then the Oath stirred, and he knew he had to return to Old Vespers. The compulsion swept through him, and he shuddered. He had the Oath. He feared he *was* the Oath, and he had no idea how he was supposed to give it to the king.

Although exhaustion dogged him, he didn't feel any different. Until his heart gave a double thump, and he held his chest in shock. As he stood up, a flush of energy revitalised him; his vision sharpened, and he shivered as his strength returned. He flexed his fist, acknowledging his power; he hadn't realised how much the Veil had sucked away his vitality, his life. It wasn't just the lack of sleep that had been dragging him down, it was the Veil's constant onslaught attacking him. It was as if the Oath had topped him back up and he breathed easily for the first time in months.

Dressing, he hissed as the material scraped the welts on his skin. Shame he couldn't heal himself of his physical wounds. There were far too many, and he wouldn't survive long at this rate. Taking a deep breath, he ducked out of the hut and joined his friends around the fire pit; the aroma of roasted fish reminded him he hadn't eaten lately.

Leyarille rose. She had been sat facing the hut, her eyes watching the door, and before he had taken two steps, she was in front of him. "Birlerion?" she breathed. "Are you alright?"

He let her love wash over him, and muscles relaxed that he hadn't realised had tensed. Leyarille carefully hugged him, lifting her face for a chaste kiss, and then led the way to the clearing.

Tagerill was waiting by the fire. His hug was fierce. "Brother mine, you have some explaining to do," he murmured as he released him.

Birlerion grimaced and hugged him back. "I'm not sure we have the time."

"That much, huh?" Tagerill shook his head. "Who would've believed you could keep a secret for so long?"

Birlerion smiled and wondered which secret Tagerill thought he knew. Sitting where Leyarille pushed him, he accepted a bowl filled with chunks of white fish in an aromatic sauce, and concentrated on eating, using the offered spoon to scoop up the fish. His stomach rebelled for a moment, queasy after so long without, but he forced it down and took the gourd Leyarille passed him.

He hesitated, sadness rippling through him as she knelt beside him. Did she think he didn't know what it meant, in Birtoli, for a single man to accept a gourd from a single woman? If he drank from it, he accepted her claim on him to join together as one. Of course she knew. Her beautiful face was open and vulnerable. He had wanted their Joining to be special, to have their family around them to celebrate their union.

His heart thumped twice in his chest; she was as stubborn as he was. She stared up at him, her silver eyes large and beseeching, so full of love, and all for him. It was so unfair; he could give her so little in return.

Caressing her cheek with gentle fingers, he held her eyes as he deliberately drank from the gourd she had given him.

"Oh, how beautiful," Lilith murmured, a catch in her voice.

"What is?" Roberion turned to her and stiffened as he saw Birlerion hand the gourd to Leyarille. She held his gaze as she drank deeply. "Does she know that she just proposed to him and he's accepted?"

"Of course she knows. As does he."

"Should we say anything?"

"No, I think this is just for them."

"But they need witnesses."

"Do they?" Lilith replied. As they watched, a silver light enveloped the couple, descending from the moonlit sky. It merged with the golden glow that began to emanate from Birlerion and coalesced around him and Leyarille. "I think they have their witnesses," Lilith said as they watched Birlerion place the gourd on the ground. He smoothed his thumbs over Leyarille's cheeks and down her neck. Drawing her into his arms, he kissed her, such a private moment on display for all.

Tagerill cleared his throat and grimaced at them. "Isn't it about time you two got joined?" he asked, shattering the moment, and Roberion laughed, shifting in his seat to draw Tagerill's attention.

Birlerion released Leyarille and grinned, a glint in his eye. "If you insist, Tage."

Leyarille chuckled beside him. "We haven't even told Pa, yet."

"Oh my, is he in for a surprise then." Roberion grinned.

Elder Tuan rose, walked over to them and held his hands over their heads. "My child," he said to Leyarille, "is it truly your wish to join with this man?"

"Yes, Elder."

"My son, is it your wish to join with this woman?"

Birlerion's heart double thumped and a shiver of excitement caught his breath. The timing couldn't have been worse, but he couldn't resist Leyarille's pleading expression. "Yes, Elder."

Elder Tuan bent, grasped Leyarille's hand and then placed it in Birlerion's. Birlerion's cold fingers convulsed around hers. "The Lady blesses you." The Elder grinned as Birlerion leaned into Leyarille and kissed her. "A toast to the happy couple. Lilith! We still have some of the special reserve. I think it's time to celebrate." He smiled. "Congratulations on your Joining. May the Lady bless you, always."

Tagerill's glance flicked around the clearing and back to Birlerion. "Did I miss something here?"

Birlerion laughed, hugging Leyarille. Happiness bubbled under his skin, threatening to explode out of him. "You, Tage? You never miss anything."

Tagerill stopped and glared at them. "Stop messing about. You are not joined. You need a ceremony and stuff!

Taelia will have kittens if you two get joined without her knowing."

"Not everyone needs all the ceremonial stuff," Leyarille replied. "Sometimes, you just need each other."

"You are joking, aren't you?" Tagerill hesitated, glancing from one to the other, and then down to the gourd on the ground. He gulped, and then a slow grin spread across his face. "You're not!" Tagerill strode forward and hauled Birlerion to his feet and embraced him. "Lady's Blessings, brother. Your timing is terrible, but congratulations. Leyarille! You should have held out for the big party!"

"I don't want a party. I only want Birlerion."

Tagerill's expression softened as his eyes gleamed. "Then he is a very lucky man," he whispered as he hugged her tight before releasing her.

Leyarille flushed at his knowing look and sat on the log beside Birlerion. Wrapping an arm around her waist, he drew her closer. His stomach was full of butterflies, and his heart double thumped again, reminding him he needed to be moving. Instead, he hugged Leyarille tighter, no doubt he would pay for the delay later, but for now, it was her time. Elder Tuan instructed his daughter to break out the good stuff, and the celebrations began.

"Don't think this gets you out of explaining what's going on. I have so many questions! Why did Jerrol try to commit you? How did Jaredion get injured? Did you rescue Leyarille in the water?" Tagerill broke off as Lilith offered him a cup; he sniffed it, and his eyes widened.

"Jaredion is hurt?" Birlerion's heart stuttered. "What happened?"

"He's fine." Leyarille hurried to reassure him. "He's recovering in Tagerill's sentinal. Kin'arol took him to Deepwater. The King's Guards shot him with a bolt."

Guilt ripped through Birlerion. He had left Jaredion to fight on his own. "It's my fault. He came to rescue me."

"Thank the Lady, he did," Leyarille said, tugging him back down to the log. "He's your sword, and he always will be."

"About that …" Tagerill began.

"Tomorrow is soon enough to discuss weighty matters," Elder Tuan declared, raising his cup. "Now we celebrate Leyarille and Birlerion, may the Lady watch over you always."

Tagerill watched them with some suspicion before shrugging and gulping his drink.

"Tonight is for family," Elder Tuan said, and Lilith filled Tagerill's cup again.

It was much later, when they were seated around the fire, that Lilith whispered in Leyarille's ear and pointed to a trail of candles. Leyarille blushed and then smiled; she stood, tugging Birlerion to his feet. Tagerill blearily watched them leave. "What is this stuff?" he asked, peering into his cup, and the Elder smiled at him.

Leyarille led Birlerion down the trail, through the fragrant greenery, to a small dell, lit by more candles and lined with soft furs and rugs. Birlerion pulled her to him and bent his head. He kissed her, and she opened her mouth under the pressure of his demanding tongue, and the kiss deepened. She molded herself to him, and then they began undressing each other. Her fingers trailed over his body to his new bandages, and she faltered. "When will it be our time?" she whispered, tasting his skin, inhaling the scent of him.

"Now is our time and forevermore," Birlerion replied as his hands smoothed over her body and they sank onto the furs, so luxurious against their bare skin. Birlerion smiled down at her, aware of the Oath thrumming inside him. "Let me show you."

Bending his head, he slowly kissed his way down her body, exploring her smooth skin, her pert breasts, her flat stomach. Her sleek muscles rippled as she bowed her back, and he trailed his fingers under her ribs and down her sides. She shivered at his touch and threaded her fingers through his hair.

"You are so beautiful," he murmured, leaving a trail of blazing kisses across her stomach.

"And you are mine," she growled as his fingers drifted south and she arched into his caress, eager for more.

"Always and forever," he replied, as his lips followed his fingers, and Leyarille hissed her breath out as she melted under his touch.

"Please," she moaned as he raised his head and he slid up her body, their slick skin sliding against each other as he finally entered her, and she gasped as she wrapped her legs around his waist and thrust upwards, accepting all that he offered, and he groaned into her mouth as they kissed, frantic and messy.

She was so hot, sheathing him in all-consuming heat and pure ecstasy. He shuddered as she plundered his mouth and pressed so tight against him; he forgot where he ended and she began. Slow, sensuous movements quickened into frantic thrusts until they peaked, shuddering into each other's arms as their brains briefly shut down and then they collapsed into the furs as one.

The candles were guttering when Leyarille finally exhaled against his chest. "I've missed you so much."

"Me too. I wish we never left Westermaine that morning. I'm sorry, my love, I left your ring there. You'll have to wait until we go home to get it."

She smiled, pressing soft kisses on his salty skin. Her smile widened. He was finally all hers. "I don't need a ring to prove you're mine, but I'm glad to hear you were prepared."

She smoothed her hand over his chest, waiting for the double thump she had noticed during their love making. "What is that?"

"The Oath." He closed his eyes and sighed. "I have to take the Oath to the king." Birlerion shifted as the compulsion stirred.

"Why would it be the Oath?" Leyarille stared down at him with a frown. "What did you do?"

"I had to bond with the Oath to pick it up."

"Bond? What does that mean?" Leyarille stiffened, and Birlerion cupped her face.

"Dear heart, I don't really know, yet. I need to speak to Marguerite. But I am here, and all yours. I will explain what I can, when I know more." Sadness swept through him as her beautiful glow faded as worry clouded her expression.

"I hope it is as easy to put the Oath back down." Birlerion didn't answer. Her fingers swirled over his shoulder, leaving his skin tingling. "There is something else you haven't told me."

Birlerion sighed; there was so much she didn't know about him. "Like what?" he said, keeping his voice neutral.

"The Shield of Remargaren," she murmured against his skin.

He closed his eyes.

"You don't have to tell me," she said quietly.

Birlerion grimaced. "I would tell you all, dearest, there just isn't the time. But the shield, yes, well ..." Holding up his hand, he rotated his wrist, and a blue sparkle flashed around his hand. "I can push out a shield to protect people, only people, not material things."

"I said it was you who protected the people of Vespers," Leyarille said with satisfaction.

"Yes, but I couldn't protect Leyandrii or Guerlaire; we lost them."

"She was pure magic. There was no way she could have stayed, as was Guerlaire; it wasn't them she wanted you to protect."

"I suppose not, but for many years I thought I had failed." He shrugged. "I was very young," he said, a bit embarrassed.

Leyarille's eyes filled with tears. "Oh, Birlerion, you never failed anyone."

Grinning, he kissed her nose. "You can be my supporter any day."

"What about the Veil? It thinks you can free it, doesn't it? Can you? How do we stop it?"

"We need to speak to your father, but I think it's time we got rid of the Veil. I think it's served its time. The Veil is turning against Remargaren. It's purpose has changed. It was always a reluctant protector, but now, it is actively attacking us. I'm not sure I can restrain it without destroying it, even with the Oath."

Leyarille nodded, thoughtfully. "The Watchers aren't able to control it. They do not see what the Veil is capable of. How do we destroy it?"

"I'm not sure, but I was hoping your father might have some ideas."

"I wouldn't count on it; wouldn't he see removing the Veil as a threat to the safety of Remargaren?"

"You're probably right, but I can't think of a way to contain it, and I won't survive its continued attentions. And much as I hate to say it, I ought to get some sleep while you are here to keep me safe. Are you sure Jaredion is alright?" His smile slipped, and she kissed him.

"I told you; he is safe in Tagerill's sentinal, and he won't let him out until he is healed. He'll meet us in Old Vespers. Sleep, Birlerion, while you can."

· · ·

The next morning they woke entwined in each other's arms, snuggled under the furs. "Well, Lady Descelles, what can I offer you for breakfast?" Birlerion murmured against deliciously heated skin. He inhaled. She smelt so divine he almost melted.

Leyarille pulled his head down towards her. "My dear Lord Descelles, you know perfectly well what I want for breakfast," she whispered against his lips as she rolled him over and began kissing him. "But this morning, it's my turn, so you just lay there and enjoy." She left a trail of kisses across his chest, her hand paused over his heart as the double thump caught her attention. "I can't get over that," she murmured and then suckled on his nipple, then moved to the other one as Birlerion shuddered as his core tightened and she continued exploring. The soft sensation of her kissing each of his too prominent ribs made him squirm as she moved down his body. He shivered at the light butterfly kisses, and she continued, smiling as he flinched when she reached the middle. He was so ready for her.

She kissed him, and his hips rose under her light caress. He couldn't help it. When he reached for her, she slapped his hand away and set to work. She stroked him, firmly, and he gasped. He was so hot and so hard for her. She kissed the swollen tip, ran her tongue around the head and then down his length before she swallowed him, and his back arched up off the ground. His hands clenched in the furs as the white-hot sensations swept through him, and she smiled as she showed him what breakfast in bed should look like.

Birlerion felt bludgeoned; he wasn't sure if he could move, let alone face anyone else. He tightened his embrace around his wife, and she slid against him as she twined her legs with his. Rolling her over, he hovered above her for a moment before he began worshipping her body again. He hadn't gotten over how amazing she was. She was insatiable and generous and loving. Being joined had broken down any final barriers, and they had opened to each other completely. He felt vulnerable and yet more protected. Weak and yet stronger. Ensnared and yet freed.

It was enlightening.

He would never give her up.

26

CHERNI

It was much later that morning when Birlerion and Leyarille ventured out into the central clearing and demurely sat on the logs. Accepting a mug of a local brew, Birlerion smiled. It was hot and fragrant and very soothing. Good for hangovers, he thought, as Tagerill staggered out of a hut, groaning, his face grey and puffy.

"Too much of the good stuff?" Birlerion asked with a grin.

"What was it he was giving us?" Tagerill asked, holding his head. His eyes were bloodshot, and he swallowed convulsively.

Birlerion chuckled. "I was expecting you to be on good form this morning. Maybe you should just sleep it off, Tage."

Tagerill snorted and then gulped his tea.

Roberion and Lilith joined them, and Leyarille flushed under their teasing eyes. "Sleep well?" Roberion asked with a grin as Lilith dug him in the ribs.

"Not really," Birlerion replied as Leyarille flushed deeper. Chuckling, he kissed her ear, and she leaned into him.

Tagerill leered at them. "What are you two like? We have

more serious subjects to be discussing. Like what do we do about the Veil?"

Birlerion observed his friends before he started speaking, "Just to be clear, I am not, nor have I ever been, deranged. When Ellie took me up to the Veil, I believe it recognised me; it believes it can use me to get free. I was one of those involved in binding it to the Lady's will to protect Remargaren, and I'm sure it believes I am its escape." He paused for a moment, collecting his thoughts. "My defences must fall when I sleep, and only Leyarille can keep it away. Jaredion is my alternate defence, but it exhausts him, and he can only defend me for so long."

"And he's not available right now," Tagerill said.

"What is it about Leyarille that enables her to protect you?" Roberion asked.

"The Bloodstone. My father absorbed it before I was born, and he must have passed some of the protection on to me," Leyarille said.

Tagerill nodded carefully. Rubbing his eyes, he glanced at his brother. "And of course you were involved with the rebinding as well."

"Yes, but it was Ellie who betrayed me; the Veil recognised me when she dragged me up with her."

Tagerill frowned at him. "The Shield of Remargaren. I can't believe you never told me."

"There was never quite the right moment."

"In over three thousand years? There must have been one moment you could have told me."

Birlerion pretended to consider. "No, I don't think there was."

Tagerill scowled. "What else haven't you told us?"

"Tage, we don't have the time. I have to return the Oath to the king, and we have to figure out how to destroy the Veil for good."

"Why for good?"

"During the Veil's last attack was when I was in Senti, it shared images, horrific images of Remargaren in ruins. I believe it wants to destroy all of us, not just me. I am its route to freedom. The Veil will kill me and then destroy the Remargaren we know and love; it's already begun," he said, keeping his voice calm as Tagerill exclaimed in horror and Leyarille flinched beside him.

"But if I'm with you, it can't reach you."

"You won't always be at my side."

Her face said otherwise, but she said, "If not me, then Jaredion."

"Would you expect me to leave a threat hanging over you? I can't live like that, my love, and nor can he."

"But to destroy the Veil ..." She hesitated.

"Say it," he said.

"Won't you have to use the Oath?"

Birlerion waited as the others exclaimed in horror. That had been his initial response. The Oath protected Remargaren and everyone who lived there. He couldn't use it. But the Oath was the only magical source in Remargaren, there was nothing else he could think of that would give him enough power to overwhelm the Veil.

"Yes."

"But you have to take it to the king," Tagerill said.

"You can't use it. You'll destroy it." Lilith was having palpitations, and Roberion glared at him.

Birlerion shrugged. "I can't see any other way. If we allow the Veil to continue, it will destroy Remargaren."

"But you are the only one who can carry it," Leyarille said, concern shining through the tears in her eyes. "Love, if you take the Oath to the Veil, there is no guarantee you will come back."

Birlerion smiled. "There is no guarantee any of us will survive one day to the next."

"There are some things that are more dangerous than others, and taking the Oath to the Veil would be one of them."

"I am the Shield, and if that means I have to forfeit my life for the people, then so be it. It has always been that way."

"No," Leyarille said.

Tagerill glanced at her pale face. "She's right. Just because you've been the shield doesn't mean you get to commit suicide; I thought you said you weren't mad?"

Birlerion grinned. "That's why I am open to any suggestions you may have. I would very much like to not commit suicide."

They hashed over one crazy idea after another, but nothing that trumped using the Oath. There was nothing else magical in all of Remargaren.

"How do you know the Oath will even work? What would you have to do?" Tagerill finally asked.

Birlerion stared at the fire and then raised his hand. "It's not just the Oath," he said as he rotated his wrist and the blue sparkle flashed around his skin. He pushed it out in front of him, and it formed a blue transparent shield, undulating between them. "The Oath would give me access and the power, and with this, I could protect Remargaren from the backlash."

"Backlash?" Roberion repeated.

"Of course. If I implode that much power, there would be a backlash."

"No," Tagerill said. "There has to be another way. I am not losing my brother."

Birlerion threw him a sharp glance. "Would you rather lose Miranda? Or Alyssa or Jaredion? Or all of them?"

"It's not a choice, dammit."

"It is," Birlerion said softly. "It has always been a choice. It is what we do. We protect those who cannot protect themselves."

"No," Leyarille's voice was cold. "Promise me, it doesn't have to be you. You can pass it on to someone else."

"Like who? Leyarille. Who can I pass it to? You? Tagerill? Roberion? Can any of you create a shield?"

"You could teach us; we could help you."

"Show me your shield and I will." He cupped her face, taking the sting out of his words.

Her face blanched. "Birlerion," she whispered.

"I'm sorry, my love." He looked around the faces watching him in concern. "I suggest we take the Oath back to the king and then have this discussion with Jerrol. He is the Lady's Captain. Maybe Leyandrii will give him some guidance."

"They'll just lock you up again. They don't believe you," Leyarille said bitterly.

"They can't lock me up from the Veil. We need to reach the Lady. Marguerite is exhausted and focused on the Land; she looks inwards not out. We need Leyandrii. Pass the word, call Leyandrii. Maybe if we all call her, she'll hear us." He shifted in his seat. He needed to get moving. The urgency to move was building. "Roberion, can you drop us at Mortelin? We can get the waystone at Marchwood."

Roberion nodded. "Of course."

"Then, unless anyone has any better suggestions, that is what we will do." The compulsion eased as he made plans to return to Vespers.

Birlerion wrapped his arms around Leyarille as they watched the port of Mortelin approach. "Let's hope there isn't a welcoming committee," he murmured.

"Uncle Tage is ready for a fight. I think he might barrel over anyone who tries to detain you."

"Seeing as we are headed for Vespers, hopefully, all will be well."

"Jennery and Alyssa went to Old Vespers. They'll already be there when we arrive. Even Jaredion should be there," Tagerill said from behind them.

"And Mir'elle and her men will help you," Leyarille said.

"She'll be too busy preparing for her Joining." Birlerion dipped his head. "It's what you should have had; a full ceremony in front of everyone. I am sorry, Leyarille."

Leyarille leaned against him. "I was the one who propositioned you, remember? And besides, I don't need one. I just want you, Birlerion. Promise me, promise you'll come back."

"Always, my love."

Roberion cleared his throat. "Alright, you lovebirds. It's time to leave." After hugging them tightly, he assisted them over the side into the small rowboat. Tagerill rocked the boat as he joined them. He quickly sat, and the sailors rowed them over to the quay. Birlerion wasn't surprised to find the quay silently filling up with King's Guards as they climbed up the stone steps.

Tagerill swore, loudly.

"Tagerill, don't, they are only following their orders."

"Orders be damned, what does Jerrol think he's doing?" Tagerill continued cursing under his breath.

"Protecting Remargaren, I suppose." Birlerion helped Leyarille up onto the quay and turned to the senior officer. "Captain Benson, we meet again."

"Yes, sir, we are your escort to Marchwood."

"Very well, carry on then." Birlerion smiled at his brother. "At least they've brought the horses, saves us having to find some."

Birlerion followed Benson through his ranks of men, and

they closed in around him, cutting Leyarille and Tagerill off. He sighed. Were they really expecting to drag him in as a criminal? Tagerill exploded, and that was when Birlerion found out he was no longer First Administrator. The king had revoked his position and replaced him.

Birlerion was quite relieved if he was honest. But he could see that was the final straw for Tagerill. He raised his voice to carry over his guards, who were being very conscientious. "Tage, it doesn't matter. I need to see the king. We'll deal with it after."

"It *does* matter. How can he treat you so behind your back?"

Shrugging, Birlerion mounted the horse they escorted him to. The guards closed in around him, and they led him out of the harbour. He wondered how long they had been waiting but didn't bother asking. Somehow, he didn't think he'd get an answer.

He mused on their destination, Marchwood. The guards couldn't go through the waystone, so were they taking him back to the healerie? If they did, he would summon the king to him. Shifting in his saddle, he looked back at Tagerill, and the guards either side of him stiffened. What had they been told?

Tagerill raised his eyebrows, his expression furious, and Birlerion faced forward again.

He was pleasantly surprised when they rode up to the Marchwood waystone. "Which waystone? The chapterhouse or the palace?" Birlerion asked as he dismounted.

Benson scowled at him. "You will go where you're taken, and to make sure, Healer Tarvin will accompany you."

Birlerion felt a prick in his neck and spun. Tarvin jumped back.

"That was quite unnecessary. The king has invoked the

Oath y'know." Birlerion staggered. "I have no choice but to return to Vespers. I was not going to cause any trouble."

Leyarille pushed her way through. "What do you think you're doing? He has rights. You just can't go around attacking people."

"He is a danger to us all," Benson replied pompously, "and the chancellor wants him detained."

"How dare you." Leyarille was magnificent in her anger. "He hasn't laid a finger on any of you. You should all be ashamed of yourselves. I will be lodging a complaint with your superiors and the king!"

"S-sorry to interrupt, but if you don't want to carry me, suggest we go now," Birlerion slurred as Anterion stepped forward.

"Birlerion," he whispered, horrified. Anterion grabbed his arm as he swayed. "They never said it was you."

"Sentinal, if you would be so good to take us to the palace," Benson snapped as Birlerion was tugged forward.

Peering owlishly at Leyarille, he said, "See you at home, my love, don't be late." As he stepped into the waystone, he felt the king invoke the oath *again*. He fell as the Oath twisted inside him. "Leyarille," his cry was cut off as he landed in a pile of hot sand, face down. He choked and rolled over on his side, spitting out grit. His head swirled as he gained his knees in the burning sands, but the sedation hit, and he crumpled in a heap.

27

OLD VESPERS, VESPIRI

Tarvin and Anterion stepped out of the waystone outside Bryce's office at the palace. When Tarvin turned to assist Birlerion, he was holding empty air. He was unceremoniously shoved out of the way as Tagerill and Leyarille stepped out. "Where is he?" Tagerill's voice was harsh.

"He cried out. What did you do?" Leyarille had Tarvin by the throat, and Deron launched upright in shock, balancing against the wall.

"He-he disappeared."

"You had hold of him. You should have gone wherever he went. Where is he?"

"I don't know. He should be here." The healer heaved.

"Outside," Deron snapped. "Don't even think of hurling in here." He pushed Tarvin out the door, and Tagerill followed him as Bryce came out of his office at the commotion.

"How much did you give him?" Tagerill demanded.

Tarvin gaped at him as he tried to control his stomach.

"Two chimes. He'll be out for at least two chimes." And he vomited over the gravel.

"Who will be?" Bryce asked, as he stood watching them from the doorway of his office.

Tagerill glared at Bryce. "This dimwit sedated Birlerion again and then lost him in a waystone. He could be anywhere, unconscious."

"You mean wherever he has landed, he will be asleep and unprotected?"

Leyarille shivered as a chill settled in her stomach. "Anterion, check all the waystones in Vespiri, Tagerill you take Birtoli and Elothia, I'll check Terolia. Meet back here." Leyarille stepped back into the waystone. She came out in Mistra, searched the surrounding area, and stepped back into the waystone to Melila. A quick search only revealed burning sand, so she stepped again and again until her frantic mind could no longer remember the locations. She returned to Old Vespers, drained and desperate.

Deron was beside her in a moment as she swayed. "I couldn't find him. I need a map. I couldn't remember any more waystones."

"Sit down a minute. You're exhausted, you can't keep using the waystone and not pay the price," Bryce said as he hovered over her.

"I need a map. I'll mark off the waystones I searched, but he wasn't there."

Tagerill appeared in the office. "He's not there."

"Where would he go?" Leyarille was almost in tears.

"He was barely conscious. I doubt he would have been able to select anywhere." Tagerill wasn't much better, his face grey and strained.

Anterion appeared, a worried scowl etched on his face. "He's not in the Watches. I am so sorry, Leyarille. He collapsed; it must have been the sedation. It hit him really quick."

Leyarille scowled at the young healer still folded over on the steps, clasping his stomach and groaning. "That's all they seem to know. You'd think they'd find another way, wouldn't you?"

Jerrol appeared in the doorway. "What's going on?" He took a step back at the angry expressions on the Sentinal's faces.

"You couldn't leave well alone, could you?" Tagerill spat. "He was on his way here. You knew he had to come back here; the king invoked the Oath on him, for Lady's sake. Yet you still had him arrested and *escorted* here." The scorn in Tagerill's voice cut deep, and Jerrol flinched.

"It was for his safety; they were his protection," Jerrol said quickly.

"Bollocks was it. They sedated him and then they lost him in the waystone."

"You mean you let him escape?" Jerrol asked, turning to the healer.

Leyarille watched as Tagerill tore her father apart; he was livid. She leaned her chin on her hand and would have enjoyed every moment if not for the fact that Birlerion was lost.

Her father took it all, like a rock being battered by ferocious waves. Leyarille was secretly impressed. She would never have been able to face down such a tongue lashing. He was pale, but he took it.

Tagerill finally wound down. "By the Lady, Jerrol, you have got to get your priorities straight; you don't treat anyone the way you've treated Birlerion. I would never have believed it of you."

"We need the map of the waystones," Leyarille interrupted. "We've checked all the ones we know. There must be others. Wherever he is, he's unconscious. The healer said he would be out for at least two chimes, and anything could happen to him in that time."

Jerrol paled even further. "You mean it wasn't his choice?"

Leyarille glared at him. "We were on our way here when your toadies surrounded us and crept up on him from behind as usual and bungled it all. He would've been here if you hadn't interfered. He was coming to see you and the king."

"I'll get the map." Jerrol whipped out the door, and Leyarille held her aching head.

"Here." Deron offered a cup of coffee.

Leyarille smiled her thanks and took the mug.

Jerrol returned with the parchment which marked the location of the waystones and laid it on Deron's desk. "Here, which ones are still possible?"

Leyarille leaned over the map, her temples pounding. "Marmera and the salt flats; I didn't know there was one up there."

Tagerill stepped into the waystone.

He was soon back. "He's not there."

"But where could he be?" Leyarille gulped. "You don't get stuck in a waystone if you're unconscious, do you?"

"No, people have travelled through fine, even when unconscious." Jerrol stared at the map. "There must be a waystone not marked on here. Tagerill, did Guerlaire create any odd waystones? Ones not used much?"

Tagerill rubbed his neck. "Guerlaire shut them down if they were only temporary. When we did the raids on the Ascendants arrays, we used them to get in and out. They were never used again." He stared out the office window, deep in thought. "There was one, only I don't know where it was. I only remember because Birlerion shut it down, and Leyandrii went berserk. Serillion would have known because he was there. *Maybe Niallerion will know. I remember him saying he had never seen the Lady so angry. He was there when Birlerion rescued Guerlaire and Serillion.*"

"Anterion, could you go and ask Niallerion to join us?" Jerrol asked.

Leyarille sipped her coffee and watched her father. He looked tired, aged. His receding hair line accentuated it; she had never noticed before. She stiffened. No, she would not forgive him. Her husband was lost, had been ill-treated, and now his life was at risk, and it was all his fault.

Anterion stepped out of the waystone with Niallerion, a thin dark-haired Sentinal. He flashed a glance around the room, and Leyarille knew he had assessed each of them. This was the man who had designed and built the harbour walls at Senti. He was a very clever man, now residing in Stoneford with his family.

"Leyarille, I'm so sorry about Birlerion." Straight to the point like a sharp knife. Jerrol winced.

She stood to hug him. "Thank you, Niallerion. We need your help to find him."

"So I hear. Whose bright idea was it to sedate him? You know how much he hates it."

"The fact is they did, and we can't find him. He collapsed as he entered the waystone. We've checked every known waystone location, and he isn't there. Wherever he is, Niallerion, he is unconscious. We have to find him and fast."

Niallerion cast an eye over the map. "Looks like they are all marked."

Tagerill spoke up. "Wasn't there one that Birlerion closed down? That time Leyandrii tore him off a strip. Do you know where that one was?"

Niallerion shrugged. "It was shut down at both ends." He grinned, raising his arm as if he held a bow. "Birlerion stood, his bow appeared in his hand, and he was gone; the next instant he was back with Guerlaire and Serillion. It was chaos. He was gone for about two minutes, and he'd emptied his quiver. Leyandrii went crazy." He shivered. "Boy, was she mad."

"Do you know where Guerlaire went?"

"The rumour was that Guerlaire went for the Blood-stone. It was somewhere in Terolia. Birlerion heard his call for help. He dragged both Guerlaire and Serillion back through the waystone and shut it down. We never spoke of it again after Leyandrii finished with us."

Leyarille sympathised with Leyandrii. She'd had a lot to contend with; Birlerion and Guerlaire, it seemed, always found trouble.

"That doesn't help us find Birlerion. And he was unconscious, so he couldn't have reopened a waystone," Tagerill said, frowning in thought.

Jerrol gaped at them. "Is the fact that Guerlaire found the Bloodstone in Terolia not of interest to you?"

Tagerill scowled at him. "Old history, it is no more. You destroyed it."

"But it was found in Terolia, an item powerful enough to destroy all magic and bring down the Veil, if Leyarille is right. The Veil is after its freedom, and Birlerion needs something powerful enough to stop it," Jerrol pointed out.

Leyarille cocked her head. Had her father read her report? The question was, did he believe it?

"The Oath would do that, wouldn't it?" Niallerion asked.

"He has the Oath?" Jerrol asked, looking around him. "Come to my office, we can't talk about this here."

Once they were all settled in his office, rather crowded with so many tall Sentinals and Bryce squeezed in, Jerrol repeated his question. "Does Birlerion have the Oath?"

Leyarille nodded. "Yes. The king ordered him to go and get it. We were on our way here when he got diverted."

"He intended on giving it up to the king?"

"Of course, he was compelled by the King's Oath. He only went to Cherni to get it because the king instructed him to."

"Cherni? He found it in Cherni? Not Senti?"

"Marguerite moved it, or so the Elder said."

"Where is Marguerite?"

"We don't know, but Birlerion said we needed to call on the Lady for help, not Marguerite."

"Could the Oath have taken over when Birlerion lost consciousness? Jerrol, does the Oath think? Could it have its own agenda?" Niallerion asked.

Jerrol frowned in thought. "The Oath protects. I believe the Lady created it when she created the Veil. The King's Oath is an extension of it. Protection from without and within," he murmured to himself. "It is separate to the Land, and it has a degree of sentiency, but it has never directly intervened that I am aware of."

"So it's unlikely the Oath can act on its own; it would need Birlerion," Niallerion stated.

"Or whomever the Oath Keeper is at the time," Jerrol agreed. "He could be anywhere. What could the Oath possibly need?"

The Sentinals looked at each other blankly.

"Or," Bryce said dryly from the corner, "the king interfered again. He has been getting impatient, Jerrol, especially when he heard Birlerion went for the Oath."

Jerrol stiffened. "That is all too likely. Anders could have called him. That would have caused the Oath to react."

"You mean this could be the king's fault?" Leyarille's jaw dropped open, and she snapped it shut. "We're talking about Birlerion's life here. Does the king not understand?"

"Not well enough, obviously. Let me go speak with him, wait here for me. I'll be as quick as I can."

There was silence after Jerrol closed the door, then Niallerion started ticking off items on his fingers. "One, we know Birlerion has the Oath. Two, we know he is currently unconscious, so the Oath is stuck. Three, even if the king invoked the Oath, we have no way of knowing how that affected Birlerion, or where he is." He shrugged, his thin face grave. "There is no way we can find him."

"The Arifels. Ari can find him," Leyarille said, raising her head.

Four Sentinals called Ari. He exploded into the air in front of them, chittering in distress. "I'm sorry, I'm sorry, we didn't mean to scare you," Leyarille soothed as she coaxed him onto her hand. "We've lost Birlerion, he needs our help. Do you know where he is?"

They were bombarded with images of rolling sand dunes. "Terolia? Where in Terolia?"

The dunes gave way to a dried-up river bed, the sides steep, the bed baked hard. A train of beige camels crested a dune and worked their way down the other side, blending with their surroundings. Men walked beside them wrapped in brown robes; little was left exposed to identify them. Chains swayed against the camel's sides as they rocked; Leyarille could almost hear them clinking. The camel train met a wagon train jolting over the sun-baked terrain.

"Slavers?" Tagerill asked, frowning at a sight Bryce couldn't see. "There are no slavers anymore; Jerrol stamped that out years ago."

"Opportunists?" Niallerion suggested.

"Now that is more likely," Tagerill agreed. "Question is, did they find Birlerion?"

The angle changed, and a honey gold stallion came into view, galloping down the riverbed, the Kharma ridge rising behind him. Leyarille gasped. "Is that Kino? How can he be there? He's in Deepwater, isn't he?"

Tagerill straightened in excitement. "That's the Kharma Ridge. Ari, can you take us to Birlerion? Is he still there?"

Ari burbled sadly. He left them with an image of Birlerion collapsed in the sand, his silver eyes half-open, his bare chest bloodied, in the middle of an arena, surrounded by rising tiers of seats, dilapidated and crumbling. His tattered cloak stirred around him as a blood red sun cast a crimson tinge over the arena and stained the swirls of agitated clouds churning above him. The crown of columns rising from the top level of seats were shattered and stone fragments tumbled down, blocking the rows—the remains of an arena reminiscent of death and destruction.

Tagerill hissed his breath out, his face paling. "There is no such arena in Terolia," he said, a tremor in his voice. "There is no such place in Remargaren. That arena is a myth."

Ari chittered at them, scolding, and then blinked out of sight.

28

SOME TIME, SOME PLACE

Birlerion stirred. A lethargy dragged at his limbs, and he was hot, thirsty, and uncomfortable. The Veil snarled at him, and he stiffened as he struggled up out of the cloying miasma of whatever they had given him. Lady help him. When would he be free of over-zealous healers and their needles?

He blinked and the Veil struck as he grappled with his unexpected surroundings. He spasmed as a strand wrapped itself around his chest, scoring his skin, and his foot caught against something hard as he gasped for breath. The Veil released him with a low snarl, and he blearily opened his eyes and peered around him.

He was being jolted against a hard metal frame. Flexing his shoulders, he tried to unscrunch himself, but there was barely room to move. A cramp struck in his thigh, and he massaged the muscle as he tried to stretch, a hiss of breath escaping his lips. His shirt rubbed his new welt and absorbed the leaking blood.

"I wouldn't bother, mate. You ain't getting out any time soon."

"Where am I?"

"Heatstroke does it to yer. Yer was found collapsed, that's why yer not tied up. They didn't expect yer to wake up. 'spect they were hoping they could offload yer before yer came round."

"Offload me?" Birlerion tried to peer through the gloom towards the speaker. The heat was stifling and the air oppressive. He was in a cage, surrounded by other cages, which were stacked on top of each other, and the stink of unwashed humanity and piss unlocked a flood of memories he'd rather not think about.

He choked as bile rose in his throat.

"They weren't sure what to do with yer. Passing yer up the line I heard."

"Where am I?"

"Lost mate, yer lost. Yer won't be found now."

"Who captured us?"

"Don't make no difference. We ain't coming back. We're all lost." The man hunched his shoulder and stopped speaking.

"Please, I don't understand. *Where are we?*"

"Best yer don't know, lad, best yer don't know," the voice was a whisper merging with the flapping of the canvas.

The wagon jolted to a halt, and the cover was lifted. A bucket of water was flung at the captives and the cover pulled back down. Birlerion stripped his shirt off and mopped up what moisture he could. It dripped on his bare skin from above, and he froze as he caught a black feral glare gleaming at him through the bars.

"Thass my water."

"It's my shirt," Birlerion replied as he sucked up what moisture he could. What a waste. Most of the water dripped out the bottom of the cages, which was no doubt their intent. Torturing them with what they couldn't have. He shrugged back into his shirt, the damp material cooling his skin. How had he ended up here? Leyandrii must be really upset with him.

Trying to shift into a more comfortable position set off a cramp in his calf, and he groaned as he massaged his leg. He was so thirsty, cramps were the least of his worries. He managed to shift around to the front of his cage, but there was no lock to pick. The weight of the cage above kept him contained. Peering through the canvas, his view revealed nothing but dried out, hard-baked dirt. He could safely assume he was somewhere in Terolia, but he had no idea where or why.

He curled back up. His long legs bent awkwardly as the wagon shuddered around them, and groans and mutters punctuated the creak of the protesting wood. It was dark when the wagon next stopped and their evening meal was thrown at them, half of it bouncing off the metal cages, followed by another bucket of water. Birlerion concentrated on collecting as much water as he could.

No one spoke to them. The cover was tugged back down, and they were left in their cages until morning, where those who had managed to sleep were awoken as the wagon lurched forward and began its jolting journey to wherever they were going.

Birlerion was stiff and cramped, and his chest stung as sweat dribbled down into the welts. He had nodded off once and woken to the gasping pain of the Veil, his hand clamped around his sword, and although he called Jaredion for help, the Veilspace was empty except for him.

Shuddering awake, he spent the night reciting the Lady's prayer and the Mother's blessing. Over and over. "Lady protect us, guard our health," he mumbled out loud, forgetting where he was.

"Hah, no point asking the gods for help. They don't care. Youse got to prove yourself here. Earn the right to speak. Otherwise, they don't listen," the man in the neighbouring cage said.

Birlerion jerked back against the bars. "What?"

"You got cloth ears or summat? You gotta prove yourself then they'll help you."

"Prove? How?"

The man cackled. "Make sure yer can pay the price first though; the sorta help you get ain't always what you want."

That Birlerion could believe. If the Lady expected him to earn her help, then he would just have to earn it. "Is any of this real?" he whispered.

"Of course it's real. You're the one creating it!"

"Me? I've never seen this place before."

"Then whatever you're facing out there has to be a right nightmare for you to come up with this as a way to escape it," the man grumbled.

"This isn't my choice."

"It must be. Who'd choose the Mother's testing to escape somewhere else? I wouldn't."

"Mother's testing?" Birlerion replied, his stomach dropping. It couldn't be. "But you're here on this wagon. Why are you being tested?"

The man huffed out his breath. "Because you brought me here. It's your fault. These slavers were going to Mistra. But no! You had to divert them *here* of all places."

Birlerion frowned in confusion. "But there are no slavers anymore and we've never met. How can I imagine you? How can I imagine any of this?" He flung his hand out in frustration and caught the bars. Stinging pain made him jerk his arm back in as he gripped his bruised fingers. The pain was real enough.

Birlerion knew *he* hadn't brought them here. He didn't know where here was. The Oath must have taken over when he collapsed and brought them here for a reason. Unease stirred in his gut. The reason escaped him. Had Kirin been right? Was he going mad? He eased his tense shoulders. Why was Leyandrii making it so difficult?

He jerked out of another Veil-induced awakening with the answer on his lips. She wasn't. Leyandrii was trying to work within the boundaries that had been set. She was trying to help him, he knew it; the certainty percolated through his bones and the Oath stirred at his shoulder. She was trying to get her mother, the All Mother, to help him.

The wagon came to an abrupt halt. The cover was ripped off, and they were blinded by the brilliant midday sun, a burnished gold, so ancient it looked bronze. Before he could react, wooden poles were pushed through the top crates and they were lifted into the air. Poles were rammed through his cage, scoring his shoulder as he tried to squeeze out of the way. From the screams it seemed someone had failed to move in time.

His cage was shunted off the wagon and positioned against a gaping black hole. One end was raised, and he was pushed out into the hole. It was all so quick; a tried and tested process.

He tumbled down the chute and landed in a heap on a stone floor. He hissed as welts met bruises. A slab thudded shut, blocking out the scintillating light, trapping him in his hole. Heavy, suffocating heat enveloped him, ragged clothes stuck to sweat-slick skin. Salt-laced moisture pooled, dribbled, and seeped into angry sores.

Searching around him on his hands and knees, he found he had room to lay down, but he couldn't stand up. The walls were smooth. They were split by a seam which suggested some sort of opening, but the stone didn't give when he pushed. He stretched out with a sigh of relief. Working his way through *Acknowledgement* lying down was a novelty, but his muscles appreciated the exercise. Resting his head on his arm, he considered what he could be possibly facing.

He had no weapons, except his sword in the Veil space, which was weird, but he wasn't complaining; it was better than nothing. He didn't know where his sword came from; could he be reaching? Swirling his hand, he stared at the blue sparkle that flowed around his wrist. For a moment, he visualised his sling on the table in his bedchamber in Westermaine, and reaching, he raised his eyebrows when it appeared in his hand. He sat up, banging his head against the stone ceiling, and the sling disappeared.

Cringing away from the stone, he held his head. "Ow, ow, ow." His head thumped in time with his curses.

There was no way to tell time, but he had completed Apeiron from Acknowledgement to Acceptance many times over before a tunnel was opened and a breath of air entered. He crawled down it towards the light. Climbing to his feet with relief, he stretched aching back muscles, and he slowly rotated.

He was in an arena, an empty arena. The air warped and shimmered, distorting the stone columns before they settled. Seated stone tiers rose around him to meet a wall of columns rising to the sky. An unfamiliar sky adorned by a bronze-red sun, which beat down on him all the same, arced above him. Swirling clouds crept over the arena, blocking some of the heat but not the weird red tinge. He wore a tattered cloak which flapped in the sudden breeze. The air was cool on his skin, his shirt shredded by blood-rimmed slashes, baring his chest. Blood seeped from the welts on his skin, staining the cloth as he slowly walked into the middle of the arena.

He stopped walking when a booming voice aggravated his headache. Squinting around him, he raised a hand to shield his eyes. He thought the voice was female, but it was too encompassing and indistinct to tell. It resonated through his bones, a vibration deep in his soul, and it reminded him of the Land and the gods. His stomach twisted. The other prisoner had said the Mother's testing. Why would Leyandrii's mother, the All Mother, want to test him? "Who are you? What do you want?"

Many leagues away, Jaredion lurched to his feet in Tager-ill's sentinal, spinning as he searched the empty room. "Birlerion?"

Birlerion froze. "Jaredion?"

"Yes, where are you, Birlerion? I'll be there as soon as I can."

"I, uh," Birlerion paused as Jaredion materialised on one of the lower tiers of the arena. He had a white shirt in his hand and his sword in the other, a thick bandage still wrapped around half his torso. "I was going to say I don't know. Are you alright? I am so sorry Jaredion. I never meant for you to get hurt."

"I'm fine. It's not your fault."

"How did you get here?"

Jaredion patted his chest and then the stone seat before springing to his feet. "I'm not sure. Am I here?" He twisted. "Where is here?"

Birlerion began to laugh. An irritated voice boomed out, and Jaredion stilled, looking up with an awed expression on his face.

"Did you hear what she said?" Birlerion asked.

"She said you're allowed one more on the testing ground. One more what? What testing ground?"

Leyarille appeared beside Jaredion, and she gasped as she jumped to her feet and dashed across the arena to Birlerion, her cloudy hair billowing around her. "Lady be praised, darling. I'm so glad you're alright. I was so worried."

Birlerion stood frozen with shock as she grabbed him. "You're real," he said in surprise.

"Of course I'm real," she said, hugging him. He hugged her back. She, in turn, frowned at the scene around her. "Where are we? Oh, this is the arena before it was destroyed."

"What arena?" Birlerion asked. "How are you here?"

A deep rumble grew louder and coalesced into words which echoed around the arena. "You have chosen." Birlerion flinched as the Oath hummed, filling his mind.

Leyarille stiffened. "Oh no."

"Tell me quick, before you're yanked away."

"Tagerill said the arena was the site of the All Mother's testing. It's some legend that says you have to pass her tests to receive that which you need to succeed."

"How does Tagerill know that?"

"Apparently, it was one of his favourite stories when he was a kid. Tagerill recognised the arena from the image Ari gave us. Oh, Birlerion, what have you done?"

Birlerion thought that was a little unfair. "I haven't done anything."

Leyarille gripped his shoulders. "You're not on your own. No matter what, you're never on your own."

Birlerion smiled at her. "With you at my side and Jaredion behind my back, anything is possible."

She gave him a brilliant smile and then disappeared before he could kiss her. She reappeared beside to Jaredion, dropping into her seat.

"Keep the Veil off me," Birlerion shouted, and they waved back at him.

"Alright then, what's next?" he murmured, inspecting his surroundings. He stiffened when Tagerill appeared in the arena and overbalanced into the stone seat next to Leyarille. Tagerill cursed and leapt to his feet, all burnished red hair and wide shoulders, a broadsword on his back.

Birlerion looked up at the unfamiliar sky. Roiling clouds gathered like some unspoken threat. "I thought you said only one more?"

"This one is also bound to you. I understand the sword and the shield, but what is this one?" the voice asked, a rumble like thunder echoing around a valley, and Tagerill straightened.

"Family," Birlerion replied without hesitation.

"I am not fighting my brother," Tagerill declared.

Birlerion's heart sank. It was going to be that sort of test, was it? "Are you testing me, or him?" Birlerion shouted, desperately hoping Tagerill's assumption they would have to fight was incorrect.

Tagerill appeared beside him and staggered in surprise. Birlerion reached out to steady him. "Do you know what is going on?"

"This is the Mother's arena." Tagerill said, gripping Birlerion's arm as he glanced around him. "She tested her guardians, her guards, anyone she wanted to, I suppose. The arena was rumoured to be near Kharma, but I never thought it actually existed; more a myth, you know, not physically here. I'm not sure I *am* physically here." Tagerill patted his body.

"You must be, because we are talking to each other and I can touch you," Birlerion said.

"That doesn't mean anything when the gods are involved; they are capable of anything. Time is meaningless. Minutes here could be days elsewhere and days could be minutes. The gods don't bother with consistency, it makes no difference to them." Tagerill hugged him. "But it is good to see you."

"How do you know so much about the All Mother's arena?"

Tagerill's face flushed and he shrugged. "One of my favourite fables. Pa used to read them to me every night. I loved all the fighting and how the men and women proved themselves." He looked up at the roiling sky. "We are not fighting each other, so don't think we are."

"Good, because you would beat me. Especially with that thing." Birlerion nodded at the broadsword.

Tagerill unsheathed it; the blade shone with a virulent crimson gleam. "Do you think you'll need it?" he asked as he handed it to Birlerion, his hair glowing like a flaring ember in the fiery light.

Birlerion pushed it back. "Keep it. You might need it."

Tagerill shimmered and appeared back in the lower tier as the voice rumbled. "That wasn't a choice; that was a discussion," he complained as he re-sheathed his sword. Leyarille pulled him down beside her.

Birlerion rotated; the arena seemed empty, but there was a prickle on his neck. Someone was watching him. His heart stopped as his best friend, Serillion, strode into the arena. Tagerill bounced back to his feet, his mouth gaping. The three of them had met in the Rangers Academy over three thousand years ago and had been inseparable. They had graduated together and become Sentinals at the same time.

Serillion looked just as Birlerion remembered; a young man frozen in time. He had never had the chance to age as he'd died protecting Jerrol at the Watch Towers over twenty years previously. Slender as a reed, his blond hair swept back off his open face—he was a quiet historian who only wanted to study what he found in the world around him.

Birlerion's vision blurred with sudden tears, and his heart

ached. He was vaguely aware of Tagerill howling behind him, but he was frozen to the spot until Serillion stopped in front of him. He raised his hand, and Serillion pulled him into a heartfelt hug. "I always said you were the best of us."

"I've missed you," Birlerion choked out.

Serillion patted his back. "You know better than that; I've always been here." Releasing him, he rested his hand on Birlerion's chest. Birlerion's heart double thumped, and Serillion's eyes widened. "Birlerion. My dearest friend. What have you done?"

"It's too complicated to explain. How are you here?"

Serillion shrugged. "You do know this isn't real, don't you?" He tapped Birlerion's forehead. "You know I'm dead. This is only happening in the All Mother's arena, wherever that is. Your body is still collapsed in the sands. You are not really here, nor am I. But here, no rules apply. This is the All Mother's test and anything is possible."

Birlerion rubbed his temple. "None of this makes sense." Birlerion clung to him, reluctant to release him. "I'd introduce you to my wife, but I'm not sure Tage will let you go."

"But you did, Birler. You did what was necessary when it was needed, just as you will now. I believe in you, don't let anyone tell you otherwise." Serillion hugged him again and disappeared in a shimmer to reappear next to Tagerill. Tagerill froze as Serillion laughed and grabbed him. Tagerill hugged him back and wouldn't let him go and after a moment started speaking very fast.

The arena undulated and Birlerion spun, reaching for his sword as the Watch Tower formed around him. He stood at the base of one of the towers, guarding the entrance as the King's Guards charged him, and he knew he couldn't kill them. They were affected by *Mentiserium*, the persuasive spell that the Ascendants used, and were not responsible for their actions. The knowledge fell like dead weights, distracting him. He mustn't let anyone in. He had to protect the Captain.

A deep, feminine voice vibrated in his head. The All Mother's voice, soft and seductive. "You can change the past, Birlerion. You just have to make a choice. Choose to save Serillion and let Saerille die. She dies anyway. Bring back your friend. Tagerill wants you to bring back your friend. You both miss him."

Tagerill and Serillion jumped on their seats, shouting and waving at him. He stared through them, frozen in the past as he swung his sword, defending the tower entrance.

"All you have to do is run up those stairs and shield him. If you'd known, you could have protected both him and Jerrol. That's what you always wished you'd done, isn't it?" The voice was persuasive. "You failed him, Birlerion. You can put that right. Drop your sword and go to them. You can wrap your shield around them both and stop what happened. You might not have ended up in Adeeron. Think of all that agony avoided. If you make one little decision now."

Leyarille listened in horror. Birlerion had been carrying this misplaced guilt for all these years? What else was he carrying? It wasn't his fault. She jumped up beside Serillion and joined in, yelling at him not to listen to the voice.

They fell silent as Birlerion spoke, his voice emotionless. His face was pale and strained as he faced Serillion. "That was not my choice to make; it was Serillion's. If I had gone up the stairs, we might have all been killed. If I hadn't caused the distraction, Jerrol would never have escaped. I made my choice, and I stand by it."

The arena faded and his holding cell appeared around him. Birlerion curled up tight, his hand clenched around a black, stone bead and tears on his face.

"One," the Oath said with satisfaction.

"One?"

"You need to get as many as you can."

"How many do I need?"

"As many as you can carry."

Birlerion shuddered as darkness descended.

Palace Infirmary, Old Vespers

Leyarille gasped and bolted upright, the image of Birlerion standing alone in the arena with tears on his face seared in her mind.

"No, we have to go back." Leyarille tried to grasp the fading image and found herself lying in a bed.

"Leyarille?" Jerrol exclaimed from beside her. "Thank the Lady. You're awake."

Leyarille patted the bed, her fist clenched in the sheets as she recognised the palace infirmary. "What am I doing here?"

"You've been unconscious for three days, you and Tagerill."

"Three days?" Tagerill's voice was full of tears, and Leyarille's heart ached at the pain in his voice. If Tagerill was distraught, she dreaded to think what Birlerion must be feeling. She was so thankful she'd had the chance to meet their friend, Serillion, but she didn't understand what was happening.

"We've been so worried. When I came back from speaking to the king, you were both frozen."

"But we were gone for minutes."

"No, it's been three days. What happened?" Jerrol asked.

"I met Serillion," Leyarille said as she pushed back the sheets, and, ignoring her father's gasp of shock, she staggered over to console Tagerill. "How was he there, Uncle Tage?"

"It's the All Mother's Testing. She can move us wherever she wants us," Tagerill replied.

"The All Mother?" Jerrol asked.

Tagerill rubbed his pale face with a shaky hand. "Leyandrii's mother," he said as if that explained everything.

Jerrol blanched at his words.

29

MOTHER'S ARENA

irlerion huddled in his cell as screams rebounded around the arena. He had no idea what was going on, but the screams tore through him. "Enough," he shouted, banging his fists against the stone walls, and he found himself back in the arena, a young woman kneeling at his feet in the sand. Leyarille, Jaredion and Tagerill sat on the lower stone tier. All glancing around them in surprise.

"What is the matter?" Birlerion asked, helping the woman stand.

"They want to take away my b-baby."

"Who does?"

"The healers say I can't cope on my own and I should give her up to the foundling hall."

"Why?"

"B-because her father doesn't want her."

"And what do you say?"

"I want her to have a good life, but I'm afraid."

"Of what?"

The woman raised her blue eyes to Birlerion's. "Raising her on my own."

"The Lady will always help those who ask her. You have to have the strength and belief to trust in her, even when it seems you are all alone."

A scornful voice interrupted them. "So, you are still spouting that nonsense? Airy fairy stuff that only the gullible believe."

Birlerion turned and faced the newcomer. A well-dressed stocky young man with a sword at his hip, blond hair elegantly cut, and a sneer on his face entered the arena. The son of Dominant Clary, the one man who had hated his existence, and his son had followed in his father's footsteps. "Tyrler Clary, you haven't changed a bit."

Tyrler laughed. "You have, going grey, looking a bit peaky, life not been treating you well lately? I wonder why that is? You gutter rats should be left where you're found. Rising above your position is not good for your health."

"Can't say your position was good for your health, either."

Tyrler flicked a glance at the woman. "You still snivelling about that baby? I told you to get rid of it."

A slow burn began to build within Birlerion. "Yours, was it?" he asked.

"She was quick enough to spread her legs. Ha, offends your sense of what? Propriety? Likes of you don't even know what the word means. Bet you wished you killed me sooner. Regretting it now, aren't you?" He unsheathed his sword. "Want to try again? Rid the world of another Clary? I bet you still can't hold a sword."

"Alas, I don't have a sword to hand, but even if I did, I wouldn't waste my time on you."

"Snivelling coward."

Birlerion turned back to the woman. "Just because her father is an arse, doesn't mean she won't grow up to be a wonderful, strong woman if you give her a chance."

The woman smiled. "You're right."

Tyrler scowled at him as they began to fade.

When Birlerion's awareness returned, he held two stones in his hand as the arena materialised around him. Although the sand beneath his feet had been swept clean of footprints, the surrounding stone tiers still looked dilapidated and desolate. The clouds roiling in the sky above were still tinged blood red and pressed down on them oppressively.

Leyarille stood beside him, and he slid his arm around her waist and hugged her tight. Jaredion and Tagerill remained in the tiers. A tall, statuesque woman stood on the sands. Birlerion gulped at the sight of the woman who must be Leyandrii's mother, the All Mother. Her long coppery-green gown shimmered and morphed from one colour to the other as she moved. Her golden hair was piled on her head, styled so that artful curls escaped, and luminous pale green eyes stared at him out of a flawless face. "Everything is a choice, but the question is, do you always make the right choice?" Her voice shivered through him, questioning every fibre of his being, every thought, every decision.

She gestured, and Tagerill and Jaredion stood as the large arena gates opened.

Birlerion's sister Marianille and her husband Niallerion walked into the arena, with baby Melisarille, a chubby bundle in her arms. Marianille, elegant and beautiful, the image of her mother, Melis. They looked around them in some surprise, though hurried to join Birlerion and Leyarille in the centre of the arena.

Birlerion's heart raced and he gasped as his father, Warren, solid, reassuring Warren, escorted Melis into the arena. It wasn't possible, they were all long dead. Birlerion tried to control his ragged breathing. Was he hallucinating?

His panic subsided a little as Leyarille squeezed his waist and leaned against him. She felt so real. "Remember what

Serillion said. Anything is possible in the All Mother's Testing."

Warren was closely followed by his other sons, Penner and Versillion. Melis approached him, warm, loving and so generous, and familiar dark brown eyes smiled up into his. She reached up and cupped his face and Leyarille's. "Know we never forgot you, my son. Leyarille, we are so pleased to meet you." Melis looked around her children. "Versill, Marian, Tagerill, and Birler. You're all here. Lady be blessed."

Warren hugged him, holding him tight and Birlerion didn't ever want him to let go. His tears fell as Melis embraced Marianille. "You have a baby, our grandchild." She cooed at Melisarille, and Marianille handed her to Melis. "We named her after you, Ma." Warren finally released Birlerion and grabbed Tagerill tight, and then Versill, and they were all laughing and crying. Marianille introduced Niallerion as her husband, and Warren hugged him too.

Birlerion's heart broke. He would have to split them all up again. Warren turned back to him and slung an arm around his shoulders. "What you have given us is a gift. We would never have known what had happened to you if you hadn't invited us here. But we can't stay, we're not really here; you know that. We love you, never forget that."

Birlerion smiled through his tears, his throat tight.

"We are so proud of you all," Warren whispered as he caressed Birlerion's face before he shimmered and appeared next to the rest of his family in the tiers.

Warren and Penner hugged Leyarille, and she was lost amongst his family. Such a loving family.

The Oath stirred within him. *"Would you give them up?"*

"Why would I have to give them up?"

"So others can live, of course."

"I already did once."

"But could you do it again? To protect them all?"

Birlerion exhaled, and his family stilled, watching him as he deliberated. This was so heartbreaking. The All Mother had brought them all back to remind him of what he had already lost and what he still had left to lose. *"Yes, I would do it again."* He said at last, watching them all fade from the tiers, tearing his heart out and leaving him alone in the arena.

Palace Infirmary, Old Vespers

Tagerill wailed as he woke up. He hunched up against the loss of his family, and Marianille gathered him into her arms, tears running down her face. Where had she come from? Niallerion stood behind her, baby Melisarille in his arms. "Tage, it's alright, we're still here, Versillion and I, we're still here. And Ma and Pa know we're all well. That's a blessing, isn't it?"

"What about Birlerion? Where is he? He is not alright. This is going to destroy him, isn't it? It's not over yet." Tagerill gasped for breath. "You know it isn't."

Healer Ewan watched them in confusion. He could explain none of what was going on. Healer Tyrone hovered over Tagerill, white-haired and grizzled as he watched him in concern. "Drink, before you go again, Tagerill. Leyarille has already collapsed. You'll be called back imminently. It's been five days, Tagerill. Whatever you are doing, you need to finish it. Your bodies can't sustain this for much longer."

Tagerill drank the liquid. He had no idea what it was, though it soothed the craving in his stomach. Five days? He gripped Marianille's hand. "Were you there too? And the others?"

"We dreamt it. Only you and Leyarille, and possibly Jaredion seem to be there with him. We came as soon as we woke."

"Did you see Serillion? And Ma and Pa? And Penner?"

"Yes, we saw them all; you didn't imagine it."

Tyrone forced another mug on him. "Drink."

Tagerill took a gulp. "How is Birlerion doing?"

"He is still standing," she said sadly, and Tyrone grabbed the mug as Tagerill collapsed back on his bed, his face emptying of all expression.

All Mother's Arena

The All Mother watched him, her luminous eyes boring into him. "Could you let them all go? The real question Birler is whether you are capable of doing this alone. Words are so easy; actions are so much more difficult. Especially when family is so important to you. After all, isn't that what you have been searching for your whole life?"

"Why?"

"You know why. You knew this day would come. Why else have you always lived through others, never committing yourself?"

"I have always committed myself, in everything I do."

"Not until now."

Birlerion looked at her, bemused. "What more do you want of me?" he asked as he rotated the three black beads in his fingers.

"Prove yourself."

Birlerion rolled his eyes. "Again?"

"Yes, my son, one final time."

"You promise this will be the last time?"

"I promise."

Birlerion felt a rush behind him, and he parried the strike

without thinking, reaching for his sword with a thought. He grimaced as he faced Tyrler Clary once more.

"Tyrler, it's all in the past, let it go."

"I bet Celia would like to hear you say that. She was one of your failures, wasn't she? You couldn't save her, could you?"

"I can't save everyone, as much as I would like to."

"Did you hear that, everyone? He admits he can't save you all."

Birlerion glanced around the arena. The tiers were filling with familiar faces. A scowling Tagerill sat in the front row. Serillion was seated next to him one arm wrapped around his shoulders, and he breathed a sigh of relief. Leyarille was sitting between him and Jaredion.

"And you could?"

"That wasn't my self-proclaimed job. You're the one with the protection problem."

Birlerion shrugged. "It's not a problem."

"I'd say it is. The little boy desperate for a family, prepared to ruin the Descelles for the sake of his own needs."

"I am a Descelle, and as my family will attest. The Descelles are not ruined."

"Too right," Tagerill yelled.

Serillion stood and walked onto the arena. He hugged Birlerion, a huge smile on his face. "Congratulations, my friend. I wish you every happiness."

Tyrler scowled at Serillion and then at Tagerill as he joined them in the centre. "You never listened, did you? We all laughed at you. Celia too. Come out, Celia, tell Birlerion what you think of him."

A young woman came out into the arena. She was petite, barely reaching Tyrler's chest. Birlerion paled, and Leyarille leaned forward. Tyrler wrapped an arm around Celia's shoulders and clamped her to his side. Her short brown curls bounced as she looked up at Birlerion, a tremulous smile on her face. "Hello, Birlerion."

"Celia." Birlerion smiled into her vivid blue eyes, his face sad.

"Reunions with old flames are such fun, aren't they? Shame you didn't have the chance to build a bonfire, isn't it? So I made up for you. Enjoyed it, didn't you, love?" Tyrler squeezed her shoulders.

Birlerion's face tightened. "She wouldn't have looked at you if you hadn't used *Mentiserium*."

"Of course you would say that, but you'll never really know, will you? After all, she died right in front of your eyes, and you did nothing to save her."

"I'm so sorry, Celia."

"What would you do to stop her dying? Right now? What would you offer? You, who are so happy. Celia, did you know he got joined? Forgot all about you."

"That's not true."

"Save her then, this time around."

"I can't." Birlerion cleared his throat, tight with emotion. Celia had never deserved any of this. Tyrler had only looked her way once Birlerion had shown an interest. It was Birlerion's fault she had died.

"But if you could," Tyrler wheedled.

"It's too late. I can't."

"Can't or won't? Celia, he won't even try. I bet he would for his wife. Let's exchange them, shall we? What's her name? Leyarille? What would you do to save her? If I told you she was dead, but you could bring her back; what would you do?"

Birlerion stared at him, his face rigid, and then he closed his eyes. "If it was possible, I would die for her, but it wouldn't change anything. I would have already lost her."

Tyrler scowled. "I so wish you would die, but dying

wouldn't be enough. That's too easy. First, you would have to give up everything, just for her; give up the Lady, the shield, who you are," he said.

Birlerion met Leyarille's eyes. "If I did that, I wouldn't be me anymore; I would already be dead."

"But if you could, just for her. Forget everyone else, they can save themselves," Tyrler persisted.

"I wouldn't be saving her. I would be killing our world," Birlerion replied. "And without a world for us to live in, there would be no point in anything."

Tyrler stamped his foot. "For once, Birlerion, just once, think of yourself. You want her, I know you do. I can feel the way your pulse speeds up just by looking at her, the flutter in your stomach when she smiles at you, see? There! The heat that's rising within you at the thought of …"

Birlerion stepped forward and punched him on the nose. "Enough, get to the point."

Tyrler's face flushed red, and he shook with anger. He held his nose as blood dripped through his fingers. "You'll regret that. I can take her away from you, just like," he snapped his fingers, and Leyarille disappeared, "that."

"No, you can't," Birlerion replied, and he wrapped his arm around Leyarille's waist as she reappeared beside him, and he tugged her into his side. She hugged him back.

"There, admit it. No matter what was demanded, you would save her, over everyone else."

"He would do what he could, but although I am his world, I am not *the* world, and there are many other people he has to protect as well. I wouldn't expect him to put me before them, nor would he, as you well know," Leyarille said, firmly.

"Exactly, little lady. He can only save the world if he lets you go. Would you give her up, Birlerion? Now you finally have her? To save Leyandrii's world for her?" Tyrler stared at him, waiting.

A piece of Birlerion died. Truly? They would take her away from him, now, when she was all he had left?

"That's not fair," Birlerion whispered. He wanted to wail and shriek, but he felt cold inside.

Tyrler cackled. "He wants it to be fair." Spinning, he raised his arms to the silent tiers. "Who said life was supposed to be fair?" Eyes like flint drilled into Birlerion's. "Go on, cut the thread that binds you together."

Palace Infirmary, Old Vespers

Leyarille opened her eyes and sat up, sweeping the sheets off her. "Whoa, Leyarille, wait a minute, you can't leave yet." Tyrone pushed her back down on the bed.

"Is he here? Where is Birlerion?"

"I have no idea; you've been with him for the last week. Don't you know where he is?"

"No, no," she tried to sit up again. "He needs me; why am I here? Tagerill?" she wailed, and Healer Ewan came running, wiping his bleary eyes.

"What's the matter?" Ewan searched the darkened healerie.

"Tagerill, don't you dare get up. Ewan, hold her down," Tyrone stomped over to Tagerill's bed. "Stay put, you'll collapse as soon as you stand up."

"Did he make a choice?" Leyarille shouted, desperation clear in her voice.

"Leyarille, please calm down." Ewan patted her shoulder.

"Don't tell me to calm down. My husband is being torn apart, and you want me to calm down?" Her voice rose to a screech.

Tagerill's composed voice overrode hers. "I can still feel him, Leyarille, can you? We are still tied together. My knots are holding." He gave her a sad smile. "I tied them in triplicate. I wasn't letting him go."

Leyarille tried to calm her panic, her heart stuttering at the thought of losing him. She took deep breaths, trying to find the thread that bound them tight. It vibrated in her senses, and she shuddered out a relieved breath. "Yes, oh yes," she whispered.

"Then he chose you."

Leyarille lay back down, curling up in the sheets as tears leaked down her cheeks. To be faced with such a choice. She wasn't sure she could make such a decision. Why should anyone have to? Could Birlerion? Had he decided? Would he hate her for it, in time?

Ewan patted her shoulder again and retreated.

She cleared her throat. "What day is it?"

Tyrone peered over his glasses, his bushy white eyebrows frowning at her. "It's the twenty-fourth. You've got a week to recuperate before the Joining. Mir'elle was worried; she wants you as her witness if you can't find Birlerion by then."

Leyarille shivered. "Tyrone?" she whispered. Tyrone bent over her. "He isn't mentally unstable."

"I know, my dear, I know. That's why I'm here, to declare him fit, but I do need to see him first. Now rest, you're expected to attend the king's reception tomorrow night, if you are still awake and well enough."

All Mother's Arena

Birlerion no longer knew what was real and what was a dream. He no longer knew if we was making a choice that mattered or if someone was just toying with him and he had finally lost his mind. Had his family joined him in the arena or had they all been a hallucination? It hadn't felt like a hallucination.

The empty red-tinged arena surrounded him, and yet the vision of Leyarille standing in the crowd at the king's reception was so clear he could reach out and touch her. She stood close to Tagerill, elegantly gowned in soft grey silk that enhanced the delicate blush of her skin. He met her eyes across the room and smiled. Giving her an elegant courtly bow from another age, he snapped the threads that so newly bound them tight.

"No, you promised," she shrieked as she lurched towards him, her hand outstretched, startling the people around her. People stilled, frozen in place as her scream died away.

Parsillion left the king's side and converged on her at the same time as Tagerill grabbed her. "Leyarille, don't let him go, for Lady's sake, hold on to him."

"He ... He ..."

"The thread goes both ways, never forget. You have a say too," Tagerill said, his voice fierce. "He is trusting you; you have to trust him."

"What's happened?" Mir'elle gripped Leyarille's arm.

"My lady," Leyarille dropped into a stiff curtsey, her mind scrambling to make sense of Tagerill's words. "It's Birlerion; he is being tested."

"As are all of us," Tagerill added. "He is not on his own, no matter what they say."

Mir'elle hugged Leyarille. "Don't ever let go of him," she whispered. "Don't you let go."

Birlerion swept his hand through the air in a cutting motion, and all the threads connecting him to those he loved shrivelled. He collapsed on the sands at the backlash, writhing as his family and friends tried to find him.

Tyrler glared down at him in disbelief. "I never thought you'd do it. You bastard. I should have got rid of you when I had the chance; you no good piece of shit. Your father was the same; weak, easily led, but you killed him, didn't you? A defenceless old man, you killed him, you murderer, you…" his vicious voice finally cut off. Birlerion shuddered as the fourth and fifth beads materialised in his hand.

"That's all of them," the Oath said with satisfaction. *"You are deemed worthy."*

Birlerion lay in the burning sands, bereft. The golden sun beat down on him and he tried to speak, but his throat was parched. Precious water seeped down his cheeks, tears he couldn't stop from falling. He had fought so hard for a family, and now he was back where he started, alone. "Worthy of what?" he managed, though as he sat up, he supposed he would never truly be alone with the Oath burbling in his head, and he faltered as a strange sensation, though muted, impinged on his senses. An echo of the world waiting for him to return. The echo grew louder and the connection to the land rose in his mind, eager to embrace him, to soothe him, to bolster him on his journey.

The Land had accepted him? Is that what the All Mother deemed him worthy of? To bond with the Land? To help Marguerite? But what did that mean for him? Would he have to reside within the Land like Marguerite? But no, he was still above ground. He rotated the back beads in his fingers as he struggled to comprehend what had just happened.

A cacophony of sound and images overwhelmed him, a burbling spring, the weighty pressure of a tall mountain reaching for the sky, raucous birds clattering through the trees, the deepest ocean trenches, silent and mysterious, a shifting fault line grating on his senses; they all merged into a mindless roar and then settled like calming water in the back of his mind. He missed Kin'arol's deep voice, the thrum of his sentinal. Those familiar memories were washed away with the physical presence of the Land, filling his mind, ever present and a weight on his shoulders.

The Oath was a humming presence in the back of his mind, light and mischievous. In comparison, the Land was a burden of responsibility. How Marguerite had managed to balance the two, he was unsure, but then she was a goddess, he was only a Sentinal. At least Marguerite was still part of Remargaren, he only had to carry half the burden, though if he was honest, he felt as if he had always carried the responsibility for protecting Remargaren.

His affinity was closer to the Oath than the Land. He was used to defending, not sustaining.

Shuddering, he accepted that his life was now entwined even more closely with the future of Remargaren. With Marguerite, he was now the Land, though he still didn't really know what that meant nor what he was meant to do. He didn't have the energy to sustain anything except himself.

Looking around him, he recognised the dried-up riverbed. He was in central Terolia, miles from anywhere. The Kharma ridge rose behind him. He rolled to his knees and took a deep breath. His heart stuttered in his chest. So many memories, too many emotions, so much loss all crowded in his chest at once. He thought he might burst. Help from the gods was always double-edged. He folded over as sobs racked him.

The All Mother's voice echoed in his head. *"You have what you need. Go, my son. You know what you must do."*

Jaredion and Kin'arol found him in the sands. A tattered figure kneeling in the burning sun, his skin burnt, eyes empty. All he had left was five black beads in his hand.

30

DESERTS OF TEROLIA

At the sight of Birlerion, Kin'arol bounded forward. *"Birlerion? Are you hurt? Where did you go? How did you get here?"*

"I'm fine," Birlerion replied.

"You are not fine," Jaredion said, and Birlerion stiffened, his eyes widening as he realised Jaredion had heard both him and Kin'arol.

"I'm as good as I'm going to be," he amended, and Kin'arol crooned in his head, his rich voice a warm embrace that relaxed tensed muscles.

Jaredion released the leading rein of the second horse, slid off his back, and, grabbing the waterskin, knelt beside Birlerion. Thrusting the water skin into his hands, he said, "Drink. You need to drink." His voice broke as he hovered over his friend, his expression tight with concern.

Numbly following Jaredion's direction, Birlerion lifted the waterskin to his mouth, Jaredion supporting his hands as they shook. Cool water slid down his parched throat, and he closed his eyes and gulped. He whimpered as Jaredion pulled it away. "Slowly," Jaredion murmured, offering it again.

Birlerion took another gulp and cleared his throat. "How did you find me?"

"Kin'arol and I pictured the arena when we entered the waystone in Deepwater, and we came out here."

"You saw the arena? You were really there?"

"I don't think we were physically there, but Leyarille, Tagerill, and I were all with you. You were never alone, Birlerion. I promise. No matter what you thought."

"I thought I was hallucinating." He rubbed his face. "I'm not sure I know what's real anymore."

Jaredion gripped his shoulders, his face tightening. "You are not mad, Birlerion. It was real. The All Mother tested you and you survived. Why was she testing you?"

"I think …" Birlerion cleared his throat and took another sip of water. "She bonded me to the Land."

Jaredion gasped. "Like Marguerite? But why?"

"Protection, I think. I believe this was Leyandrii's way of helping us. The Lands sustains as the Oath protects." Birlerion held out his hand. "She also gave me these."

Jaredion peered at the five black beads. "What are they for?"

"I don't know, though the All Mother seemed to think I did."

"Then you'll know what to do when you need them."

Birlerion considered Jaredion for a moment. Gaunt features, too thin body, too many scars hidden beneath his loose clothes. Constant belief, no matter what was thrown at him. "I don't deserve you," he whispered.

Jaredion twisted his lips. "No matter what anyone else says, I'm yours, Birlerion. I'll protect you until my last breath if necessary."

"You truly *are* my sword," Birlerion breathed as Jaredion's eyes luminesced in the golden sunlight and the silver drained away, leaving a deep indigo blue. The same colour Birlerion's eyes used to be. Jaredion had just placed his life, his allegiance, into Birlerion's hands, giving up the goddess Leyandrii and choosing Birlerion.

Heart stuttering, Birlerion took a deep breath. His heart double thumped again, the oath giving its approval. The land beneath his knees shivered in his awareness, and concern rippled through him, along with images of mounted patrols in the desert, searching for him.

"We need to leave," Birlerion said, lurching to his feet, glad of Jaredion's helping hand.

It took two tries, but Jaredion managed to get him into the saddle, and as Kin'arol's rich voice filled his mind, he relaxed, sagging over his Darian's neck. Jaredion moved his horse in closer as if afraid Birlerion would fall off.

It took four days to reach Mistra. Although Jaredion had found Birlerion via a waystone, they couldn't find one for a return trip. Birlerion slid off Kin'arol and leaned against him to hold him up as his limbs trembled. Exhaustion swept through him, his body hurt, his head ached, and his eyes were dry and gritty. He had hardly slept since Jaredion had found him.

With both the Oath and the Land within him, he had thought he would be stronger, but in reality he was even more exhausted. Assimilating the Land was draining him, he didn't know how to control it or use it. He wasn't a god no matter what the All Mother had done. The Veil was getting desperate, and Jaredion was carrying the injuries as proof. Birlerion couldn't sleep knowing Jaredion would pay for every minute.

His clothes hung off him. He couldn't eat the food they managed to scavenge. It didn't seem to matter anymore. Jaredion wasn't in much better shape. And that hurt Birlerion even more, the knowledge that he was causing Jaredion so much pain.

He had no idea how Jaredion had found him. His explanation made no sense, but then he supposed there was little that made sense anymore. It shouldn't have been possible, but Jaredion had been determined.

Jaredion reminded him a little of himself when he was younger. He had been able to achieve the impossible on occasion.

"The waystone is guarded. Are you sure you want to use it?" Kin'arol asked.

"We don't have a choice. I have to return to Vespers. Now."

"Wouldn't it be better to speak to Kayerille? Maybe she could help divert the guards at the other end. We won't get past them. What's the point of getting hurt if we can avoid it? Please, Birlerion, let's speak to Kayerille first."

Birlerion wasn't sure what the Lady or the All Mother expected of him, but he was terrified he would fail them both. The lack of sleep dragged at him, tempting him to close his eyes and lie down right there.

The King's Oath swept through him, and Birlerion staggered, the command freezing his limbs and tearing through his battered self-control. Collapsing to his knees, he tried to resist. *Not now, please, I'll go back, I swear I'm trying, just not now.* The compulsion eased as he accepted the command. The Oath shimmered through him, and he breathed deeply as Jaredion held him up.

"Birlerion? What happened?" Jaredion asked, searching the street.

"I swear," Birlerion said as he tried to control his breathing, "that when I find Anders, I'll break his Oath into so many pieces, he'll never be able to put it back together again."

Jaredion grunted as he helped him stand. "I'll help you," he promised.

The need to return to Old Vespers and the king ran through Birlerion overlaying his current need to hide. He stiffened, battling the compulsion. *Later, we'll turn that way later, just not yet,* he soothed.

"We need to find Kayerille," he said through gritted teeth.

A sharp voice split the night air. "Hey, isn't he that Sentinal with the golden horse. They said detain him at all costs; quick, stop him."

Kin'arol galloped off, drawing the soldiers away as Jaredion dragged Birlerion into an alley. They hid in the shadows and then made their way through the narrow passages, Jaredion allowing Birlerion to lead the way without protest. Really, the lad was a treasure. Birlerion knew he wouldn't have survived without him.

Avoiding patrols and searching soldiers, they had hidden in the Lady's temple for a few chimes where he had finally been able to relax for a moment and dose; not sleep; Lady forbid he slept, but it was enough to soothe tired limbs and weary aches.

He had searched for Leyandrii and Marguerite, but they were both absent. He felt the echoes of their concern, but he couldn't make the connection. It was if they stood on the other side of a waterfall, but he couldn't make out what they were saying. Their mouths moved, but the water drowned out the sounds and blurred their faces.

Was it his error? Had he let them slip from his grasp? Had he cut his connection to them as well? He had clung on so tight he was afraid he had snapped the link in his fear of losing them. And now he was all alone and had no one but himself to blame. Shutting down that line of thought, he focused on the door. What should do he do? Would Kayerille let him in or turn him away? Would they help him or report him? He could say he was returning to Vespers. He just needed a diversion and if he couldn't use the waystones then some money to get there.

Peering out of the shadows at the painted door that led to Kayerille's home, Birlerion stiffened as the door opened and Kayerille appeared. Lustrous black hair curled around her bare shoulders; she looked exquisite. She stared across the street, frowning; her gaze ran the length of the road and returned, and he eased out of the shadows and waited, Jaredion hovering behind him. A stray vagabond hoping to be thrown a few sops. Kayerille's beautiful silver eyes widened, and she jerked her head, opening the door wider. They darted across the street, and the door closed behind him without a sound.

Soft arms embraced him, and he stiffened, unsure of how to respond. Kayerille leaned back and inspected his face. "Oh, Birlerion, what have they done to you?" she whispered, loosening her arms. Sadness filled her eyes as she took in his debilitated state. Filthy and desperate, he was skin and bones; the once assured man a mere memory, his silver eyes sunken and furtive. Jaredion looked little better. She found he was just as thin as she hugged him.

Carefully, she eased Birlerion into a chair and crouched beside him. A gentle hand on his arm to keep him in place, to stop him fleeing. "What do you need, Birlerion?"

Easy tears started in his eyes, and his throat tightened; he didn't know what to ask for. "I don't want to cause any trouble," he whispered, his voice scratchy.

"You won't. What do you need? Food? A bath? A place to sleep? Tell me, and it's yours."

All the above would be bliss, he thought, though maybe not the sleep. "I can't stay. I have to return to Vespers."

"Why Vespers? Surely that is the last place you should go; they are searching for you."

"I have no choice. It's time. I can't last much longer. Jaredion is doing his best but the Veil is relentless, and he is tiring." He gave Jaredion a weak smile. "I don't want to drag you down with me." Kayerille's grip tightened as a tremor shuddered through him. "I-I need a diversion and some money. I'll pay you back, I swear, only-only maybe not in this lifetime."

"It's yours," Kayerille promised. "Take the time to bathe, Birlerion. You'll feel better. Eat, then leave. It won't take long. Oscar will bring a horse round."

She held him in place as the door opened and her husband entered, his blue eyes glittering in the lamplight. "You have nothing to fear from us, I swear," Kayerille said firmly as Oscar froze and then shut the door.

"By the Lady, Birlerion?" Oscar breathed, his face reflecting his shock, though he did try to hide his horror at the state of his friend. He slowly stepped into the room as if conscious of the fragile condition of the man seated before him. "What is going on? We keep getting conflicting orders regarding you; first to help you and now to detain you at all costs. What is happening to you? Why is everyone chasing you?"

Birlerion grimaced, his skin taut across his hollow cheeks. "I can't explain it. It's too complicated. I need to go to Vespers."

"I'll go with you."

"No, just a diversion please; they'll attack you too. I-I can't protect you; I can hardly protect myself anymore." He clenched his hands as they shook. Jaredion gripped his shoulder, his knuckles wrapped in blood-soaked cloth.

"More reason for me to go with you. There must be some misunderstanding. I don't believe you are a threat to anyone, least of all the Oath. And anyway, if you travel with me, they won't realise it's you; we can disguise you as one of my men. There would be no reason for them to attack us."

"He's right, Birlerion. Have a bath, eat. Let Oscar go with you; let us help you. You don't have to do this alone. The Lady would never desert you. She wants us to help you."

Birlerion wavered. Their concern buffeted him, shaking his resolve. It reminded him of the inclusive sense of belonging amongst those of the Family. Oscar and Kayer-ille breathed it as if it were in the very air around them. To be safe and cherished; it called and coaxed, and he couldn't resist the chance to lose himself in it one last time, even though he knew he would miss it even more once he left.

Oscar helped him undress and steadied him as he stepped into the bath tub. His horrified gaze catalogued the mass of welts on his body, some abraded, some infected; they looked raw and sore and none were healing. Birlerion hissed as the warm water covered him, and he relaxed as Oscar washed him down. He did nothing. He just existed as someone else cared for his body. It wasn't really his anymore; he had mistreated it so much he didn't deserve it. Soon, he would leave it and then it could rest, as could he. He was so tired.

The Veil snared him, and his eyes flew open as a bright red welt slashed across his ribs, and Oscar gasped. "I'm so sorry, Birlerion, I didn't realise you drifted off."

Birlerion cursed himself. He had let his guard down, almost fallen asleep under Oscar's soothing hands. The new welt stung in the water, and he sat up, shivering. Easy tears glistened in his luminous eyes. "The Veil, it's sucking me dry. It needs the Oath to break its chains, and I'm it's chosen prey."

"How do we stop it? How do we stop it from attacking you?"

"I have to stay awake; it can only get past my defences if I sleep. Make sure I don't fall asleep. Jaredion can't take much more, but he won't stop trying to defend me."

Oscar sat back on his heels. "That is not a long-term plan. You have to sleep at some point."

"I will," Birlerion whispered, "when I get to Vespers."

Oscar led him unresisting back out to their living space, and Kayerille began to smooth salve over the raw welts as she continued her conversation with Jaredion.

"Why did you resign?" Kayerille asked Jaredion, keeping her voice calm, though her fingers shook as she moved to the next welt.

Jaredion finished his mouthful and said, "Uncle Jerrol wouldn't listen. He wanted to reassign me away from Birlerion."

"He wanted to do what? Why?"

"They thought I was a bad influence," Birlerion said with a harsh laugh. "They were probably right. Jaredion has had a tough time of it. He always seems to get the thankless jobs."

Oscar helped him dress in light tunic and trousers; the cloth stuck to his cream coated skin, but Birlerion barely noticed. He sat where they told him to as Jaredion went off for a bath.

"And Leyarille?" Kayerille asked, tentatively.

Birlerion stiffened and didn't answer. Reaching for a piece of bread, he concentrated on tearing it in half and then half again. He nibbled it, barely touching the rest of the food on his plate.

"You need to eat," Kayerille said, catching her husband's eye in desperation.

"I need to go. I can't stay." Birlerion shifted restlessly in his chair.

"But you've not eaten; you need more than a piece of bread."

"Birlerion?"

Birlerion lifted his head. *"Kin'arol?"*

"I'm here."

Birlerion rose. "Kin'arol is here."

Oscar stood. "I'll get Jaredion and my things, then. I am coming with you, so don't argue."

Birlerion turned and hugged Kayerille, snapping the thread that connected them. The pain lashed him, and he absorbed it until it tingled out of his fingertips, and her arms tightened around him. He needed to leave. "Take care, thank you for everything."

Kayerille traced his hollow cheeks with her fingers. "You take care, Birlerion. I want to see you back here eating a proper meal. I'll cook a Tanjia just for you."

"That would be lovely."

Kayerille hugged her husband tight as Jaredion appeared, stamping into his boots. "Don't leave him on his own."

"I won't. I'll stay with him."

Kayerille watched them leave. She wasn't so sure. Birlerion was so thin and gaunt, she wanted to wrap him in her favourite quilted blanket and never let him go. Her stomach fluttered with unease. They were losing him, and there was nothing they could do.

31

KING'S PALACE, OLD VESPERS

The morning of the king's Joining dawned clear and bright. The first day of the new year and it was so cold that plumes of breath followed the guards as they patrolled the ornately decorated palace. The swathes of white and gold material draped over the walls were rimed with frost, making the building glimmer and sparkle in the early morning sunlight.

Jerrol walked through the surprisingly silent corridors, his formal red robes swirling around his ankles as he dodged servants intent on their duties. Considering the palace was full of honourable guests and influential people, he ought to be with Bryce checking their security one more time, but he was drawn to the king's throne room for one last check.

He had been monitoring the Oath. The golden glow *was* diminishing; it was obvious now. A good handspan around the edges were dark, and there was no explanation for it. He had closed the throne room as out of bounds for the duration of the Joining; they didn't want word of the Oath's demise to spread. Lady knew what people would assume and, worst of all, what it meant for Birlerion.

He wondered where he was. Birlerion was supposed to have been back in Vespers by today. Leyarille and Tagerill had tried to explain what they had seen. They had frozen in time. But the All Mother's Arena? It was beyond comprehension, beyond belief.

Ewan had been unable to wake them or explain what was happening to them. Healer Tyrone had returned to help him, and Jerrol had squirmed under his clear gaze. Three times Leyarille and Tagerill had frozen, for days at a time. Supporting Birlerion. He should have been at Birlerion's side, supporting him as he had supported Jerrol so many times. Now he was missing again; on the run from his guards.

Kayenion had been too efficient; he had delivered the new order to help and aid Birlerion, before his original order had even arrived. He should have been more specific in his new order to prevent units still pursuing Birlerion. It was all such a mess and it was all his fault. If only he'd listened to Birlerion from the beginning and helped him without question as Birlerion had helped him on so many occasions. At least Birlerion wasn't hurt. The Oath was not flushed pink.

Tagerill had been so distressed, Tyrone had sedated him just to calm him down. He was in the palace somewhere, reunited with his wife Miranda, who had him in hand now. Leyarille had been unnaturally quiet as if she had suppressed all her emotions. No matter what he said, she just stared at him with dry accusing eyes. It made him shiver just remembering.

Of Jaredion there was no sign. He was no longer in Deepwater, but no one knew where he was. As a result, Jennery was giving him the cold shoulder as well, and Alyssa had been furious that he had set the guards against her son, that they had injured him while he did his duty. Reminding them that Jaredion had resigned would only make matters worse, and he couldn't face their condemnation. He had never thought of himself as a coward, until now. But there it was.

Birlerion was alone. He understood now why he couldn't sense him; no one could. Why would he sever that which he had protected so fiercely? Why would he join with Leyarille, only to break it off a few days later?

Leyarille was becoming increasingly frantic and barely able to hide her anger with him. She didn't think he was doing enough to help her husband. Jerrol was shocked and saddened that they had joined in such desperate circumstances, but Tagerill had confirmed it.

Taelia would be furious when she found out, missing her daughter's Joining. He wasn't looking forward to telling her. He didn't think Leyarille should attend the king's Joining, but Mir'elle was insistent. Leyarille was one of her witnesses in place of her brother.

He sighed. How had he made such a mess of everything? No matter what he tried to do, he only made it worse. His failure to recall that damned order curdled in his stomach. Attempting to undo the damage had compounded the problem; even the palace guards still gossiped about Birlerion as if he was a danger. Recalling the orders had not changed what everyone now thought. Even if Birlerion made it to Vespers, he wouldn't be safe. To be honest, he was surprised Birlerion was so determined to return. Why didn't he deal with the Veil once and for all instead of suffering? What was he waiting for?

He stared at the King's Oath until it blurred. Where was Birlerion? And more importantly, what would he do?

Turning away, he gently closed the double doors behind him. He locked them and hung the key around his neck, concealing it in his robes. "No one enters. No matter what," he said to the sentry on duty and then went to the king's chambers.

Slumping in his saddle, Birlerion was relieved when Oscar and Jaredion closed in on either side of him. Between them, they were determined to keep him on Kin'arol and their presence was comforting.

"Birlerion, we're approaching Old Vespers; we're nearly there," Jaredion murmured as they began the rise from the harbour.

Birlerion jerked upright and squinted down the road. They had waystoned from Mistra to Greenswatch. He had felt the pull of his home in Westermaine, all the more strongly with Melis and Warren vivid in his memories. He missed them so much, it had been tempting to stop at Greenswatch, and only Oscar's determination, once he and his men had recovered, had kept him on the East Road.

"Oscar is worried," Kin'arol said at the same time.

"So he should be," Birlerion replied. *"The hardest part is yet to come."*

"We should have gone home."

"Home?"

"Westermaine, it waits for us."

"We will, after."

"Good."

Birlerion smiled at his Darian's calm acceptance. His smile faded as they began the long pull up the hill past the harbour town. A barricade came into view blocking the road. Oscar rode forward and dismounted as his men closed in around Birlerion.

A King's Guard strode down the road, observing them. Pausing, he inspected Kin'arol intently. His gaze rose to the rider, and Birlerion kept his eyes down. "You, step down."

Birlerion eased back in his saddle. *"You know, you need to be less noticeable."*

Kin'arol snorted as Birlerion gathered his reins. "Be warned," Birlerion said softly, "we have been riding far and long. If I get down, I may not be able to get back up."

The man raised his crossbow, and Oscar strode back, knocking the bow down. "Don't you dare. Your orders are to stand down."

"He's wanted, the Lord Chancellor has been looking for him. Stop or I'll shoot."

Kin'arol had been sidling back through Oscar's men, but Birlerion held him still. "There is no reason to hurt anyone. We will come quietly. I need to speak to the Lord Chancellor."

"The road's shut until after the Joining."

The situation deteriorated after that as the King's Guards charged Oscar's men. Birlerion slid off Kin'arol in the melee and ran back down the hill cutting in towards the harbour town. If they weren't going to let him reach the palace, then so be it. He would stop trying.

Oscar was livid. Searching for Birlerion, he only came up with a squealing Kin'arol, desperately trying to escape the guard holding his reins. "Enough," he roared, and the men stopped fighting. "Release that horse before you injure it. I am the Commander of the Terolian Guards. You had better hope you don't rotate under my jurisdiction, because I can assure you, I will make you regret it. Every single one of you."

The guards shrank back under his glare and froze as Commander Nikols of the King's Rangers arrived. "Oscar, what is going on here?"

"The King's Guards are trying to kill Birlerion, again."

"What?" Nikols swept a glance over the chaos. "Where is he?"

Oscar gestured at the King's Guard. "Why don't you tell him?" he said, his voice cutting.

Anders waited nervously in his private rooms as his attendant tweaked his ruffles and set the final gems in his cravat. His valet slapped his hand as he went to adjust it and Anders glared at him. The man ignored him and carefully brushed his deep blue jacket over his shoulders, tweaking the red sash draped diagonally across his chest. He was determined that the king would be perfect, and not even the king would stop him.

"I should have followed your daughter's example and just told everyone we'd got joined," Anders said, fidgeting as he glanced at Jerrol seated in one of the ornate chairs by the fireplace.

"Your majesty, please," the man held his hands up to stop the king moving.

Jerrol laughed. "And spoil everyone's fun? There won't be another event like this until your son or daughter gets joined."

"Any sign of Birlerion?" Anders asked as the man finally stepped away from him.

"No."

"It doesn't seem right without him here. This day would never have happened without him."

"A lot of things would never have happened without him, Anders."

"No, I suppose not."

He took a deep breath as the door opened, and Bryce grinned at them. "Ready when you are."

Anders exhaled. "This is it then."

"Yes, Your Majesty."

Bryce stood back, and Jerrol followed the king out of his chambers and along the corridor towards the palace entrance. His coach awaited him at the bottom of the steps with four gleaming white stallions harnessed to it. Jerrol joined him inside the plush interior.

The king smiled out of the window, waving his hand at the staff crowding on the steps to see him leave. Jerrol concentrated on arranging the folds of his robe. The king's escort closed around them, and the carriage smoothly rolled forward.

People lined the roads, waving colourful flags as the procession passed. Anders waved his hand in return.

Jerrol escorted Anders into the Lady's temple. It seemed like everyone was there, but in reality, the list of participants had been pared right down as there just wasn't the space. The temple gleamed, the white marble a beautiful backdrop for the exotic flower arrangements Mir'elle had insisted on. Brilliant reds and yellows were interspersed with the elegant white lilies found on the borders of Elothia.

The temple father stood on the steps and opened his hands. "Your Majesty, welcome."

Anders smiled nervously and stood to one side, nodding his head as he caught the eyes of his Administration, the Duke and Duchess of Elothia, the Emperor and Empress of Birtoli, the Lords of the Watches, and the list just kept going.

There was a stir at the door, and Jerrol hurried over. "Nikols, what are you doing here?"

"We missed him. Birlerion was here, and the patrols challenged him."

"Where is he now?"

"We lost him in harbour town."

"Very well, try to find him." He rested his hand on Nikol's arm. "Without harming him. He is not a wanted man; he is our friend, and we need to help him."

"I know. I'll deal with those fool enough to ignore their orders."

Jerrol nodded and scuttled back to the king as he caught sight of Mir'elle's carriage arriving. The people lining the streets let out a roar as she emerged. Anders ran a hand around his collar.

Jerrol chuckled. "At least she turned up. Imagine being left at the altar."

Anders blanched and turned to the door. His jaw dropped as Mir'elle entered, a vision in brilliant red, swathed in glowing gold lace as fragile as butterfly wings.

Birlerion slipped in the mud, landing heavily as he misjudged the distance. Exhaustion fogged his mind as he tried to decide where to go. All he wanted to do was lay down and go to sleep and never wake up again.

Gloop squelched through his fingers, cold and revolting. He was still being pursued; he couldn't shake them. The crash of the waves against the beach had been growing louder. He was going the wrong way. The roar of the sea was superseded by the crescendo of voices; the Joining must have begun.

Lurching to his feet, he wiped the mud off his hands and ignored the seductive pull of the sea. It would be so peaceful, just to let go and not worry anymore. Another roar intruded, and he shook the thought out of his head.

The Docker's tavern was around the corner. He would find help there.

Except it was all closed up. Jim must have given the staff time off to see their new queen. He banged on the door, but it echoed emptily. Turning his back to the door, he knew he was running out of options. His fingers found the beads in his pocket, and he began rotating them, a nervous habit he had acquired. He couldn't stay here. Pounding boots sloshed through the streets, growing closer, and he staggered down an alleyway headed for the warehouses.

32

KING'S JOINING CEREMONY

Jerrol chuckled and nudged Anders, who snapped his mouth shut and straightened as he ran damp palms down his trousers. The haunting notes of a flute filled the temple, rising in an exquisite aria as Mir'elle entered. She paused in the doorway, the sun's brilliant rays a halo of light around her, causing her gown to shimmer. Swathes of golden gauze accentuated the tight fitting gown of crimson red hugging her body. Gold lace draped down her back, in an elegant waterfall of filigree and decadence. Goosebumps shivered over Jerrol's arms and made the hair on his neck prickle.

Anders' gaze never left Mir'elle's as she slowly walked up the aisle, accompanied by her Medera and Sodera. The swish of her skirts was loud in the awed silence. Sweet floral scents gently perfumed the air, and as Mir'elle approached, her black eyes sparkling, a broad smile on her face, the aroma of roses intensified.

She came to halt, escorted by Medera Elisande and Sodera Andisse, her gaze never leaving Anders. Jerrol's lips twitched. It was if they were the only two people in the temple and they couldn't see anyone else.

"Who requests entry to the Atolea?" Elisande intoned as they arrived, her voice echoing around the temple.

Anders cleared his throat. "I, Anders, King of Vespiri and Terolia do."

"And will you swear to protect your Family? To nurture, to hoard, to protect. All are responsible for ensuring the other is safe and well."

"I will."

Jerrol stepped forward. "Who gives this daughter to be joined to this son in the eyes of the Lady?"

Elisande smiled. "I, Elisande, Medera of the Atolea am honoured to stand with my sister on this her Joining day." She offered Mir'elle's hand, and Jerrol took it with a slight bow. He turned to Anders and almost laughed at how quickly Anders extended his hand. Jerrol placed Mir'elle's hand in his and stepped back.

His part in the ceremony done, Jerrol moved to his seat beside Taelia and he clutched her hand tight as the Father raised his hands to start the service.

"We are gathered in the presence of the Lady to join these two people as one. Anders and Mir'elle, you stand before the Lady and your chosen witnesses to commit one to the other today and for eternity.

"We ask our dear Lady to grace this union, to bless this couple as they venture on the path of one life." The Father paused as an aide approached, clasping a lit candle. "With this flame we light the path," the Father declared as he took the candle and lit the large ivory tapers on the altar behind him.

Facing the congregation, he spread his hands wide. "Join us as we take a moment to thank the Lady for her constant guidance and say with us the Lady's prayer.

· · ·

Lady protect us, guard our health. From beyond watch o'er our land.

Our oath to you will bind us all, Lady, Land, and Liege we stand.

Life and death, a Sentinal breathes, a last defence well done.

Our lives are yours, and ours, and theirs, joined together as one."

Jerrol faltered as he chanted the words, 'a Sentinal breathes, a last defence'. Could that really mean Birlerion? And not all Sentinals as he had always thought? Why would Leyandrii keep that quiet from the Lady's Captain?

"Lady keep him safe," he murmured at the end.

The Father smiled at the dignitaries sitting in his temple and then at the radiant couple standing before him.

"Anders, do you take this woman to be your wife? To honour and protect in the name of the Lady?"

"I do." Anders' voice resounded through the temple, deep and firm, and there was a faint echo of cheering as the ceremony was relayed to the people waiting outside.

"Mir'elle, do you take this man? To honour and protect in the name of the Lady?"

"I do." Mir'elle's response was just as firm.

"Then let that which the Lady blesses be celebrated as the Joining of Anders and Mir'elle unites us all. Lady bless you all."

More cheers penetrated the temple and the flautist launched into a celebratory hymn that filled the vaulted ceiling with joy as Anders and Mir'elle lost themselves in a kiss for a moment and then turned more self-consciously to acknowledge their witnesses.

. . .

The carriage with their king and queen pulled away. Jerrol, and he was sure quite a few others, breathed a sigh of relief. It was followed by a procession of other dignitaries. The ceremony had been poignant, and Taelia was all starry-eyed in memory of their own Joining. Only Leyarille had been pale and sad. She wore a cream gown, adorned with glittering crystals, her hair piled elegantly on her head. She had never looked so beautiful, nor so stern, and Jerrol shared her anguish and her fear.

Jerrol escorted his wife and daughters into the grand ballroom, currently set for the Joining feast, a vision of white tablecloths, sparkling crystal, and gleaming silver. Guests from around the world milled about with glasses in their hand, waiting for everyone to make the journey from the Lady's temple, and then they would be directed to their seats. Taelia gave a little shriek of delight as she pounced on their son, Mikkeal, and his wife Saranne, Lord and Lady of Stoneford Watch. And so it went on as he circulated around the room, greeting guests. Stiffening, he heard Leyarille's voice from across the room, strident above the general chatter.

"You dare sit here, expecting to enjoy this wonderful food, when there is a man you abused, fighting for all of us? You have a nerve."

Jerrol hurried to join her. She was standing over Healer Kirin, who shrank back in his chair away from her visible anger. "Leyarille, stop."

Leyarille shrugged her father off. "Who gave you the right over life or death?"

"I am a healer, young lady. Life rests in a healer's hands every day," Kirin replied.

"Then you should honour it for the very miracle it is. You should heal, not torture. You should sustain those who protect the world that you have the luxury of living in. Instead ..." she stopped, raising her head.

"Leyarille? He needs you. Now."

"Leyarille, I will deal with this." Jerrol tried to pull her away.

"Kin'arol? Where are you?"

Kirin inhaled. "Young lady …"

Leyarille flung up her hand in front of him, making Kirin stutter to a halt, and turned away, her eyes distant. *"Kin'arol? Where are you?"*

"In the harbour town alleys. He runs."

Leyarille met the queen's eyes across the room as she entered the ballroom. "Go," Mir'elle mouthed, and Leyarille picked up her skirts and ran.

Jerrol stepped into the gap. "I'm afraid the King's Administration is withdrawing its support for your anxiety disorder program until you can prove that it is in the best interests of the patient. Reports of your treatments have left much to be desired, and Healer Tyrone has agreed to oversee the investigation into your practices."

"You can't do that. It is enshrined in the law."

"The need to support our people is enshrined in law, not the method by which you treat them," Jerrol said softly. "Your healerie is closed down until Healer Tyrone clears it to reopen."

"I will speak with the king about that."

"I suggest you tread carefully on his Joining day. I doubt he will be interested in your petty complaints."

"I have influence. I can make things difficult for you; difficult for your friend."

Anger flared through Jerrol, and he stiffened as he glared at the healer. "Unfortunately, you have already achieved that. Hopefully, Tyrone will be able to undo whatever damage you have done."

Kirin raised himself up. "I can assure you, I have not done any damage, nor could I; the man was in denial. He is violent. I will see him locked up. He shouldn't be allowed on the streets."

"Kayenion, please escort Mr Kirin out. I believe he has said enough. He is a threat to the peace of the king's special day. Make sure he does not come back."

"With pleasure, Lord Chancellor."

"You'll regret this. I am a man of means. You can't do this …" Kirin's voice died away as Kayenion strong-armed him out of the hall, and Jerrol turned back to the guests, staring at them in horror.

"I apologise for the disturbance. Please be seated, we have a wonderful occasion to celebrate."

33

HARBOUR TOWN, OLD VESPERS

Birlerion spun into the building, the force of the arrow striking his thigh overbalancing him, and he slipped in the mud. He braced himself against the wall, finally cornered, nowhere to go. Pain spiked through his leg, drawing him back from panicked despair. He had failed. He hadn't been able to return the Oath, but maybe that was a good thing. Anders wouldn't be able to call him anymore.

His skin pulsed faintly with the beat of his heart, almost translucent, fading. His heart skipped a beat as a grey mare barrelled around the corner and skidded into the alleyway; Leyarille sat astride her, skirts bunched, a vision of cream and sparkles. "No," he whispered, sliding awkwardly to his knees. He snapped the arrow off, pain lancing through his leg and bringing the alleyway back into focus. "Please, Lady no." He was back where he started, alone in the gutter, dying, a beautiful woman reaching for him. But she couldn't save him this time.

Leyarille shouted his name in horror, released her skirts as she slid off Per'enne's back, and rushed towards him.

Heedlessly dropping in the mud, she gathered his limp body in her arms.

"Sweet Leyarille, you look so beautiful." Shuddering, he pulsed again, a brilliant blue flash spreading over his skin, and his eyes closed as his vision faded.

Leyarille reached for him, following him to the Veil, and drew her sword as she found him engulfed by the glistening threads. It swirled around him in excited agitation, burrowing its strands in his skin. His blood flowed freely, and he did nothing to stop it.

She launched herself at him and, just as quick, his bow appeared in his hand. Nocking his arrow, he pointed it at her, and her heart stuttered at the expression on his face; the pain and loss were etched so deep they cut.

"No, Birlerion. Don't you dare," she screamed, her essence rippling in despair.

He released the arrow, and it struck true, and she fell out of the Veilspace and collapsed in the mud beside Birlerion's body. The thud of running feet made her stir. An iridescent, black arrow was still embedded in her chest; she couldn't breathe, yet she could. The arrow dissolved under her horrified gaze. She took a deep breath as Jaredion careered around the corner.

"Leyarille? What happened?" He slid to his knees beside Birlerion and reached.

"Jaredion, no!" But she was too late. His face stilled, empty of life and expression; he had gone. In desperation, her heart thrumming in her chest, she drew Birlerion's body to her. "Birlerion, whatever it is you're doing, please stop. I love you; I need you, don't leave me. Oh, Lady, please don't take him, not now." Kneeling in the mud, she rocked, her gown spread out around her, sparkling like the stars above. "You're mine; you swore it, Birlerion. You swore you wouldn't leave me."

She flinched as a black feathered arrow thunked into Jaredion's chest, and he shuddered as he collapsed beside them. "He shot me," Jaredion gasped in shock as he opened his eyes. His hand strayed to the arrow, and he took a painful breath as the arrow dissolved. Trying to reach for the Veil, he found his way barred. "What is he doing? Birlerion? Let us back in!"

"He is protecting us," Leyarille said sadly, the tears trickling down her cheeks. "It's what he does best."

Birlerion nocked his final arrow. He knew there would be one more, and he waited as the Veil devoured him, the pain an echo of the agony roiling inside him as he watched those he loved weep over him. The last of his threads connecting them shrivelled as if burnt. Finally, he was alone, just him, the Veil, and the Oath. His family were all safe now.

Jerrol left the celebrations and walked towards the king's throne room. Leyarille's anguish prickled his conscience. How had he misread everything so badly? How could the Lady have let him go so far astray? Though it wasn't her fault, it was his; he had allowed his office to replace his humanity. His horror at his friend's suffering, coloured his opinion of him. Wincing, he acknowledged he wouldn't have been able to overcome the shame, the anger, so he hadn't expected Birlerion to. His failure was not trusting him.

Pulling the key out of his robe, he unlocked the doors. He leaned against the solid wood and pushed them open. Halting on the threshold, he gazed at the Oath in shock. His stomach dropped as the crimson flush from the Oath spread across the room. Birlerion was hurt, and it was Jerrol's fault.

He knelt on the steps before the Oath and tentatively reached for the Veil. Roiling chaos filled his vision, and he flinched back. A golden glow stood steady in the middle, and he met Birlerion's iridescent eyes. The Veil was entrenched, writhing through Birlerion's transparent body, but Birlerion stood waiting, his face calm, his bow and arrow in his hands.

"I knew you'd come," Birlerion said, raising his bow. "But it's too late." He released the arrow and it struck Jerrol in the chest. Jerrol collapsed on the mosaic floor as Tagerill burst into the throne room. He gaped at the black arrow protruding from Jerrol's chest. It dissolved as Jerrol heaved a desperate breath, his face tight with grief.

Tagerill gathered Jerrol in his arms, kneeling before the Oath, much as Leyarille and Jaredion knelt beside Birlerion's empty body. He was done. Birlerion tossed his bow aside. He had done what he could. He made one last effort as the Veil crawled up his chest and found his heart; it thumped, twice, and he crushed the remaining two black beads in his hand, and the glowing Oath in the king's throne room went out, pitching the room into darkness.

And then he exploded.

He shattered into minute fragments that flew out in all directions, shredding the Veil, which writhed as the splinters drew it away from Remargaren and then back into the golden human form that glowed so bright, and then everything pulsed.

A spark of blue flickered and solidified as it raced around the world of Remargaren, forming an impenetrable shield. Once, twice, a blinding golden flash enveloped the planet, and then there was silence. The clear blue shield faded and the world of Remargaren hung in empty space. Stars twinkled overhead as if nothing had happened. The Veil was no more. There was no longer a barrier between Remargaren and whatever lay beyond.

A deep detonation vibrated through the land, followed by a brilliant golden flash, and then a second that lit up the sky. A fine rain began to fall, and Leyarille convulsed around Birlerion. She looked up as Jaredion rose, his sword drawn. Anger coursed through her. Still, they wouldn't let him rest. Laying her husband's lifeless body in the mud, she gently smoothed his hair off his face, kissed his cold lips, and then stood.

"I swear by the Lady, you so much as touch him and I'll chop your hand off," Leyarille growled, her sword steady in her hand as she stood over Birlerion's body. Her mind was shrieking in despair, but she had weaved *her* thread tight, joining her to him; she would never let him go.

Her sword followed the approach of a man in healer robes, who jostled the soldiers aside. Healer Ewan. How had he found them so quickly? Had her father assigned a healer with every patrol? She twisted her lips. More likely word of Birlerion's arrival in Vespers had spread like a wild fire, unhindered by anyone with common sense.

"Sentinal Leyarille there is no need to be so melodramatic. You must let us pass; it's obvious he is in need of aid." The healer's voice was condescending.

"I mean it. You didn't care for him before. You can't have him now. He's the Lady's, and he's mine."

Jaredion prowled forward, his face grim as anger rolled off him in tangible waves, and the air around him crackled with blue flashes. "Leave now or I will kill you," he said as he strode down the alley, death on his face, and the soldiers pulled the healer behind them and backed away from him in fear.

Oscar pushed his way through the gathering crowd. He paled as he saw Jaredion's face and behind him Birlerion's limp body. "Leave now, it's all over. There is nothing else to see." He ordered his men to form a perimeter, pushing the guards further back.

Jaredion nodded at him and took a deep, steadying breath before turning back to Leyarille. Stone-faced, he watched as Leyarille tenderly lifted Birlerion out of the mud and cradled his head in her lap.

Fingers trembling, she smoothed his face. He looked so gaunt, so ill. His skin was waxy with a yellow tinge that didn't look right. A snapped off arrow still protruded from his thigh, ignored. He had gone; he had left her. She had promised to protect him, and she had failed, again.

She looked up as a disturbance scattered the people at the end of the alley, and Jaredion flattened himself against the wall as a muddy honey-gold stallion skittered towards her. He stopped, quivering, blocking the alleyway. His liquid black eyes stared at her, and he nosed Birlerion's shoulder.

"He's gone, we've lost him," she thought in despair. Birlerion's Darian had come to find him.

"He promised he wouldn't leave. Tell him to wake up." Kin'arol's voice was rich and deep and smoothed off the sharp edges of Leyarille's growing hysteria.

"H-He can't."

"Of course he can, we just need to call him."

Leyarille began rocking. *"He's dead. It's too late."*

"The Oath protects, it does not kill. Birlerion told me that once. He thought it was all the goodness in the world rolled into one, always prepared to leap to the defence when needed. It sits within him. Protects him. Can't you feel it?"

Leyarille stilled and bent over Birlerion. His face was so

cold, lifeless. She reached, searching for the man she loved. He wasn't there. His body was resoundingly empty. A transparent thread flashed before her eyes, spinning away from her into a dark abyss, a suffocating place without light that Birlerion would hate. Her heart clenched at the thought of him trapped in the dark, helpless. She followed the thread she had bound so tight and never released.

The image seared Jaredion's mind. A lifeless Birlerion wrapped in Leyarille's arms. His face hidden by her hair, his arm stretched out at his side, hand cupped to catch the misty rain. They were both far too still. It was as if neither breathed. The droplets sparkled in Leyarille's hair, on her back, and she began to glow. Above them, a golden stallion stood guard.

Jaredion ducked under Kin'arol's neck and knelt beside Birlerion. Grabbing his hand, he held it to his chest, and reached.

King Anders halted on the threshold of his throne room, his eyes wide with shock. His throne room was a shambles. The wall behind his throne had shattered, the words of the Oath destroyed. The back of his mind was empty, no sense that someone was watching over him, no reassuring hum. His chancellor lay in the arms of a Sentinal in the middle of the debris, surrounded by a faint blue shield which began to fade as he watched. A guard stood to the side holding a torch aloft, his eyes wide.

"What happened to the Oath? It's gone."

"It was Birlerion," Jerrol whispered. "He was in the Veilspace."

"Why didn't he come?" Anders asked. "I called him."

Jerrol looked up, his silver eyes dull and empty. "He did."

"Where is he, then? What did he do with the Oath?"

"They're gone, along with the Veil." Shuddering, he closed his eyes. When he opened them again, Anders flinched at the desolation he saw. "You know what he once said to me? He said, 'Jerrol, remember. We protect those who can't protect themselves. We die so they don't have to.' He knew he was going to die, and he still did it. I didn't help him, Anders. I stood there, and I didn't help him. And look," he gestured at the empty air above him, his tears falling. "He protected us anyway."

34

HARBOUR TOWN

Leyarille followed her thread into the darkest shadows. She didn't care that she'd left her body kneeling in cold mud, her dress ruined. All that mattered was Birlerion. She had sworn she would protect him. He was hers, and she loved him so much she knew she wouldn't survive without him.

If the Oath protected, as Kin'arol said, then he was still alive, sustained by the Land and nurtured by the Oath. No matter that he had intended to sacrifice himself for them all, she wouldn't allow it. The Land would have to put up with him living on top of it with her and not encased within it.

She found him huddled in the depths, surrounded in velvety darkness, cocooned in the Land's concern. Genuine worry hovered in the rock strata. Eyes blinded, essence shaking, barely existing, Birlerion had taken the back lash from the Veil, absorbed it so no one else would have to until the Oath had taken over and the Land had pulled his essence back into its core and encompassed him in its protection.

Wrapping him in her love, in herself, she gently drew him out. He resisted, pain-ridden and confused. The Land protested, a deep threatening rumble that shook Remargaren, and Marguerite's voice soothed the trembles away.

"Keep going," Marguerite said, a powerful presence hovering at her shoulder.

"He's mine!" Leyarille hissed, throwing out a collection of images of her and Birlerion together, and the Land hesitated. Leyarille coaxed and whispered, tugged on that fragile connection, whispering sweet endearments and reminders of who he was and where he belonged. In *her* arms, forever.

Jaredion's presence arrived in a sudden flurry and laid a gentle hand on Birlerion's shoulder. "I promised I'd never leave you trapped in a dark box," he whispered, and Leyarille shivered at the tight emotion in his voice. "I'm here to keep that promise." If voices had tears then Jaredion's was drenched in them, and they seeped into Birlerion's awareness, and he unravelled slightly.

Leyarille tugged him into her arms, and with Jaredion's help, they guided his wavering steps out of the dark and back towards the light, back up to his body. But Leyarille knew he wasn't the same man. He didn't fit.

She shuddered back into her awareness, bent over Birlerion's body, clinging tight to the glistening thread that bound them, vowing never to let go. Kneeling in the mud, icy cold seeping through the ruined material of her gown, she hovered over his body, aware of his unnatural stillness, and her heart stuttered. "Birlerion?" she whispered as Jaredion lurched beside her. Looking up, she gave him a wavering smile, ignoring the silver tracks trailing down his cheeks.

"*I told you he wasn't dead,*" Kin'arol said from above them.

Leyarille hiccuped a desperate laugh. "*I'm not sure he's quite alive.*"

"He is," Jaredion said, steel in his voice. "*He just needs time to … to reassemble.*"

Birlerion's chest rose, and Leyarille caught her breath as

a vibrant blue glow began to emanate from his body, spilling over and surrounding them in light. Dark lashes fluttered on too pale skin, and under her hand his heart did its double thump and then stilled.

When his eyes opened, she knew he didn't see them. Colours swirled, and his body visibly shimmered, beginning to fade before solidifying as she whispered his name again. His eyes briefly settled into a deep indigo blue and then shifted back into the dizzying maelstrom of colours.

He mumbled something, and she bent closer. "What was that?"

"*His leg hurts,*" Kin'arol said, and Leyarille choked on a laugh. She cut it off when she heard the hysterical edge to it.

"There's an arrow in it, my love. We'll get it seen to." Sensing his slight withdrawal, she hurried to add, "Tyrone is here. Only Healer Tyrone."

"No."

"Birlerion, you need help," Leyarille whispered.

"No. Only Marguerite." His hand moved, and before Leyarille could stop him, he grabbed the arrow and jerked it out. Blood spurted out of his thigh, still a crimson red she was relieved to see. She clamped her hand over it, desperate to stem any further blood loss.

"Birlerion! You'll do more damage."

"It's better out," Birlerion replied, his voice barely a breath of air.

Marguerite appeared in the muddy alley, glanced around, and then knelt beside them. Her deep green skirts swirled around her. "Neither of you let go of him; you tie those threads so tight he can't undo them. If you do, we'll lose him."

"Lady Marguerite? Where have you been? What happened to him? He ..."

Marguerite patted her shoulder. "Not here, my dear.

We'll have plenty of time to discuss what he did and what he's become." She hovered over Birlerion. "Dear one? Can you hear me?" Birlerion opened his eyes and Marguerite hissed her breath out. "Dearest, I am so proud of you. But you need to control your presence, it's leaking out everywhere."

Leyarille observed the blue glow more closely; it sparkled and resonated of Birlerion's … what? She didn't know, only that it was familiar and him. The blue glow began to dim, and Leyarille felt the loss deep in her gut.

Marguerite patted Birlerion's shoulder. "Well done." Tutting, she inspected the wound in Birlerion's leg. "We need to move him out of this mud."

A shadow loomed over them and Leyarille glanced up. It turned out to be Oscar Landis. His face pinched as he inspected Birlerion. "Tell me what you need."

Leyarille stared at him in shock. He didn't question what Birlerion had done, only how he could help. Swallowing down the sudden lump in her throat, she said, "He doesn't want the healers."

Lips tightening, Oscar nodded. "Understandable. Where does he want to go?"

Leyarille blinked at him. Where could they go that was far enough away from healer or Vespiri interference, come to that?

"Senti," Birlerion whispered.

Glancing down at him, she unconsciously nodded in agreement. His heart double thumped under her fingers. It was so slow it was painful. She lifted her gaze back to Oscar. "Transport down to the port and Roberion's ship. We need to go to Senti."

Oscar nodded. "I'll go with you."

Jaredion called for Lin, the little black and white Arifel. After a quick cuddle of reassurance with the little creature, he sent her off to Roberion, requesting he dock in King's Port and pick them up. She returned almost immediately with Roberion's assent.

Oscar flew into action, and she watched in awe as he rapped out orders, sending men scurrying. They soon returned with a stretcher and no healers, though he did drop a field kit beside Marguerite. Not that Leyarille thought it would be much use. Birlerion was beyond their help. If his leg hurt, she couldn't imagine what the rest of his body felt like after what he had just done. As she watched, Marguerite tied a field dressing around his thigh, though it had stopped bleeding on its own. Marguerite patted Birlerion's cheek. "Rest, dear one. The only thing you should be doing is holding on to your wife. She will anchor you here until I can teach you how to do it yourself."

"I'll watch him," Jaredion said, and Marguerite smiled. Leyarille knew Jaredion wouldn't let go of him either. It was a reassuring thought.

It was terrifying, just the thought of what he'd done. And the knowledge that he was now more, walking with gods and the Land itself, truthfully, made her angry. Angrier. What had they done to her beloved husband? If she saw her father right now … Birlerion squeezed her hand, and she took a deep breath, controlling her sudden spurt of fury.

Leaning over him, she said, "We'll get you out of here as soon as we can, my love."

"Not Jerrol's fault," Birlerion whispered. "It is the Veil you should be angry with."

Leyarille snorted. "Seeing as you destroyed it, darling, there's nothing left to be angry with."

Birlerion's lips twitched. "Then there's no reason for you to upset yourself."

Leyarille kissed him. Always the peacemaker. She wasn't ready to forgive her father just yet. Briefly, she wondered what the Watchers thought of it all. Had they been witnesses? They had all effectively been made redundant, there being no Veil left to watch.

Shrugging, Leyarille shelved that thought and gripped Birlerion's hand tight as Jaredion and Oscar carefully lifted him onto the stretcher. With Oscar's help they whisked him away before anyone could get a clear view of him. No one would know what had happened to him unless he deemed it so. This was the last time Birlerion would risk his life to save them. He was done. She didn't care what the rumour mills said, the Administration could manage that.

Her lips quirked for a moment, imagining her parents trying to explain everything that had just happened. She doubted anyone would hear much past the fact that the Veil was no more. What would that mean for Remargaren?

It didn't matter. Well, she knew it did, but for now, it was time for Birlerion to live his life, with her in Westermaine.

35

ONE MONTH LATER

Tagerill glared at the chancellor seated behind his ornate desk. He clenched his fists and then released them as he hissed out his breath, frustrated with Jerrol's refusal to visit Birlerion in Senti. "Jerrol, stop being such a stubborn arse."

Jerrol stiffened, his face suffusing red. "I think you forget yourself."

"Bullshit. You've forgotten *yourself*. This is not about you, nor Birlerion. This is about Remargaren; a wonderful magical world that needs diverse people to help her limp along. The Lady created the Veil, and it has done an amazing job, but the time for it is over. There are no Ascendants left; we don't need it anymore. It's gone, so it doesn't matter. It is no more.

"What we do need are people who understand this new magic and how it works, and Birlerion is the one person who has the most of it. We need him. He needs to help us understand it and how to control it. You need to create a new position, one to oversee magical powers, part of the Chapterhouse even, and Birlerion needs to be leading it."

"Why would he want to help us?"

Tagerill cursed, violently. "What will it take to get through your pig-headed pride and get you to accept that Birlerion doesn't blame you for what you did. You did what you thought was right for Remargaren. He would never fault you for that."

"Then why is he in Senti and not here?"

"Because the Oath is strongest in Senti, as you well know, and he feels most comfortable near the Oath. Marguerite is keeping an eye on him."

Jerrol exhaled all his frustration. He didn't know how to approach his friend. He had failed him so badly for all the right reasons, but still, his own daughter, his nephew, and most of his Sentinals had run counter to his orders and helped Birlerion; even Zin'talia admitted to helping Kin'arol. Why hadn't he seen the truth as well?

"I didn't believe him."

"Because you see the larger picture, Jerrol."

"What is larger than saving our world?"

"True, but you have to be impartial."

"Leyarille won't even speak to me."

"Set Taelia on to her."

"It's not that simple; Taelia isn't happy with me either."

"Then you need to resolve the key issue, which is the fact that you are not speaking to Birlerion. He is not allowed to travel. If you want to sort this out, you have to go there."

Jerrol closed his eyes. What a mess.

Leyandrii stirred at his shoulder. *"You miss him. You need him, and he needs you. You are two halves of a whole. He will not heal without your forgiveness."*

"My forgiveness? What do I have to forgive him for?"

"He believes that he caused this situation; he is horrified that Leyarille won't speak to you. She won't listen to him. She is still angry.

Marguerite is struggling to hold him in Senti. He is threatening to travel here, and it won't go well; he is not grounded enough."

Tagerill's fear percolated through Leyandrii's voice. "Birlerion wants to speak to you. If you don't go there, he will come here, and Marguerite says he won't make it. Something about his grip on Remargaren being too tenuous. Please, Jerrol, for the sake of our friendship, for my brother, please go to Senti. I don't want to lose him again."

"Alright."

Tagerill blinked. "What?"

"I said, alright. I'll go to Senti. Tell him I'm on my way."

Jerrol hesitated in the Senti sentinal and took a deep breath. His sentinal embraced him, pleased he had returned. He took a moment to savour the welcome. He was sure it was the only one he was going to receive.

Stiffening his shoulders, he stepped out onto the headland and inhaled the balmy sea air. The humid heat swirled around him, and his shoulders relaxed. The silver shimmer of the sea stretched out before him, meeting the azure sky on the horizon. Overhead an amethyst tinge softened the once blue sky. Senti never failed to overwhelm his senses.

Looking down over the harbour, he stared at the impossible storm walls curving inwards and outwards; they glittered in the sunshine, vibrant and strong, sheltering all within. Jaredion strode up the headland to greet him. He looked tanned and healthy, though he still would not put the uniform back on. He had been clear. He reported to Birlerion and no one else.

"Lord Chancellor, it was good of you to come. We were starting to run out of excuses to keep Birlerion hogtied. He is very stubborn." Jaredion's voice was cool but welcoming.

Jerrol smiled. "I am sure he is. I am surprised you succeeded." Jerrol swallowed at the sight of Jaredion's deep blue eyes. He truly had placed his allegiance firmly behind Birlerion and not the Lady.

"He is not as strong as he makes out, so don't let him fool you. He needs to rest, but he won't. Leyarille keeps him in order; at least he listens to her." They reached the house with the white veranda, the place they so often retreated to, their safe haven, the place to tend their wounds. He wasn't surprised to see Leyarille guarding the entrance.

Her silver eyes were unrelenting, but she stood aside without comment, and Jaredion escorted him inside. He was surprised Birlerion wasn't seated out on the veranda enjoying the sunshine, but he halted in shock as he entered a sunny room with a single bed in it. The man lying in the bed was a pale reflection of the man he knew. This couldn't be Birlerion. He was even more surprised when Marguerite rose from beside his bedside, petite and vivacious, her face grave. "Jerrol, at last, we've been waiting for you. See, Birlerion, I said he would come." Birlerion smiled, but he was far too pale, almost translucent as if he was merely an image and the real Birlerion was elsewhere.

Marguerite gave Jerrol a vivid blue glare full of import. Jerrol had no idea what it meant. Approaching Birlerion's bed, he met his eyes; luminous eyes that saw more than the world around them. They weren't silver; he couldn't describe what else they could be, but they were no longer silver. "Birlerion, they didn't tell me." He gestured at the bed.

"Don't worry, I'm improving. Having trouble with the 'being here bit' at the moment." His voice was breathy, sibilant, not quite formed.

Jerrol frowned. "What do you mean?" Dropping into the seat next to him, he hesitantly reached for his friend's hand.

His skin was like fine paper, so fragile it would tear. He held it carefully in his hands.

"It's hard to anchor here in this dimension; the others call me."

"Others?"

"Many others," Birlerion said as he sighed.

"What is in the other dimensions?"

"Wonders that would amaze you, but they are not part of Remargaren. They are distracting, makes it difficult to concentrate. Makes it difficult to *be*. Marguerite is trying to teach me. I am getting better at it."

"I'm glad to hear it. Birlerion, I am so sorry, I never meant to make it more difficult for you."

"I know, I suppose I wasn't making much sense. I'm not surprised everyone thought I was mad."

"Not everyone."

"No, fortunately for me; enough to keep me sane. If it hadn't been for Leyarille and Jaredion, I wouldn't be here. That boy is talented. His swordsmanship is truly amazing; just thinking about it exhausts me."

"Well don't think about it, then; you need to conserve your energy."

Birlerion chuckled weakly and began to fade.

"Birlerion, focus, you're leaving again." Marguerite's voice came from the veranda.

"What's happening, Birlerion? What happened to you?"

Birlerion struggled to keep his form, blurring around the edges as a bright blue glow began to seep from him, and as he gripped Jerrol's hand, his eyes swirled in a myriad of colours. Jerrol reached for him, searching for the man he knew, for the bright spark that used to hang in his awareness. He grabbed a glistening tendril questing in the air and drew it into him, binding it tight. Birlerion gasped as he solidified.

Jerrol watched him shudder as his skin tone deepened

and his body settled back in the bed. The tendril resonated within him, and he fed it love and comfort, whatever Birlerion needed. Relaxing, Birlerion closed his luminous eyes. "Thank you," he murmured, his voice stronger. "I wanted to say I'm sorry. I never meant to cause strife between you and Leyarille, nor anyone else."

"It's not your fault, Birlerion, please don't worry. We are adults; we can work it out ourselves."

"That would be good. She misses her family." His breath crackled in his chest. "The Veil is gone. I'm sure you've realised that by now. I had to destroy it …" he took a deeper breath, "… before it destroyed me."

Jerrol squeezed his hand. "I'm sorry I didn't help you. I should have believed you from the beginning instead of being influenced by those healers."

Birlerion's smile was wry. "Not your fault."

"Why did you keep your connection to the Veil a secret?"

"Leyandrii said to never speak of it. Less who knew the better. Never crossed my mind to mention it."

"Leyarille figured it all out."

"Smart woman."

"What happens now?"

"Up to you. I'm retiring. Leyarille insists, and I find I agree. Once I'm recovered, we'll return to Westermaine."

Jerrol watched him with concern as he closed his eyes and then relaxed. His crackly breath deepened, and he slept.

Jaredion came up beside him. "I'll guard his sleep," he said, his eyes on Birlerion. "Marguerite is on the veranda."

Standing at the unspoken request, Jerrol looked down at his friend. He was unrecognisable, even in sleep. Gently, he squeezed Birlerion's hand in farewell and let Jaredion take his place. The air shimmered, and Jaredion stiffened. His blue eyes glowed and Birlerion sighed as he settled more firmly in the bed.

Jerrol backed out of the room and stood on the veranda, still staring at Birlerion, his mind in a whirl.

"Sit," Marguerite said gently. "It's a bit of a shock, isn't it? We couldn't warn you. I mean, how do you explain it?" She waved her hand towards the room.

"Will he be alright?"

"Depends what you mean by 'alright'. He severed all his links with this world. When he took the Oath to the Veil, it was just him, the Land and the Oath. The Oath brought him back, and the Land sustained him, but he is not actually here yet. Don't ask me how he did it because I have no idea, but between him and the Oath, they released the Veil. It is no more. Magic is now percolating through Remargaren as it was once supposed to. I hope you will treat it better than the last time."

Jerrol waved his hand in the air, unable to encapsulate his thoughts into words. "Is there anything I need to be worried about?"

"About Birlerion? Don't even think it, Jerrol. He is no longer under your remit." She chuckled softly. "In fact, I think you'll find you are all under his."

Jerrol swallowed and briefly closed his eyes. "People fear the unknown," he whispered.

"Then you'd better do a good job of explaining that he saved this world and without him, all would have been lost."

"Are you here for good now?"

"I never left. I am Remargaren, much as Birlerion is now. We are both anchored here by the Oath and the Land. Between us, we will protect this world. Without the Veil, I can manifest more easily now; even Leyandrii will be able to visit, though she and Guerlaire have other duties elsewhere, so don't expect to see her that often."

"I don't even know where to start. How do we know what the magic is, or what it can do, or who can do it?" He paused, absorbing Marguerite's comments. "If Leyandrii and Guerlaire can visit, will there be others too?"

"One day, maybe. That's the fun bit, though, isn't it? Learning something new. Meeting new people. Isn't it exciting?"

36

SENTI, BIRTOLI

Leyarille was seated on the veranda, absorbing the sun's last rays when she became aware of a presence. It wasn't Marguerite. She had gotten used to her being around now, such a powerful aura for such a small package. She was a lovely woman who Leyarille loved all the more for her single-minded concern for Birlerion.

If it hadn't been for Marguerite, she didn't think they would still have Birlerion with them. Not that he was really with them even now; his hold on the world was still tenuous, and without Jaredion guarding his sleep, he would have left them long since. Not deliberately, she knew, but still, his grip would have failed no matter his intentions.

No, it wasn't Marguerite, which meant … her eyes flew open as she realised who it must be. Jerking to her feet, her legs tangled in the light blanket that Marguerite must have tossed over her; it was later than she thought.

"My Lady," she gasped as she saw the slender young woman leaning against the post at the top of the steps. Masses of golden hair curled around her shoulders, and the greenest eyes observed her. She was dressed in a simple pale blue shift dress, her feet bare, and yet she overwhelmed the senses.

Leyandrii smiled. "My dearest Leyarille, I didn't mean to startle you."

"We weren't expecting you. Marguerite never said."

"We thought we'd surprise her, and anyway, we came to see Birlerion."

"Of course, he is inside. He is improving. Not as fast as we'd hoped, but he is here more than he's not."

"I know, that's why we came. I am sorry we couldn't come sooner."

Leyarille stuttered, and Leyandrii laughed and reached behind her, pulling the man standing on the steps below her up beside her. He was taller than her, with wavy brown hair that reached his broad shoulders. Sliding his arm around Leyandrii's waist, he smiled at Leyarille, his matching emerald green eyes gleaming with amusement. Straight eyebrows rose as Leyarille gaped at him.

"Y-You're …" Leyarille couldn't get her words out. The legendary Lady's Captain was standing on her porch, and his presence was just as overwhelming as Leyandrii's.

The man extended his right hand and grinned. "I'm Guerlaire. It's a pleasure to meet the woman who managed to snare our Birlerion." His voice was deep, and the rich tones vibrated through her bones.

Leyarille smiled at his possessive tone as she shook his hand. His grip was firm, and he squeezed her hand before releasing it.

"Captain Guerlaire. It's an honour to meet you."

Guerlaire flicked his fingers. "Just Guerlaire will do. I haven't been the Captain for many years."

Leyandrii watched them, a small smile on her lips. "We're here because Birlerion wants to go home."

"Are you sure? He never said."

"He'll recover faster at Westermaine, and he would be anchored more securely with you in your own home. He's never had his own home before, Leyarille. One that is his and yours will help him the most. Having your own home gives you a sense of belonging that can't be beaten."

"I thought he needed to be here because the Oath is stronger here."

"Not really. He *is* the Oath. He bonded with Remargaren at a time of need, much as Marguerite did. The Oath will be present wherever he is. He is just learning how to control everything. How to be himself."

"I don't understand. How can he be the Oath? Will he disappear like Marguerite does?"

Leyandrii smiled. "No, he won't leave *you*, Leyarille. You are the reason he is here at all. The Oath protected him when he used it to destroy the Veil. But to do so, Birlerion had to absorb it, become one with it instead of carrying it like Marguerite did. The Oath took him into the Land, where he would have stayed if you hadn't pulled him back out."

Leyarille frowned in confusion. "Is he replacing Marguerite? Will she leave us?"

"No. Marguerite is bound to Remargaren, the same as Birlerion. She will never leave, though she and Taurillion can relax now and have some time together. Birlerion is ..."

"More," Guerlaire interjected. "He always surprised us. Only Birlerion would think to use the Oath to destroy the Veil."

"Which is why he is struggling to keep his form. He is hosting untold power, and it doesn't like being constrained in such a small container. It is used to spreading throughout Remargaren and it is constantly trying to escape."

Leyarille stared at her in horror, and Leyandrii chuckled,

reaching to pat her cheek. "Don't panic so. He is still the man you know and love."

"Just with some interesting extras," Guerlaire added, irrepressibly.

Leyandrii rolled her eyes, and Leyarille smiled at such a familiar expression of loving exasperation on her face.

"That's better," Leyandrii said. "Birlerion doesn't want to be a burden. Not that the silly man has ever been a burden. Just this once, I am prepared to be high-handed and relocate you all to Westermaine if you want me to."

"But Westermaine isn't ready; we haven't finished furnishing or anything."

"I took the liberty of making sure everything Birlerion needs is in place. I spoke with Mary; a lovely young woman. Birlerion chose well there. She is expecting you."

"We have to ask Birlerion first. We are not deciding without him."

Leyandrii inclined her head. "Of course, I wouldn't expect it any other way."

Leyarille led the way inside and crouched beside Birlerion, who was dozing in a chair next to the bed. He was much stronger, physically recovering, though they had to prevent him from overdoing things. The more exhausted he became, the more likely he would lose his grip on Remargaren. "Birlerion?" Leyarille caressed his face, and he opened his eyes. They roiled with a myriad of colours that swirled into unending depths, before they solidified into a deep indigo blue.

"Yes, my love?" His voice was still breathy, but it sounded more like him. Jaredion stirred in the corner, blinking as he refocused on the room.

"Do you want to go home to Westermaine?"

He squeezed her arm gently. "It would be nice to go home, but I don't want to be a bother."

"You are not, nor will you ever be, a bother. Westermaine is waiting for us if you are ready."

Birlerion smiled. "Then, yes, I'd like to go home."

"Leyandrii has offered to relocate us."

Jaredion lurched to his feet, his face pale as Leyandrii entered the room with Guerlaire behind her.

Leyandrii glanced at him, her eyes bright with mischief as she patted his cheek and then turned back to Birlerion. "Only on condition that you do nothing but lay there. I mean it, Birlerion. No reaching or you could end up somewhere you can survive but Leyarille and Jaredion can't."

Birlerion's face lit up, the most animated Leyarille had seen it. "Leyandrii?"

"My dearest Birlerion, did I tell you how amazing you are? I am so sorry about the arena and the All Mother's tests, but it was the only way I could get my mother to help you, and you did brilliantly. She was most impressed with you."

Tears sprung into his eyes, and he shimmered. Leyandrii was suddenly beside him, flinging her arms around him. "Oh no you don't. You belong here, with your wife. Don't you go leaving her behind."

"I-I'm sorry. It is difficult to remember to hold on all the time."

"So I see. It will become second nature. It takes a little time, and Westermaine will anchor you much better than here. I will take you home as long as you promise not to interfere." She kissed his forehead and he relaxed in her embrace.

"I promise. I won't do anything at all."

She scowled as she released him, and he chuckled at her suspicious expression.

"And no trying to transition yourself somewhere else later, just because you'll see how it's done. It doesn't mean you are ready to try it. I have no idea where you would end up. And Leyarille would be most upset at losing you."

"Promise me you won't try," Leyarille said urgently

"I promise I'll be good."

Leyandrii patted his chest. "You were always such a good boy."

Guerlaire laughed from behind her and said, "Not so much a boy anymore."

Birlerion struggled to his feet and swayed as his eyes filled with tears. Guerlaire pulled him into a hug, and Birlerion clung on to him as Leyandrii replied, "No, but I'll always think of him as that scruffy young urchin who had so much potential."

Leyarille's throat constricted as she watched their reunion. Birlerion was crying into Guerlaire's shoulder, and as Guerlaire soothed him, Leyandrii joined them in their embrace.

"And did he deliver," Marguerite said from behind them.

Leyandrii laughed, throwing a bright glance at her sister over her shoulder as she rubbed Birlerion's back. "That he did," she said, and the surroundings shimmered and solidified into Leyarille and Birlerion's bedchamber in Westermaine. The walls had been painted a soft grey, and colourful cushions were scattered around, brightening the room. Thick, deep green rugs covered the floor, and rose-pink curtains hung either side of the tall windows, burnished to a rich gold by the setting sun.

Marguerite steadied Jaredion as they appeared in the room, and he shuffled back until he hit the wall, watching Leyandrii and Guerlaire with wide eyes.

Guerlaire helped Birlerion lay on the bed, reassuring him that they would stay a while as Leyandrii tucked a thick quilted blanket around him against the cooler Vespiri air.

Leyarille climbed on the bed, lay beside Birlerion, and

tenderly smoothed his hair off his heated face. His skin was red and blotchy, but his obvious happiness soothed her concern. Birlerion hugged her tight.

Leyandrii sat beside him, holding his hand. Guerlaire hovered behind her, a broad smile on his face, his hand on Leyandrii's shoulder. Marguerite sat on the other side, and Jaredion tentatively perched on the end of the bed, his eyes wide as he watched them all.

"Welcome to Westermaine," Birlerion said, his voice vibrant and deep, and then he kissed Leyarille.

EPILOGUE – WESTERMAINE

"Birlerion, you're fading." Jaredion's voice interrupted his concentration, and Birlerion snapped his attention back to himself as he solidified on the jetty. That's all it took; one distraction and he forgot to hold his shape.

"No, he's not," Kin'arol said.

"He is. He's gone all wishy washy around the edges."

"Wishy washy? What's that?" Kin'arol sounded confused.

Birlerion grinned as he sank his awareness back down into the land. His Darian was very literal; you were either there or you weren't, there was nothing in between. He was glad Kin'arol continued to include both Leyarille and Jaredion in their conversations. It saved so much time when he didn't have to repeat everything.

He flicked an idle thought around the boundaries of Westermaine, caressing the tall sentinal trees standing outside the front door of his home and then deeper into Greens. He smiled at the soft greeting from the Ancestor tree as it dozed in the golden sunlight.

Returning to the jetty he sat upon, he sank his thoughts

through the clear waters of the lake. He paused as sunlight gleamed on bronze scales.

"It's when people go fuzzy around the edges, you know, lose definition." Jaredion's voice faded as he hovered, waiting.

Rubbery lips mouthed the water as the fat carp drifted through the thick fronds of weeds, observing the shimmering reflection which had been seated on the end of the wooden jetty for a long time.

Birlerion sent the slightest tickle over his scales and the carp stirred, easing out of the weeds. A bug skimmed across the water, its feet pressing down into the surface, and the carp sucked him in with a soft plop. *"You wait."*

"For what?" Birlerion asked.

"That which you haven't found."

"I didn't realise I was looking."

The carp mouthed the water, almost as if he chuckled. *"Of course you are. You will always be searching."*

"Always?"

"Always."

"Will I find what I am searching for?"

"Some you will find, some will find you, and some are already found."

"And those I can't find?"

"Will suffer for it."

"Birlerion, you're fading again." Jaredion's voice interrupted his conversation, and Birlerion sighed.

"He's not," Kin'arol insisted, stirring in his stall.

"He is."

The trouble was, when he let his human form go, he felt more comfortable. Maintaining the form felt like he was all squashed up in a tiny box which pinched in the most uncomfortable places. Just because he wasn't compressed didn't mean he wasn't anchored; he had yet to convince Marguerite of that.

Though if he was honest, he knew most people were uncomfortable when he dissipated, especially Leyarille and Jaredion, so maybe it was better to hold on to normalcy for as long as possible; it wouldn't be right to scare the family after all.

"He is still right here; he hasn't changed."

"To you maybe, but you can't see him, I can, and he was all fuzzy around the edges."

Birlerion stared at his reflection in the smooth water. Another bug skated across the surface, and the carp moved lazily and there was another soft plop. "I am sitting right here, you know," he said, observing the hollowed face that stared back at him through the gentle ripples. He needed to put on some weight; maybe that would help with the being here bit. He looked like he might fade just through lack of nourishment, even though Leyarille tried to feed him every chance she got.

Smoothing himself out a bit might make him look healthier; he hadn't really thought about his appearance. He supposed, he could look however he wanted. Something to think about, though he had a feeling Leyarille would get upset if he suddenly appeared a lot younger. Maybe he should do it gradually.

He rose to his feet in one fluid movement. His wooden jetty remained firm beneath him and he smiled. He was quite proud of his new jetty. His smile faded. Just as he could create with a thought so he could destroy; it was a humbling thought he hadn't voiced out loud. He raised his eyebrow as he stared at his companion.

Jaredion was laid out on the grass, enjoying the sunshine. The lad was a picture of rare indolence. He was usually on high alert, standing behind Birlerion's shoulder, trying to keep him safe. Birlerion grimaced; not that he made it easy for him.

"Are you supposed to be guarding me or what?" he asked, a small smile hovering over his lips.

"Or what," Jaredion replied, opening his eyes. They were a deep indigo blue, the same as Birlerion's. Birlerion winced again at the fact that Jaredion had given up the Lady for him, though he wasn't sure Jaredion realised that yet. "Not that you really need me anymore. The Veil is gone, you are nigh on indestructible; what do you need a guard for?"

"You'd be surprised. Who knows what the newly magical world of Remargaren will throw at us?"

"You should know. It's your world, now."

Birlerion cringed. Leyandrii had been clear about that before she and Guerlaire had left. A warmth simmered in his core at their unequivocal love and belief in him. The knowledge that they would return to visit them one day filled him with joy. "If only it were that simple. You forget this wonderful world is populated by thousands of unpredictable people, none of whom know or care about me."

"Yet," Jaredion said with a grimace as he rolled to his feet. Adjusting the sword at his waist, his gaze flicked around the peaceful glade.

"Or ever. Leyandrii is their Lady and nothing will change that."

Jaredion snorted. "They know something has changed. You can't go around blinding everyone with brilliant explosions and expect them not to notice. Magic will return now, and you and Marguerite are the only ones who know anything about it."

"Makes you want to cry, doesn't it?" Birlerion said, beginning the walk up the slope to his home.

"With laughter. Who'd have thought you'd be our magical expert?"

"Beggars can't be choosers."

Jaredion rested his hand on Birlerion's shoulder. "They are lucky to have you," he said, his face suddenly grave.

Birlerion grinned. "As fortunate as I am to have you. Come, dinner will be ready."

"Thank goodness, I thought you were going to stare into that pond forever. I'm starving."

They found two young women chatting in the kitchen. Even though they had a huge mansion, everyone preferred to congregate in the kitchen. Mary, the young woman Birlerion had employed as his housekeeper was chopping up vegetables, and the auburn-haired deity, Marguerite, who scowled at them as Birlerion moved over to the sink to wash up.

"Marguerite, you worry too much. Your face will stay like that, and then what will Taurillion say?" Birlerion said with a low chuckle.

"You know the risk, Birlerion. Learning to control your power is too important to experiment with."

Birlerion concentrated on washing his hands and didn't reply, aware of Marguerite's eyes boring into his back.

"I mean it, Birlerion."

"I know you do, and so do I. You worry too much. Westermaine anchors me, as do Leyarille and Jaredion and the rest of you, as you know so well. But I will endeavour to restrain my activities to Westermaine, just to please you."

He sat at the table as Marguerite scowled at him again. She didn't look like a goddess, much as he didn't look like a god, he supposed. Marguerite was a vivacious bundle of energy topped by bright auburn curls and vivid blue eyes, though her presence could be overwhelming when she forgot to rein it in. A bit like him, Birlerion thought with a quirk of his lips. He frowned in thought. Maybe that was it; he had been looking at it wrong. It wasn't his physical shape he needed to control, but his *presence*.

Marguerite's eyes gleamed in the light of the onoffs Birlerion had created for Mary. The onoffs were the first thing he had made when he had been well enough to come downstairs; silver globes of light suspended in the air were much safer than a naked flame, especially when there was a precious baby crawling under foot and grabbing your ankles.

Scooping Mary's child, Sybil, into his arms, he crooned in her ear. She chuckled in delight and tried to grab his nose. Marguerite threw her hands up in the air and left the kitchen.

"Birlerion, you spoil her, she is supposed to be having a nap," Mary complained, though she had a smile on her face.

Birlerion grinned. "My darling Sybil, you didn't escape again?"

Sybil gurgled as she grasped his finger tight.

He whispered in her ear, and she snuggled in his arms and her long lashes drooped as she fell asleep. A shadow paused in the doorway, taking in the scene.

Birlerion looked up and caught a gleam of silver eyes as his wife stepped into the kitchen. His throat tightened at her pensive expression. Standing, he carefully passed Sybil back to her mother. He crossed the room and smoothed his fingers over Leyarille's cheeks and then across her lips, before gently wrapping his arms around her, and as he kissed her, they disappeared.

Jaredion stared at the empty doorway. "Marguerite is going to be upset."

Mary snorted. "About what? She's his wife. They need time together after what they've been through."

"Yeah, but he's not supposed to do that transporting thing."

"He's perfectly capable; more capable than most realise. I don't know what you are worrying about. He won't get lost." Mary laid Sybil in her basket.

"And how do you know that?" Marguerite asked from the doorway.

Mary flashed the vibrant woman a stern look and placed her hands on her slim hips. "You know he won't get lost. This is his home. He is rooted, anchored, whatever you want to call it, right here, and you know it."

Marguerite sighed and joined Jaredion at the table. "I know, but he needs time to adjust, recalibrate. To find his balance before they start pulling him in all directions, as they will."

"I thought you said it would take years for magic to find its way back into Remargaren," Jaredion said.

"Into Remargaren, yes. Into Westermaine? It's already here. It will cluster around Birlerion because of who he is. He is the Oath, bonded with our world and brimming full of power. He must learn to control it."

"It's been months, Marguerite. I would suggest his control is amazing considering where he started. He is a different person since we came home. He rarely fades, and even then, Kin'arol says he is still here. Kin'arol doesn't see him fading at all."

Marguerite looked thoughtful for a moment. "Still, he can improve."

"'Tis a hard task master you are," Mary said as she seasoned a pot hanging over the fire. "Are you and Taurillion joining us for dinner tonight?"

"If that is one of your famous stews I can smell simmering, then yes."

"Seven for dinner then."

"You sure Birlerion and Leyarille will be back in time for dinner?"

"Of course," Mary said comfortably. "He is always on time."

Marguerite stared at her before frowning again. "Always?"

"Always."

Jaredion held up his hands as Marguerite began muttering under her breath. "It's nothing to do with me."

They lay on the beach, the surf tugging their entwined legs as the sun began to set. "I never want to leave," Leyarille breathed into his ear, her arms tight around his bare back, the weight of him reassuring. He hadn't faded once while they had been on their island. She smiled into his slowly tanning skin. Not once.

"Why not?"

"Because here you are mine, and no one can take you away from me." She hid her face in his neck, knowing she sounded selfish.

Salt encrusted her sensitive skin as she lay on the warm sands with the man she loved. They had been here all day, even though she knew the day had been well advanced when they'd left Westermaine. That was, if they had left Westermaine. She wasn't sure where they were. She shivered as his finger traced her jawline and down her throat.

His eyes were a swirling mystery when she raised her face to meet his gaze. "No one will ever take me away from you again," he said as he bent his head and kissed her. The need for him swelled throughout her body, their kiss deepened, and he absorbed her, cell by cell as they joined as one, his inherent glow swirling around them in a sea of bliss, nerve ends tingling with desire. She gasped, or she thought she did. She wasn't sure where her mouth was anymore; they were joined as one in a glorious confusion of sensation and desire. Pulsing waves of heat and need flooded through them as Birlerion took them over the edge and all their love entwined together and wrapped them tight as they united in one exultant release.

An insistent wave lifted them off the sand and dragged them up the beach. Frothy warm water fizzed as it swirled around them, tickling their bare skin. Leyarille regained her senses and her body, which was tight and tingly with delight. "What was that?" she breathed as she clutched him. His hot skin, firm and slick, slid against hers, and she inhaled his exquisite scent as her aching core tightened again in anticipation.

"Us," Birlerion replied, looking at her with such a tender expression she wanted to cry.

"Can we do it again?"

"Whenever we want to."

"Thank goodness." She kissed away his smug smile, and he tightened his embrace. Warmth spread through her, along with a sense of belonging, of being loved, and she breathed him in, content with the knowledge that he loved her just as much as she loved him.

"Marguerite will be worrying. I suppose we should head home." She couldn't help the reluctance that tinged her voice.

Safe in each other's arms, she smiled as he kissed her nose, her cheeks, her lips. She shivered as his warm breath caressed her skin and his whisper tickled her ear. "You're my home."

The End

And so ends the Sentinal series. But no! You cry. That can't be the end. There is so much more story to be told, after all, there's magic! Untold misunderstandings, catastrophes and mishaps can occur with magic. This is true, and as such, I agree, there are many more words yet to be written.

But the tale of the Sentinals is over. Well, I lie! There is a prequel still to come, but this tale is over as the Sentinals are no longer needed to protect Remargaren. They can retire and live their own lives if they so choose.

I debated about continuing the Sentinal series, but as I just said, the story no longer centres around the Sentinals, so I think it's time to end here and begin a new related series focused on Westermaine and those magical newbies Birlerion will be searching for. It's a new world, and who knows what will happen next!

Make sure you sign up to my newsletter via my website www.helengarraway.com to find out first about my next book release, all the inside info about my books and free downloads of novellas/short stories set in the world of Remargaren.

If you enjoyed Sentinals Destiny, please do leave a review. Reviews help indie authors like me gain visibility in Amazon's algorithm.

GLOSSARY

Deities

Leyandrii (Lay-ann-dree): Guardian of Remargaren

Marguerite: (Mar-guh-reet): Leyandrii's sister, Guardian of the Land

Guerlaire (Guh-LAIR): Original Lady's Captain

Westermaine

Birlerion (Bur-lair-ri-on): First Administrator, Sentinal

Leyarille (LAY-er-rill): Jerrol's daughter, Sentinal

Jaredion (Juh-red-ion) Sentinal

Kin'arol (Kin-ah-roll): Birlerion's Darian

Old Vespers

King Anders: Ruling monarch of Vespiri and Terolia

King Benedict: Former monarch of Vespiri (dead)

Jerrol Haven, Lady's Captain and Lord Chancellor

Taelia (Tay-lee-ah) ScholarDeane, Jerrol's wife

Kayenion (Kay-en-ion): Sentinal

Commander Bryce: Commander of the King's Justice

Commander Nikols: Commander of the King's Rangers

Parsillion (Par-sill-i-on): Sentinal
Frenerion (Fren-nair-ri-on): Sentinal
Zin'talia (Zin-Tar-lee-ah): Jerrol's Darian Mare
Tom: Birlerion's contact at Docker's Tavern
Jim: Owner of Docker's Tavern

<u>Chapterhouse</u>
Taelia: Scholar Deane of the Chapterhouse, Jerrol's wife

<u>Deepwater Watch</u>
Lady Alyssa (A-liss-ah): Guardian of Deepwater
Leander Jennery: Lord of Deepwater
Tagerillion (Tagerill) (Taj-er-rill-i-on): Sentinal
Miranda: Tagerill's wife
Denirion (Duh-near-ri-on): Sentinal

<u>Marchwood Watch</u>
Lord William: Lord of Marchwood
Anterion (Ant-air-ri-on): Sentinal

<u>Stoneford</u>
Mikkeal (Mick-i-all) : Lord of Stoneford Watch, Jerrol's son
Marianille (M-a-ri-an-ill): Sentinal
Niallerion (N-i-al-air-ri-on): Sentinal
Healer Tyrone
Jason: Former Lord of the Watch

<u>Watch Towers</u>
Margareth (Mar-gar-eth) Jerrol's youngest daughter
Tianerille (Tee-ann-er-rill): Sentinal (Watch Towers)
Venterion (Vent-air-ri-on): Sentinal (Watch Towers)

<u>Terolia</u>
Maraine (ma-rain): Medera (retired)

Mir'elle (mi-rell): Maraine's daughter
Elisande (Ell-i-sand): Maraine's daughter, Medera
Andisse, (Ann-deece) Elisande's Sodera
Fer'ilan (Fair-il-an): Captain of Terolian Guards
Cor'ilno (cor-ill-no): Andisse's brother
Oscar Landis: Commander Terolian Guards
Kayerille (Kay-er-ille): Sentinal, Oscar's wife

<u>Elothia</u>
Owen – Commander of the Elothian Army
Taurillion (Tor-rill-ion) : Sentinal

<u>Birtoli</u>
Elder Tuan, (Too-an) leader of the Tu'ani clan
Roberion (Roe-bear-ion): Sentinal
Lilith, Roberion's wife, Tuan's daughter

ACKNOWLEDGMENTS

Three years ago, I self published my debut novel, Sentinals Awaken, the first book in the Sentinal series. Today, I am releasing Sentinals Destiny, the sixth and final book in the Sentinal series.

The last three years have been an amazing experience. Learning the world of self publishing and book promotion. I now have nine books published, became a USA TODAY Bestselling author, and my books have received multiple awards. I have loved every minute of it, and I hope you have enjoyed accompanying me on this journey.

If it hadn't been for readers like yourself, buying and enjoying my books, I wouldn't still be publishing. Your support and feedback has made all of this possible.

I have to thank my editor, Maddy Glenn of Softwood Self-Publishing for making me think harder about my stories and writing even more. To Michael Strick, my alpha reader extraordinaire who has the best ideas! Jeff Brown, for creating my amazing covers. My amazing ARC readers, Jan, Daisy, Johnny, Ellen, Dr Pam, Pat, Chastity, Jackie, Leah, Barbara, Pierre and Kris who absorb my books in a flash and make me very happy when they love them! Thank you.

I look forward to sharing new worlds and more stories in the old worlds as more and more ideas bubble. The saga of Remargaren is not quite finished as I have a prequel I am writing, set three thousand years previously, and I have various requests from readers for more stories about their favourite characters. So if there is someone you want to know more about, then me know!

Make sure you sign up to my newsletter via my website www.helengarraway.com to find out first about my next book release, to let me know who else you want me to write about, all the inside info about my books and free downloads of novellas/short stories set in the world of Remargaren.

Thank you so much for your continued support.

Helen

ABOUT THE AUTHOR

Helen Garraway is the USA Today Bestselling author of the award winning epic fantasy Sentinal series which was first published in 2020, followed by the first book of the fantasy romance SoulMist series, SoulBreather, first released in 2022 as part of the Realm of Darkness boxset.

An avid reader of many different fiction genres, a love she inherited from her mother, Helen writes fantasy novels and also enjoys paper crafting and scrapbooking as an escape from the pressure of the day job.

Having graduated from the University of Southampton with a Degree in Politics and International Relations, she remains an active member of their alumni. You can find out more at www.helengarraway.com.

Patreon

Become a supporter or Join Team Arifel, Team Darian or Team Sentinal and get access to the first chapters of my new books first, free bookish downloads, polls, and early sneak peeks.

patreon.com/HelenGarraway

bookbub.com/authors/helen-garraway

amazon.com/author/helengarraway

instagram.com/helengarrawayauthor

1
SOULBREATHER
THE SOULMIST SERIES
HELEN GARRAWAY

SOULMIST SERIES

Interested in my Romantic Fantasy SoulMist series? Find out more at www.helengarraway.com

Start the adventure now with book one, SoulBreather. Available in the format of your choice from Amazon.

- Audiobook
- Ebook
- Paperback
- Hardcover

If you fall in love with the shadows, does that mean you are fallen too?

A dying angel. A fractured realm. The SoulBreather who might be able to save them both.

Solanji has a secret. One that is becoming increasingly difficult to keep. She can touch souls and see into a person's inner thoughts. Soulbreathing is exhilarating and addictive, until the day Solanji caresses the wrong person's soulmist.

Dragged into a long forgotten angelic mystery, she is

forced to venture into Eidolon, the godforsaken last resort for those without souls. In order to save her brother, she must rescue a broken and tortured man. Can she save him from the shadows? Does he even want to be saved? And can she find a way to return to the light before the darkness engulfs them both?

SoulBreather is the first book in the paranormal fantasy SoulMist series. Winner of a Global Book Award Silver medal, a Readers' Favorite Finalist medal and a Readers' Favorite Five Star Review.

Order: https://Books2Read.com/SoulBreather